GOOD ENDEAVOUR

A Maryland Family's Turbulent History

1695–2002

A HISTORICAL NOVEL BY
NED TILLMAN

Good Endeavour

A Maryland Family's Turbulent History 1695-2002

Copyright ©2023 Ned Tillman

ISBN   978-1-7324841-2-2   print
ISBN   978-1-7324841-3-9   ebook
LCCN   2023903874

Book design by Nan Barnes, StoriesToTellBooks.com
Cover design by James F. Brisson
Published by South Branch Press

Publisher's Cataloging-in-Publication Data

Names: Tillman, Ned, author.

Title: Good Endeavour : a Maryland family's turbulent history, 1695-2002 / Ned Tillman.

Description: Columbia, MD : South Branch Press, 2023.

Identifiers: ISBN 978-1-7324841-2-2 (paperback) | ISBN 978-1-7324841-3-9 (ebook)

Subjects: LCSH: Maryland--Fiction. | Baltimore (Md.)--Fiction. | Tobacco farmers--Fiction. | United States--History--Revolution, 1775-1783--Fiction. | Race relations--Fiction. | Historical fiction. | BISAC: FICTION / Historical / General. | FICTION / Family Life / General. | GSAFD: Historical fiction.

Classification: LCC PS3620.I45 G66 2023 (print) | LCC PS3620.I45 (ebook) | DDC 813/.6--dc23.

About the Painting on the Front Cover

The painting of Good Endeavour Farm, created by the author's wife, Kathryn Tillman, captures how the homestead looked in 2000. It was a real house built on a real tract of land registered in 1695 in the Maryland colony. It lay adjacent to the Little Gunpowder Falls, just a couple of miles west of the Chesapeake Bay. It was located at the end of Bulls Lane, which once connected the farm to Old Philadelphia Road/Old Post Road. The now-developed land, Gunpowder, can be accessed from Manchester Drive. In 1695 it was an average-sized tract for an average European settler, and it was farmed up until 2000. Its story is similar to the stories of thousands of other small farms across the country. The author grew up on this farm.

Praise for Ned Tillman's Books

Ned's books lie at the nexus of the human struggle to coexist with each other and the natural world.

Good Endeavour an engaging look into our past that reveals wisdom for dealing with the challenges we face today.

> *I highly recommend this book as an enjoyable and enlightening read."*
> —The Honorable Liz Bobo, Maryland House of Delegates

> *"Reminiscent of Edward Rutherford's or James Michener's books but on a more accessible scale. Good Endeavour is a great read, hard to put down, and draws the reader in to care about the characters and the issues they deal with. I highly recommend it."*
> —Tracey Manning, University of Maryland

> *"The book is inspiring and encourages us to reconsider what we know about our ancestors and how they - and now we - are caught up in responding to the issues of the time."*
> —John Caughey, University of Maryland

> *"I loved this book… and the stories stay with you."*
> —Audrey Suhr, Howard County Conservancy

The Chesapeake Watershed introduces you to the challenges a single ecosystem faces as the human population continues to grow and impact our precious natural resources.

AWARDS

Winner of the Excellence in Journalism Award from the Renewable Natural Resources Foundation

Winner of the Best Book on Environmental and Natural Resources selected by The American Society for Public Administration.

REVIEWS

"...takes you on a fascinating journey through nature and time, illustrating the importance of experiencing nature and the urgency of preserving it."
—Richard Louv, author of *Last Child in the Woods*

"These essays touched my soul."
—Bernd Heinrich, author of *Mind of the Raven*

Saving the Places We Love reveals that these man/nature conflicts occur all across the country and around the world.

AWARDS

Selected as the Book of the Year by Howard County Library, Howard Community College, and the Howard County Poetry and Literary Society.

REVIEWS

"It is a book that has transformed my life, inspiring me to make changes that are more caring of the Earth. After reading it, I became more aware of my footprint on the planet and how can I reduce it.
—Ramsey Hanhan, author of the memoir *Fugitive Dreams: Chronicles of Occupation and Resistance*

～

The Big Melt is a surreal look at what might happen to our climate and how the younger generations might respond to it. Suspend your disbelief and come along for a hyperbolic ride into a warmer future.

AWARDS

Shortlisted for The Green Book Award, The One Maryland One Book Award, and selected for the NASA Book Club.

REVIEWS

"I couldn't put the book down because it was so intriguing. I loved the mixture of the real and the surreal."
—J. Kari

"Marley's just like us, so readers connect with him."
—S. Fuller

"Lots of humor… made it fun to read."
—B. Vanthoff

CONTENTS

PART FOUR
Creating America: Robert and Josie

PART FIVE
Rebuilding America: Nathan and Nellie

PART SIX
Adjusting to Change: Andrew and Kate

PART SEVEN
End of an Era: Edward and Jessica

Acknowledgments

I would like to thank the following reviewers for their invaluable suggestions to manuscript drafts: John Caughey, PhD; Tracey Manning, PhD; Debbi Duel; Kathryn Tillman; Leigh Tillman; Henry Posko, PhD; Bill Tibbs; Donna Mennitto; Kathy Leonard; Laurie True; Mina Hilsenrath; Max Buffington; Ed Dudek, MD; Dina Boogaard; PhD, Karen Learmouth; and Biff Barnes. The reviewers represent many perspectives and offered insight to the author on how the characters in the stories were portrayed. Parts of the stories were inspired by the writings of Abbey, Doerr, Emerson, Berry, Kimmerer, Coates, Whitehead, Bass, Barth, Powers, Doyle, McPhee, McKibben, Lanham, Proulx, and Kingsolver. I would like to thank Biff and Nan Barnes and Jenny Margotta for their assistance during the publication of this book.

Dedicated to our ancestors and our descendants

PART ONE

The Keys to the Past

Edward

Chapter 1

THE LAST CHANCE

2001

As Edward drove up the dirt lane for one last look at the family homestead, he recoiled in horror. Flames and smoke erupted from the buildings at the top of the hill. "What the hell's going on?" he shouted, his words echoing in the emptiness in the van. "They're burning it down! Now I'll never know any more details about what really happened over the centuries here at Good Endeavour Farm."

He was shocked and angry. Today was to be his chance—his *last* chance—to explore the homestead in hopes of finding answers to haunting family questions. He was sure there were more clues about life here at this Colonial-era crossroads. Clues hidden in and around the old log cabin.

"Damn it." Edward ground his yellowed teeth. The developers had promised him this one-day window to check behind the walls and beneath the floorboards. He and other members of his family had a slew of unanswered questions about their past, and he had hoped to find answers hidden in the original seventeenth-century cabin and the eighteenth-century addition. But now it was all going up in smoke. He was pissed.

Edward stomped on the gas pedal with his steel-toed boot. The worn tires spun in the loose gravel, and his blood pressure rocketed. Sweat started beading on his bare, sunburned forehead. As his tires gained traction, the wild black-cherry trees, day lilies, and multi-flora rose bushes along the lane became a blur. His neck and head stretched forward as he desperately tried to see what was happening. After all this time, was he too late? Could he save anything?

As Edward's van slid to a stop in front of the weathered, green grain shed, he saw that the four smaller outbuildings behind it were already gone. He shook with anger. The debris had been pushed into a pile and set afire—a part of his past turning into smoke. But then he noticed that the house was still standing. His face brightened. Maybe he could delay the burning of the old home and the big barns for just one more day.

Two men were watching the old, dry wood burn. Who are these guys, he wondered? He slid out of his van and hurried over to them. He saw their white construction hats stenciled with Henkels and McCoy, Inc. So they were legit. This wasn't some random arsonist—just somebody jumping the gun. Why don't people tell you when there's a change in plans? He charged over to the man closer to him and almost growled, "Who's in charge?"

The short man turned to face him. "I am. I'm Mario Juarez. Can I help you?"

"I thought I had all day to look around the old homestead," Edward blurted out. "And now you're burning it down." He kicked a scorched board back toward the flaming pile of wood.

"I heard you cared only about the farmhouse. We've left that intact. But we'll be back first thing tomorrow to demolish the house and the two big barns. We're saving the old outhouse until the end." Mario smiled. "We might be needing it."

Edward took a couple of deep breaths to calm down. They were correct; he was mainly interested in the old farmhouse, but he hated to see any of it go. "Okay, you're right. But I'll be here the rest of the day, exploring around the house, and I'll be back in the morning. I understand you have an eight a.m. start."

"Yes, sir."

"Please don't start before I get here. I have this gut feeling that something of value has been preserved for centuries in or around these buildings. It could be important. If I don't look now, it will probably be destroyed—lost forever. I'll always wonder what I missed." With that, Edward turned and began to wander around the farm, trying to get his bearings now that some of the building landmarks were gone.

The scene took him by surprise; it was unsettling. The homestead already looked so different. The farmhouse and the two remaining barns still loomed large at the top of the hill. But without the old sheds, the pine, spruce, and fir forest loomed larger and appeared closer to the farmhouse than he remembered. Thankfully, the house was still intact, as were the tall trees and the overgrown and unpruned shrubs in the yard.

Calming down a bit, Edward walked across the clay-packed soil and took a closer look at the large boxwood bushes and the bulky clusters of lilac trees, as well as sycamores, mimosas, walnuts, oaks, several tall, narrow ginkgos, and one majestic pecan tree that dwarfed them all. His body relaxed as he reached out to touch these old friends he had known throughout his life. They had each been a character playing a role in his imagination, as well as landmarks in his everyday life. It felt as if he was saying goodbye to each of them—and of course, he was.

Edward looked around, trying his best not to picture what this ridgetop would look like by the end of the next day. There would be no trees, no buildings, and no signs of the past. The source of all his memories erased. It made him sad to think there would be nothing left of this once vibrant, historic homestead but fallow fields. When the new families moved into their new homes, there would be nothing to inform them about the past. No one would know that the first structure on the one-hundred-acre tract had been a tiny log cabin. A cabin that had housed his family for three centuries. He wondered if anyone would care.

The massive, yellow bulldozer that had leveled the sheds earlier in the day crouched in the weeds off to one side of the empty farmhouse. It looked like a giant predator waiting for the morning, poised to spring out of its slumber and pounce on its defenseless prey. With hands pushed deep in his pockets and a scowl across his face, Edward walked around, stalking the beast, eyeing the destructive potential of the massive machine. The dozer looked menacing, smelled like diesel, and its mud-covered steel tracks had already churned up the overgrown, grassy lawn. A lawn Edward had mowed hundreds of times as a teenager. All those hours of his life doing chores to make his parents' home look nice—and to what end? No one would ever know or care about the effort he had put into the farm so long ago.

Edward's hands shook and his breath quickened as he walked around the barns. He hadn't thought it would be this hard. His body hunched over as he tried to absorb the reality of the moment and the imminent loss of the seventeenth-century farm. One side of him was still deeply disappointed it had come to this, but there were no other options, no other descendants standing in line to farm Good Endeavour. The farm had done its job and now society had different plans for the land.

This machine and the people who hired it were ready to destroy the past, his past, in the name of progress, and he wished that he could stop that day from coming. But he couldn't. The papers had been signed, and the land no longer belonged to his extended family. They had all left the family homestead and its land-based universe and moved away to get on with their lives in this modern, auto-centric, and digital new world.

As Mario and his colleague left the site in their white Ford pickup, they stopped next to Edward, who was standing lost in thought in the middle of the lane. Mario still wore his white construction hat and casually lit up a Marlboro as they talked. "Cigarette?"

"No thanks."

"Was this your place?"

Edward hesitated. He felt like he was consorting with the enemy even though he felt no personal grievance with this man. When he was younger, he had worked on numerous construction sites. It had just been a job for him, never thinking about the bigger picture. What was happening here was just one aspect of the times—building the American Dream for others by converting small farms of the past into the suburbs of the future. Land was either preserved or developed, and he could not find anyone to farm, protect, or preserve Good Endeavour Farm for the future. It was that simple.

Taking another moment to think about it, Edward relaxed a bit and pushed up the front of his hat, revealing his thinning hair. "Yep, I grew up here, but it's been thirty-some years since I've lived here. I built a home over in Ellicott City, near Columbia, on the west side of Baltimore. That's where I raised my kids. It's where my wife and I both work."

Mario nodded. "Tomorrow's going to be noisy, dusty, and maybe a little disappointing for you to watch the demolition."

"Yeah." Edward said, a little bit of wetness at the corners of his eyes. "But I've got to be here. I'm hoping you'll turn up something of historical value. This old farmhouse has been sitting here as a witness to our past for a long time. I think it's likely that my ancestors left something here for future generations. I plan to find it."

"A lot of people want to do that, but it's rare to find anything. I'll let you know if we do. Of course, we can't spend much time digging through debris. We're on a tight schedule."

They each signed off with a gentle nod, a wave, and an understanding, a tentative trust that often grows between two men trying to work together.

The sound of Mario's pickup truck dissipated as the

contractors drove down the lane. Edward stood there, watching the dust rise and then settle back down onto the fields adjacent to the lane. A sense of loneliness came over him as he listened to the call of a solitary mourning dove cooing in the empty barn and a crow cawing in the distance. Yes, he was alone with the farm — probably for the last time.

He thought back to his conversation with Mario. There was more to it than what he had mentioned. The desire to be here for the demolition was more complex than just finding family records. Edward wanted to know how his ancestors dealt with the moral issues of their time. Who were these people he descended from? Could he learn anything from them that might apply to his life in the twenty-first century? He was looking for answers to some of the basic questions he faced in his life. Questions about democracy, equality, and being good stewards of the land. These were not questions new to the twenty-first century, and he wondered how his ancestors had struggled with them in the past.

Growing up, he had overheard fragments of family stories, off-hand remarks, and a mix of respect and jokes about his long-dead relatives. Some of them had been literate people who had read and cared deeply about these same issues. Evidently, there had also been an old sea captain who had brought in exotic trees for the lawns and who had allegedly buried a chest on the farm. His father had never mentioned it, but his mother had been a true believer ever since she had heard the story from Edward's grandmother. It was now up to him to take one last look at the homestead to see if he could find any hidden messages.

Going through the emotional process of selling the farm was tough and made him even more interested in the truth behind the stories. There was little known about his earliest ancestors. All he knew of his roots was that the family had held on to the land through wars, droughts, plagues, and the growth of the nation. But now, in the twenty-first century, raising livestock was no longer considered the "best use" of small farms close to big cities like Baltimore. The 300-year farming era was over for Good Endeavour, and Edward had to accept that reality. But without the farm he was beginning to have this vague sense of being uprooted, afloat on constantly changing seas of an evolving society. It was complicated.

As a result of rehashing all the old stories, Edward had recently turned his attention to the past. He had told his wife, Jess, "We should collect all the family stories and find some way to share them with others. It's a good way to pay tribute to our ancestors and what they had to live through. I hope it will also give our children ample roots for understanding their past."

"That's quite a goal. Do you think you have enough information to write these stories?"

"You never have enough, but I have this sense, a hunch, that the sea captain or others might have left messages in the house for future generations to find. If that's true, we need to find those records before the house is destroyed. It's our last chance. I plan to take time off to be there before and during demolition to check for any missives from the past. I owe that to my ancestors and to our descendants. It's like a calling, an obligation that I want to answer."

Jess had smiled at his fervor to pursue this new interest in history. "I understand. I've had the bug as well, ever since we emptied out the homestead last year. I have many questions about your ancestors and the things they did."

When Jess and Edward had emptied the house prior to the estate sale, they had discovered boxes of old letters, records, and diaries. They had spent hours sorting through the papers and documents left by his parents and grandparents. They pulled together what they had started to refer to as the "bones" of the family's history.

Jess was intrigued by his family stories as well as her own. She was a tall, red-headed artist and teacher, and they had been married for thirty years. She was going to miss the farm, and she also wanted to learn more about the stories that had been passed down through the centuries.

For the past year, they had dedicated Sunday nights to reading the old letters. One night Jess looked up with a quizzical look and said, "Some of these letters make me wonder if something historically significant happened here. After all, the farm was adjacent to Joppa Towne, back when it was a bustling port on the Chesapeake Bay."

"It's possible," Edward replied. "Philadelphia Road was the main land route that eventually connected the colonies, so this area was a strategic crossroads. Makes me think there's more to this homestead than old buildings about to be torched."

"Do you have any idea how Good Endeavour Farm was impacted when Washington and Rochambeau marched thousands of their troops along this road on their way to Yorktown, Virginia?"

"I don't know, but the family probably sold provisions and offered lodging to the troops or officers. It would be fun to know that." Edward leaned back in his chair and started to wonder if he was related to any notable men and women. Or were his ancestors all thieves and scoundrels? Did any of them accomplish great deeds? Or did they struggle just to get by, like most people at most times in history? "I would love to have the chance to talk with some of my ancestors to find out how they dealt with the evils they encountered. How did they manage when faced with frontier justice, tyranny, plagues, and a society dependent on the labor and skills of indentured and enslaved men and women?"

"I see the benefits of seeking more information, but what if you find evidence that documents something horrible in your family's past?" Jess asked. "My father used to say that you could make a great case for *letting the dead lie in peace.*"

Edward had also been wondering what he would do if he discovered inherited traits in the family—such as genetic diseases or encounters with mental illness, depression, or aggression. What if he found proof about family members who had committed murders or enslaved others? What would he do with that knowledge? "Good question," he told Jess. "I don't know, but I feel compelled to charge ahead and find whatever there is to discover. We'll just have to wait and see how what we find affects who we are and what we do with that knowledge."

Chapter 2

THE OLD FARMHOUSE

After watching Mario leave, Edward walked up the overgrown footpath to the chalky-white farmhouse. For as long as he could remember, any stranger getting this far along the flagstone sidewalk would have had a pack of English Setters yipping at their heels. The dogs were enough of a threat to keep vandals away and to keep solicitors in their cars with the windows rolled up. Yet today, all was quiet—no dogs, no livestock, and now that Mario and his associate had left, no other people either.

Edward scanned the rolling hillside pastures overgrown with orchard grass and honeysuckle vines waving in the breeze. This farm had served as his portal to the past. He would miss it. This was his last chance to stand on the land his relatives had cleared, sense their presence in the cabin they had built, and rest in the shade of the trees they had planted. A lifetime of sounds, smells, and emotions washed through his body. All the family stories were rooted in this tract of land, and soon, it would be unrecognizable.

As he approached the house, he remembered that back in the fifties he had helped paint the old brown shingles on the house barn-red. In the sixties, a "Tin Man" salesman came, jabbering about the wonders of aluminum siding "guaranteed for life." The house changed color to white with green shutters, as it was on this final day.

Before entering the house, Edward decided to relieve himself in what everyone called *Eli's Privy*. Nobody seemed to know who Eli was, but the tiny shed looked like it had been there

forever. Edward recalled encounters with spiders and bees
while visiting it late at night or during a sweltering day. It was
a well-maintained, sturdy little structure that had probably been
rebuilt many times over the years. It was located downwind
from the house and hidden behind several *very* healthy box-
woods—probably the healthiest bushes on the property.

Once he was relieved, Edward walked up the uneven stone
walk to the original, two-story log cabin. Someone had left the
door ajar, almost as if the house were welcoming him home. He
pushed the door with his hand. "Ugh." It was stuck again. The
doorframe had continued to collapse as the old, once durable
chestnut timbers deteriorated into an organic dust flowing like
deltas out onto the floor at the base of the walls. Termites and
time had finally taken their toll on the empty structure. It was
time for the house to go.

When Edward leaned into the door to shove it with his shoulder, it gave way. The top board of the frame came loose, and six,
baby, black rat snakes fell into his untidy hair. A scream erupted
from his throat, but he cut it short as he remembered there was
no one there to hear him except the snakes. He brushed off the
tiny reptiles and watched as they wiggled to safety among the
cracks at the base of the broken doorframe. For just a moment
he wondered where their momma might be . . . probably in the
basement. Over the years he had pulled a number of five- to six-
foot black rat snakes out of the foundation by hand.

Once his nerves had calmed down, Edward gingerly stepped
through the door and into the compact kitchen, the main room of
the old log cabin. The room reeked with the mustiness of decay,
and he noticed dark-green, pistachio-green, and black mold
clinging to the smoke-darkened walls. Only twelve short months
had transpired since the house had been abandoned and already
everything was deteriorating. How quickly nature begins the
process of reclaiming her own, he thought.

Edward stood there, his five foot, ten inches tall, 185 pound frame filling the collapsing entrance to the old kitchen. He reached up and touched the low ceiling overhead. Immediately, a tinge of claustrophobia washed over him. He tried to imagine the settler family, just happy to have shelter and food, fighting to survive in this cramped, single room back in Colonial days.

Every view of the kitchen brought back memories. Edward could picture his mother's old shotgun hanging over the door, the flyswatter by the window, and pots on the stove. Looking to the left, he imagined her rotating the waffle iron and rolling out crusts for apple pies.

Closing his eyes, Edward could smell the nutmeg in the shepherd's pie and the aroma of a salted ham hanging in the corner. His memories were so intense that the sweet smell of blanched peaches filled the air. There had been hundreds of pint, quart, and gallon jars canned in this room and stored in the cool basement below. Old red Formica still covered the counters and tan linoleum squares covered the floor. Wear tracks in the linoleum revealed decades-old, family traffic patterns around the room.

Edward took a deep breath and recalled his father's Concord grape wine exploding in the fermentation vats in the basement. The rich, red wine aromas had seeped through the cracks into all three floors of the old wooden addition, permeating up and out into every room. Even now he detected the fermented grape residue at the back of his throat.

Then Edward spun around, thinking he'd heard his mother asking the usual questions as he came in the door.

Did you collect the eggs? Are the animals fed? Did you turn off the water? Her questions hung in the air, and even now, he felt the urge in his gut to run back outside and finish one last task he had forgotten to do.

Turning his attention to the right, he felt her presence as if she were sitting in her white wicker rocking chair, staring out the window and down the lane. She had often sat there, watching for his dad or some other loved one expected for dinner to come rumbling up the gravel lane. Edward recalled her hands fearfully fidgeting with her knitting while she anxiously awaited their arrival. There had been many times she had remained sitting there after the timer had gone off and the dinner was ready, with still no sign of his dad, who was often stuck in traffic with no way to call.

These rare recollections were triggered in Edward's mind by being present in the house that day. He worried about what would happen to these memories when there was no longer a farm to visit, no physical portal into the past. Would these smells, sounds, and feelings all drift away and disperse into the ether without a tangible anchor to reawaken them?

As Edward's scattered thoughts returned to the present, he knew he had to get busy. This was his chance to explore and discover more of the past. Grabbing his crowbar, he began his search for clues in the nuances of the kitchen linoleum and the weathered-pine floorboards of the addition. He pulled up a few boards that looked loose, striking out time and again. He kept asking himself where would he have hidden something if he wanted someone to find it in the future.

Having no luck on the first floor, Edward climbed up the well-worn staircase with its smooth, mahogany banister and entered his old bedroom. Immediately, he noticed several dents below the window that had been poorly patched with plaster. Aha, he thought, this is a little more promising. What could be hiding in here?

Smiling, he knelt down on the floor and reopened the indentations with the crowbar. Reaching in, he pulled out handwritten notes on lined, spiral notebook pages that didn't look that old.

He noticed that the penmanship was awful, as was the sentence structure. When he pulled out a 1959 edition of *MAD Magazine*, he concluded that the notes must have been written by his nine-year-old self back in the fifties. He chuckled, not remembering the papers and embarrassed by his poor penmanship. But the magazine and notes helped him recall how his father had been angry with him at first but then patiently showed him how to patch holes with plaster.

After scouring the second floor without much luck, Edward went to the bottom of the attic steps. Opening the door, he stopped dead in his tracks. The recurring fear he had experienced as a child when mounting these same steep steps up to the attic came over him. The attic was an uninviting and uninsulated space, sweltering hot in summer and bitterly cold in winter. It was full of bees, spiders, and bats, especially in the wavy-glass window alcoves at both ends of the large open room.

As he started to climb the stairs, he could once again hear his mother's voice calling, *Be careful, those steps are steep. Watch out for the bees. They have nests in the light fixtures. Don't touch the guns.*

When Edward was growing up, his dad had stored shotguns and rifles in an unlocked cedar wardrobe, off limits to Edward when he was young. When Edward was twelve, he got his own Remington double-barreled shotgun for a Christmas present, and he proudly kept it in the wardrobe as well. It was a big deal and added another element to his after-school forays around the farm.

Half-empty ammunition boxes and kits for cleaning gun barrels had sat open on the shelves next to the guns. There had also been boxes of clay pigeons in the cabinet and a hand-held trap sling for launching the disk-shaped clay targets in an arc across the sky. He had fond memories of his dad, a man of few words, teaching him about gun safety, how to aim with one or both eyes open, and the importance of cleaning your gun after each use.

The family's collection of real and ceremonial swords from the Civil War and various secret societies like the Knights Templar, Masons, and Shriners had also been kept in the cabinet. Edward didn't know anyone still living who was a member of those organizations, and he wondered what they did. No one ever discussed their activities aside from their social fundraising events for local charities. The family's arsenal of swords and guns was fortunately never needed or used during Edward's lifetime, except for trap and skeet shooting, quail, goose, and grouse hunting, and sword fighting by Edward and his friends. If there were stories connected to any of these weapons, they had not been passed down to him.

Edward climbed up the steep, narrow steps and scanned the barren walls and floors of the room. "There's got to be something here," he muttered.

The attic seemed so much smaller than he remembered, its slanted ceiling forcing him to bend over throughout much of the room. Above his head were flaky-plaster-covered laths underlying the asphalt-shingled roof. He remembered many cold December nights up here assisting his dad as the printer's devil when printing their holiday cards. They had used the heavy, cast iron, hand-printing press the family had owned since the 1920s.

"Add more ink," his father would say as the imprints became lighter and lighter. "Not so fast on the hand crank . . . you almost got my hand flattened in there that time."

Edward could still smell the rich aroma of the printing ink as the rubber rollers spread ink from the top plate across his dad's original woodcuts and typeset, holiday greetings. Creaks from the back-and-forth motion of the hand-cranked press reverberated throughout the house each winter, announcing that it was the holiday season once again.

Scanning the bare floorboards and ceiling, Edward's eyes settled on the three-foot-high side walls. He figured they were probably installed to keep items from getting lost too far back under the eaves. What's behind the walls, he wondered, and why haven't I explored them before?

It was time to find out, he thought, and using the crowbar, he ripped open gashes that then became holes large enough for him to climb through. Carrying the flashlight in his mouth, he crawled on all fours into the first hole. It was a dusty and cramped space. The floor was covered with desiccated mouse droppings and dead, crispy crickets, moths, bees, and a range of insects he didn't recognize. Edward held his breath, not wanting to breathe in any of the dust from these departed lives.

Shining his flashlight into the far reaches of darkness, he saw multiple piles of magazines stacked behind the half-walls at one end. Feeling like G.I. Joe, he crawled back on his belly and found that they were old copies of *Harper's Bazar*. Flipping through a few of them, he was shocked to see that they hailed back to 1867. Knowing nothing about the magazine, he could only assume their presence was a clue revealing something about the residents of Good Endeavour Farm during the late 1800s. Next to the magazines he discovered a fancy, polished, wooden toilet chair with a removable, porcelain chamber pot. It was a lovely version of an essential item from the days before indoor plumbing.

Since the toilet had been hidden away, he surmised that the occupants installed the short sidewalls after the installation of indoor plumbing and venting. These modern conveniences must have been installed sometime after December 1898, the latest edition that he could find of the dusty magazines stored there. They must have kept the portable toilet, thinking they might need it one day when the plumbing failed or if the well went dry.

Taking the oldest and newest editions of the magazines, he moved over to climb into the hole in the south wall. There he found stacks of *National Geographic Magazine* from the 1890s, each year bound together in a book of twelve issues. He saved the oldest and the newest, climbed out, dusted himself off and, heeding his mother's earlier warnings, carefully climbed down the steep steps. With magazines under his left arm, he scanned the second floor again but found no more leads. What more could he do? Start tearing random holes in all the walls and floors? A stirring of disappointment grew in his head. Was he just on a fool's errand, wasting a valued vacation day in his hectic life?

Right before Edward descended from the second floor, three words floated into his head: *the other attic.* His whole body froze at the top of the stairs, his right foot suspended in air, his mouth agape. Looking around, he wondered who had spoken to him. It was as if the house itself spoke, or his mother or some other ancestor was standing there with him . . . or maybe it was just his subconscious mind speaking to him.

Then he started thinking about what he had heard. Another attic? That's right, there must be another attic —or at least a space —over the two-story log cabin, which had a pitched roof. But he was perplexed. Why had he never thought about its existence before? He stood there wondering how to get into it; there were no stairs, doors, or windows that he could see.

Excited about this new possibility, Edward walked back into his childhood bedroom and eyeballed where the attic to the smaller log cabin should be on the adjoining wall. Adrenaline pumped through his veins as he picked up the crowbar and attacked the wall. Within minutes, plaster dust was everywhere, causing him to sneeze, so he stopped to wrap a handkerchief over his mouth and nose. It didn't take long until his body ached and he was sweating profusely. Dust and sweat covered his glasses.

Then the crowbar struck red brick—the disintegrating chimney to the wood stove in the cabin and the oil burner in the basement. Moving to one side of the brick, he continued until his bar broke through into a void. Working faster, he cleared out a large-enough passageway to climb through. His whole body tensed with excitement as he wondered if he was right on the edge of a significant discovery. What would he find in this hidden room? Using his flashlight as a guide, Edward crawled into the darkness of the closed-up attic. Fear and excitement ran through his body; he felt like a spelunker climbing into a dark, unexplored cave.

It was dark. The room was eerily quiet, filled with stifling air and dust that had been entombed there for generations. But then his ears seemed to pick up the whispers of times gone by, as if he had stumbled into an ancient mausoleum. He almost expected to see mummies . . . or at least a coffin.

Edward surveyed the room's contents with his flashlight, hoping its batteries wouldn't die. A cedar cabinet leaned against one wall. Opening it, he found it was full of linens. Then he glanced at the far corner of the room, and there, behind a few boxes, was an old chest. He moved closer to it and saw that it was made of brass and ornately painted leather covered with decades of dust.

A smile surfaced from under the grime on his sweaty face. "Now, this is more like it," he said as he walked over to inspect it. He wished Jess were with him to share in this discovery.

Someone had already sprung the latch on the chest, so it was easy to open. Slowly lifting the lid, he bent over to peer inside. Two beady eyes stared back at him. Yanking his head back, he dropped the lid in alarm, thinking he must have seen a raccoon or opossum . . . or something worse. Catching his breath, he listened carefully, and hearing nothing, took a second, more hesitant look into the chest, ready to recoil again if needed. The eyes did not move. He reached in and found an exquisitely carved mask with eyes made from glass beads.

Edward carefully removed several masks, an armful of colorful clothes, and early-eighteenth-century books about Africa, India, China, and the South Pacific. He decided the old chest probably belonged to a sea captain—and probably the source of the stories he had heard growing up. After all these years of speculation., he had proven his mother to be right.

Edward was excited but also a little disappointed that there was no treasure or messages from the past. The trunk had already been raided. Maybe such things had existed at one time, but their absence now just added to the questions he still had. Slowly turning around, he continued his search, scanning the room from floor to ceiling with the fading beams from the flashlight.

On the opposite wall a primitive typewriter sat on a writing desk, along with stacks of magazines and newspapers. Bending over, he carefully made his way across the room, trying his best not to trip on anything or hit his head. Finding another pile of magazines, he thumbed through the articles. He also examined a wooden file box containing birth certificates, obituaries, discharge papers, manumission documents, and bills of sale. These were original documents about his ancestors and events that had impacted the family on Good Endeavour Farm. Holding the documents in his hands, he smiled. This must be it—he had unearthed a motherlode of information.

Another wooden file box contained a treasure trove of handwritten letters signed by or addressed to either Nathan or Nellie. He had heard these names before but knew nothing about them. His grandparents would have known them. Who were these people who had written hundreds of letters from the 1870s to the 1920s? He was excited to delve into the files, but a bigger question invaded his thoughts: why had this writing room been sealed off from the rest of the house for so many years? What were they hiding? What were they scared of?

Glancing at a few of the articles, he smiled at their flowery prose, excellent penmanship, and formal nature. It was clear they were advocating for some issue or another. The letter-writers had been passionate, well-read, and had written dozens and dozens of letters on various topics. They had found a way to reach out and engage in a community much more extensive than Joppa; they had found a way to have a national impact. There were also written responses from the governors of Maryland and Colorado, two presidents of the United States, and other government and business leaders.

It was thrilling to be holding the life's work for not just one but two of his relatives. He stood there, trying to soak up as much as he could from Nathan and Nellie's secret little hideaway.

Delighted at the discovery of their correspondence, Edward took all the files, a few placards advertising town hall performances, a *Vote for Women* banner and veil, and a few of the magazines, including several editions of H. L. Mencken's *The Jet Set*. Along with all the contents of the captain's chest, he carried everything out to his van. He also took some of the linens he thought Jess or his sister might like to have.

It was getting late and time to go home. He smiled, knowing he had saved a great deal from the jaws of the dozer and had gained a peek into the past. Thank goodness they had not burned down the old house before he had made it back to the site today.

When he finished packing the van, he looked up and was struck by the brilliance of the cobalt-blue sky overhead and a thin vermillion line on the western horizon. The sky seemed to shine down on him even though he was only a speck on the surface of the planet. He hoped the treasures he had found that day would remind him of the beauty and all of the intangible gifts that the farm had provided him over the years.

Upon his arrival home, Edward unloaded the van and sat down with Jess. "Look at these treasures. Can you believe these artifacts would have all been lost forever if I hadn't been there today?"

"I'm glad you were able to be there," she replied. "There's a lot of family and even American history here. These items should help us flesh out more about the past."

"You know, I'm still perplexed on why it was hidden. I hope we find that out."

They brainstormed ideas on why someone would go to all the effort to seal off an entire room to hide their writings. What were his ancestors afraid of? It was puzzling. Who—or what—were they trying to protect? Neither Jess nor Edward had any idea, but Edward was committed more than ever to get back early the next day to find out what else was hidden on the site.

Chapter 3

DIGGING FOR TREASURE

Edward rolled out of bed early the next morning and pulled on the same dusty jeans and work boots he had worn the day before. A deep groan escaped his lips as he stood up; his whole body was sore from knocking holes in the walls the previous day, and he still had a cough from breathing in the mortar dust. His cough had kept him and Jess both awake during the night.

"Jess, are you sure you can't go with me today. We might find more treasures?"

"I would love to, but I have to teach."

Jess taught English and history to immigrant students who came from dozens of different countries. She had become a surrogate mom to many of them, helping them learn about and navigate the customs in America. She felt her dedication to her students was of primary importance, and even though she would have loved to go to the farm that day, her classroom was calling her.

Edward grabbed several muffins Jess had baked, filled his travel mug with hot chocolate, and then hurried out the front door, chewing and drinking on the way back to Good Endeavour. Concerned about not being there on time, he barely stopped at several intersections and spilled his chocolate on his lap as he accelerated through a stop sign. When he finally drove up the lane to the farm, he noticed that he was on site well ahead of the proposed start time.

When Mario arrived, Edward was more gracious and talkative than the day before, offering the contractor a muffin and explaining what he wanted to do. It was evident from Mario's more reserved body language that he wasn't as excited as Edward. In fact, he seemed slightly on edge by Edward's presence, expectations, and requests. Edward got it: this was just another demolition project for Mario, not a treasure hunt or a search for clues about the past—at least, not Mario's past. Edward knew he needed to get Mario interested in the project.

"Last night I discovered an old sea captain's chest and a file of old letters and articles sealed in the smaller attic—it's a real trove of information. I don't think anyone has been in there since the 1920s. Come take a look at one of the masks I found. I brought it back today just to show it to you."

Mario became more intrigued. When they walked upstairs, he was equally impressed that this older man had created such a large hole with just a crowbar. But even after Mario saw the hole and the chest in the attic, he still was not convinced that the day's efforts would be worthwhile. Probably just another time-sucking tangent to getting the job done, he thought. But he was also ready to cut Edward a little slack and work with him. "Okay, let's get going," Mario said when he had looked at everything.

"I'll stay out of your way," Edward promised. "But I'm planning to keep an eye peeled along the foundations and around the old root cellar."

"Don't get too close to the root cellar; they tend to collapse."

"You're the expert. Where do you think someone might hide a message?"

"Time capsules are often built into foundations or fireplaces. It's easy for stone and brick masons to build out a sealed-off chamber as they're building chimneys. They have fun with it, makes their jobs more interesting."

"That's exactly what happened when I built my home. The contractor threw in an old phonograph and a current Yellow Pages listing of phone numbers."

"Let's see what some old stone mason has left for us." Mario gave Edward a white construction helmet and showed him a couple of hand signals to use to communicate over the sound of the bulldozer.

The first target was the addition that had been built onto the log cabin. Edward kept moving around, trying to find the best view of the debris as it came crashing down. Several times, Mario waved him away from precarious walls and falling material.

Mario next focused on the two chimneys. The older chimney, built with local fieldstone, had been repaired with handmade, red-clay bricks bonded with oyster-shell mortar. It tumbled down quickly. When Mario took a break, Edward grabbed a spade and shoveled through the debris. All he found were bricks, paper scraps, and pages from more old magazines, nothing of real interest to him.

After the break, Mario used the dozer to knock down the newer brick chimney. Edward watched closely but again saw nothing of interest. This had been his prime target, but nothing was hidden there as far as he could tell. How disappointing, he thought, grimacing as he scanned the demolition site.

Mario then pulled up the rock foundation with the dozer, reaching deep into the basement to extract all the remaining copper and iron plumbing. Edward was having doubts again, wondering what he was doing. Then silence engulfed the site—the dozer had been shut down. Edward glanced over at Mario, who waved to him and pointed to where the foundation was twice as wide as elsewhere. Dust had filled the air, but Edward didn't notice. His eyes were on the suspicious part of the foundation.

"This could be it," Mario said in his gravelly voice. Together, they carefully lifted a wide slab of rock off the foundation.

"YES," Edward shouted, reaching into the rock-lined cavity and lifting out a tightly sealed wooden box. Thinking the contents might be fragile, he placed the box on the edge of a clean, blue tarp he had set off to one side of the demolition site. He gently opened the box and found that someone had left a worn leather satchel containing a slew of handwritten letters. His hands shook with excitement as he carefully laid out the items on the tarp. "Mario . . . this is just what I was hoping for."

Gingerly lifting the corner of one document, he saw a beautifully sketched family tree with names and dates of his ancestors who had lived in England, Ireland, and Scotland. Edward was in awe that one of his ancestors had so much talent and had taken time to share their artistic flair in drawing this document. What prompted him to send it down through the decades to be discovered and read by someone like him? The artist's signature on the lower right side of the page revealed that "Eli" had created this illustrated family tree.

"I wonder if it's the same Eli who built the privy," Edward said aloud. "It's a well-made piece of artwork too, but it can't be the original, can it? It must have been rebuilt many times during the past three hundred years."

Mario glanced at him but didn't ask for an explanation.

Thrilled beyond belief, Edward held the family tree at arm's length to fully appreciate this gift from a long-deceased ancestor. Examining the papers, he found there was one with a listing of Native American names. He did not know how that fit in, so he set it aside for later.

Wrapping the bundle up again, he carried it over to his van, holding it tightly to his chest and marveling about the miracle of it all. This package had traveled through time from people who had struggled and survived in this primitive cabin centuries ago, ancestors who had recorded their stories to share with future generations. The satchel had been "sent" on April 29,

1731, according to the letters inside it, and he "received" it on August 9, 2001. So much had transpired in that period of time, but the messages had been safely preserved, buried beneath the house for all those years. Edward wished Jess was here with him to share in the excitement of this discovery. He couldn't wait to show it to her when he got home.

Mario's deft hands got the bulldozer rumbling again and started to level the old chestnut-wood log cabin. He stopped when, much to his surprise, he uncovered a cornerstone, which he quickly carried over to Edward.

The cornerstone was a trapezoidal-shaped block of black rock with the year 1695 chiseled into it. Edward held the block with both hands, his fingers tracing the chiseled grooves as he walked it over to the tarp. The dark crystals in the rock reflected light back at him, and the white veins followed fractures that zig-zagged across the block. He would definitely save this piece. Just holding the block in his hands made him feel physically connected to his forebears, like walking on the worn, wooden stairs of the old cabin.

The only other artifacts found around the cabin site were clay pipes, broken pottery, and cobalt blue "medicine" bottles found in an old refuse pile near the back door. Holding the blue bottles, he wondered if one of his ancestors had had a serious addiction. Or had they taken opium just to get through painful experiences like childbirth or serious injuries?

There were no obvious Native American relics except for two, large clay pots full of grain in a sealed-off part of the basement. The room had been blocked off by his grandfather when installing the oil boiler early in the twentieth century. If there had been more time, Edward would have hired an archeologist, who would probably have found more items.

Mario used the bulldozer to push the house debris into a large pile and moved on to knock down the two, large, faded-green barns. Edward sat down to sort through the fragile and flaky letters written by family members from the mid-eighteenth century. He understood that this pile was a collection of messages intentionally stored in the leather satchel and put in a cache for someone to find. And Edward had found it. What were the odds? He was excited and satisfied with the find, even though there was no monetary reward. He accepted that and relaxed; he had found messages from the past and was excited to get home and read all the documents.

While replacing the letters in the leather satchel, Edward noticed what appeared to be a rough map scratched on the outside flap with a knife or quill or some other sharp object. It looked as if the rough drawing represented the four corners of the log cabin, with measurements extending out onto the lawn. He laughed. Was this yet another clue or just his imagination running wild? As unlikely as it was to find another treasure, he picked up the satchel and paced off the distances shown on the map. The markings led him right to the ancient pecan tree. He paced back and forth, wondering what it meant. Was it the location of a well, a dump pile, or maybe just the pecan tree—the most prominent landmark on the property? To Edward, this did not seem to be just a coincidence.

He went to find Mario and asked, "What are your plans for the trees?"

"We're running late. I'll knock the trees down tomorrow."

"Would you mind felling the pecan tree today while I'm here? I hate to see it go, but for some reason, I would like to be present when you do it."

Mario hesitated then gave a slight smile. "Okay. It won't take too long . . . unless we find something."

Edward missed the humor in Mario's comment because he was slowly backing up the hill and staring at the reach of the massive branches of the ancient tree. The pecan had grown to become a magnificent landmark on the farm and, based on the circumference of its massive trunk, could easily be over 200 years old.

Recalling past harvests, he estimated that his immediate family had collected thousands of nuts during good mast years. This single tree had fed his family for generations. Someone's thoughtful action in the distant past had continued to feed hundreds of people down through the years. He murmured a heartfelt blessing in its honor. The tree just stood there in silence.

Then it was gone. Mario had knocked it over in a matter of minutes. Edward watched as the ancient tree trunk shimmied for a moment and then fell, extracting a host of tentacle-like roots from the matted grass lawn and the bright orange clay beneath. The tree crashed with a thunderous sound echoing across the valley, and the tree trunk bounced twice before settling solidly on the ground. The downed tree opened a new vista across the front fields, a view Edward had never witnessed before.

As it fell Edward thought he saw a tiny glint, a reflection, in the roots. Probably just a piece of flint or mica in the clay, he thought, but something told him he needed to take a closer look. Waving to Mario to join him, he went closer to the tree and broke up the clay-encrusted root ball with a shovel. His lower jaw dropped, not believing what he was seeing. There, amidst the clay and rock fragments, was a chest entangled in the roots. Edward chuckled to himself as he turned around to show it to Mario. Although smaller, it was similar in design to the one he had found in the attic the night before. He just stood there, wide-eyed in disbelief, smelling the freshly disturbed, pecan-enriched soil.

Bursting into laughter, Edward thought about all the pecans he had picked up from around the base of this tree, never dreaming there was a buried chest just a few feet below. He tried to imagine how excited he might have been if he had found the chest as a kid. Of course, even now, at fifty, he was pretty darn excited at his discovery.

With the help of Mario and a chain saw, they extracted the chest from the centuries-old grasp of the tree's protective roots.

"Want me to pry it open?" Mario asked.

"Sure. But be careful. We have no idea what's inside."

"I bet it's full of gold coins, Spanish coins," Mario said with a big smile on his weather-worn face. After finding the right tool, he sprang the encrusted metal lock. It was tough, but he smiled with pride when it opened.

Edward brushed off the clay with a broom and a rag, and then, with his eyes wide with the excitement of a lifetime, he lifted the lid of the old chest. Shoulder to shoulder, they both peered inside.

"There's no gold bars or even gold coins," Mario said. It was one of the great disappointments of his life.

"But look, there is a dagger," Edward said, "and a gold pocket watch, a sextant, a brass telescope, and a lodestone-and-needle compass kit. That's pretty neat."

Closing the lid, they carried the chest over to the tarp, where Edward discovered that the chest also contained an extensive collection of yellowed, ships' logs covering the years from 1707 to 1730 and still in readable condition. That era, he recognized, was the heyday for pirates along the Atlantic Seaboard.

Examining the entries in the log book, Edward said, "There's a long list of cargo items crossed out with an X and noted with 'STOLEN' in capital letters. The owner of this chest must have been attacked by pirates." He showed the page to Mario to cheer him up.

Looking over the rest of the items, Edward discovered a captain's commission, detailed sea charts, descriptions of ports visited, and lists of transactions made. Just glancing at the logs about life on the high seas, written by one of his ancestors, was fascinating. These ancient records would provide a deep look into a sea captain's mind and travels during Colonial days. As much as Edward wanted to devour the logs, he refrained, deciding to take steps to preserve the documents for a professional to evaluate.

With no more leads, Edward wrapped up the treasures, secured them in his van, and went to find Mario, who had kept digging around the roots of the pecan, hoping to find another chest or even a few loose gold coins. Edward thanked him for his help, gave him his phone number in case Mario or his crew found other treasures, and turned to leave. As he drove down the lane, he noticed that Mario had already torched the pile of debris that had once been Edward's home. His last image of Good Endeavour Farm was of yellow and red flames and sparks tickling the evening sky.

After years of family speculation, Edward was quite pleased with himself that he had taken the time to pursue the rumors. Without his efforts, these seventeenth-, eighteenth-, nineteenth-, and twentieth-century records would have been destroyed and lost forever, like so many artifacts on historical sites. Was it his curiosity or his persistence that had paid off? Probably a little of each; they were qualities he had inherited from both of his parents.

When he got home to Jess, he was jubilant. His eyes welled up as the miracles of the day started to sink in. "Jess, my ancestors reached across the centuries to share a small part of their lives with us."

"It's incredible how much you were able to find and to save. What if—?"

"Yes, it's a good thing I went today. It is my good fortune to have found all of these treasures, and now I need to do something with them. I want to honor my relatives by fleshing out their stories and preserving them for future generations. Maybe

I'll learn something in the process. It could be a good way for me—and my cousins—to find closure in the messy process of selling the family homestead. It's time to write a book."

. . . And so, the stories begin.

PART TWO

Establishing a Foothold

Eli and Chenoa

Chapter 4

A Breeze in the Woods

Maryland Colony, 1696

A twig snapped. Eli's limber body froze in a crouching position and his heart began to race. His eyes scanned the rolling land before him as he peered back into the still, green, shadowy darkness of the forest.

Glancing toward the snapping sound that had caught his attention, a quick movement caught his eye—a mere flutter of a single leaf along the far side of the clearing. What was that, he wondered? Could a breeze be so slight as to move only one leaf, while all its companions did not bother to stir? Or was it something else—a shadow, a deer, or even a person along the forest's edge?

Eli did not have enough experience to know. After all, he was relatively new to this job of harvesting the forest's gifts. There was a great deal to learn, and his mind often played tricks on him during these long, lonely days spent foraging for food. Anything was possible here on the frontier of the Maryland Colony. You had to be alert at all times.

Could it have been a human standing there behind the trees watching him? But if so, how did they vanish? Where did they go? The movement had happened quickly, at a time when he was not expecting to encounter anyone, least of all another settler in this unsettled land.

His family's land, which they had named "Good Endeavor," was the most remotely occupied tract west of the emerging port of Joppa Towne. Eli's family believed their land was still wild and uninhabited except for the wild beasts that roamed the woods at night. His father had shot elk and deer and had seen wolves and panthers, but now they were rarely seen this close to their cabin. His father had fed his family on their flesh over the past year, so there were fewer large animals left to hunt.

Eli knew that natives once lived here, might live here still or occasionally travel through hunting for food. The movement he saw could have been a hunter from the mighty Susquehannock Nation coming down from the north or the Piscataway coming up from the south. It might have been an Algonquian hunting party from the east or Senecas from the west. They all traveled through these parts, but few stayed now that the white man had come.

There were no major native settlements here in Joppa, but there were a few small native encampments scattered around. They were largely inhabited by the old, the young, and the weak. All the healthy men had perished from disease, shot by other warring nations or by European settlers, or had moved west to escape the settlers. His family had built their cabin fully aware that it was possible, maybe even likely, that they would encounter native people at some point. Eli was excited and a little scared to meet one here in the forest. The only ones he had encountered so far were the old Indian men who traded in town.

Intrigued, Eli crept toward the spot where he had seen the movement, but he found nothing. He listened for running footsteps but heard nothing unfamiliar. There was birdsong, squirrels chattering, and the tops of hundred-foot-tall trees brushing against one another and waving at the powdery white clouds passing by in the sky. He wished his eyesight was better, that his focus on details was stronger. He looked hard, trying to discern if there was any evidence of what had caused the twig to crack or the leaf to flutter.

Eli saw no signs on the forest floor of anyone having passed through, yet there was a scent. What is that, he wondered? There was a fragrance in the air he couldn't place. It was foreign to him, just like so much of the air he breathed in this wild frontier land.

The unusual scent hung in the air, spreading slowly outward, mixing with the clearing's fresher air. At first, he hadn't noticed it, but the airborne dust or pollen sparkled when it caught the sun's filtered rays, and then the scent it carried hit him. It was a pungent, musky aroma that filled and excited his nostrils. He sat down on a log to reflect on what had just happened.

It was late in the day when Eli stood up and rambled home in a daze, continuing to ponder the forest's mysteries and what he might or might not have seen. This reverie faded away when he remembered that his bag was empty. Once again, he had failed at foraging food for his family's dinner. His parents and his two brothers would be angry with him for not doing his job. They needed him to be better at foraging, much better, or they would not make it through the winter. They had saddled him with a lot of responsibility, and today he could feel his failure in his bones.

He was new at the job. Just a few months earlier, when they had first moved into the cabin, his parents had sat him down and said, "Eli, at sixteen you are a grown man now. We need you to take on more of the burden of feeding the family. That means we need you to bring home dinner . . . every day."

"How am I going to do that? Do you want me to take the musket and go hunting?"

"No," his father had responded. "I will still go hunting once or twice a week to bring home meat. Your job is to go out every day and collect whatever is edible to complement what meat we can shoot or grains we can buy."

"We want you to collect seeds, berries, mushrooms, nuts, shoots, roots, and fruit," his mother explained. "And any birds, reptiles, and small game that you can trap."

"It's hard," Eli had protested. "The animals and plants here in the Maryland backcountry are new to me. I don't yet know what plants are good to eat and what might be poisonous."

His father's voice was stern as he replied, "You can learn. Talk to people in town. Pretty soon you'll be good at it."

From that point on, Eli's family counted on his contributions for dinner each day. His father and his two brothers couldn't help, as they were busy all day clearing the forest on their one-hundred-acre tract of land. The trees had to go before they could plant tobacco and earn a living off their land. It was tough carving a farm out of the wilderness.

Now Eli headed down the hill away from the cabin toward a marshy and stagnant-smelling oxbow pond, where he pulled up all the cattails he could find, roots and all. He knew the cattails would be enough to take the edge off their hunger. His mother had developed multiple ways to cook the stalks and roots—and even the catkins on top, which she used like flour. Eli was hopeful that his father had taken time today to shoot something more substantial. When his dad was lucky, he would bring home a quail, turkey, or even an elk. But Eli was not optimistic. He had not heard a gun go off. If his father had found game nearby, the blast would have ricocheted off the trees and reached his ears. Then again, his father could have left the tract to hunt farther west where game was more abundant. His father had already shot most of the game on their tract.

When Eli returned to his family's cabin on top of the ridge, he stopped for a moment, taking pride in the front door he had made all by himself. He smiled. The other project he had constructed was the privy, a two-holer with a few hooks and shelf space. He had located it about a hundred feet downwind from the cabin. The three sons and their father had built the two-and-a-half story cabin with their own hands and now all lived there with his mother.

Eli hung his satchel by the cabin door and hustled over to the privy to relieve himself before entering the kitchen. His older brother, John, was just coming out and warned him, "I wouldn't go in there if I were you."

"Why not?"

"Something must have died, it stinks."

"Very funny. At least it's sturdy enough to withstand what-ever you left."

"You're right. That privy ain't going anywhere."

When Eli finished in the privy, he returned to the cabin, which was a twenty-foot by twenty-foot room, complete with a stone fireplace and a built-in oven and spit. Central to the room and life on the farm was a table with five stools built by their father from the wood of a large black-walnut tree. Two addi-tional stools, pushed up against one wall, were surrounded by rough shelves holding rudimentary tools and serving bowls.

Simple shuttered windows had been placed on the east and west walls. The room was dark most of the year when the wooden and cloth shutters were closed to keep the wind, the sun, and the insects at bay. But the cabin was their shelter from the elements, and it was their home.

Eli, along with his younger brother, Peter, had dug the root cellar for the cabin. This underground room provided storage for food and drink and kept everything cool in summer and warm enough in winter to keep the preserves from freezing. The cellar was dark and dank and had a spring in wet seasons when water would run down the uphill wall from the top of the clay horizon. It would then flow across the cellar floor and disappear into the fractured bedrock that lay under the downhill wall.

The digging had been easy at first but had gotten harder after they had dug through two feet of rich, brown topsoil. They then encountered several feet of hard, orange clay full of increasingly large and angular fragments of black rock. This subsoil was mixed in with a maze of intertwining tree roots. At the base of the clay was solid rock. Eli and Peter had removed the black rock piece by piece from the hole and used it to build a solid foundation for the wooden cabin. His family had cut chestnut logs for the cabin walls and beams, split cedar shakes for the roof, and collected fieldstone for the fireplace.

After completion, the family moved into the cabin. They were overjoyed; it was the first house they had owned. Eli's parents slept on the second floor of the cabin, and the sons had to scramble up an even narrower ladder to the windowless attic, which was miserably hot in summer.

They had everything they needed, and Eli's father was fully committed to doing whatever it took to keep the land. He had borrowed money to get a start in the Maryland Colony, and now they would have to grow enough tobacco to pay off their debts. They all knew this would require a lot of work, but anything was better than conditions in England, where there had been no hope of a future after they were pushed off their land when the Land Act passed.

Eli's mother, Molly, had selected "Good Endeavour" as the name for their tract when they acquired the land, hoping their efforts here in Maryland would someday pay off. Most of them would say it had been a good endeavor so far, but Eli silently worried about the future. Life was never easy or predictable on the frontier.

When Eli came into the cabin, Molly, who rarely smiled these days, was deeply troubled by his mostly empty satchel. She stood there in her dark, full-length dress, hands on her hips, looking at him. She was a rail-thin woman, always dressed in dark colors, an apron, and a bonnet.

Molly had been raised as a strict Quaker and believed in hard work. She no longer considered Eli to be a boy and thought he should be taking his responsibilities for the welfare of the family more seriously. Tonight, she was angry with him, and when angry or tired, she often slipped into the more formal old English practiced by the Quakers, including the use of thee and thou. "Eli," she scolded now, "we've got to eat. What were thee doing all day?"

"I foraged all day, Mother, and collected what I could find. There's not much left around here." He handed her the cattails he had gathered.

"What? We cannot live on this. Thou hast to find more food to feed this family. This is the time that food should be abundant. Surely, thou can do better than this."

Eli was defensive. It was as if she was never satisfied with his efforts. "I've picked all the edible food on our tract."

"It's not enough."

"Then I need to go farther west ... which you told me not to do."

She scowled at him and said, "Let's ask your father when he returns. We'll never make it through the winter at this rate."

Eli knew that she counted on him, her reflective son, the curious one, for foraging. He had lots of patience and a good eye for nature, but no one had taught him how to forage and what to eat without getting sick here in the New World. He had already taken ill twice from eating berries he had picked.

Molly sighed. Once again, she would have to rely on the dwindling stash of food from her small backyard garden, the preserves in the root cellar, and the pease and flour they had purchased in town. Setting the catkins aside for tomorrow's baking, she started cutting up the slimy cattail shoots and roots. Along with the cattails, she would have to fall back on their everyday staples of pease porridge and the coarse dark bread she had baked that afternoon. She knew there would be disappointment if not grumbling at the table that night.

Dinner that evening was meager. The family's diet shifted dramatically with the seasons and their luck hunting and foraging. Eli's father, Caleb, returned home right at dusk that night, coming into the kitchen like a beaten man and silently putting his musket behind the door. Eli greeted him but did not stare when his father sat down at the end of the table, obviously pleased to be off his feet but quite solemn. Caleb had taken the entire day off from clearing the land in order to hunt, but maddeningly, he had even less to show for his labors than Eli.

His father's full beard hid much of his disappointment from coming home empty-handed. But Caleb remained quiet, and his family did as well—they had learned not to question him. His fear of failure had resulted in the past in periods of anger and depression; he struggled with his demons, his limitations, and his responsibilities whenever things looked bleak.

Eli's big brother, John, had come in covered with sweat and sawdust after a long day of cutting wood and sharpening his blades. That's all he ever did, seven days a week. It was the most demanding job of all in the seemingly endless effort of clearing the forest. The family had already cut several acres of massive trees, but it seemed there were an infinite number of trees remaining to be tackled. But John, as the eldest son, would inherit the land and the cabin one day, so he was fully committed to clearing the land.

In contrast, Eli and Peter were not quite as committed to cutting down as many trees as possible. But they knew better than to question the norm of inheritance rights with their parents. They did discuss it between themselves, and neither thought it was fair. But they understood it would take them all working together to clear the land and get a tobacco crop planted by spring. It was a high-stakes game they were playing—one they had to win.

John was determined to do his part and set an example, so he kept at it, day in and day out, in the heat, in the mud, in the rain, whatever the weather. He rarely complained but often came home covered with bites from mosquitos and other biting and stinging insects that had been meddling with his progress. The black flies fattened on his blood. The worst bites were the minuscule no-see-ums, whose welts burned for hours.

John's hands were heavily calloused year-round and turned purple in winter, but he kept swinging his ax. He had become known as the best woodsman in Joppa. Over the past year, he had grown taller than his father and had broad, muscular shoulders. But he had a near-impossible job. First of all, he needed to clear a much larger area for planting tobacco. He also needed to clear a large area for Molly so she could expand her kitchen garden to plant corn, beans, and squash, along with herbs, roots, and medicinal plants.

The produce Molly had planted in her small garden during this first year was all gone by October, and they had stored only a meager amount of food for the coming months. As a result, it was going to be up to Eli and his father to bring home enough food to feed the family throughout the winter, and today, they had both failed to bring home even enough for one meal.

Peter came in the door last, singing and smiling as usual, and pushed Eli off his stool. The two wrestled around on the floor until they got so loud that their father shouted at them, "Sit up at the table and fold your hands."

Peter sat down and immediately started talking about all he had learned in town that day. As it turned out, he had not cut wood that day either, since he had been hired out three days per week to one of the local merchants. It was just another way to keep the family going until they could all support themselves on the farm.

That night, John was angry. He always got angry when he was hungry and especially when he had to work alone. "I wish you all would have worked with me today," he groused at his father and brothers. "I needed the help. We could have gotten a lot more done with a two- or three-man team."

No one said a thing. There was nothing to say.

The meal that night only partly satisfied the hunger pains in Eli's stomach, but he couldn't complain—it was his fault. He had this nagging sense of doom, so he silently recommitted himself to bringing home twice as much the next day. He had to find some way to do better.

Over dinner, Eli mentioned his mysterious encounter. Molly didn't look at him but said, "Probably just a shadow in the trees. Is that what distracted you?"

Caleb looked at Eli and then at his wife and said, "It could have been an Indian. They know their way around these woods, and they're hungry too. Best you be careful, son. They're not like us. Many of 'em round here are sick with the pox. They're desperate people living in disease-ridden villages. If you see one, keep your distance."

"Are you mixing it up with savages?" John demanded. "Damn it, you must be crazy. Did you see what happened to Joe Tucker? He got shot with three arrows and now he can't use his right arm or turn his head. He's basically useless. They ambushed him right over on Foster's Neck and left him for dead after taking his shoes right off his feet and his waistcoat."

Eli ignored his brother and turned to his father. "Mother needs me to find more food. I'll have to go farther west."

Caleb looked at Molly, who nodded to him. "Go where you need to go, son, but be careful and always keep your knife handy. There's no telling what you might find out there. It's not like back home in England, there are wild things back in the dense forests here in Maryland."

Chapter 5

CHENOA

E arly the following day, Eli took off into the woods accompanied by the pre-dawn chorus. He was excited about revisiting the clearing where he had had his encounter the day before. Today, he was wondering if it had been an Indian. Just think about it, he said to himself, the person would have to be so attuned to the land that they could vanish into the woods. He would love to meet a person like that, if for no other reason than to learn from them—they would know what was good to eat. After all, how dangerous could it be to meet one of the natives?

Eli found a cluster of dogwood trees and spicebush about fifty yards away from the clearing and stood there motionless for some time. One of the basic rules of the forest that he had learned was that the less he moved, the more he saw, and he enjoyed observing the wildlife activity throughout the year. He eventually sat down on a fallen tree trunk and waited.

After ten motionless minutes, he noticed the birds had stopped singing. Something's up, he thought. Then he got a whiff of the scent from the day before and sensed someone was watching him. He spun around on the log, and right there, ten feet away, was a native girl, silent, motionless.

Eli sprang to his feet. He was so surprised that he did not know what to say, so they both stood there examining each other's faces and clothing. He couldn't figure out how she had gotten so close to him without him knowing.

She looked nothing like the girls in town. The clothing she wore was sparse and rough looking, her face was darker, and she seemed as foreign as the forest had when his family first arrived. Braids of black hair extended to her shoulder blades, and her calves were as trim and muscular as the legs of a deer.

Unencumbered by a lengthy dress, she appeared streamlined and ready to hunt. Eli noticed that her clothes were sturdy and their colors blended in with the undergrowth, much different from the women and girls he knew who wore shoe-length dresses with long sleeves, aprons, and bonnets. The girl appeared to be totally relaxed and was casually sizing him up at the same time as he was assessing her.

Eli sheepishly wondered what she was noticing about him. She would see a tall, thin boy with unkempt, dark-brown hair hanging down over tanned skin that was lighter and blotchier than hers. The girl might have noticed the hair just starting to grow above his upper lip and chin and his knee-length breeches, stockings, linen shirt, and waistcoat. Could she sense his bewilderment at seeing her?

The urge to run like a startled wild animal filled his chest, but at sixteen he was beyond running away from things. So Eli stayed and stared at the girl, feeling a great deal more awkward and out of place than this graceful creature of the forest who blended right into the shaded understory. She had probably grown up in the woods and was totally at home here, whereas he thought of himself as an intruder. His natural inclination in public was to stare down at his feet, but he refrained, afraid that if he glanced away for even a moment, she would vanish again.

Eli was intrigued by this encounter and excited to see her at so close a distance. Then he remembered the warnings from his mother and father. Searching her for weapons, he noticed that she carried a knife hanging from a rope around her waist. But he also noticed she had a basket, already half-full of food this early in the morning. A smile came to his face. She was out foraging as well, so he decided to talk with her. She seemed to be about his age, and he figured there was a great deal he could learn from her about the woods and where to forage. Whatever the risk, he was fascinated and wanted to know more about her.

Eli tried to smile as an offering of friendship, but his boyish face revealed only shyness. But that was enough to put her at ease. She knelt on the ground, and he sat back down on the fallen log. The forest which had been quiet came alive with song.

"H-hi," he stammered. "Uh . . . do you speak English?" It was a silly question. There was not much chance that she did, living out here away from English-speaking folks.

After a moment or two spent looking at his angular face and listening to him speak, she replied, "Yes. And Algonquian."

"What? How did you learn English?"

"My father taught me."

Eli was surprised, "How did he learn?"

"He was like you—a white man and a beaver trapper. He smelled like you too. But he is gone. He followed the rivers west to find more beaver."

Eli shifted his seat to get a ray of sunlight out of his eyes and then struggled with what to say. "You know these woods well, don't you?"

"This is my hunting ground. I have to know it well. I live off the fruits of this valley."

"Was that you yesterday?"

"Yes. Was that the first time you saw me?"

"I barely saw you then, and I didn't hear you approach me a few minutes ago."

"You have a lot to learn."

"You were so quiet. I could never move like that."

She got up to leave. "I must go."

"Will I see you again?" Eli asked.

The girl hesitated and then turned toward him and said, "Yes. Tomorrow."

"What's your name?"

Again, she hesitated but finally said, "Che-no' a."

"I'm Eli."

She smiled, "Yes, I know." And then she was gone.

The next day they met again and sat down in the same place.

"I'm glad you came," he said.

"I am here every day. I have been watching you and your family ever since you moved here."

"What! I've never seen you or any evidence of you. Why are you doing that?"

"To see if you were a danger to me. I wanted to judge if it would be safe if we met. I have learned not to trust many whites. I thought you might be different."

Eli had to think about that, how strange it was to know someone else was judging you from afar. Judging your character just by how you looked and your actions. But he did not feel threatened at all. In fact, he was attracted by her nature. She was calm, warm, and as curious about him as he was about her.

"Where do you live?" he asked. "I didn't know there were any Indian villages left in this area."

"I live in a small camp with my mother, my grandmother, and a few other elders. I try to feed them all."

"Are you part of a larger nation?"

"We are Lenape." Chenoa explained how her people were from the other side of the Great Shellfish Bay and the Susquehanna River. They were river Indians who had lived on fish they caught and corn they grew along the banks of a river the English called Brandywine Creek. The Swedish, Finnish, Dutch, and English traded with them. Then, without checking with the Indians, the Europeans built dams across the rivers, flooding the lands and blocking the fish from running up the Brandywine. The Indians were forced to change their whole way of life.

"My father moved us here to escape those white men and find a new way to feed ourselves," Chenoa told Eli. "Where are you from?"

"We left a place called Kent, England. We lost our land as well. Our father brought us here where we could start over and earn a living off the land."

"That is possible . . . but you have a lot to learn. I will see you tomorrow." With that, she stood up and vanished into the woods.

Chenoa and Eli kept meeting over the next few weeks, each time a little longer than the previous time. He kept asking questions about foraging because she always had more in her basket than he did. She avoided his questions about sources for food.

Then one day Chenoa said, "We used to share these hunting grounds with people from other nations. We formed alliances with the tribes we could trust. It worked. But they have gone north and west to escape the whites. There is enough food here for both our families. I am willing to share the secrets of living off this land with you, but you have to promise me two things."

Eli was ecstatic. He had been hoping they could work more closely together, and he was eager to spend more time with her. "What two things?"

"First, you cannot tell others about where I hunt and forage."

"Yes, I can make you that promise."

"Second, you must agree to be wise in the ways of the forest. You cannot take everything you find all at once. You have to think about the future."

"What do you mean?"

"I have watched your father kill all the larger animals close to your cabin. He killed the mothers and even the very young last year. Now there is nothing left."

"I don't think father thought about that," Eli protested. "He was just trying to feed his family, to keep us alive. I'll talk with him. If I can bring back more food from foraging, there will be less pressure on him to shoot game."

Chenoa held his gaze in silence and, after a long pause, said, "Come."

They rose together and set off into the woods. Their first stop was by the oak where he had first caught a glimpse of her.

"What's that scent that's so strong right here?" he asked her.

"Those are hidden mushrooms. My grandmother loves to cook with them because they have strong aromas and make other foods taste better. I picked a few this morning." She showed him her basket.

Eli looked into her leather-lined, woven basket and coughed, overcome by the intense aroma. "I haven't seen that kind of mushroom anywhere out here."

Chenoa laughed. "That is because you search like a white man—just at the surface of things. These mushrooms lie beneath the forest floor. You have to smell them first and then root around in the leafy thatch. Looking is the last thing you do."

He watched as she walked over to the big oak, squatted on her heels, and ran her hands beneath the leaves. Black-and-white tubers popped to the surface. He got down on all fours in the thatch next to her and tried the same thing. He found a few to keep but did not have the well-honed skills that she possessed.

Chenoa stood up and said, "Next spot." And with that, she was off like a breeze, jumping over blowdowns and zipping through the underbrush.

Eli followed but quickly fell behind. He was not used to running quickly in the woods. He usually sauntered, looking for clues for anything that might be good to eat. Now he watched with amazement as Chenoa moved through the understory with barely a sound. She followed animal trails, tree trunks, and rock ledges.

She seemed to seek out stream bottoms and moss-covered banks. It was clear she knew these woods, knew where she was going, and was able to run and keep her eyes on her surroundings at all times. His cautious movements were clumsy compared to hers.

They left the river valley and stopped to forage at several places new to him. They then ascended a ridge covered in sandy soil. Soon he was losing his footing as his ankles rolled from side to side on large, prickly nut husks. Coming to a stop, he looked up in awe at a grove of one-hundred-foot-tall chestnuts with equally broad canopies. They were massive trees, and there were many more here than back on his family's land, where he had picked them clean. He quickly filled his leather bag with the large nuts, complete with their prickly shells, and then watched Chenoa deftly shuck the nuts from their prickly outer layers with a sharp tool made of white flint. Because of this tool, which allowed her to separate nuts from their husks, she could carry many more nuts in her bag than he could. He sat down, picked up a piece of black rock and tried to learn how to shuck the nuts. It wasn't easy.

Once her basket was full, she turned to him and said, "Can you find your way back along the river?"

"Yes. I can picture the way we came through the valley."

"Good. I will see you tomorrow." Chenoa took flight over the ridgeline and into the denser parts of the forest.

Eli wasn't about to follow her but took a moment before leaving to reflect on the day. Chenoa was a godsend, and with her help he was starting to believe that their foraging might be able to feed his family through the winter. But he still had a lot to learn. The most important event of the day was that Chenoa had welcomed him into her world. She trusted him. Eli had a sense that Chenoa was going to be important in his life here in the wilderness.

In a triumphant state of mind, he headed home, smiling.

There was a little more bounce in his step, even though he was carrying a bag heavy with food. His mother would be excited that he had collected enough mushrooms and nuts for several days; he had never been this prolific. But how was he going to tell her about Chenoa? Should he keep it a secret? What would his mother say? What would his father say?

When he got home, his mother and father were shocked and delighted at seeing his satchel so full. Molly sensed something had changed and wanted to find out the cause of his record yield. She looked right at him and asked, "How did thee find so much? Thee gathered more food today than thee usually finds in a whole week."

Eli hesitated, concerned what his mother might say or do. He had made big strides but knew it was all due to Chenoa. He *had* to keep seeing her. They had made a pact.

Molly sat down and waited, knowing that Eli had something to tell her.

"Remember that shadow in the woods I mentioned? It turned out to be a girl, an Indian girl, and today, she offered to help me find these foods, both right here on our tract and farther west. She knows the land well and I'm learning a lot."

Molly was tongue tied, confused about how she should respond. She was concerned that her son was spending time with an Indian girl, somebody Molly didn't know. It could be dangerous. But on the other side of the argument, his relationship with this girl might help him feed their family this winter and ensure the family's success here in this new world. She tried to balance the risks they were taking. "I can see that," she finally replied. "She's doing a great job teaching you. What do you know about her? What's her name and where does she live?"

"Her name is Chenoa. Her father is English. I don't quite know where she lives. We just meet up at this big oak tree each morning."

"Do you know anything about her or her family? Is it safe for you two to be working together?"

"I don't know a lot about the family. Her father was a white trapper who has moved west. She learned her English from him. Aside from me, she hunts and forages alone. She does talk about getting food and medicines for her mother and grandmother, who she lives with upstream."

Eli's father had been sitting at the table, listening to this exchange. Now he said, "Learn as much as you can from this native girl, but be careful. Many colonists are scared of Indians, and I don't want it to get around that we work with one. You must tell me if you're ever threatened by the natives—or by the settlers. Do you understand? We can't take on too many more risks."

Molly turned to face Eli and gave him a firm hug. "Thee might be able to help feed us this winter, but please, my son, be careful."

Chapter 6

Pirates on the Bay

A few days later, Chenoa was not at their meeting spot, and Eli walked around and around in a blue mood, trying to find her or, at least, some trace of her. She was knowledge-able and fun to be with, and aside from his younger brother, Peter, she was becoming his only other friend in the colony. As a result of missing her, he was distracted all day and went home empty-handed. Eli struggled to understand his reaction of not connecting with Chenoa that day—he had never missed someone like this before.

As pleased as his mother had been with his full satchel earlier in the week, she was equally disappointed with him for return-ing empty-handed today. "What happened, Eli? What were thee doing all day?"

Eli looked down at his feet. "Foraging is getting harder as the weather gets colder."

"Is that all?"

After a few moments, Eli said, "Chenoa didn't show up today."

"I thought she was teaching thee how to find food. Haven't thou learned anything yet?"

"There's lots to learn."

The following day, Eli was anxious to go foraging with Chenoa again, but his father told him he needed his help picking up large bags of flour, beans, and other supplies in town. Visiting town would generally be an exciting opportunity, but not today. Missing Chenoa two days in a row made him wonder if he would ever see her again. That would be devastating for him and the family.

Eli and his father followed a rocky path along Little Gunpowder Falls that ended at the tidewater settlement known as Joppa Towne. It was a small, developing port near the north end of the Chesapeake Bay. As they walked, Eli was mesmerized by the fresh, clear waters splashing over a series of cascades and around rocky ledges. He and his father both bent over and washed their hands and faces in the cool waters of the river. They walked along neighboring, one-hundred-acre tracts of land that also adjoined the river. These tracts, marked with ax blazes on trees and cairns of rocks, were not yet cleared or occupied. The Good Endeavour Farm was the only property this far from town with a cabin. The farm was part of a larger area known as The Forks of the Gunpowder, so named because two branches of the river came together there as they emptied into the mile-wide tidewater portion of the Gunpowder River. All the area around the town and the forks were part of Joppa.

Caleb stopped to admire a gigantic oak, a chestnut, and a tall pine along the forest edge. "These trees are so majestic, and the forests are so vast . . . nothing like trees in the sparse forests in England. Most of the forests back home have been cut down to build shelters or ships or to use as firewood."

"I doubt that could ever happen here in the New World," Eli replied. "These forests are endless."

"I'm not so sure, son," Caleb said. "Just take a look at what we colonists have already done close to the bay in just a few decades. The poor and desperate men and women of Europe are going to become the lumberjacks of America. And there's no telling how many more settlers will come this way from all around the globe. This is a paradise compared to so many other parts of the world."

As they left the heavily-wooded backcountry, Eli could see for himself that most of the trees were gone—replaced by tobacco—on the flatter, sandier, and more cultivated tidewater areas. It made him stop and think about his own family's relentless pursuit of cleared land. Everyone was driven by some inner instinct for survival.

Eli followed his father across the dusty Philadelphia Post Road and entered the port of Joppa Towne. It had taken them less than an hour to get there, but it would take them longer to return, loaded down with heavy bags of staples and supplies.

Along the way, they passed the bloated remains of a whitetail deer. The musket shot had missed the heart and penetrated the haunches, so the deer had been able to get away but had died soon after. Caleb examined the deer, trying to determine whether he could scavenge anything of value. He hated to see all the meat and the hide wasted, but its abdomen was vibrating with maggots, so he left the carcass to the vultures watching them from a dead oak branch nearby. Caleb was devastated after encountering the deer and, looking directly at Eli, said, "What a sin to wound a deer and not track it down and harvest the meat. That doe could have fed us for weeks."

As they arrived in town, Eli and Caleb were welcomed by the smells of saltwater and seaweed delivered on the wings of an onshore breeze. They listened to the sounds of hundreds of shorebirds hovering over the docks and debris dumps along the water's edge. Closer to the waterfront, Eli encountered a more complex mix of odors, from rotting fish guts to manure-covered paths. There were also smells from tanning, brewing, and butchering operations. All the residue from these businesses went directly into the harbor.

Eli knew it was best to go to town on days with a strong westerly breeze or after a major storm that would have cleared the air and flushed the fouled waters out of the port. It was hard for him to believe that the aromas of the backcountry and the odors of the harbor, separated by just a couple miles, were so different. He was glad he didn't work in town.

Caleb and Eli walked to the docks. A dirt road and several sheds lined the waterfront, and a few wood-framed houses lay on the other side of the road. Hand-hewn wooden docks and piers stretched out into the wide, brackish estuary like arms welcoming seagoing ships to slip into an open berth and sell their wares.

"Do you realize that Joppa Towne is just one of several burgeoning ports on Chesapeake Bay, each competing to earn the rights for serving the needs of the immigrants while making money for the Crown," Caleb said. "Life is all about commerce. You've got to have something to sell and someone to buy it from you. Ships from both sides of the Atlantic are starting to include Joppa as one of their ports of call. That's good for us. The port and the surrounding area are becoming the largest agriculture and commercial center in the northern reaches of the bay."

Eli nodded. He was more interested in seeing the people in the port. They walked by several large private homes and passed the tiny jail, an inn, and a large tobacco warehouse. Farther along, they passed buildings with wooden signs advertising barber-surgeons, apothecaries, and midwives. Eli knew these common words since Caleb and Molly had taught their sons to read using the Bible and pamphlets they found in town.

They then passed the Anglican Church, which his family attended when they could; it was a good way to meet townsfolk and get to know the other settlers better. But the church was also a place of great loss for the family. Eli's younger sisters had both died shortly after the family arrived from Europe, one from smallpox and the other from yellow fever. The family had held their funerals at the church.

Those first six months in America had been a devastating time for all of them, especially his mother. Eli remembered his mother's touch, her smile, and all the good times before his sisters died. After their loss, Molly wore her sadness across her face instead of a smile and in her slumped shoulders every day of her life. It made Eli angry. He missed his old mom and the gaiety she had brought to their lives. Eli remembered his sisters' deaths as the time his mother lost her smile.

After the funerals the family came to town less often. Staying on their land was also a way of avoiding the various diseases that ran rampant through Joppa Town and the other colonial settlements.

Caleb continued explaining to Eli that the port was their critical lifeline to the outside world. Roads were rare and not as necessary for connecting settlements growing on the shores of a vast estuary like the Chesapeake. He pointed out the town's three public wells, each hosting a bucket for people to use and a wooden watering trough for horses and oxen. "It's essential to make sure your water is clean to avoid dysentery, the scourge of our time," Caleb reminded his son. "Don't drink any water in town. It's no good. The milk here will make you sick, too, because it goes bad quickly. We can't afford for you to be taken sick."

"What can I drink if I'm thirsty?"

"The safest drinks in town are hard cider, beer, ale, rum, and whiskey. The alcohol makes you stronger and kills whatever it is that makes a person sick."

"But mother gave me a beating the last time I drank cider."

"That's because you drank too much and made a fool of yourself. You were a bit fishy-looking with bleary eyes and turned-down lips. If you're going to drink the hard stuff, you've got to know when to stop."

"How about tea and chocolate? They use boiled water."

"Yeah, but those drinks are costly. I always have a few swigs of water at the farm before going anywhere, or I take water with me. There's no better water than what we draw from our spring."

Eli had heard all this before, so he glanced behind his father and watched several tall, ocean-going merchant ships at anchor in the harbor. He could not take his eyes off them. The sleek vessels were things of beauty with long, swooping gunwales, tall masts, and rigging like threads in an intricate spider web. At the very top were crow's nests and the English Red Ensign, the flag of the Royal Navy. He wished he could take the time to sketch one of tall ships.

When ships were in port, the little town usually bustled with the unloading and loading of cargo and the bartering and selling of goods and materials. Eli found it exhilarating to see all the activity every time he came to town. But today, he noticed an eerie calm—few people were on the streets. It was as if everyone was in their homes, waiting for something to happen.

When Caleb and Eli arrived at the waterfront, they spoke with several merchants but found few supplies available. The lack of supplies was a grave disappointment, and Eli could see the concern in the wrinkles on his father's brow. Caleb had thought he would be stocking up on critical supplies in plenty of time for winter, but there was no flour available since no new ships had come into the port for days.

Eli could sense that his father felt a pang of hopelessness at the situation. His father withdrew a bit and looked down at the ground, probably contemplating what to do next. Moments like these helped Eli understand that his family had little control over their lives. His father desperately needed the Crown to come through with a regular merchant fleet if he, his family, and the colonies were going to survive.

A merchant friend named Benjamin came over to talk with Caleb, sensing his confusion and frustration. After a cordial greeting, the older man said, "A crazy Frenchman named Louis Guittar decided to become a pirate. He's commandeered a French cutter, ironically named *La Paix*, and has been raiding

British merchant ships down at the mouth of the bay. He has taken control of several ships by now."

"Oh no. Not another flaming pirate," Caleb exclaimed.

"Yes, indeed, and his aggressive actions have shut down all commerce on the bay."

"That bloody bugger. Who does he think he is, another Captain Kidd? No wonder the town's quiet. The Royal Navy needs to capture his arse and hang him."

"You're right, but that might not be too easy," the merchant replied. "Guittar has a formidable crew of a hundred and fifty cutthroats and twenty cannon, and he has attacked three vessels in the past week. The word is he boarded the ships, plundering the cargo and taking men captive, stealing sails and rigging, and even burning boats. Captains throughout the Chesapeake are hiding their ships in ports like ours, scared of being attacked in open water by this monster's armada."

"I wouldn't go out either, with a madman on the loose," Caleb concurred. "But I wonder how well we could defend ourselves if he sailed into port here."

"It would take a while to gather a hundred and fifty men, and I doubt they would be as fierce or as bloodthirsty as the pirates."

"Most of us would do anything to protect our homes. I would bring my three sons down to defend the port, but we only have one musket."

"To fight a pirate sloop or frigate, what we need are cannon, a lot of them, not muskets."

"How do we get our hands on a cannon?"

"Don't lose sleep over it," Benjamin advised. "I'm sure the Crown will act to regain control of the seas. That's their job to go out and capture these pirates. I wager shipping will get back to normal in a few days."

Caleb took a deep breath and nodded. "I can get by for a few days, but we'll be needing flour, beans, and other supplies to get through the winter."

"We all need supplies from England and the Caribbean. My bones are telling me it's going to be a bad winter"

On their way home Caleb took the opportunity to talk with Eli about the events of the day. Eli knew right away that his father wanted him to listen to what he had to say, because his father's pace slowed and his voice had deepened. "Now that you're a man, you need to be thinking about the risks we face here on the frontier."

"Yes, I know. We can't count on anything or anybody but ourselves," Eli responded.

His father put his hand on Eli's shoulder. "What makes it worse are men who think they can cheat, steal, or even kill without consequence. This pirate sounds like one of those people. He's not just stealing from the owners of those ships that he's plundering, he's also shutting down all commerce around the bay, making it hard on every one of us. We've got to have laws and learn how to enforce them to discourage these villains."

Eli looked at his father's wrinkled face and asked, "Can't the king help us with the pirates?"

"We have Crown-appointed governors in each colony who need to act quickly to re-establish law and order. If they don't, we're all in trouble."

"What do we do if they fail?"

"Our family has to be ready for anything. We need to build trust with our neighbors, build up our food supplies, and you boys have to be ready to fight as a last resort."

Eli stared at the ground as he took this all in, not quite ready to accept that things could change at any moment. "Is there any place we can go and be safe from people like that?"

"We left England to get away from dangerous men in our hamlet who took away our lands. You know we intended to settle on the James River in Virginia but were unable to secure decent land there, so we moved here to the Maryland colony."

"Is it better here?"

Caleb took a moment and then said, "You know that, with me being a non-conformist and Mother being a Quaker, we're not always welcome. But at least here there is more opportunity and less religious squabbling, so, yes, I think it's better."

When they returned home, Molly was alarmed that they had been unable to bring any supplies back from town. She was not a worrier, but it was hard to make dinner with little food in the pantry. Eli sensed she was scared about the coming winter, too.

That night at dinner, his older brother, John, said, "It makes me sick that you went on a wild goose chase today with nothing to show for it. I can't level the forest all by myself."

In contrast, Eli's younger brother, Peter, was excited to share more about the pirates. Many young people thought there was something romantic about life at sea, and the pirates cut dashing, larger-than-life figures. "They're not afraid of the Spanish, French, and even English fleets," Peter proclaimed.

The stories of their escapades fueled the picture of them as swashbuckling rebels, stealing from the wealthy merchants and divvying up the loot among the impoverished pirate deckhands. But it was clear to Eli that the pirates' actions were hurting the poor, starving settlers the most.

"I sure would like to know more about Louis Guittar and his battles at sea," Peter continued. "I might have seen or heard of some of those ships that he has attacked. I have seen a number of Crown-sponsored privateers come into port and have often wondered if any of them have gone rogue and become pirates."

Caleb did not respond, and Eli wondered what his father thought of Peter's romanticizing the pirates' lives. "You won't be so happy with the pirates if their actions cause us to starve this winter," Eli warned his brother.

Peter was the one in the family who had a growing sense of wanderlust, and being the third in line, he knew he would not end up with the farm. He therefore focused his interests elsewhere and often shared his dreams with his brother about traveling to far-off places. But Eli never took any of it seriously. He was happy being right here on dry land, exploring the woods of their backcountry home.

A few days later, when he came home from town, Peter reported that the British governor of Virginia, Francis Nicholson, had quickly dispatched military frigates to capture the pirate. After a twelve-hour battle, Guittar had surrendered. The pirates who didn't jump ship and disappear into the marshlands were captured and sent to England to be tried; their prospects were bleak. It was the custom for the king to hang pirates along the Thames in London to set a clear example of what lay in store for all future would-be pirates.

A week after the capture of the pirates, Peter announced that supply ships had arrived at Joppa Towne. Eli and Caleb set off the following day to walk back to town and stock up on the basic staples they would need if they were to have any chance of making it through the winter.

Chapter 7

WINTER BEGINS

Early in November, Caleb told all three of his sons that they were needed for clearing the land over the next several weeks. It was not going fast enough for his liking, and he was concerned that they were in for a long, cold winter, which would slow down the work even more.

Eli, anxious to get back to the woods to see Chenoa, asked his dad, "What are we going to eat if I don't go foraging?"

Always practical and often the mediator, Molly quietly encouraged Caleb to let Eli go back to foraging until their supply of provisions had been built up. She knew that putting food on the table each day was just as important as having a tobacco harvest the following year. Caleb finally agreed but with a stern warning. "You've got to gather much more food this week because the snow's coming soon, foraging will be harder, and we need your help with clearing."

Eli could sense his father was anxious about the progress of clearing the land, but he did not know all the details about the risks they were facing. He knew the soil was fertile and well-drained—they had picked a good location. But Caleb had underestimated how much time it would take to clear the land.

The next morning Eli was out of the house early before his father could change his mind. He went to the buried mushroom patch and didn't have to wait long before seeing Chenoa. He relaxed, relieved to see her, and his fear of never seeing her again drained away. "I'm sorry I couldn't make it the other day," Eli said.

"Me too. That happens. If I do not show up by dawn, there is no need to wait long."

"Dad wants me to bring back a lot of food this week. He's scared winter might be coming early and wants all of us to focus on clearing the land."

"Well then, let us get started."

Eli just marveled as Chenoa glided silently down the hillside and stopped by a cluster of short trees he had passed by before. Laying a hemp cloth on the ground under one of them, she climbed up to the treetop and shook it vigorously. Eli stood back, amazed as a rain of orange and purple bite-sized morsels fell onto her cloth. In no time at all, she was down on her knees, collecting the sticky fruit.

"What are these?" Eli asked as he examined one of the soft, strange-looking fruits.

"My father called them persimmons. Be careful, they may not all be completely ripe, and they can pucker your mouth." Chenoa picked one up, tasted it, and stuck out her tongue.

Eli ate one and liked the sweet taste. But on his second try, he picked up a harder one and immediately spit out the skin, flesh, and large seeds. His mouth had a dry, cotton-mouth sensation that he couldn't get rid of, no matter how much he tried to spit out the remains. "I see what you mean, but the ripe one was good."

"Take the softest fruit home to eat, they are the sweetest," Chenoa instructed. "We also dry them for winter. The bitter ones go into a fruit bread—I will tell you how to make it. And be sure to collect a few seeds in your pocket before we leave."

"How come?"

"See the gap in the canopy where the big tree fell over?"

Eli noticed a sunny patch on the forest floor and a large array of new growth. Chenoa walked over to it and planted a dozen persimmon seeds, along with several chestnut seeds. "Planting things we will use in the future is how we manage the forest. Every day, I plant something. Someday, our children will be harvesting these fruits and nuts and thanking us. Who knows, the fruit we gathered today could have come from trees planted by raccoons and birds or by my ancestors. Either way, those efforts have benefitted us."

"I've never thought of it that way."

Chenoa smiled. "We should head down along the river. I will show you where there are cascades of vines draped over small trees and dead snags."

"What kind of vines?"

"Grapes."

He kept up with her this time—grapes would be a real treat. He could almost taste them on his tongue. Now that he knew what he was looking for, he quickly saw the vines and wondered how he could have missed them before. Hundreds of long, straggly vines had climbed their way up both short and tall trees and were draped over the branches, looking like monks wearing dark green robes.

But when they came close to the vines, Eli was disappointed. The grapes were small, picked over by the birds, and many were dried out. Others had fermented and were surrounded by bees. If only he had found them a week earlier. Before long, however, he saw that the large, leathery leaves hid the best grapes from sight. He kept searching, reaching into the thicket until he found large grapes filled with sweet juice. "Father's going to love these."

Once his satchel was full, he said goodbye to Chenoa and started to head home. He stopped after a few paces and turned halfway around to thank her, but she was gone. He called out to her, but there was no response. Disappointed in his failure to be gracious and show his appreciation, he wondered what the best way would be to thank her for all her help.

Eli headed back to the cabin, proud of all he and Chenoa had gathered and wanting to show his father and mother that he could contribute in a significant way to the family.

When he arrived home, his dad asked, "Where did you get all this food?"

"Chenoa is showing me more ways to live off the forest. She knows where to look for things when they're ripe."

"Why is she doing this?" Caleb asked. "It only takes away from her own food supplies."

"I've learned a little more about her life and how her father was able to work here among the Indians. They form alliances that help both parties. She knows she can help us but she sees more white men coming and believes she will be safer if she is aligned with a white family, one she can trust.

"She also believes that our family's presence here may keep other whites from invading these foraging and hunting grounds. I think she's right that we will both benefit if we work together. I've made promises to her not to tell anyone where I'm finding the food and that we'll work with her in managing the land."

Caleb listened with a furrowed brow, grateful for the help Eli was receiving but also concerned about what that might mean.

After everyone cleared their plates that night, Caleb gathered the whole family together. "Eli's made a deal with Chenoa for food that we desperately need," he told them. "In return he has promised not to reveal the places where he is harvesting all these items." Caleb glanced at the dishes all around the table and then at each of his sons. "I support this alliance. None of us can break that promise. Is that clear? We cannot even mention that we know her—or any Indian—to anyone. If people find out, that threatens her life and ours. We need to make this new alliance work for both sides."

❧

Caleb was right about the weather. November and December were worse than anyone in Joppa could remember. The winter cold came early and stayed lodged deep in the ground. When the sleet and snow came, it hardened into ice on the frozen topsoil. The winds buffeted the cabin, and the white sun seldom showed its steely face.

The snow and ice made walking and foraging difficult, if not impossible. The family burned large quantities of wood to keep the cabin warm; fortunately, they had lots to burn. So much so that John sold cords of wood to the merchants and residents in town. But delivering wood was not easy. He had to pull sled loads through the woods or down the uneven, icy path along the river. They had no money for a horse or ox, which would have made his life easier.

Even the brackish-water port became icebound, stopping all shipping. Peter lost his job in the warehouse since there was no work as long as ice prevented ships from landing. Times were desperate with no merchant ships to bring food and supplies to the hungry colonists. There was barely enough food to go around, and it was a tough time for all the settlers in the northern sections of Chesapeake Bay.

Chenoa showed Eli how to catch fish through holes in the ice. It was cold, hard work, and for a while he suffered from frostbite. At the end of each day, he warmed his fingers in a pot of water by the stove. The most helpful skills he learned from Chenoa were how to read the habits of the animals all around him and where to set traps to capture small game. They managed to capture rabbits, squirrel, and quail. Chenoa also introduced him to the slippery elm, which had a layer beneath the bark that could be eaten. "If you have nothing else, it will keep you alive."

No matter what Eli brought home, the men craved meat, so Caleb began taking two- and three-day excursions west into lands that still contained wild game. He took Peter along to help him clean, carry, and drag carcasses home. When he shot a large elk, the house smelled of grease and game for weeks; it was a heavenly smell to hungry bellies. They knew they were lucky to have any meat at all.

A second but unspoken reason Caleb took Peter along on these hunting trips was to train his son to be a good shot. Peter needed to learn how to stalk, shoot, and clean a carcass because Caleb's eyes were failing. He was starting to miss too many shots with his musket. Peter had a nose for game, patience for taking a clear shot, and a good eye.

In mid-December the weather took a turn for the worse. Bitter cold winds swept in just as the food supplies of the most recent settlers ran out. It was a desperate time. The families without adequate food or money started begging from their neighbors. They were often met with locked doors and silence when they came calling—or a volley of buckshot. Life in the colonies depended on how much food you could put away during the summer for the following winter. With commerce grinding to a halt at the port, there were no good options for those recent settlers with limited supplies.

Reports started circulating in town that the few remaining native villages in the region still had food. The colonists smelled the aroma of fish floating downwind from the Indian campfires. These rumors spread quickly, making many hungry settlers envious and bringing out the worst sides of human nature. Desperate men and women, shivering and starving in their homes, started plotting ways to steal the Indians' food supplies. The hungriest of the colonists—or the meanest—decided to move the Indian villages farther west, claiming it was for "their safety."

A few days later, Eli heard that fifteen vigilantes with guns had shown up one night at the village where Chenoa, her mother, and her grandmother lived. The village occupants were forcefully loaded onto one open wagon and their food supplies onto a second. The old village was razed and burned, leaving only a few signs that it had ever been a settlement.

The vigilantes transported the Indian women and children as far as the road was passable by wagon, some miles to the northwest. The men abandoned the Indians in the woods with no shelter or water. The wagons carrying the food supplies never made it to the new destination. The barrels of dried fish, stores of nuts, flour, and beans, as well as blankets all *disappeared* into the night.

As word spread about the removal of the village, there was a lot of headshaking but no action. The vigilantes were never identified or brought to justice. The courthouse stayed eerily idle, and the sheriff remained silent throughout this time. No one cared enough to punish the men who had stolen the food, and no move was made to compensate the Indians. The settlers were all too concerned about feeding their own families to worry about justice for the Indians. The residents in town were also increasingly scared of what might happen to them as the vigilantes got more desperate. As a result, they did not publicly express any moral outcry about what had happened.

Shocked and scared, Eli took off to find the old village. After searching for half a day, he found the burned remains. Walking around the leveled site, his boots kicked up ashes and broken tools. Bending over, he picked up what looked like one of Chenoa's baskets, now badly burned. There was no other evidence to confirm she had been there when the vigilantes had raided the village. He wondered what they might have done to her if she had been there that night.

Eli was sickened by what his fellow settlers had done. His gut was tight and his throat was sore, and he didn't know what to do, so he took off to follow the wagon tracks westward. By mid-afternoon he had to admit that he had lost the trail, so he headed home, his shoulders drooping. He had failed at finding her and he felt powerless.

The next day, Eli ran to the woods, searching the spots where he and Chenoa had foraged, looking for some sign that she had been there since the relocation of her village. He found nothing. No sign of her at all. Of course, he knew she would never leave her mother and her grandmother. At one point he slumped to the forest floor in despair. There was nothing he could do to bring her back.

Eli asked around town but could not learn any details of where the settlers had taken the Indians. No one would even talk to him about it and acted almost as if it had never happened. All knowledge of the event disappeared, buried deep in the town's frozen soul. This type of injustice was all too familiar on the frontier. Humans could be cruel and selfish; they would do anything to each other in order to survive. Worrying about what had happened to Chenoa made Eli so angry that he could no longer focus on foraging. His emotions sabotaged his job, putting his whole family at risk.

Eli continued to stumble through the woods in a stupor as the days passed. He missed Chenoa's presence, his life empty without her. Her enthusiasm and confidence had become part of his life. Cursing the world, he even let his mind wander to a very dark place, wondering if Chenoa and her family were even alive.

His father finally sat him down. "Eli, pull yourself together, son."

"How can I? Chenoa's gone."

"Moping around all day won't bring her back."

"What will?"

"You have to stay alive in case she does come back. You need to keep foraging in the woods. If she returns, that's where you'll find her. Don't forget, you have an alliance with her. She will be back if it's at all possible."

"I've stripped all of the best spots for food."

"Then go farther west. You've got to keep trying. Use the skills Chenoa taught you."

"But what about her?"

"I don't know, but right now the family needs you to put food on the table, or we'll all starve and will be of no value to her."

Chapter 8

A PLAN TO SURVIVE

One night at dinner in early January, John eyed his father and spoke very slowly and with a somber tone. "Father, at the rate we're clearing land, we won't have an adequate tobacco crop next summer to pay our debts. We will lose the farm."

Eli had known this discussion was coming, and he watched his father's face out of the corner of his eye. He knew his father had already been thinking about all the ramifications of what John had just concluded. They all had.

Caleb's response was slow in coming, but finally, he turned to his oldest son and asked, "What do you propose?"

"We need money for oxen, a wagon, and hired hands."

Caleb sat still for a few moments, smoking tobacco in a soapstone pipe he had gotten from an old Indian in town. He did not challenge John's premise but asked in an even tone, "What can we sell to get the money to hire help?"

"They need wood in town right now to keep from freezing, and we have plenty," John said. "We also have lots of hard rock from the cliffs along the river. They have nothing like that down in the tidewater. There's a market for rock riprap for reinforcing the shoreline, building wells and bridges, and for house foundations as more people move into town."

Eli spoke up, "Wood and rock are hard to get into town along that rough path by the river."

There was silence all around the table. "What we need is a good road," Caleb replied.

John had been thinking of his options during his long, solo days cutting trees, but many of them had come to a dead end for lack of funds. "I agree. So how do we pay for that?"

"That's where the Crown comes in and the local merchants," Caleb said. "They could invest in the future by building a road out here to where there's plenty of wood and rock and, hopefully by next summer, tobacco."

John nodded. "This is clearly a crisis where the Crown should act. The cold weather threatens our settlement and our port."

"The short-term urgency would be to get firewood to the people in town as soon as possible so they don't freeze."

"We could get paid for providing rock and wood to build the bridges for the road, and then we can use the road to deliver wood, rock, and tobacco to town," John said.

"In the long term, a road will open up this whole backcountry region to logging, quarrying, and farming," Caleb said. "A road will benefit everyone. Tomorrow morning we'll go to town to test the idea out on the local burgesses and the merchants." For the first time in a long time, a ray of hope crossed his face.

Listening to his older brother talk about the plan made Eli appreciate how excited John was. His older brother had a vision, was enthusiastic about it, and their father was right there with him. Maybe they had found a way to raise money for clearing and planting. It gave them all hope at a time when none of them had much hope left. A glimmer of light flickered in the cabin that night as they all retired for the evening with the wind howling outside.

John and Caleb rose early the next morning, put a few biscuits in a bag, and drank several mugs of water. They were out the door before anyone else stirred. In town they met with several different groups and laid out their plans. As they expected, they were told that the town's coffers were low due to the iced-in port, but they found a receptive if cautious audience. The majority of people agreed that building a road was an excellent way to get firewood distributed to those who needed it during the crisis. A road-building project might be just what was needed in the community to distract the hungry masses and get money into their hands. It might also reduce the likelihood of further violence.

To build the case for a road, John went around to the key citizens in town and offered them a good deal on firewood delivery. He would deliver it to them as soon as they could build the road. One man was so enthusiastic that he offered John the use of a pair of oxen and a wagon in return for wood and stone. John also enlisted the support of all his neighbors who would also benefit from a road directly to the port. By the end of the week, the road proposal was passed.

Caleb was delighted when the flat ridgeline between his cabin and the port was selected for the new road because it was "high and dry," making it the easiest, cheapest, and quickest place to build. You could drive a wagon through a lot of the woods already since it was a mature forest. The main challenge was the need for bridges across a couple of streams.

John signed a contract to provide rock and wood for the bridges. He lobbied for the road to start at its west end—which was nearest to the farm—so he could use the wagon to take rocks from the cliff to the closest bridge first. This plan allowed him to earn cash right away.

Caleb decided to use the money the family earned to buy the equipment and the manpower needed to clear trees on the farm. To better understand his labor options, Caleb met several times with Benjamin, his merchant friend who was a sot-weed factor—a tobacco broker. The majority of the workforce in the northern part of the Maryland were indentured servants from Europe, although there was an increasing number of enslaved Africans being brought into the colony as well. Caleb ended up making a deal with two, ex-indentured men.

Eli, who always liked talking to new people, was excited to meet them. The two men, Jacob and Marcus, claimed to have logging experience and agreed to work for room and board and a pittance of coin, at least until spring. The men moved in with John, Eli, and Peter in the cramped attic, bringing lice, loud snores, and horrific smells. They also brought strong arms, a desire to work, and great stories.

Marcus told them, in very broken English, "I indentured to mean man. He beat me and did not give enough to eat. So I leave. The local sheriff knew how bad that man treat his people, so he not try hard to find me."

"You were smarter than I was," Jacob said. "I completed my full indenture and then received nothing. The indenture promised me land of my own and a gun in return for all those years of labor, but the man who held my papers claimed to have no money."

Both of these men had been lining up each day at the docks in Joppa, looking for work. They decided that working for Caleb and John was a godsend in the middle of a freezing winter. The first night in the attic, Jacob told Eli, "A hot meal, a warm room, and good company are worth a lot in a mean winter like this. Better than living day by day down by the docks."

Eli knew all too well that the overall plan had a critical flaw: finding enough food for everyone. He and Peter now had seven mouths to feed during this frozen winter. Peter went on hunting trips each week because the men craved meat. Caleb told him not to return until he had bagged something of substance. When Peter's luck failed him and he did not return for several days, the family had to count on Eli's ability to forage and Molly's ability to stretch the flour, beans, and rice. It was a balancing act for them all. Eli could have eaten twice as much during these frigid days. His stomach growled day and night like a starving beast. They had to find more sources of food.

✐

On one foggy morning when the cloud cover hung low, Caleb took Eli and headed east to the marshes and then out onto a frozen part of the bay. Usually, Caleb would have taken Peter, but he was sick in bed.

As they walked out on the ice, Eli could hear but not see geese squabbling and calling to one another. His father moved as quietly as possible in order to get close enough to the geese to get a good shot. On clear days it was hard to hunt geese. On those days, the birds would be flying higher, out of range of their musket.

Eli and his father walked gingerly on the ice, trying to find open-water areas where ducks and geese congregated to rest or feed. Walking on top of the ice was risky, and they were both scared of falling through. The ice kept talking to Eli as he walked. It rumbled, adjusting to the tides as they rose and fell. The shifting ice sheets created whale-like sounds, and occasionally, Eli heard musket-like shots as large sections of ice cracked. As the day grew brighter, he could see the cracks beneath his feet. These large cracks extended for hundreds of feet laterally and maybe a foot or two vertically.

Eli stopped, held his breath, and listened, hoping the ice would not open up and plunge him into the bay's salty, shivering depths. Caleb came over to him and tied the ends of a thirty-foot-long rope around each of their waists. He told Eli to stand as far away from him as possible in case one of them should fall through. The rope would give them a chance of pulling the other man out.

Caleb saw the fear in Eli's eyes. "Listen son, this is scary to me as well. We don't want to fall in. But my greater fear is not being able to feed the family."

Eli responded by taking a deep breath and stretching out the rope that tethered them together. He wondered if the rope would end up pulling them both into the deep. Then they started once more across the hard, slippery surface and silently approached a stretch of darkness—an opening in the ice—where geese and ducks were floating in the water. Moments before the birds would have taken flight, Eli's father shot at the largest bird. The blast momentarily silenced the birds. All that could be heard was Caleb reloading as quickly as possible, hoping to get another clear shot. But moments after the first shot, the waterfowl exploded into the air with a cacophony of honks and beating wings. The birds scattered in all directions and disappeared into the fog. They were gone by the time Caleb was ready to shoot again.

Eli orbited his father at the end of his rope tether, lay down on his stomach, and scooted close to the water's edge. Using a long oak branch, he had picked up back on shore, he reached out and collected the large, lifeless, gray, black, and white goose that his father had shot. Father and son then moved on, looking for more open water patches full of geese.

After walking some distance, Eli's father stopped still and whispered, "Freeze!" He raised his musket and pointed it into the fog. The distant sound of geese calling grew in volume, and then Eli heard wingbeats just seconds before two birds erupted out of the fog bank and flew right over their heads. Eli jumped when he heard the musket fire. Caleb had been ready for them and bagged another goose. But his father's quick movements also made his feet slip out from under him and he fell on his arse. Eli was concerned, but the first thing he heard was a belly laugh erupting from Caleb. The older man got up, smiling at his ability to aim and shoot while falling.

Later that morning, before the fog burned off, Caleb shot a canvasback and a hooded merganser as well. They headed home, triply rewarded by the waterfowl: there would be fresh meat for the table, broth for a soup, and feathers for a quilt.

∂ιρ

There were no days off for any of them during that winter; they were too scared of running out of food and not clearing enough land. Eli expanded the range of his foraging and was gone from before dawn until after dusk each day, but without Chenoa he was less successful. He knew the family was disappointed with him, which was frustrating, knowing he could be doing better with her guidance. He picked the ground clean of nuts under all the trees she had shown him and now was setting traps and scouring the woods farther west. One day he brought back a couple of woodcocks, which were tasty but small. He cursed the vigilantes who had destroyed Chenoa's village, blaming them for his failing attempts at foraging.

His mother had learned how to open and process every type of nut he could bring her, including chestnut, hickory, beech, walnut, hazelnut, and acorn. Marcus would sit down and help her, listening to the ebb and flow of the kitchen conversations. He liked to keep busy in the evenings, and she needed the help. Molly showered kindness on both hired hands, something neither of them had experienced since leaving their homes in Europe. Eli wondered if his mother's kindness was even more effective than John's example of hard work in motivating Jacob and Marcus to put in long days in the unbearably cold weather.

Clearing the land was hard work. The men girdled trees by cutting a broad collar of bark all around the bottom of each tree trunk, causing the trees to die and dry out faster. Several days each week, the team burned brush and would return at the end of the day with their faces, ears, and hands blackened with soot. They would cough all night from the ash in their throats and lungs.

Eli found it nearly impossible to sleep with the coughing, gagging, and spitting from the exhausted bodies all around him. But most members of the household were so tired that they welcomed sleep, even a fitful one, as an escape from the cold, the wind, their callouses, and their aching muscles.

On many a night, Caleb's three sons would fall asleep listening to Jacob's stories. As a down-on-his-luck Irish immigrant, he was full of stories of his travels as well as life back in Ireland. He would sit with his back against the log wall and deliver his stories with a lyrical cadence that mesmerized them all.

"I left an adoring wife and two imps in Ireland because I had no job there, no way to support them once they took our land away. We moved to Belfast, which proved to be a horrible place to live—dirty, noisy, and overcrowded. There was no work to be had in that piss-hole either. I was forced to sign on to come here, where there seemed to be more opportunity. If this doesn't work out, I hope your father will help me find another job. It makes no sense for me to go home to my wife with nothing to show for my years in America. And by now, my children are all grown up and wouldn't know me, even if I could find them."

Jacob had signed a contract for four years in return for free passage to the New World. It had seemed like the only way to get to the colonies and have a chance —or maybe a second chance —at life, but it hadn't turned out that way.

"While traveling in search of work, I've been beaten up, taken advantage of, and robbed of everything I had, including my dignity. Many desperate and greedy men have become predators, preying on the less aggressive souls—the trusting, the weak, and the hopeless. It's not fair. It's a tough life, an ugly life, and I hope I can do better in the future."

Jacob's stories provided invaluable but quite stark lessons to the brothers. It became pretty clear to each of them that if they lost the farm, they too might be destined for even more challenging times ahead.

In contrast to Jacob, Marcus rarely said a thing. He sat in the corner, with his rheumy eyes, crooked nose, and bad teeth, listening and nodding his head. Marcus had one wandering eye from a lumbering accident and often cursed under his breath but proved to be a steady worker. Eli would occasionally hear Marcus singing to himself in the woods, but Eli could not decipher the words. In the close quarters of the log cabin, the two hired hands became part of the family, and the family treated them as such throughout that devilish winter.

Chapter 9

THEY CAME AT NIGHT

By February, life had become desperate for everyone in the northern part of the Maryland colony. Even with money, food was hard to procure. No deliveries had arrived by sea in months, leaving all the import warehouses bare. Settlers began eating their dogs, horses, and oxen and continued to steal from one another.

One night, Eli woke up startled by the sound of voices just outside the cabin walls. Caleb had warned the family that they should be ready for hungry visitors as more and more people sank into desperate states of mind. The family's high profile while building the road, and the easier access the road now provided to their cabin, made them a likely target for hungry vigilantes.

When Eli heard his father get up and go out the front door, he threw off his covers, put on his coat, and went outside to join him. He was shivering from fear of their late-night callers but figured his father could use all the help he could get. Eli noticed that his father's gun was no longer by the front door.

Once Eli was on the porch, he saw his father standing tall in the darkness and holding his loaded musket. Facing him was a ragtag horde of men and boys clustered around the clearing. It was hard to see them all in the shadows, but several had muskets, and each had an empty burlap gunnysack for hauling home their bounty. This was clearly not their first time at paying midnight visits to their neighbors.

Eli couldn't tell how many men were there, but none of them said a thing. They just stared at him as he walked up and joined his father, and like a pack of starving wolves circling its prey, the vigilantes' eyes gleamed with hunger.

A small man in front held a lantern in his right hand and a musket in his left. But even with that light, it was hard to identify any of the men. Some wore masks and caps, and others wore scarves to hide their faces and to protect them from the bitter cold. Eli thought he might have seen one or two before but couldn't be sure. He stood up as tall as he could next to his father and waited to see what would happen next.

Caleb cleared his throat and spoke to the mob. "Evening. Mighty late to be out. What can I do for you fellas?"

Eli saw minute snow crystals falling from his father's breath as he spoke. The sap from a tree in the woods exploded from the cold.

The small man carrying the lantern took a step forward. "Our families are starving. We're here to take a share of your food."

From the man's tone, Eli knew this was not just a request. It was clear that this pack of men would do whatever it took to take food home to their families that night. He wondered why the vigilantes thought his family had any more food than they did.

"I'm afraid I can't help you, brother," Caleb answered calmly. "We're as hungry as you, and like you, we're living hand to mouth. We were not here early enough in the year to have planted enough to carry us through the winter. I can give you firewood, but I have no food to offer."

The men took a few steps closer, brandishing their weapons. It was clear they were wondering whether to shoot or charge this old man and his son. The odds were in favor of the visitors.

At that moment the door opened. Eli's brothers, his mother, and even Marcus and Jacob came out onto the porch, their hands clutching whatever they could grab to defend themselves. John held the ax he had swung at least 10,000 times, Peter had a butcher knife with a long blade that reflected the lantern light, Marcus had a *cant dog*—a lever with a metal spike for rolling logs—and Jacob had a pitchfork. Looking down at his own hands, Eli saw that his left hand held a crowbar and his right held a knife. He had no memory of grabbing them and no idea what he would do with them. Even his mother had a red-hot poker from the woodstove. She came right out to Caleb's side and bravely stood her ground. The yellow light from the vigilante's lantern reflected like live coals in Molly's eyes. It was clear to everyone in the clearing that this would be a life-or-death confrontation, win or lose, and neither side could afford to lose.

A tense silence hung like fog in the darkness. It may have lasted a minute or maybe two. Eli's knees were shaking, his heart was hammering in his chest, and he could not breathe. He remembered his father's comments that at some point when civil authority fails, your family's safety comes down to just you standing up for what is right.

Caleb broke the terrible silence in a low but firm and empathic voice. "Why don't you men turn around now and head home. It won't be long till the next ship comes into port. There's no need for us to tell others what happened here tonight. I know that desperate times require desperate steps, but I'm afraid that I can't help you."

The silence crept back into the clearing, punctuated by heavy breathing. The marauders eyed each other. Another minute went by, and then Eli saw the small man nod his head to Caleb and then turn around, pushing his way through the others and vanishing back into the darkness. After a few moments of hesitation, the others followed. Caleb did not stir until the mob and the swinging lantern were well out of sight and earshot. Light snow began to settle on the ground as he turned, looked kindly at each member of his household, and then went back inside the cabin.

Once inside, everyone huddled around the woodstove, trying to warm their shivering bodies. "That was close," Caleb said. "Our unified front convinced them they couldn't win without serious casualties. In case any of them changes their mind, we'll post a sentry. I'll take the first shift. We can't afford to let our guard down. All of us are desperate."

When Eli climbed the stairs to the attic and lay down on his bedding, he had a terrible time falling back to sleep, and it wasn't due to the snoring or the smells. Adrenaline kept pumping through his veins as he lay there in the darkness, reliving the whole awful encounter with the vigilantes. Every time he tried to fall asleep, he would remember the gleam in the men's hungry eyes. His father's words kept repeating in his mind as he reflected on all the ways the meeting could have turned out differently.

Life here on the frontier was fragile. He had lost two sisters in the blink of an eye, and he still missed them terribly. But that was an act of nature. All sorts of diseases existed and people died. Nothing you could do about it. But tonight's events were different, he thought. These men, planning to steal the last of the family's food, came to deliberately hurt his family. They would have let his family starve so their families could live. Was this how all humans would behave and treat each other in similar circumstances? Was the fledging colony here in Maryland that weak, that vulnerable? Could he ever trust other people again?

Eli stared into the darkness of the attic and wondered what he would have done if the vigilantes had opened fire or had charged them in the dark. He could have died, or maybe he would have killed one of them while defending his mother. He had never killed anything larger than a rabbit or been in a fight with another person except for a tussle on the ship to America.

But tonight, he had been in a situation where he might have killed a man.

In contrast to what he had just experienced as the dark side of the evening, Eli also noted the respect Jacob and Marcus had for his father. They had stood up and been willing to risk their lives, along with his family. He wondered if all men and women had a dark side as well as a good side, depending on the situation.

Eli was also struck by his father's wisdom and almost kindness when talking with the vigilantes. They were human too. Their families were hungry, and they believed they had no other choice. Caleb had done more than just show a display of strength. He had shown compassion, reaching out to their better selves, and he had been able to resolve the standoff without resorting to the use of weapons. Eli felt it was the tone his father had used that had proved effective. For the first time, Eli understood how valuable a person's empathy could be. He promised himself to remember his father's example if he ever found himself in a similar situation.

The following day, Eli was up early. After taking several long gulps of water, he set off into the woods, determined to forage with a greater sense of responsibility. It was even more apparent that they all had to work harder to ensure that the family and the community would never be in the situation of near starvation again.

A fresh blanket of snow covered the ground, recording footprints of the other early risers. Eli saw squirrel, raccoon, and rabbit tracks and followed quail tracks until he flushed the bird by coughing. The quail took flight like an arrow through the spicebush understory.

Eli checked his crude snares to see if he had bagged any game. They were empty. He took advantage of the fresh tracks and relocated the snares in a more heavily traveled area. He wished he had paid better attention when Chenoa had taught him how and where to set snares. Thinking of Chenoa made him miss her even more, and he hoped she would return one day. But for now, he had work to do and could not let thoughts of her distract him.

Eli kept an eye on the horizon, as his father had instructed him to do. It was always wise to play it safe in these daunting times when everyone was hungry. He rarely saw signs of people in the woods. He had been surprised once or twice in the past but saw nothing today. He smiled, knowing the snow was his friend. It was an absolute comfort to have a fresh cover of untrammeled snow to assure him that he was alone and safe.

As Eli approached the crest of a hill, this sense of comfort vanished. He noticed a small, light-gray beech that still held on tightly to most of its tan leaves. However, the sparkling white snow had fallen off the leaves on the lowest, elbow-high branch. The bare leaves could be a sign that someone or something passing by quite recently had knocked the snow off the tree on this still, windless morning. Eli froze in his tracks and scanned every aspect of the forest, from the snowy leaf thatch on the forest floor to the naked canopy high overhead. There were no signs of deer, hawk, or fox. Then he saw the tracks . . . fresh, human footprints in the new-fallen snow.

The tracks continued down the hill toward the river. The person must have been moving quickly, judging by the spacing of the tracks. Should he follow, he wondered. Or should he do his best to avoid any contact out here in his foraging pantry?

Eli squatted close to the ground and took a closer look at the tracks. He did not recognize the pattern of the footwear. But the shape, size, and depth of the tracks reminded him of Chenoa's moccasins. These tracks were different but, in many ways, the same. He almost expected to get a whiff of dark mushrooms. He stood up, his heart pounding. "She's back. I must find her," he said softly.

Following the tracks downhill, he recognized the zig-zag scouting pattern she often used. It had to be Chenoa. When he arrived at the riverbank, the footprints stopped. He looked all around for other tracks. It was just like Chenoa, he thought, picturing what she would have done to lose a pursuer. He stood there, perplexed and absorbing all the signs of life in the forest around him. Then he noticed a long sycamore branch with smooth, dry bark right above him. There was no snow on it. He smiled. Jumping up, he grabbed the limb and pulled himself skyward. He shimmied along the tree limb until he came to the main trunk. He bent over to an opening in the trunk and whispered, "Chenoa?"

"Eli?"

He heard a rustling from inside the hollowed-out trunk of the big tree, and there she was. She looked older, but it was clear she was excited to see him. Sliding along the limb, she came up face to face with him and looked softly as if nothing else mattered in the world. She leaned forward and hugged him for a long time. Words weren't necessary. The hug said it all.

His whole body warmed, and all the tension and fears of the recent past melted from his shoulders. Letting her go, he looked carefully at her face. It was as if she were reaching into his soul. Eli couldn't hold her gaze for long, so he started talking. "It's so good to see you. When did you get back? I haven't seen any sign of you for weeks."

"I got back this morning and came right here to set up a place to live."

Eli thought that was good news, but what did it mean? "You've been gone a long time. I was scared I would never see you again."

"Yes, it has been two cycles of the moon. But it looks like you have been able to feed yourself."

"We've been getting by, but tell me what happened."

"When the white men came and stole our food, my mother told me to run."

"That must have been awful. Did you run?"

"No. I chose to stay to see where they would resettle us. The men just dropped us off, leaving us nothing to eat, so we all had to forage for food to keep us alive."

"So what happened to bring you back here?"

"When it became clear that nothing good would come of the relocation, and when we saw the other elders passing on, my mother and grandmother each decided it was time for them to pass through to the other world. They told me that all their thoughts were about the past, that they no longer had dreams of the future. It was their time to go, they said, and they wanted to free me of any further obligations to them. They said I had a life to live, but it was no longer with them."

"Chenoa, I'm so sorry."

"My mother thought I should head west and find a nation I could fit in with easily. But my grandmother disagreed strongly. She thought I should honor my alliance with you and make a home here in the colonies. She said the white man is the future."

Eli didn't know what to say to that.

"We only had a little time together after that because they stopped eating. Even the food I found for them while foraging, they passed on to others. We held a sacred ritual where they called to the great unknown of the world to accept them and to protect me. The other women in camp echoed the songs and chants we were singing. My mother and grandmother said their final goodbyes with broad, silent smiles. Eli . . . it was so peaceful. They sent you their blessings and then just closed their eyes and passed from my consciousness."

"I wish I had met them."

"I touched their foreheads with my breath, turned around, and left. I did not stop running until I collapsed. I found a cave to shelter me while I mourned my past and pictured my future. I spent several days there dreaming on and off until the vision of my future became clearer."

"Then what?"

"When I left the cave, I quickly learned that I was still in the same river valley as this one, just farther upstream. Up there it has not been picked over as much and still has game. I could easily have stayed. But I found that I missed these lands where I had spent so much of my time. I missed foraging and talking with you. I decided I had to make a decision."

"How did you decide?"

"You were in my dreams, Eli, and so were these woods. My alliance with you and your family is the only one I have now. You and your family are the only people I have agreed to trust and work beside, and it seems to have worked well for both parties. I chose to come back here, even though I will always be angry with and wary of many of the white men in town."

"I'm thrilled you came back."

"This morning, I returned and left the tracks. I figured you needed to make a choice too. If you wanted to find me, I knew you would."

Eli was excited with her decision and pleased that the alliance they had made was now so significant to them both. She would be more vulnerable and totally on her own without it. He could finally pay her back for all she had done for him and his family. "I'm so glad you came back," he blurted out. "And I'm mad as hell at the men who did this to your family. A similar group of vigilantes tried to take our food last night. We stopped them, but they are to be feared. Many families are still desperate for food and can't be trusted."

Eli had no idea what else to say. Chenoa had simply spoken the truth, so he opened his mouth and spoke from somewhere deep inside. "I've thought about you every day. These woods are empty without you here." He touched his chest and said softly, "And I've had this hollow feeling, here inside of me, ever since you vanished."

Chenoa looked at him and said, "I know our alliance is strong, and it will get us through this winter. But I want to tell you that I have stored away the details of everything I saw on my trip back. I know where the beaver has built his dams, where the eagle flies, where the elk still thrive. I learned a lot on my journey, and I hope to return to those places again. I have been wondering if one day you will go there with me."

Eli was struck dumb by her stories: the loss of her family, the ceremony, her mourning, and that she had come back to be with him. He pondered her question of whether he would want to go away with her. Of course, he would . . . someday . . . but he struggled to find the right words to say. Finally, he just smiled and said, "It's time for you to meet my family. Maybe even move in with us."

"I do not want to rush that. They need to be ready to invite me in. I am fine here in this tree. Let us continue as we were for now."

"I'll leave that up to you. It's just so good to have you back."

Chenoa took his arm, and they jumped down to the forest floor. "I am here now. Let us see what food is still left in these woods."

Chapter 10

THE THAW

L ater that day, they passed her tree again, and Chenoa took Eli into the hollow sycamore where she had planned to live. Eli was surprised to see how much of the heartwood had rotted out. There was room for both of them to either stand up or lie down inside the trunk of the tree. There was also a basket of food and supplies she had brought with her. Standing so close together, he recognized her familiar scent, similar to the buried mushrooms he always associated with her.

"Are you going to be okay living here?" Eli asked.

"It will be good for now. Our people have used these large ghost trees for years, especially on hunting trips in new areas. It is easy to find them. They are the biggest trees in the forest, and although the bottoms are camouflaged with darker bark, the top branches are the whitest in the woods. You can see them along stream valleys from miles away."

Stepping on his knee and shoulder, she climbed out, he followed, and they headed downstream. Chenoa showed him locations that he had not seen before. Some were even close to his home, and he kept wondering how he had missed them.

Over the next week, with Chenoa's help, he rarely came home empty-handed. The family noticed the difference in his attitude and his yield immediately, so he told them Chenoa was back and what had happened to her.

They were saddened and deeply concerned when they heard how she had lost her family but delighted she was back to help Eli fill his satchel. They also knew she faced significant risks living this close to town. Caleb and Molly wanted to meet her, and they discussed how they could reach out to her and provide her with shelter. Everything they thought of was risky.

Eli did not tell his parents about his and Chenoa's plans to go off with each other at some point. But he knew that was in their future. Of course he couldn't leave now and go with Chenoa, no matter how much he might want to. At least not yet. This was a desperate time for the family. If he left now, the odds of success for the others would be slim. Eli also knew that with time the farm would pass to his brother John, so at some point it was likely he would have to move on from Good Endeavour. He wanted that move to be with Chenoa.

As winter ran on into March and April, many colonists started to fear that spring would never come. Then, one day, Chenoa stopped in her tracks and said, "Eli, look!"

He followed her gaze and saw a delicate white flower on one of the understory trees.

"It's shadblow," Chenoa told him. "The first blossom of the year. The shad will be running up the rivers soon. Winter is over."

Over the next few days, everyone saw the flowers, and spirits started to rise. Those colonists living in town by the waterfront began to hear deep rumbles resonating from the bay as the large ice sheets in the broad estuary shifted and began breaking up. It was spring, and the strong, radiant rays of the sun were beckoning people and creatures alike to come outside.

Chenoa showed Eli how the rapids along the Little Gunpowder Falls had opened up and were carrying ice floes downstream. The two young people were excited and happy that they were back together and that spring was coming.

"Tell your family to prepare the nets and the drying racks. The largest bounty of the year is coming!" Chenoa said.

Eli immediately understood. He had witnessed this event the

previous year and had almost given up on it happening again. His family had not known the previous year how to take full advantage of the free fish running up the falls. But this year, if the shad returned, they would be ready for them. Their arrival would be just in time to save both the people in town and the backwoods settlers. Shad had been feeding the natives for eons.

Eli got the family, aside from Marcus and Jacob, to stop lumbering long enough to prepare for the shad harvest. Caleb and Molly made more nets. John and Peter brought large wooden barrels out to the riverbank. Eli sharpened knives and brought canvas bags of salt up from the storage cabinets. They all kept their eyes peeled downstream, watching and waiting.

Eli noticed how his family's frowns had become smiles of anticipation. The wrinkles etched into his father's weathered face slowly converted to symbols of joy, and even his mother's face had softened and her mood was lighter. They eagerly awaited the fish and the feast that would save them from starvation.

The whole family now knew that this was the time to renourish themselves and start laying in the supplies of dried fish that would carry them through the following winter. Life on the frontier was all about planning ahead, and they now had learned firsthand what it takes to get through a harsh winter in Maryland. The whole settlement had learned—from the horrible incident involving Chenoa's family—that kegs of dried fish were critical for survival.

The runoff-engorged river broke up the ice jams and carried the last floes of river ice out into the semi-frozen bay. The flowing river was a beautiful sight, and it made it all the more exciting that the fish were returning.

Peter was the first one to shout, "I see one! There's another!"

They all let out yells as the silver flashes in the water showed that the shad were working their way upstream. By the end of the day, the brothers were catching fish. The first retrieval of the dip-net revealed two, twenty-inch-long, flopping fish. When they deployed the longer nets, each haul collected dozens of shiny fish, some as long as three feet. The harvest was underway and would dominate life in the colony for the next couple of weeks. That night they had a fish fry and gave thanks for this harvest from the sea.

The folks in town eagerly awaited the ice in the tidal parts of the bay to break up. They watched as open areas started to splash with schools of fish doing what they had been doing forever. The annual migration was a miracle that made Eli, and probably every settler catching fish, believe in something greater than themselves.

As the ice broke up around the port in Joppa Towne, dozens of men boarded their wooden skiffs loaded with long nets and pushed off into the ice-floe-dotted waters of the tidal part of the Gunpowder. Onshore, their wives and children would clean, salt, and dry the fish in the spring sunshine. Neighbors were working collaboratively to catch, dry, and store the fish in barrels. Merchants began to buy and sell fresh or dried fish to local farmers and residents. They would ship the surplus to other destinations not blessed with this annual spawning event. In just a few days, the Joppa community had come out from hibernation, and commerce was alive and well. The fear and isolation that had grown with the competition for food during the winter began to fade away. Eli's family and many of the residents of Joppa had made it through another winter in America.

Two weeks later, Caleb had trouble getting up for the fourth day in a row. He had pushed it too hard, trying as usual to clear more trees and catch more fish than was humanly possible. Now his body was doing its best to let him know that being human had its limitations.

Eli came up the stairs to see if he could help his father. Caleb lay there, grumbling, claiming his limbs and back were stiff and sore and that sharp pains were firing down his right leg to his toes. Eli could sense that his father was angry at himself, knowing he had overdone it and that he was not rebounding quickly. In this state of mind, Caleb confided to Eli that they had not made as much progress on clearing the woods over the winter as he had hoped. The tobacco crop would still be too small to pay off their debts.

"How about the money from the bridge and road construction we earned this winter?" Eli asked.

"Not enough," Caleb mumbled and then dozed off for a few more moments of tormented sleep, wondering how he had gotten his family into this deep hole.

The sounds of men walking up the hill to his cabin stirred him from his restless sleep. When Molly called up to them, Eli, fearing the worst, helped his father stand up and hobble down the stairs. They went outdoors to where Molly was standing on the porch. Were the merchants coming to take the farm away? Where would they go? Were these intruders more vigilantes coming to take their food? Or was there some other bad news the family would have to face that day? The family was tough, but how much could a body stand?

Musket in hand, Caleb hobbled outside to the edge of the porch and stood his ground. He blinked his eyes and tried to focus on the sight coming up the lane. What he, Molly, and Eli witnessed was the second miracle of the spring. A dozen tough-looking men, each as rough-hewn as members of his own family, were leading their oxen up the road. Each of the massive beasts pulled wagons full of lumbering supplies: axes, saws, rope, and crowbars of various lengths. Caleb recognized each of the men.

They were his closest neighbors, poor farmers like himself, just trying to get by. Men he had worked side by side with to build the road and the bridges over the winter. They respected him for being the leader who got the road built, a road that would benefit them all. Now they knew he needed help, so they came.

John, Peter, Jacob, and Marcus all stopped what they were doing and came over to see what was going on—they had to see it to believe it. After experiencing the desperate side of people over the winter, it was heartening for the family to observe the better side of human nature. Molly stood in the doorway in her apron, wiping tears from her cheeks.

The closest neighbor came up to Caleb and said, "Heard 'bout your back. We're here to help get this farm ready to plow. Where do you want us to start?"

Caleb could hardly keep his eyes from tearing up, too. After so much stress, fear, and pain, here were his closest neighbors, many as destitute as himself, ready to help him and his family survive. He shook everyone's calloused hands and shouted to John, "Set these teams up to pull all those big trees off to one side of the field. Stack any good lumber or firewood up by the side of the new road. Anyone wanting to take a load of firewood home is more than welcome to take it." He turned to his wife and continued. "Put the kettle on, Molly, get some biscuits in the oven, and let's serve up the last of the venison. These men will deserve a good meal."

The oxen, equipment, and human muscle did the trick. Eli watched, wide-eyed, as the oxen pulled the giant downed trees into piles along the edge of the track. They dragged all the dried underbrush into the middle of the opening and the men set it ablaze in huge bonfires. The oxen also helped to pull stumps out of the ground and line them up on the edges of the newly opened areas as stump fences. The farm was a beehive of activity from the misty dawn well past the darkening of the skies. To Eli it was like an army had arrived just in the nick of time to save them from starvation.

The folks in Joppa Towne had heard about the plans for the logging bee and smiled when they saw the smoke rising to the west. Benjamin, Caleb's merchant friend, sent his son in their wagon with a barrel of cider to share with the men. The neighbors all agreed to come back for several more days to get even more work done. It was gratifying to them all to see the dark forest slowly turn into a sun-lit field.

Eli had always known how important each family member was in meeting their dreams here in the New World, but now he appreciated how vital each of their neighbors were as well. It was a dramatic effort, one that brought them all closer together as a stronger and better-connected community. After losing everything in England, now they were on their way to being landowners and tobacco farmers. The whole family gave thanks and a collective sigh of relief. Although still wary of the future, they now had a better chance to make a go of it on their tract here in the New World.

Chapter 11

Malaria Strikes

Spring 1697

The family had made enough money over the winter from building bridges and delivering wood that they could buy their own ox. Along with the ox, John procured a leather harness, wooden yoke, and plowing rig to turn the soil. This gentle beast, whose withers were taller than Molly's head, could move a mountain and never seemed to tire from pulling the wagon, hauling trees, and plowing. When he did tire, he would lie down wherever he was and call it quits for the day.

Once his back was better, Caleb took turns with John on the plow. They worked the root-infested topsoil into roughly parallel ridges and furrows in preparation of planning their crops.

After the family completed the spring planting, Caleb knew that he and his sons could handle the rest of the work without their hired hands, so he sat down with Jacob and Marcus and told them it was time for them to find better-paying jobs. They understood and were happy to have had room, board, and companionship throughout the long, frigid winter. Peter and Eli were sad to see them go; they had loved listening to Jacob's stories and had grown fond of each of the men.

Once she finished planting her newly enlarged vegetable garden, Molly found she had a little more energy and turned her focus to her sons' education. She required Eli, John, and Peter to read or write an hour a day whenever possible. Caleb also took the time to make sure his sons understood the concepts of bartering, honor, keeping records, and the mechanics of debt. The sons liked the break from hard physical labor. Unfortunately, there were few books or gazettes to read, aside from the Bible, so Molly asked several of her neighbors to lend her books for the family to read.

The good times on Good Endeavour Farm did not last long. One night in late spring, Caleb woke to the sounds of his wife moaning and tossing in her bed. Molly had chills that soon turned into a severe fever. Her body ached, she was nauseous, and had coughing spells. In the small quarters where they lived, her continuous coughing kept everyone awake.

Caleb's face was contorted out of fear and frustration. He did not know what to do except hold her quivering body. Just watching her suffer made him fall into a state of despair. He whispered to the boys that he thought she was dying. They shouted back at him to "Do something!" He didn't trust the apothecaries in town since they had done nothing useful when his two little daughters had taken sick. He was scared the same thing would happen to Molly. He couldn't image losing her, too, so he sat there on their bed, holding her and sobbing.

"Chenoa knows about these things," Eli told his father. "She kept her mother and grandmother healthy for years while many others died. Let her come and see what she can do."

Caleb had developed a lot of respect for Chenoa even though they had not yet met. He had initially been cautious of Eli getting too entangled with her, but she had clearly saved their lives by teaching Eli how to forage. If anyone knew what plants to use to combat illness, it would be Chenoa. He looked at Eli, his eyes filled with faint hope. "Ask her if she will come."

Listening to them talk, John erupted in anger. "You can't bring her in here. What if word gets around that we're harboring a savage. That puts us all at risk. No one will trust us ever again."

"Keep your thoughts to yourself, son," Caleb snapped back. "We're talking about your mother's life, and that Indian woman has saved us from starving over the winter. Hasn't she earned your respect yet?"

John clenched his teeth and didn't reply.

Fearing for his mother's life, Eli ran out the door at first light. When he came up close to the giant sycamore, he called Chenoa's name gently so as to not startle her. "Chenoa?"

"Eli?"

"Mother has a terrible fever. You're the only one we trust to help."

"We?"

"Yes, Father has asked for your help. He thinks you're our best hope to save her."

"Give me a minute to collect a few things. I will need wild ginger root, basil, sassafras bark, and mustard seeds. I have dried bloodroot for her fever. We will need to go out later today to find witch hazel and other plants that will help."

Moments later, Chenoa climbed out of the tree with a bag over her shoulder and then began to jog towards the farm. "We should hurry," she called over her shoulder.

When they arrived at the cabin, the sun was brightening the morning skies. Caleb came to the door and greeted them.

"Father, this is Chenoa," Eli told Caleb.

"Thank you for coming, Chenoa. I greatly appreciate all your help."

Chenoa looked at Caleb and saw the fear for his wife in his tired eyes. She could see that his concern for Molly trumped all his other fears and prejudices and that he was willing to entrust his wife's life to Chenoa's care. They held each other's gaze for several moments, and then Chenoa's face softened as if they had been friends for months or years. "Where is she?"

Caleb invited her inside and led the way upstairs to the second floor. Chenoa sat down next to Molly and held her hands for a few minutes.

"How can I help?" Eli asked.

"We will need a bowl of hot water and one of cool water. I will need to make a paste of a few herbs and roots to apply to her chest and forehead—that will cool her down. And I will make a tincture for her to drink that should soothe her cough."

"What do you think's wrong with her?"

"She has malaria. It has been so wet, and it is common this time of year." She wiped Molly's forehead with a wet towel.

When Molly opened her eyes, Eli said, "Mother, this is Chenoa."

Molly smiled, then closed her eyes and said softly, almost to herself, "Chenoa. What a beautiful name." She then went back to sleep.

John and Peter joined them, and Eli introduced his brothers to Chenoa. Neither John nor Peter had seen an Indian up close, and they were trying to make sense out of it all. Peter was intrigued there was an Indian in their house, sitting with their mother and offering her comfort.

Chenoa's presence, there on the second floor of their log cabin, brought a calming influence to the room and to each of the men in the family. She spoke to them like someone who was used to illness and caring for others. "This sickness will take several days to work its way through her body and may produce bad dreams, but your mother looks strong. Noticing your blood-shot eyes, I suggest you should all get some sleep. I will stay here with her."

The men listened to Chenoa, greatly relieved that she was there and praying that she had a cure. They were scared and feared the worst. Each of them went about their work but checked in regularly to see how Molly was doing. Even John got over his anger and fear in Chenoa's presence and spoke briefly with her whenever he came in to check on his mother.

Chenoa was constantly by Molly's side, often taking naps on the floor by the bed. Molly's clarity of thought came back after several days, but she still had vivid dreams in which she called out her daughters' names. When Molly was awake, she was able to talk and asked Chenoa about the Indian girl's life and family. She asked about the chants Chenoa had sung to soothe her fears.

In turn Molly told Chenoa about their challenges in England and Virginia before moving to Maryland and about the two daughters she had lost. She said how happy she was that Eli had met her. Eli joined them at times, reading to his mother from the Bible. Like Chenoa's songs, the familiar verses seemed to calm Molly. When he was reading, Chenoa sat close to Eli, trying to connect the words he spoke with the words on the page. Her father had not been literate and only taught her how to speak English, not to read or write.

Chenoa took over the kitchen during Molly's illness and while she was recovering. She told Eli how intrigued she was by the cast iron cookware that Molly used in the fireplace. She tried out all the spices Molly had collected, grown, or purchased and asked where Molly had gotten them. Chenoa loved how the large fireplace projected shadows across the room, allowing the light to dance on the walls and across the ceiling.

After a week, Molly had recovered enough so she could get up for short periods to help in the kitchen. Chenoa stayed a few more days to make sure the symptoms were gone and that Molly's strength had returned. Throughout this whole period, Eli marveled at how the two women worked side by side without getting in each other's way in the small cabin. It was not like mother and daughter but more like trusted friends. As they worked, Molly asked Chenoa how she prepared the medicinal herbs and whatever else she had used to treat her malaria.

"Hast thou thought of selling these materials to the local apothecaries?" Molly asked. "Malaria is common. It would be nice to be able to reduce the suffering of others."

"I have never sold any cures. And I do not know if the white merchants in town would want our native medicines any more than they want us. Caring for others is a gift my mother and my grandmother have given me. The cures are more than just the herbs. It is the care in treating each stage of an illness and the songs that make the medicine effective."

Over the next week, a wave of malaria spread throughout the settlement. Word of Chenoa's treatment of Molly spread around to their neighbors. Husbands, wives, fathers, and mothers walked or rode out to the cabin to ask for Chenoa's treatments. Chenoa was happy to help, visiting several cabins for days on end and asking for nothing in return. These settlers grew to respect and appreciate Chenoa and overcame some of their fear of native people.

While Chenoa was out treating people with malaria, Caleb rallied his sons, and they built a tiny cabin for her on the far side of the property near the river. Eli was delighted. His family could finally live up to their side of the alliance he and Chenoa had made by providing her with shelter and friendship. He was pleased that she was now so close to their home and had a better place for drying herbs, sewing clothes, cooking, and sleeping.

Chenoa accepted the home graciously, and when she was not out tending to the sick or working in her new cabin, she often took evening meals with the family. Eli noticed how much Chenoa liked working with his mother and talking with his father. It was clear his parents had grown to love her company and found her perspectives on life of great value. Her presence enriched their lives and helped fill the hole in their hearts from losing their daughters.

When she came for dinner, Chenoa would often bring an aromatic cedar branch to throw on the fire. It would freshen the air and revive everyone's weary spirits at the end of the day. As tired as they all might be, Chenoa's presence made their table discussions livelier. She became a trusted and energetic member of the family.

Eli's parents respected how Eli and Chenoa worked together and watched as their care and love for each other grew with time. They didn't talk about Eli spending more and more time at Chenoa's cabin. Caleb and Molly were getting used to the idea that the strengthening bond between Eli and Chenoa might mean they would marry one day. At first this possibility of an Indian daughter-in-law and half-breed grandchildren alarmed them, but as they grew to love and respect this talented young woman, they warmly accepted Chenoa into the family. The alliance was strong.

Spring, 1698

By the next spring, life on Good Endeavour Farm had stabilized. Their first tobacco harvest was good enough to keep the lenders at bay, and the family had enlarged the fields even further during the second year. Thanks to Chenoa and Eli, they had stored plenty of food in the root cellar, and when it turned out to be a moderate winter, there was enough to share with others. Caleb and Molly had accomplished what they had set out to do in the New World. They had conquered their small part of the forest and had begun to understand how best to work with the land.

Family routines were evolving. There was more time for socializing and helping their neighbors. John was off many evenings courting a young woman named Sara who lived not too far away. He proudly brought her by a couple of times so that everyone had a chance to meet her. When they came for dinner one night, John spoke so much about her virtues that Eli thought John was showing her off as if she were a prized turkey. But most of the time they either dined with her parents, who lived closer to town, or they went out on carriage rides.

Eli assumed they would marry one day in the not-too-distant future and wondered where they would live. If John and Sara took over the third floor, he and Peter would need a place to stay. He discussed this with Peter and told Peter that he planned to move in with Chenoa, and he said Peter could join them. It was clear that all of their lives were about to change.

Chenoa's and Eli's relationship had continued to grow and mature. She was becoming more than his loyal friend and foraging partner. They were together much of the time, and he began to spend nights in the cabin his family had built for her, exploring the nuances of their friendship and their growing love for one another. Chenoa had grown into a full-fledged woman and was fully committed to Eli and her new family. Eli tried to express his deepening feelings for her and made it clear it was getting close to the time when they would go upriver together.

One evening after dinner, when it was just Chenoa, Molly, Caleb, and Eli, Molly spoke up, asking, "Now that John and Sara may marry, are thee two planning to marry as well?"

Eli blushed. He still had a tendency to be a little shy on personal matters, but because of Chenoa's love for him, he felt pretty grown up and thought it was a good time for the discussion he had been putting off. "Yes, we've been talking about that and are hoping to get your blessing. We're thinking of holding a small ceremony here at Good Endeavour after the crops have been planted. We're planning a common-law wedding to avoid any problems with the people in town."

"What does thee think about that, Chenoa?" Molly asked.

With a huge smile, Chenoa replied, "I already feel like I am part of the family. Thank you so much for treating me like a daughter. As far as a ceremony, I do prefer something out here on your land, maybe something by the rock ledge or down by the river, rather than something in a church. I have no need for any official blessing of our marriage by the white men in town—unless you think it is important for our children. I would like a sacred ceremony with just the six of us."

"After the ceremony, we'd like to go upriver for a couple of weeks," Eli added. "Would you want us back after that? We could build a new home or make our home right here in Chenoa's cabin."

Caleb stood up. It was clear that he was a little choked up, so he pulled Molly up as well. Placing his arms around his wife, he stumbled over the words. "Ch-Che-Chenoa. We would love for you to be an official member of this family in any way you want. I think our alliance has been strong, and we would be pleased if you could keep it going for generations to come."

"I would like nothing better than for thee to raise your family on Good Endeavour Farm," Molly told them. "And as far as town is concerned, thou hast already won over the hearts of our neighbors that thou nursed through malaria. Yes, there will be tough times ahead, but we'll stand together in facing the future."

On a warm spring night a few weeks later, when the family had just finished dinner, Peter cleared his throat and stood up with a smile across his face and a mug in his hand. "I'm excited to say that I've just signed up as a cabin boy on the *Halifax*. We leave port next Tuesday, heading north for the Maritimes."

The room fell silent. Each of them had been thrown off balance with this sudden decision They looked at one another with expressions of wide-eyed disbelief. Then John asked, "When will you be back?"

"We should be at sea for at least a couple of months,

depending on what products we pick up at each port, so I could be back for a visit by fall."

Everyone was speechless. The family had assumed that Peter would want to get more involved in the shipping business, but this decision seemed to be so hasty, so drastic, so final. Surely, he was too young to leave. Eli glanced at his mother. She looked pale, grief-stricken, and old. He remembered that look from when his sisters had died. Her expression was one of deep sadness, as if someone were taking her youngest son away from her forever and there was nothing, she could do about it.

Molly spoke, her voice shaky. "What does that mean? Thou said thee should be at sea for only a couple of months."

"It might be longer. We could get a cargo headed for England, then a cargo from England to the Caribbean before returning here, so it could be a year. Just think about it, Mother. I'll be visiting all the places I've heard about and that we trade with. I'll be full of stories when I return."

"Thou art too young to run off to sea."

Caleb looked directly at his youngest son and said, "Have you committed to this, Peter?"

"Yes, sir. I signed a paper."

"Well, I guess that's settled then. Your word is your bond. Your word and hard work are all you have to offer, but it will be enough. I wish you had talked to us first before signing the papers. But you made a decision and we wish you the best. Of course, you know we'll miss you greatly, and never forget you always have a home here with us."

Molly got up from the table without another word and climbed the creaky stairs to her room. Eli could hear her crying into her bedding. He shifted his weight by leaning forward in preparation for standing so he could go comfort her. He glanced at his father, who put his hand on Eli's back and said, "Let her be, son, she needs time to cry." It was clear that Molly was heartbroken about losing Peter to the uncertainty of life on the high seas, and she must be wondering if she would ever see him again. After all, she was getting old.

John chided Peter, saying, "I can't believe you're moving on to the easy life where the sailors let the wind do all the work and the fish just jump into your pot." He laughed at his own joke and then, more affectionately, said, "I'll miss you too . . . and especially the venison and other meat you bring home from hunting. I guess we'll be eating cornbread, beans, and cattails from now on."

Eli sat there tongue-tied. Peter was the youngest, and now the first to leave. He didn't get it. Questions bubbled around in his head, but he didn't know where to start. Why couldn't things just stay the way they were? Life seemed to be just one loss after another. Two months was a long time; a year was like a lifetime. Slumping on his stool, Eli watched Peter, trying to figure out why he was so eager to leave.

Eli now knew that his life was going to change dramatically. Peter had always been there, ready to join Eli in wrestling matches, long talks, and working on jobs together. Peter had been his best friend and confidant and now he was going away. Then he got it. Peter probably felt he was being abandoned by his two older brothers and thought it was time to strike out on his own. Good for him, Eli thought, and thank goodness for Chenoa. She would always be there to help fill the void in his heart created by his sisters' dying, John getting married, and now Peter leaving. Eli couldn't imagine losing Chenoa, too. It was time for them to take the next step in their relationship, time to go on their trip west up the Gunpowder, and a good time to move into Chenoa's cabin by the river.

Eli got up from the table, raised his glass, and said, "Peter, you're a great friend and brother. I'll miss you terribly. You better come back often to visit." He felt that he was about to cry, so he said, "Let me absorb this for a little while, and we'll talk more later." With that, he walked out the door.

He wandered in the dark for a few minutes then worked his way down toward the Little Gunpowder as if something was drawing him there. Eli found the ledge overlooking the river. It was a secluded spot he had just recently started to visit when in need of time alone to think. It felt safe, and his emotions quieted down as he listened to the sounds of the night.

After about half an hour, he heard faint footsteps approaching. Chenoa joined him on the ledge and sat down beside him. Eli reached over to hold her hand, and she rested her head on his shoulder.

"Aside from Dad's fits of frustration, Mother's sadness, Peter's wanderlust, and John's anger, they're all good people," Eli said quietly.

"You have a wonderful family."

"Are you ready to join us?"

"Of course. I have been committed to you and your family ever since we agreed to form an alliance, even before I knew what it was like to love someone. I have never wavered from that decision. And as for Peter, he needs to do this. He will come back one day."

"I sure hope so."

PART THREE

Building a Future

Peter and the Esmerelda

Chapter 12

THE SEA CAPTAIN

1730

A rather stout, forty-seven-year-old man, outfitted in full captain's regalia, walked down the gangplank of the tall ship *Esmerelda*. Swaying as he walked, the captain proceeded along the dock; he did not turn around and did not idle. He was a man on a mission, and the first step in his plan was to explore the town he had left over thirty years before.

Yes, Peter had returned. It was the first time he had been back since leaving as a wide-eyed cabin boy before the turn of the century. When Peter boarded the *Halifax* all those years ago, he never imagined he would be gone for so long. A twinge of guilt fluttered in his heart as he remembered his promise to his mother that he would return in a few months or a year or two at most.

Joppa Towne had grown so much that he barely recognized it. To get his bearings, he decided to walk the streets. As he passed a fine Anglican chapel built on the location of the church his family had attended, he stopped and reflected on his two sisters who were buried there.

Continuing his exploration, he walked by a large courthouse, a modern racetrack, and a goodly number of warehouses and stately homes. The town had grown into a busy port and seemed to have all the amenities of a modern settlement here in the Maryland colony. The sounds, smells, and sights compared favorably with many of the ports he had visited. A smile crossed his face. It would do. This bustling town could become his home once again—only time would tell if he'd be happy settling here.

First, he needed to adapt to walking on land after all those years at sea, and next, he needed to find out what he had missed while he was gone.

After exploring the cobblestone streets, the captain headed to the best inn the town had to offer. No matter what port he visited, there was always someone at the better inns who could tell him everything he needed to know.

On his way he stopped to watch the Africans working the docks. A pair of these men loaded a wagon with his two chests and three, worn canvas satchels. These items contained all his worldly possessions. The longshoremen dropped the chests and bags off at the warehouse in the bin labeled "Good Endeavour Farm."

Peter looked out with pride and a little bit of nostalgia over the vast expanse of the tidewater part of the Gunpower River, now full of ships and moorings. Even though he recognized very little, he was glad to be home, and after thirty years at sea, he was ready to retire. In fact, he had seen all he wanted to see of the world and now had no interest to go to sea again.

Fortunately, his coffers were full and he was in good health. He also owned part of the *Esmerelda,* which would bring a good price in a booming port like this one. That would give him enough assets to acquire property and live well. But first of all, he wanted to know what had happened to his family and Good Endeavour before deciding his next step.

After no contact all these years, he wondered who lived there now and whether he would be welcomed. Could he even fit back into life on a farm? Remembering his folks dearly, he could only hope his mother and father were still alive. Where were his brothers? Chenoa? Full of questions, it was finally time to discover the answers.

Dressed in his captain's best, Peter chose to sit down at the inn near a well-dressed gentleman. Few people were seated this early in the afternoon, but the gentleman looked like someone who might want to engage with him in conversation. Just the type of man to answer some of Peter's questions.

The gentleman nodded and then welcomed him. "Ahoy, Captain. What brings you to our fine port of Joppa Towne?"

Peter's face brightened; his instincts about this man were accurate. Here was a man with time to talk and probably plenty of local knowledge and gossip in his head. These types were always eager for an entertaining exchange. Peter was always willing to swap a few sea stories in exchange for valuable information about whatever port he was visiting. Good advice was worth a great deal to him, especially when trading in a foreign port with suspicious characters he did not know.

"I grew up around here and wanted to see how the family is doing," Peter replied. "The town's certainly grown in the past thirty years. I barely recognize it. Lots of brick buildings have replaced the clapboard ones."

"Well, let me be the first to welcome you back, Captain. I am Sir George Rumsey, one of the local magistrates. I arrived here twenty-eight years ago, a few years after you left."

"I'm Peter, captain of the merchant ship *Esmerelda*. Well, I *was* captain, until just a little while ago. I've retired." Peter ordered a rum, and when the serving girl brought it, he raised his mug to the gentleman and said, "I wish you good health, sir."

"Well, thank you. And to you as well."

"My pleasure to meet you. Please tell me what I've missed."

"Aha. How long do you have?" The man beamed. "The big news is that we've become the county seat for all of Baltimore County—the biggest and busiest county in the colony. Anyone from the Susquehanna River on the north to the Patapsco River on the south comes to Joppa Towne to conduct their official business."

"Sounds like it might be just the place to spend my twilight years."

"Indeed, our port is the reigning mistress of the Chesapeake. People around these parts say that all roads lead to Joppa. Sit in this inn long enough, and you'll see all the leaders of our colony — and the scalawags, as well."

The gentleman was right. The primary, north-south highway for the colonies was Philadelphia Road, which ran right along the western border of Joppa Towne. Joppa Road connected people to all points west, such as Towson and Woodstock. The third route was the Gunpowder River ferry, which connected travelers to Annapolis.

Peter was astounded by how his frontier town had grown. It looked like it would be a nice place to live. Even the wharves looked safe. At least they did in broad daylight. At night no self-respecting citizen would be caught out along the docks anywhere in the world. Sir George explained how the more impressive buildings such as the courthouse, the church, and the inn had all been built by Africans during the winters. The Crown had paid the planters for the services of these men, some of whom were real craftsmen when it came to construction.

Peter listened but was anxious to learn more about his family, even though he knew it couldn't all be good news. "If you don't mind me asking, sir, what do you know of my family homestead? A place called Good Endeavour Farm."

"I know it and have been there. I remember Caleb and his wife, Molly. I'm sorry to have to tell you that they ran into some tough times."

Peter sighed. "Ever since I left, I've been afraid to hear that outcome. Let me buy you a drink . . . if you wouldn't mind filling me in on the details."

"I'm happy to tell you what I know, but there's family still living around here, so best you go talk with them."

"How would you suggest I find them?"

"Hire a horse and head out the rolling road to the old place. There are four homes on the lane before you get to the main cabin."

"Thanks, I'll do that. My parents, are they still alive?"

"No, they both passed about five years ago. Some disease or another, and unfortunately, the Indian woman wasn't around to help. She was tending family farther west when they took sick. The community was sorry to lose your folks; they were the best settlers and the best of neighbors."

Peter looked into his mug and was quiet for a few minutes. "They were fine people and good parents. I've missed them every day since I left."

"I'm sorry for your loss, Captain," Sir George said.

"I learned a lot from them, much of which has kept me alive in some very challenging times. I owe them a great deal."

"Were you coming home to see them?"

"I guess I was coming home in large part to see them and help them in their old age. I'll have to live with the fact that I came too late. Tell me about Eli and Chenoa. Did they marry?"

"Eli's a fine man everyone likes, except for a few devout Indian haters. Marrying Chenoa caused quite a stir around here."

"How could anyone not like Chenoa?"

"You're right. Chenoa's a wonderful woman. Most folks have a lot of respect for her. Unfortunately, their family still has to keep a low profile. There's fear and hostility toward Indians in the souls of many settlers."

"It's sad those prejudices are still here, but it seems to be the nature of man," Peter replied. "I'm looking forward to seeing them. They were such an amazing pair."

"They still are."

"What's happened to John? He must have inherited the farm when my folks died."

"That's the other tragedy. We better have another drink." Looking around, Sir George asked, "Where's that maid?" When he saw her coming, he called out, "Two more rounds of rum."

When the drinks were delivered, and after taking another swig of rum, Sir George continued. "A few years before your parents died, a hogshead of tobacco rolled over your older brother in a freakish accident. He broke his leg and was never able-bodied again. He probably wouldn't have lived if Chenoa hadn't been there."

"Oh lordy."

"John didn't take kindly to being laid up. That's tough for a big, strong man who could always get the job done faster than anyone else. After the accident, he shrank in stature and grew in meanness, driving his indentured servants hard. Some would say too hard. Several of them ran away."

Grimacing, Peter responded, "I can picture that. John was a proud man you could always count on to get things done. Hard work was his life. I hate to think what he might have been capable of under those circumstances." He turned and stared out the window at the ships in the harbor.

"That's when he bought three Africans to get more work done on the farm. His mother, Molly, was livid at him for owning slaves and for treating them badly, but he ignored her. That transaction, on top of a failed harvest, depleted his coffers. With time he became crueler and crueler to his wife, Sara, their neighbors, merchants, and especially the Africans. One night he got into a fight with one of the Africans and killed him with just his bare hands. Nobody bothered to press charges, but that's about the time he began to drink too much." Rumsey stopped, apparently trying to figure out a delicate way of telling the rest of the story.

Sensing this hesitation, Peter said, "Go on. I need to hear the whole tale."

"Well, the story I've heard goes like this. One night Sara heard a commotion in the kitchen. She poked John to wake up. He went down the stairs, and she heard a blast. Scared, she didn't move. By the time she climbed down, the intruder had gone. She found John lying on the kitchen floor in a pool of his own blood. Shot by his own musket."

Peter was subdued, staring into his mug. Over the years he had heard many stories of murders all around the world and had seen his share. But this was his family, his brother. This awful series of events was hard to listen to and even harder to accept. The nature of John's demise conflicted so greatly with Peter's memory of his oldest brother that he almost wished he hadn't asked. Maybe it would have been better, he thought, if he had stayed at sea and never known the truth.

Peter looked at Sir George and said, "My god, that's a horrible ending to a man's life. I remember him as being so competent, so strong, so responsible. Maybe a little too rigid, but he was a good man. Life must have been so hard for the family. I should have been here for them."

"Well, I'm afraid the story gets worse."

"How could it? But, please, proceed."

"Phillip, the most senior of the Africans, was arrested the next day. They sentenced him to death for John's murder. Phillip's wife claimed that upon hearing the shot, he got up and ran to the house with several other men to see what had happened."

Peter was speechless, knowing where this was going to end.

"In the trial at the courthouse, the lawyers entered none of this evidence into the court records. The only connection was that a neighbor had heard Phillip talk back to John, and he was the first one at the site of the crime after Sara.

"Other names were talked about as suspects, since John had made many enemies over his last few years—but none of them were African. Some people think it could have been suicide; John was that despondent. Even Sara could have shot him. He had been very cruel to her toward the end. I also heard a theory that the Indian woman, Chenoa, could have done it because he was so far out of line. She was always in the kitchen helping out, and he had a reputation of being cruel to women."

Peter stood there with his mouth agape. He had no idea what to think with all this speculation spinning around in his head. "What happened to this man Phillip?"

"When the judge read the guilty verdict, several local citizens dragged Phillip out of the courthouse and hung him in the public square—with residents, farmers, African families, and children present."

Peter was horrified. "You're right. The story just gets worse. It sounds like you don't think Phillip did it."

"I don't wish to spread rumors here, but six months later, Sara married a neighboring farmer and they moved west. There were questions about how long the relationship had been going on. But once they went west, no one bothered to raise the issue again."

"John and Sara had no offspring?" Peter asked.

"That's another sad part about all of this. John left no heirs, so the property reverted back to the colony's proprietors. No one seems to have picked it up yet, as far as I know. Even Eli hasn't laid claim to it. I don't know why."

Peter shook his head and drummed his fingers on the table. He wondered how one family could have so much death in such a short time. All of Peter's good memories of John when he was younger were now tainted by his brother's actions later in life, the questions about his death, and the tragedies that followed.

Turning to the gentleman, Peter said, "Thank you, friend, for the information. I'm glad I knew this before showing up at the cabin. I wouldn't want to put them through that whole sad part of their lives again."

"Well, good luck to you. I don't know what you should expect when you get there. Except for Eli, none of those folks get to town much anymore. People here in town don't know what to make of them all."

Peter thanked the man, paid for the drinks, and headed over to the livery stable to book a horse for the following day. Then he checked in with the courthouse clerk and inquired about the ownership of Good Endeavour Farm.

"Yes, sir, you are correct," the clerk confirmed. "The land has reverted to the control of the Crown and the local Maryland proprietors. But all they want is the land to be well managed and generate revenue for the Crown. Are you interested in it, sir?"

"I don't know. Is it productive?"

"Let me see. Why, yes. It seems to be yielding as much tobacco and hemp as ever."

"Thank you for your help. I'm sure we'll talk again. And let me know if anyone shows any interest in it."

Peter couldn't believe they would have let the title eschew. That was just sloppy management. Eli could lose the whole farm. What's going on over there? He couldn't wait to find out.

Lost in thought, Peter walked to the warehouse where he had stored his things. The manager came out to meet him and ask about the items that had been dropped off there. "Are you related to the family at Good Endeavour Farm, sir?"

"Yes. I grew up there and am returning there shortly. Would it be all right with you if I left my things here for a few days? I would be willing to pay if necessary."

"Why, of course you can leave your belongings here, and at no cost at all. The family pays for this space on an annual basis. Please let me know the next time you're in town, and we could have a drink."

"I will. Thank you."

Peter headed back to the inn and turned in for the evening. There was a great deal to think about and to mourn. That was enough for one day.

Chapter 13

THE WAYWARD SON

That night Peter slept fitfully, unaccustomed to yapping dogs and a bed that didn't rock him to sleep. His mind kept rehashing the stories he had heard, hoping they were just bad dreams. The following morning, after waking late, Peter dined at the inn and then went to find his rented horse. He took the reins and led the fine dapple gray to the mounting block. After stroking and patting the horse's thick neck and long mane, he fastened two of his leather satchels to the back of the saddle and then mounted the mare. His bottom settled snugly into the worn leather saddle, and he let his body ease into the rocking motion of the horse's gait, so different from the swells on board the *Esmerelda*.

The slow, leisurely ride gave him the chance to see what else had changed along the way. He saw very few trees, and the land was flat at first, with deep gullies that had cut into the sandy soil. Houses and sheds were scattered about all the way up to Philadelphia Road. Crossing the main road, he continued up the rolling road, heading west toward Good Endeavour Farm.

The ride allowed him time to go over what he had learned the night before and to grieve for his family's losses. Yesterday's talk with Sir George Rumsey had provided him with many answers, but now he was full of new questions. Peter hoped that when he got to the farm, he would find Eli and Chenoa on the old homestead. After thirty years away and the deaths in the family, there was nobody else left that he would know.

Peter watched as the land got hillier, and he started to see black rock exposed in the ditches instead of just sand and gravel. Heading up the ridge road, he smiled with satisfaction when he saw that the rock-and-wood bridges they had built were still standing. A wave of nostalgia flowed through him. Those days of living on the edge had prepared him well for his years at the helm, fighting raging battles at sea and riding out tempests in the pitch blackness of a stormy night. How was it possible that he had lived through all those challenges while here at home so much had been lost?

As Peter approached Good Endeavour, the first thing he noticed were the four new cabins along the side of the road. They each had flourishing gardens that looked well kept. He wondered who lived in them.

At the top of the hill, he spoke to the dapple gray. "Whoa there." Pulling on the reins, he stopped the mare so he could take in all that had changed. The first thing he noticed was that his family had cleared the land of many more trees and had planted a great deal more tobacco and grain. He took a deep breath, smiling that his family's dreams had become a reality. A working farm was much more than his family had owned back in England where their smaller piece of land had been stripped away from them. Like many immigrants in the New World, his family had worked hard and had eventually succeeded. Sadly, his parents and his brother, who had worked the hardest, were not here to enjoy it. What a loss. What a sacrifice.

As he approached the main cabin, he was surprised at how small it was. There was more room on board the *Esmerelda* than he had had as a boy sharing this cabin with his parents, brothers, and the hired hands. Distant memories of the time spent here with his family flooded his mind. This cabin had been his home and it was good to be back.

A rail-thin man stepped from the cabin, reading a ledger he held in his hands. Peter's mare snorted and pawed the ground, and the man looked up. The men stared at one another, first in confusion and then in total disbelief. The face they each encountered was different from what they remembered, yet the faces were animated in such a familiar way that the brothers quickly recognized one another and burst into laughter.

Peter got off the horse, tied the reins to a tree, and sauntered over to his brother. "Eli . . . is that you under all that gray hair?" Peter's voice was gruff but there was a huge smile on his face.

"Peter?"

The brothers paused and tried to let it all sink in. They each were looking at a long-lost brother and oldest friend.

Peter took a few moments to look a little closer then commented, "Look at you. You're taller, thinner, and a lot older. You look more like father than the big brother I remember."

"You must be having trouble seeing through the wrinkles and the tuffs of white hair," Eli replied with a smile.

"Have you been here all this time?" Peter asked.

"Yes, and look at you, all dressed in your captain's uniform. How many seas have you been sailing on?"

"Most of 'em."

The two men stopped talking and hugged one another for the first time as adults.

Eli was the first to break from the embrace. "Let me put your horse in the paddock," he said, "and then let's go inside and see Chenoa. She'll be delighted to see you."

As they walked toward the cabin door, Eli kept shaking his head. "I just can't believe it. After all these years, you're alive and you came home, as you promised."

Inside the cabin it was as if the haze of age had weathered the room. Everything was a bit darker, smaller, and older. A more mature version of Chenoa stood by the fireplace. She turned enough to see who it was, just like his mother had done countless times when someone entered her kitchen. After a moment of bewilderment, her eyes twinkled and a wide smile crossed her face. She set down her ladle and came over to take Peter's hands in hers. She wanted to sense who he had become during all those years at sea. She closed her eyes for a long moment, and when he saw her eyes open, they had come alive with tears of happiness.

"Welcome home, Peter. Have a seat. Your mother always set a place for you at the table, and we have continued that tradition on Sundays, knowing you would come back one day."

"It's good to be back and to see you both keeping our parents' dreams alive."

"You look well."

"I'm getting old and creaky, not nearly as spry as the young and trim lad you once knew."

"But you're still our Peter. Where have you been all this time?"

"I've been at sea and in many distant lands. But my thoughts have often drifted back here to the family and to Good Endeavour."

"We have missed you deeply," Chenoa admitted, "but I hope you know you have always been with us."

"Yes, and I hope you know that my heart never left this farm. I sorely wish I had come sooner. I would have loved to have seen my parents again."

"Molly and Caleb mentioned you nearly every day. They were proud of you and would be delighted to know you returned to this place, their home in the woods, the one they struggled so hard to create."

They all sat down at the old black walnut table that Caleb had built and which now recorded the years of use in its rough finish. Peter ran his hands across the worn surface, remembering his role in polishing it. He also noted the well-worn floorboards, numerous new containers on the shelves, and pots hanging from the low ceiling. But it was the same log cabin he had helped build decades ago.

"Why did it take you so long to come back?" Eli asked, breaking the silence.

"My wanderlust, and the desire to sail on bigger and bigger ships, kept me going for years. At some point I came to understand that I was good at both leading men and skippering a ship. Sailing became my profession. Nothing else ever appealed to me. I loved the wind in the sails when we were out in the open ocean. I always found it exciting to pull into port in a new country. It's a vast, beautiful, and dangerous world we live in . . . and I wanted to see it all."

"Mother was right to cry when you left," Eli said. "She knew better than the rest of us that you might never come back. She missed you—we all missed you."

Peter looked down at the table. "I do regret that I left for so long, and I wish I could have come back more often, but that's not the way of life at sea. We're just cogs in the gears of commerce. I was naïve to think I had much choice where the ships were heading. If there was an opening, I took it. If there was cargo that needed to be shipped, I loaded it."

"Well, I hope you're back for good. You left a big hole in our lives, but at the same time, Peter, we traveled with you. It was exciting for me to think of you at sea, and I made up stories for our children about your adventures."

"Yes, I'm back, and I'm looking forward to meeting your children. I'm just trying to absorb all that's happened. It was a shock to see the port. It has certainly expanded. Looks like you've finished clearing the land, as well."

"Yes, there's much to show you. We'll walk around after dinner."

"I hope you are planning to stay, Peter," Chenoa said. "You can live on the second floor of the cabin as long as you like."

"Thank you. I'd like to stay. Let's see how that works out. I need time to get to know the flow of life here at Good Endeavour.

In the meantime, put me to work. I have a few skills."

Eli laughed. "Sure, but you don't look like you could carry your share of the load these days.

"You're probably right. I don't think I could carry a deer carcass for five miles anymore." They both grinned at each other and then Peter asked, "What is that delicious aroma I smell?"

"It is a pudding that Molly and I concocted," Chenoa told him. "Cornmeal and molasses with a number of spices. I call it Hasty Pudding, which is a recipe that Molly's mother made. Molly called in Indian Pudding since it is similar to something my mother made."

"I can't wait to taste it."

Chenoa smiled. "First, let us celebrate the return of the wayward son. It is noon, we will gather the family for our main meal and introduce you to them."

Peter smiled as he listened to Chenoa. Despite over thirty years spent with his family, she still retained a slight accent when speaking English.

Eli walked outside to a cast iron bell mounted on a post and rang it five times—the signal for everyone to come.

As the family started to flow in, they all eyed the old gentleman, wondering who he was. Chenoa took Peter's strong, calloused hands and introduced him to their two daughters and the daughters' husbands, who lived in the first two houses down the lane. Then a redheaded Irish couple and two Africans, a father and an almost-grown son, came in the door. The redheaded couple lived in the third house with their young son, and the Africans—William and his son, Abe—lived in the fourth house down the lane. Peter was surprised when he noticed that Chenoa and Eli treated the four of them as family.

Peter found Chenoa and Eli's daughters thoughtful like their father and competent and engaging like their mother. He was saddened and disappointed to hear that some people in town thought of them as half-breeds and less than human. Fortunately, this prejudice was not as much of a problem in the outlying area, where most people respected Chenoa's knowledge of native cures and willingness to help others. The neighbors, in fact, liked Eli's family because they were all hardworking people. But the girls and their children experienced taunts on the streets in Joppa Towne, where people used the term half-breed in a derogatory manner. This hatred against Indians and half-breeds was the main reason that Eli and Chenoa's two sons had moved to Western Pennsylvania. Despite this ugliness, the girls had grown into engaging young women and married young men from the neighboring farms.

Chenoa told Peter, "Here come the children. Do not be surprised, but they all know you from the stories Eli made up about your travels. It was a good way to keep you in our thoughts. They will love to meet the real sea captain."

When Chenoa introduced Captain Peter to her grandchildren, she told them that he was a great storyteller, so he took this as an invitation. He sat down and invited them to sit on his lap. He had two takers and two who sat on the floor. He first asked them what they knew about him from the stories Eli had already told them. He let loose with a great belly laugh when he heard the stories, and then he spun new tales that kept them all entranced. Of course, Peter sometimes modified his real adventures, but there was always a kernel of truth in his ramblings. Even though he had encountered several pirates, he was careful not to talk about them with the children. He didn't want to romanticize the evil men do.

In his stories, Peter tried to engage the children's interest in geography, different cultures, and reading the stars. He was careful not to encourage too much wanderlust, remembering his own naïve desire to go to sea and how cruel life at sea could be. He was a survivor. Not every cabin boy made it to captain.

From that day on, the children idolized their Uncle Peter. They were always following him around, asking questions.

"What 'cha planting, Uncle Peter?"

"Come play with us."

"Teach us some card games."

"Let's saddle up the horses."

"Did you sail all the way around the world without falling off?"

Peter had not been around children very much but loved their enthusiasm as much as their curiosity. He would always stop whatever he was doing to answer a question or help solve a problem.

After lunch, Eli took Peter on a walk around Good Endeavour. Peter noticed many changes on the farm, but it was still just a cabin cut out of the woods, surrounded by fields of tobacco and grain. "Molly's garden," as Chenoa called it, was much larger than he remembered and full of plants like maize, beans, and squash, as well as spices and herbs. Everything seemed to be flourishing.

"The place looks great," Peter remarked. "Who runs the farm?"

Eli responded with a nod of thanks and said, "We do."

"What do you mean?"

"That's a little complicated. Where should I start? Do you know about John and Sara?"

"Yes, I heard it last night in town. What a sad story."

"Yes, it was awful." Eli paused for a few moments and looked down at the ground. "During John's problems, Father turned to me more and more to run the farm and make the decisions. John was not pleased with me stepping in . . . but the last thing that Father wanted was to lose the farm."

"I'm sure you were a big comfort to him."

"That time was hard for each of us. After John died and Sara left, Chenoa and I felt an obligation to step in and keep the place going."

"I'm glad you did," Peter cut in. "I'm sure Father was as well."

"To keep the farm, we decided we needed a new way to manage it. The way John ran the farm towards the end didn't work for us. We were about to lose our indentured servants, and we never liked the practice of using slave labor. In fact, Mother, with her Quaker upbringing, was always dead set against it."

"What did you do?"

"We gave the enslaved men their freedom and released the indentured servants from their contracts."

"What? You gave up a small fortune."

"We told them that if they were interested in farming, we would deed or lease them one acre of land and the cabins we had built for them if in return they would help farm the rest of the property with us for a fair share of the profits."

Peter was intrigued but concerned. "That doesn't sound like the usual way to run a farm in an English colony. I'm not even sure it's legal without approval from the governor."

"It's a bit tricky, but it's worked well enough for us."

Chenoa and Eli had come to know the families well, having worked and lived next to them for years. Chenoa had tended to their needs when they were sick or when one of the women was giving birth. They had all worked together to build and maintain the cabins and had helped each other out numerous times. Eli and Chenoa felt they deserved their freedom. They also firmly believed the farm would be more productive, not less, if everyone shared in the profits.

Both of their daughters' families agreed to this plan, as well as the Irish family. William, who lived with his young son in the last cabin, was proud of the house he had built and had always dreamed of owning land. Gaining his and his son's freedom was important to him, but his wife was still a slave on a separate farm nearby. Chenoa and Eli had agreed to help him gain her freedom, too, but that had not happened yet.

"Did the community just accept this cooperative approach to farming?" Peter asked, voicing his concerns. He had spent his life in a hierarchy aboard ships where the captain ruled with the power of his experience and often the Crown, so he was fascinated that this approach was working well.

"The immediate neighbors have grown to respect William and Abe, as they did Chenoa and our daughters years ago. In fact, the local farmers will hire William directly when they need his skills."

"How about the folks in town?"

"Some of the plantation owners and townspeople are threatened that we freed William and Abe. We're wary of what those people might do. That's why we tend to keep to ourselves."

"Tell me about your role in all of this."

Eli smiled sheepishly and described his role as the farm manager, a role he performed largely from behind the scenes. "My job is to listen to everyone share their opinions and then, in consultation with Chenoa, I set up planting, cultivating, harvesting, fertilizing, and crop rotation schedules. As a result of careful management, the fields have become more productive, producing higher quality tobacco than the plantations down in the Tidewater. I've developed close relationships with several merchants who will pay us top price for what they call *Good Endeavour-grade* tobacco."

Eli's smile was proud but the smile faded when he continued. "When Mother and Father passed away, it was devastating for all of us. We thought about whether we should move into the main log cabin, but we chose not to leave our cottage down by the river. We had expanded it to accommodate our four children, so it felt roomy to us once they moved out. We maintain the original log cabin as an office, a place for meetings, and family meals. The upper two floors have been kept available for guests and storage. It would be a great place for you to move into."

"You've done a great job."

"It's working. We've paid off John's debts."

"Father would have been proud."

"The only thing that isn't clear is ownership. John had no heirs. When I tried to resolve the issue, the powers that be stone-walled me because I'm married to an Indian. I don't have the patience to deal with people with so much prejudice."

Peter thought for a moment. He was impressed with what they had accomplished. He respected the integrity of the people he had met at the noon meal and decided that he would like nothing better than to be part of this community. Peter looked at Eli and said, "Maybe I can help."

Peter and Eli sat in the kitchen, talking late into the night, each consuming several mugs of cider. The shadows in the room brought back many memories of times long ago. The bayberry candles burned down, and then they watched as the coals in the fireplace consumed themselves. The light in the room subsided.

The kitchen was the room where Peter and Eli had learned about the complexities of life from their parents' stories of the past, the daily challenges they faced, and the dangerous men they encountered. The kitchen was a good place for the recon-nected brothers to reflect on their more-recent histories and share their hopes for the future.

"I've certainly had my share of encounters with desperate and greedy men," Peter told Eli.

"Do you remember Father talking the vigilantes down from

raiding our house and taking our food?" asked Eli.

"You bet I do. That was a terrifying night. He must have had nerves of steel."

"Maybe, or maybe not. He might just have been a desperate man trying to protect his family."

Peter smiled. "You might be right. But that scene made him a larger-than-life hero to me."

"I was never so scared for my life and what I might need to do—and so impressed and relieved at how he handled that tense standoff. He showed me how to listen to and empathize with others."

"I've tried to imitate his voice and his words every time I've been in a tight spot," admitted Peter.

Eli laughed. "Hah! So have I."

"I've also encountered men who were not desperate but who would do anything to win. They would cheat, steal, and even kill people, with little or no concern for others. From my experience, they tend to be more devious and therefore more dangerous than the desperate man down on his luck."

"I recall Father saying that it's important to recognize and avoid those types of people or help direct their energies to something positive."

"That's good advice," Peter replied. "But it's often hard to know what drives men like that to be good and what drives them to commit awful acts. We just need a country big enough where there's opportunity and room for all of us without turning against one another."

"And a set of rules and laws that we agree to live by—and ones we can enforce." After a few more sips of rum, Eli continued. "I would like to hear your stories about the tight spots you found yourself in."

"I have a lifetime of stories. Some of which I will not tell anyone . . . except maybe you."

"Well, at least tell me about the places you visited, the things you saw, and of course, the women you loved. Did anyone steal your heart?"

"Aren't you the curious one? You always were. I wouldn't know where to start."

They eyed the dying embers as they absorbed the stories and warmth from each other. After another drink of rum, Peter's floodgates opened. He told Eli of his unglamorous life as a cabin boy sailing with merchant vessels carrying tobacco to England and bringing manufactured goods back to the colonies. In contrast to the daily drudgery, Peter shared how exciting it was for him to be on deck, clipping along under full sail on the open ocean with the salty, moist wind in his face. He tried to describe to Eli the apprehension of encountering another ship at sea, not knowing if it was friend or foe. And of course, there was the excitement and the hustle and bustle when coming into port.

"It sounds like an exciting life," Eli said. "I can almost picture you at the helm. You always enjoyed seeing new ships coming into the port here at Joppa."

"At times it *was* exciting. But much of the time, it was dreary work, swabbing decks, cleaning the galley, and hosing down the head."

"Did you like the sailors you worked with?"

Peter smiled. "There was a real mix of people on board the ships I crewed on. Most of them had not planned to become sailors. Many had lost their homes, lands, and livelihood when the Enclosure Acts passed in England. As usual, the landed gentry in England got more prosperous, and the poor lost the land their families had lived on for generations."

Eli nodded. "That's why there are so many immigrants flooding into the colonies. England is shedding its criminals and it's poor."

"With few job prospects, desperate men signed up to be

indentured servants, or they joined the Royal Navy."

"At least some of them got a job."

Peter looked seriously at Eli. "A job where men are treated harshly. They commonly are not paid wages after long voyages, and they often die young from disease and scurvy. It's a tough life, and many jump ship to try to make it here in the colonies. Others find themselves on pirate vessels just to support their families back home."

"How did you get to be a captain? You knew nothing about sailing when you left here."

"Through those early years at sea, I watched the crew. I filled in whenever men went missing or, more commonly, were too drunk to be up on the shifting decks. Once you've proven yourself, most sailors are happy to teach you the tricks of the trade.

"For me, visiting ports in distant lands made up for the hard work, the rivalries, and the monotony of being at sea. It's exciting to see how people live and what they eat in other, more exotic countries. But being in port could also be risky. I saw plenty of fights where people got knifed and thrown into a scummy harbor."

"We've had similar experiences when ships land and the crews take shore leave here in Joppa," said Eli. "How long were you on the *Halifax*?"

"After a year, my captain traded me to another captain to fulfill a gambling debt."

"I bet you were angry."

"I was. But of course, everyone's expendable. Whatever the case, I woke up the next morning on an old Portuguese ship heading to the slave coast of Guinea. I was miserable. The boat was filthy, in need of repair, and the crew members were the rejects of the seas. Overnight, I had become part of that dismal crew."

"So, you figured it was a step down."

"The worst thing about joining a new ship is that I had to start all over again, learning the ropes, sizing up the men, and building trust with the crew and captain. I learned too late that this new captain was known for his brutality."

"Wasn't there an honor code on those ships?"

"Ha! Just your fists. I had to defend myself twenty-four hours a day. Fortunately, by this point I had grown into an agile and muscular seaman and could calm most situations down before anyone got hurt. Not being as drunk as my assailants helped, too."

Eli had never left Joppa so was fascinated by Peter's stories. "Tell me about your stops in Africa."

Peter got up to refill their mugs and then relaxed on his stool. All sorts of pictures came to mind. He tried to remember his first visit there. "Landing in an African port was a whole new experience: the homes, villages, vegetation, and food were all foreign looking. I liked walking along the paths and dusty roads. I loved tasting the colorful fruits in baskets that were stacked in perfectly balanced piles in crude, roadside stalls.

"One day, shortly after we arrived, I heard the sound of loud shouts and chains. Turning around, I saw groups of healthy African men and women, bound by chains, being whipped by other Africans. They were forced to board one of the European ships heading to the Spanish Main of South and Central America and the Caribbean. If any human cargo was left after those stops, the ship sailed on to the American colonies.

"The Africans were the dominant cargo on many of those ships. By watching their eyes, gaits, and stern faces, I knew they were proud, indignant, angry, and scared. I remembered seeing similar men and women at the end of their trans-Atlantic passages in places like our port here in Joppa Towne. But by then those men and women had had their pride stripped from their bodies and minds. Their gaunt stares and unsteady gaits spoke volumes about how much they had lost in transit."

Peter stopped his storytelling and turned to face Eli. "Brother, that experience is why I was so taken with your choices here on the farm. You freed the enslaved men John had bought and abused, and now you treat them as family. That is highly unusual. I'm sure there is more that I can learn from you."

The next evening started the same way—with dinner and a few drinks. When they were alone in the kitchen, Eli asked Peter to continue his story.

Peter was hesitant but relieved that he had finally found someone to help him unburden his soul. "After serving at the whims of that abusive captain for more than a year, I jumped ship one night and quickly signed up with a British merchant fleet. I boarded the ship I was assigned to right away so I would not be recaptured in port by the old captain. The merchant fleet consisted of eight ships heading off to Arabia, India, and China, where I thought it would be safer, being far away from the slave trade."

Peter scowled and took a moment to reflect on this point in his career. "It was a spontaneous and foolish decision . . . one I have regretted ever since."

"It seems to me that you've led multiple lives and learned much about men in the ports you visited," Eli offered.

"Yes, I have. I know some of the evil that man can do, and as a result I try my best to do as little evil as possible."

"How was life with the British fleet?"

Peter took a deep beath. "By that point I was an able-bodied seaman and a master navigator, so the captain of our ship soon chose me as his first mate for those skills and my writing and record-keeping talents I learned here in Joppa.

"Our orders were to round the Horn of Africa, run up the east coast to Arabia, sail east to India, and eventually arrive in Canton, China. Our main goal was to trade Mexican and

Bolivian silver for silk, tea, and other spices from the Far East, but the captain also traded other commodities along the way. There were rumors of opium."

When Peter paused, Eli urged, "Please, tell me more. That sounds exciting and dangerous."

"The trip proved far more horrific than anything else I have personally experienced, before or since." Peter took a slow sip of rum, looked off at the coals' reflections on the wall, and continued as if he was seeing it all happening again right before his eyes. "The first half of the journey worked out well with much trading. But then the British flotilla entered the Cantonese harbor, our last stop on our way east. As we arrived, I was amazed at the number of people lining the banks. The density of people was far greater than anything I had seen in Europe.

"Later that afternoon, our anchored fleet was attacked by a host of Chinese men in dozens of Chinese junks and several large Dutch ships. The British ships were heavily armed and blasted a dozen Chinese junks into splinters. But the Chinese were fearless in their swarming of the British ships that were now trapped and anchored in an unfamiliar port, and there seemed to be no end to them. The junks came right alongside the British vessels and successfully used dozens of grappling hooks to climb on board, overrun, and commandeer four of the British ships.

"The dominant images of that scene are still stuck in my mind. It was an intense, half-day, full-on, chaotic battle. Hordes of men poured like giant fire ants over the gunwales and onto our ship. They had sabers and pistols by their sides and daggers in their teeth. This freed up their arms to climb the grappling hooks. The smaller ships had bound their boat to ours and were now climbing aboard for hand-to-hand combat. It was a life-or-death battle for all involved, with no thought or opportunity for negotiation."

Peter was sickened, reliving this battle. It was clearly a turning point in his life.

"Scared of losing my life and the ship I served on, I grabbed a sword in each hand and shouted to our men to battle the Chinese along the gunwales. I must have yelled 'Don't let 'em board' hundreds of times as I ran along the gunwales, slicing at anything that moved.

"It was an exhausting battle, with blood and body parts washing back and forth across the decks and flushing out the scuppers. Luckily, we repelled the attack, raised our anchors, and turned to fight the captured British ships that were shooting at us. Fortunately, the Chinese couldn't fire the British-style cannons effectively, giving us time to sink the four lost British vessels and escape with our remaining vessels and much smaller crew."

"You lost half your ships?"

"Yes, the fleet was down to four ships from the eight we had initially deployed. And only skeletal crews to sail them. The British lost so many officers that I was appointed captain of my ship for the rest of the journey. Fortunately, I had earned the respect of the crew for my courage in the battle at Canton. It had been quite a battle. I can't even imagine the number of people who died or were injured."

Peter looked at Eli with tears in his eyes. "That was not the end of our challenges. As we headed home, our ill-fated fleet ran into a typhoon where two more of our understaffed ships were lost battling the winds, gigantic waves, and torrential rains. During the storm, I tied myself to the helm and watched enormous waves wash sailors overboard. We limped home to England, and I did not re-enlist. I needed a break from sailing to recover from the turmoil and mental agony of the trip."

Only a few tiny embers still glowed in the fireplace, and darkness had settled across the kitchen. The brothers could barely see one another's faces; only their eyes shone in the dark. They were quiet, slowly absorbing the tales they had shared. After reliving his adventures at sea, Peter was exhausted. He stopped talking. After about ten minutes of silence, he said, "That's enough for tonight. I'm going to turn in upstairs."

"It's good to have you home, brother," Eli said. "I'm so glad you made it back alive."

Chapter 14

A Country Gentleman

The following day, Peter got up late and came downstairs to the rich aromas of Chenoa's cooking. The scene filled his head with childhood images. How many times had he stumbled down these well-worn stairs with half-closed eyes? How many times had he fallen asleep at sea dreaming of his parents and brothers sitting at this very same kitchen table?

Eli poured him a steaming cup of hot chocolate and asked if he cared for a splash of rum, as was common. Peter declined, taking the bitter chocolate as is. Then Chenoa served him a plate of rabbit with biscuits and gravy. She laughed. "I bet you didn't eat much fresh game while on board those flying ships."

Peter agreed. "It's been a long time since I've had rabbit. As I recall, Eli wasn't that good at trapping them until you came along. Our staples on board ship were dried fish, mush, bread, and cider. The only exceptions came when we went ashore and bartered for limes and other local foods. But I've eaten alligator and monkey. I bet you don't get those delicacies here too often."

"You're right, but we eat well," Eli replied. "Do you remember how bad that first winter in the cabin was? Now our root cellar is full, and with better roads, there's always food to buy."

"That is a good thing, because foraging is harder now that all tracts here in The Forks are cleared and have cabins on them," Chenoa chimed in. "We now have many nut and fruit trees in our orchard that we once harvested for free in the woods.

"To train the grandchildren these days, we have to go farther west, where the forest treasures are still plentiful and free. I take the children each year, and by the time they are ten, they have become good trackers and foragers. They know how to read the land, and they know the Gunpowder well, all the way to its headwaters."

Of course, they know the land, Peter thought. Having grown up with a woman like Chenoa, she would have made sure they developed basic survival skills. As prosperous as life had become, who knew when such skills might come in handy. Life in the colonies was still fragile, and there continued to be a lot of fear and hate out there directed toward Indians and Africans.

A few weeks later, Chenoa, Eli, and Peter were sitting outside, continuing their discussion on what had changed and what they had learned in the years they had been apart. Peter sat quietly and listened carefully; Eli and his wife were full of wisdom. They had learned much about the land and how commerce worked in the colonies—maybe as much as he had learned about global trade. He decided to take a more businesslike tangent in their discussion. "I have a proposal, and I want you to know that you can say no without any hard feelings. I'm hoping we can work something out with my return. And if not, I can always go back to sea."

"Let us hear your proposal," Chenoa said. "But we both agree we do not want you disappearing again into that vast ocean. So that is not an option."

Peter laughed. "I would love to move back to this area. I could afford to buy a nearby farm, so that's a back-up plan. But I would like nothing better than to live here with all of you. I'm a man of some means, and I would be happy—in fact, more than happy—if I could share that with others."

"What would you like to do?" Eli asked.

"I propose that I fix the title of this property so it will pass to your heirs. I don't think the ownership of Good Endeavour is something to leave to the fates, especially knowing people are trying to grab anything they can. I'd hate for you to lose the farm."

As he spoke, Peter observed them, trying to read their hearts through the intensity of the wrinkles on their faces. He had already observed that when they were concerned about something important, Chenoa had intricate crow's feet crevasses radiating out from her eyes, and Eli had deep furrows across his brow. Peter watched them closely for any sign of rejection. Eli looked relieved. Chenoa had a knowing smile and a twinkle in her eyes, almost as if she were channeling Molly, who would have been ecstatic that he had come home to stay.

Peter continued. "I would like to build a bigger house here on the farm. After living most of my days cramped on board a ship, I would like more room to stretch my legs. I envision hosting our family meals and meetings on the first floor, and I would use the second floor for my quarters."

"I would love to have you build a place here," Eli said. "You could easily add it on as an addition to the cabin if you wish."

"I was wondering what you might think about that. We could keep the kitchen as is. That works for me."

"We want you to be part of the family," Chenoa told Peter. "I support your proposal to build a home, or an addition, whichever you would like."

Peter looked at them and said, "It's good to be home. Thank you. How do we present this to the other members of the farm?"

"We will discuss it at Sunday's meeting," said Chenoa. "I am sure everyone would like to see the ownership cloud removed from over our heads. There are many white men who will change the laws to suit their interests. We need to be careful."

Chenoa smiled and continued with a twinkle in her eyes. "It also would not hurt our reputation to have a respectable English gentleman living on this property as well."

With a smirk on his face, but trying to act indignant, Eli jumped in. "Who are you referring to when you say 'respectable'? This pirate?"

On Sunday, after a spirited discussion on everyone's thoughts and dreams for the future, all of the members of the Good Endeavour community agreed to the plan. They all enjoyed having Peter around because he added levity and energy to what was often a lot of work.

The next day, Peter asked Abe to go with him to town. They drove the family's wagon and brought back Peter's two trunks and his remaining satchel from the warehouse. There was quite a stir when they removed the canvas tarp and some family members saw the two sea chests. He asked one of Eli's sons-in-law to help Abe deposit them both in the attic, and somehow, they got them up the narrow stairs. He didn't bother to open either of the chests and deferred any questions with a shrug and a comment. "Just my fancy breeches, waistcoats, and a few things I picked up in various ports that I might hang on the walls when we expand the cabin."

He did reveal the contents of one of the leather satchels, which contained numerous tree pods, nuts, and seeds he had collected from around the world. He was excited about having a place to plant them.

As it turned out, no one got to see what was in the trunks while Peter was alive.

Over the next year, Peter was true to his word and worked on securing the titles to the original tract and the one-acre plots. He quickly learned that Chenoa and Eli had been right about the prejudices in town. Some citizens in Joppa still resented the presence of Indians, half-breeds, and freed black men living and working together with white immigrants. It took Peter time to win over the authorities in order to reduce any threat to the family's ownership of the property. But he did it, much to everyone's delight.

Fortunately, everyone seemed to like Peter, both around The Forks of the Gunpowder and in town. He was respected as a sea captain and spoke to all people without bias. He had grown into a man who judged character based on a person's integrity and hard work, not skin color, religion, or nationality. He attended town meetings and sat in on the weekly Good Endeavour community meetings, where he learned to respect the members' beliefs and their differing viewpoints. Somehow, they all got along, probably because Chenoa and Eli were their role models.

In addition to his nieces, their husbands, and the grandchildren, Peter got to know the Irish and African families living on the lane. William, who was good with plants, offered to help Peter plant the seed pods and nuts Peter had brought with him. Peter was delighted.

The mix of native and exotic seeds Peter and William planted fell into three categories: trees that produced food, trees that provided shade, and trees that brought Peter comfort throughout the year. The food category included a pecan from a majestic tree in Charleston, South Carolina. Other food-bearing trees were black walnut, chestnut, shadblow, persimmon, pawpaw, and apple.

They planted elm and sycamore for strategic summer shade and dogwood, mountain laurel, holly, and sassafras because Peter liked them. He had hoped that one day, decades into the future, the fully grown trees would produce a vista when driving up the lane that would make the viewers catch their breath in awe.

Peter also planted several ginkgo seeds he brought home from Canton, China. He had acquired them the day before the battle and thought the trees possessed magical qualities because of the joy they evoked in Cantonese children. The trees he had seen in China had been straight as an arrow with short lateral branches, and their fan-shaped leaves turned a deep, butter yellow in the fall.

He told the children once the trees started to grow, "The trees are magical. All the leaves fall in a single day and pile up in a circle at the base of the tree. When that happens, the Chinese run around the tree trying to catch the leaves and then make a wish for the coming year." Years later, he would watch the children at Good Endeavour Farm screaming in delight as they ran around the trunks on a brisk November day, collecting leaves during the annual, single-day leaf fall. It reminded him that no matter how awful things may seem, children can always find a reason for laughter and a reason for hope.

When Peter asked William to help him dig a five-foot-deep hole after dark one night, William looked at him, wondering what he was planning. All Peter did was to look back reassuringly and nod his head. Later that night, after everyone else had gone to bed, the two men moved the smaller of Peter's two sea chests from the attic, and they buried it in the newly dug hole. They then took great care filling in the hole and planting the little pecan directly over the hidden chest. Peter dusted off the yellow dirt on his pants and then watered the ground above the planted nut.

William was curious about the chest's contents and why Peter wanted it buried. But Peter did not say anything, and William knew better than to ask. The chest was never mentioned by either of them again.

Peter buried the chest in part to make it harder for him to go back to sea on the spur of the moment. He had placed all his important papers and licenses in it, along with his ship's logs. These would be necessary to secure a commission on another ship. He figured that he might be tempted at times, but he would have to be very serious to go to the trouble of digging up the chest beneath a pecan tree.

Peter also hoped that burying the chest would keep all the details of his life, his voyages, and the decisions he had made safe and hidden until a time well beyond the passing of his generation. He hoped someone in the future would find historical value in their contents without passing judgment on him or any of the souls and actions described therein. And if nobody ever found it, so be it—some things were better left unknown.

"I propose adding two large rooms on the first floor and four bedrooms upstairs." Peter laid out the detailed sketches he had made so Eli and Chenoa and the rest of the family could approve them. "If you let me do this, I will be delighted to cover all costs. I also agree to host any gatherings you desire."

When they saw the plans, most of the family had to agree it would be nice to have more space, especially when they gathered on rainy days or in the winter. The family had outgrown Molly and Caleb's cabin. At the end of the discussion, everyone turned to Chenoa, who nodded her consent.

Peter clapped his hand and said, "We'll start tomorrow. Please, all of you let me know what skills you have so I can get things organized. And thank you all."

During construction of the foundation walls, Peter called the whole family together. "I would like each of you to contribute something to a message-to-the-future box that we'll hide in the foundation of the new building. Something that your children's children might find a hundred years from now. This is a chance to tell them who you are, what you like, and your dreams for the future."

This challenge created quite a buzz over the next week. Peter went to each family member and said, "This is your chance to reach out and touch people in the distant future. Think of what message you want to send them. Your letter is your chance at immortality."

Chenoa dictated a letter to Peter, celebrating her ancestors. He was surprised that she knew more about past generations of her family than he knew about his own ancestors. Eli designed a family tree as best he could for both his mother's and father's sides of his family. He also summarized why they had left England, the trials at sea and in the Virginia colony, and how they made it to the Maryland colony. Peter wrapped up all the items and letters, put them into one of his leather satchels, and placed it in a wooden box he had made. Before closing the lid, he sketched something on the leather flap of the satchel which he did not show to anyone. He then put it all in a cavity in the black-rock foundation, added a few copies of the local gazette, and covered it with a large slab of rock. For weeks after the internment, the whole family speculated about who might discover the box in the future.

Chapter 15

William, Maisey, and Abe

P eter often talked with or worked alongside William. They seemed to have similar interests. As they became more comfortable with each other, William shared what he remembered of his home in Guinea, West Africa. Peter listened quietly.

"When I think of home, I remember my mother singing, both in our hut and in the fields. When I heard her songs, I knew where she was and I felt safe. She and my older sisters worked most of the time in the fields, bringing home enough to feed all six of us. We lived in a small village, and the market was owned by another tribe an hour away on foot. Each week, she would take food there to sell or trade. I remember her smell, rich with aromas when she came home from the market. It was an exciting time to see what she had brought home for us. I still remember our smiles and laughter when she came back on market days.

"Then the Europeans started to stop at our port to resupply their ships with water and food, and that made food expensive and scarce, causing conflict between tribes. The Europeans also paid some of the tribes to supply them with people they could enslave and sell in the New World. Mother sat us down and told us not to stray so far from our homes that we could no longer hear her sing. We were to always come home immediately if we saw white men or if she changed her song to one of warning. I started to go to sleep every night scared that I might be taken away from my family forever."

William took a long time before he continued. When he did, he told Peter that one dark night he was dragged from his compound along with his older brother and a sister. In the torchlight, he could see his father lying unconscious and bleeding on the forest floor and could hear his mother screaming at her captors while she was being dragged away into the jungle. William called out to his family as he was bound with rope. He recognized their captors—they were from an adjacent village—and they sold his family to European merchants. The white men used iron chains to ensure William would not escape and loaded him onto a big dark ship. He never saw any of his family again. The last thing he remembered hearing was his mother singing the family story of their proud ancestors as her voice got softer and softer.

William turned to Peter. "I can still hear her voice—but it has become very, very faint."

Peter listened without interrupting William, letting it all sink in. After a while he said, "I've seen those slaver ships and could not bear to think how anyone could survive on a long trip chained with so many others in the dark hold."

"Just the thought of that trip and then being sold at auction has filled my body with a permanent sense of fear," William admitted. "I am always evaluating everyone around me and planning an escape route, if necessary. I have learned to do almost anything to keep from the ropes, the chains, and the manacles I lived in during that dark passage here."

"Would you mind telling me more about your first master, Sir Henry, and my brother John."

William thought about this, not wanting to dwell about the evil people do to each other, but he decided to share what he knew. "Plantation life was better than being manacled on a ship, but Sir Henry had terrible moods. John was better at first—he appreciated hard work. But then he got cruel. Toward the end he acted like a crazy man. I can show you the scars inflicted by both Sir Henry and John. Take a look at my wrists and forearms."

Peter struggled with the knowledge of what his brother had done to this man. He pledged to himself to do something to make William's life better. He then asked about John's demise. "Did Phillip do it?"

"Captain, there was no way Phillip was guilty. As soon as we heard the shot, we both ran up to the house and arrived there at the same time—definitely *after* the shot had been fired. It was terrible. Phillip was an honest and hardworking man. My first job here was to help Phillip dig the thirty-foot-deep well behind the cabin. It is a masterpiece, lined with fieldstone and covered with a slab of black rock. It's never gone dry like the spring in the basement. It reaches down below the clay layer, down to where the permanent water is clean and fresh. To this day, I call it *Phillip's Well*."

"From now on, I will too. Let's carve his name in the caprock. I think that's the least we can do to honor Phillip and his contributions to our community here at Good Endeavour."

Peter appreciated hearing William's stories and gave him a book about Africa that he had in the large chest in the attic. Although reading was difficult for William, he worked through the book multiple times, learning more from each reading. Peter shared his memories of the Slave Coast and how he had seen Africans in almost every port around the Atlantic. He described what he remembered about his trips ashore at the Lagos and Grand-Popo slave ports. He described how freed and enslaved, Africans played an important role in the mercantile system all around the Atlantic and Indian oceans.

One day, shortly after that conversation, while they were alone in the kitchen, Chenoa told Peter, "Do you know that William's wife is still enslaved on a farm down in the Tidewater?" She looked at Peter and asked, "Can you help?"

Peter understood that freeing Williams's wife was the most important thing he could do for William. His first step was to get to know more of the townspeople and the planters. He started visiting the inns with Sir George, his magistrate friend, and quickly met members of the landed gentry of Joppa. Sir George invited him to join a weekly whist game where Peter befriended a man named Sir Henry, who was the owner of the plantation where William's wife, Maisey, was enslaved. She often came to town with Sir Henry to do the shopping, so Peter had seen that she carried herself with a sense of dignity. Fortunately, she had not lost it working for Sir Henry.

One day at whist, Sir Henry complained about her sassiness, and Peter said, "Well, if she's that bad, I would be happy to take her off your hands. You may recall you sold her husband and son to my brother John a few years back."

"Well, she's not for sale."

"I appreciate that, and I'm not particularly interested. But if she were for sale, what would you want for her? I'm just asking because I'm new to the market value of people. Forgive me for appearing rude."

Sir Henry looked at Peter but did not say anything. Two of the other players at the table suggested prices they thought were fair for a house servant.

Sir Henry simply said, "Well, maybe so, but she's not for sale."

The following week, Peter attended the horse races, a major attraction in town. It was an exciting affair and betting was rampant. He was tempted to bet but was not knowledgeable about horses or what mischief might be going on behind the scenes. His experience had taught him that most gambling was rigged in some way to fleece money from the naïve. He was about to leave when he saw Sir Henry stomping away from the track, clearly in a foul mood.

Above the fray of the betters cheering on their horses, Peter shouted, "Well, how are you today, sir?"

"Not so good. I'm on a losing streak and spent all the money I brought with me. The racetrack is the one place in town that won't take a note for tobacco as collateral. They're demanding cash."

"I'm sorry for your misfortune. Is there any way that I can help?"

Sir Henry did not answer. He tried to cool down and think. Then he said, "Are you still interested in Maisey?"

"Well, if she were for sale, I could convince myself to offer the price that our two compatriots mentioned last week."

"If you have the cash on you, let's go find a clerk and document the transaction. That will allow me to turn my luck around this afternoon. You can pick her up tomorrow morning."

The next day, Peter and William took a wagon over to move Maisey to her new home. Peter was almost as excited as William. When they arrived, the expression on Maisey's face was one of the high points of their lives.

On the way home, William and Peter explained how she would be a free woman and a landowner. Maisey couldn't understand why some old white man bought her just to set her free. She was also having a hard time understanding the communal aspect of the farm. But she was delighted that William received a share of the profits from the larger farm and that she would too.

As they came up the lane, Abe came running out of their house, ecstatic about seeing his mother again. Chenoa didn't waste any time coming down to welcome her either, and from that point on she treated Maisey like one of her daughters.

Peter's next task was to get official manumission papers to prove that William, Abe, and Maisey were all free. Just because the family gave them their freedom didn't mean the law or the community would respect that. All Peter had to work with was the original bill of sale for each of them. As the owner of Good

Endeavour Farm, John had bought William and his son. Now they, as well as all the other property on the farm, had been inherited by Eli, and Maisey had been purchased by Peter.

Peter went back to the clerk in town and filed for the official papers to show that William, Maisey, and their son, Abe, had been set free by their owners and the Maryland colony. It was another long and complicated process, but once papers were in hand, they celebrated the end of an awful period of their lives. Unfortunately, they would still have to keep a low profile in town to avoid being challenged and questioned all the time. When William asked Maisey if she wanted to move farther north, she responded that they had a pretty good deal right there in Maryland. She quickly became a strong and positive force in the farm community.

One day, about a month later, William came running up the hill. Peter stopped watering the trees and went to see why William was running so hard. There must be an emergency. William stopped a few yards short of Peter and tried to catch his breath. "They took Abe," he finally managed between gasps.

"Who took Abe?"

"The sheriff and his deputy. They claimed he stole some silver and molested a white woman. But it ain't true. He's been here on the farm all week, working hard. I'm scared to death of what they'll do to him. You know what they did to Phillip a few years back. There's no justice in the colony for a black man."

"Saddle up both horses! I'll be right out."

As he turned to go into the house, Peter was furious and scared. The news that someone had stolen silver flatware and molested a planter's wife had been floating around for a couple of days. But this was the first time he had heard there was a suspect. Of course, he shared William's faith in Abe and

William's concern about frontier justice. Timing often became judge, jury, and executioner in cases involving nasty accusations like this one. So he went inside and quickly changed into his captain's uniform, complete with sword and loaded pistols. Peter had always assumed they would be necessary one day—and this was the day.

William brought the horses up, and they took off at a gallop toward the courthouse in Joppa Towne, intent on getting there before a mob could gather.

They were both breathing hard as they arrived in town. It was a good thing they had rushed to town, because a large, angry crowd had already assembled and were shouting, "HANG HIM, HANG HIM." The son of the woman who claimed she had been molested had rounded up and incited the mob with lies about Abe. The sheriff, who had just returned to town himself, led a petrified Abe, his hands tied behind his back, toward the jailhouse to lock him up and keep him safe from the crowd. However, that plan was disrupted by a group of rough men who knocked the sheriff and deputy aside, grabbed the ropes, and dragged Abe toward the empty gallows, where they put the noose around his throat. The mob yelled louder when they saw Abe being strung up, and the air was full of calls for vengeance. The sheriff and his deputy, totally neglecting their duty, just stood back and let the mob govern the day. They were not going to put their welfare at risk to save a young black man from an angry mob of white citizens.

Just as the leader of the vengeful crowd started to move the platform from under Abe's feet, Peter let loose with a blood-curdling battle cry as he and William charged their horses hard into the crowd, scattering the fired-up onlookers. Peter reached under his captain's jacket and pulled out one of his two flint-lock pistols. He took aim and shot just above the self-proclaimed executioner's head. The man dropped the rope and disappeared into the mob, realizing the captain might fire at him next.

Peter then brandished his sword, waving it over his head just as William, musket in hand, collected his shell-shocked son. Peter rose up as tall as he could, standing in his stirrups, looking many years younger and more potent than he was, and stared down at the mob. His uniform made him look like someone in control, someone who should at least be listened to in order to see what he had to say. He addressed the crowd, which had quickly quieted down following the gunshot. "I know you're hungry for vengeance. We all want to know who's responsible for the heinous crimes this week." He paused to catch his breath. "But I swear with my life that this young man is innocent."

Peter slowly scanned the crowd, trying to draw everyone's attention to what he had to say. "Now, you don't have to take my word for it. This should be a law-abiding country. Have a trial, look at the evidence, and then decide. For his safety, I'll keep young Abe under guard until the trial."

The crowd was quiet, the people absorbing what Peter had said. "None of us should cast doubt on the fabric of our colonial society by taking the law into our own hands. Our lives depend on following the law and seeking justice. That's the essence of a civil society. If any one of you disagrees, come forward, but you better have solid evidence. Now go home and let justice do her job."

With that, he turned his mount with a flourish and followed William and Abe, both astride William's horse, out of town. They left the deflated mob in the street, talking among themselves, wondering what the evidence was that pinpointed Abe.

The following day, Peter was back in town with an English Common Law lawyer, to meet with the sheriff and review the evidence against Abe. There was no credible evidence that Abe had been in town or had any motive to perpetrate the crime. The sheriff claimed he had arrested Abe to calm down the crowd and discourage vigilantes from coming up to Good Endeavour and rounding Abe up themselves. He hadn't expected he would lose control of the mob and endanger his suspect.

The sheriff thought the accusation was probably made by locals who didn't like that Abe's whole family were free. Some of the locals would do anything to keep the Africans down. Peter was sickened by the incident and knew this was the weakest part of their local government and one that put them all at risk. It was disheartening to see how quickly people believed false rumors, ignored due process, and were ready to put an innocent man to death.

In contrast to the crowd's rush to judgment, Peter's lawyer spent time investigating the case, trying to find the truth. His search turned up a traveling merchant who had passed through town that week. The merchant was in possession of the silver and claimed to have bought it from a woman in need of cash. He even had a receipt with her signature on it. When confronted with this evidence, the planter's wife confessed to making up both crimes. She didn't want to tell her husband that she had sold his mother's silver. The magistrate, Sir George Rumsey, dismissed the case. The townspeople who had been in the mob never spoke of it again. Peter wondered if they had learned anything from their role in "mob justice" and the near execution of an innocent and hardworking young man.

After Abe had recovered from the shock of this incident, he wondered what kind of future awaited him in such a hostile community.

Chapter 16

END OF A GENERATION

E li, Chenoa, and Peter grew old together, watching with pride as the younger generation took over. The land was secure, the farm was well managed, and they had built a vibrant community with a strong work ethic at Good Endeavour Farm.

Their success may have impressed the broader community, but it also made many embedded prejudices even greater. When Abe married Isabel, Eli and Chenoa's oldest grandchild, there was a lot of talk throughout Joppa. But the three elders loved all the children and their extended family.

Peter, Chenoa, and Eli, along with Maisey and William, knew their children and grandchildren would have a long and dangerous battle ahead. Abe had talked with them about how to escape the hatred and how best to protect his wife and children from the contempt of some of the people in Joppa. It was disheartening that Abe could not walk by himself or with his family in town without the threat of being attacked verbally and even physically. He wondered if it would be safer for his family to live in a mixed-race neighborhood in Baltimore. Eli wanted him and his family to stay on the farm, thinking that was the safest place to be—it had worked out for Chenoa. But like all people, Abe wanted the freedom to walk around his community, go where he wanted to go and eat where he wanted to eat. They chose to settle in the freedmen enclave near Fells Point, and then Maisey and William moved there as well to be near their grandchildren.

When they left, it was a sad day for the family, and they all promised to visit each other. They encouraged Abe and Isabel and Maisey and William to come back on Sundays. But even travel by carriage between Fells Point and Joppa was dangerous for a mixed-race family. Although the members of the family had good intentions, most contact was lost with Abe and Isabel's line of the family tree. Peter was the only person who traveled into the city, but even that was infrequent.

Eli and Peter would discuss these and other issues at length on quiet nights while sitting by the ledge overlooking the river. They watched the sun disappear behind the trees, they listened to the locusts, and they smelled the mist forming in the valley. The brothers had never been closer.

Eli was the first to pass. During his last coherent conversation with Chenoa, he held her hands and said, "I've lived a long life, and at fifty-nine years my body is telling me it's time to go. I want you to know you meant everything to me. I hope our alliance worked out well for you too."

Chenoa just smiled and then lay down beside him so she could keep him warm with the heat from her soul. She started a chant and sang him into a deep sleep, a sleep he never woke up from. A sleep that must have soothed him, because a smile formed across his face and never left.

Peter was devastated. Eli had become his closest friend and was the only person with whom Peter had shared the details of his life. Fortunately, he had Chenoa and there were always the grandchildren, who never grew tired of listening to the ever-changing versions of his sea stories.

After checking with Chenoa, Peter asked Eli's sons-in-law to dig a grave down by the ledge overlooking the Little Gunpowder. Everyone agreed that Eli would be happy there; he had always loved the solitude of the ledge. It had been a good place to struggle with the issues he had faced and find peace.

After Eli's death, Peter spent many an afternoon sitting on the ledge, often talking out loud, telling Eli the stories that were locked deep in his heart, ones he had not dared mention to any living soul. He also found himself talking with their parents and brother, John. Peter was now the last member of the original family who had settled on the Good Endeavour Farm.

Before he died, Eli had told Peter, in confidence, "I want you to take care of Chenoa. Keep the clouds of hate away from her. She's a wonderful woman." Eli then told Chenoa, "Please look after Peter. I love you both, and he needs someone to share the rest of his days with."

Of course, Chenoa didn't need anybody to take care of her. She still considered herself the head of the family and took care of everybody. Later on, when she and Peter decided to live together under one roof in the big house, the family was delighted. It just felt right to everyone. It saved Chenoa the walk back and forth to her cabin, and everyone on the farm knew they were kindred spirits, both doing their best to take care of the family and the farm.

Peter had loved Chenoa as a friend. She then became a sister and now a partner at the end of his life. He fondly remembered what a beautiful mystery she had been when Eli first described her and then more so when her spirit flowed through the cabin door and into their lives. Even after all these years, she still had a mythical quality about her presence, actions, and words. She was far more than a friend—he found that he could share his deepest emotions with her.

Late one night, sitting by the fire, Peter told Chenoa about Esmerelda, not the ship, but the woman he had fallen in love with in London. "After returning from Canton, I struggled with drink and memories of my part in the battle along the gunwales. I was disgusted with myself, having killed and maimed dozens of men that day, and I kept having vivid nightmares of watching the hordes with their grappling hooks surging onto our ship.

"Esmerelda helped me reconnect with reality and regain a little self-respect. Because of her care, I started to drink less and sleep better. When I got back on my feet, we married and had a wee son whom I named Caleb.

"But times were hard, and I struggled for two years trying to support the family, working as a clerk in the underbelly of that crowded port. Finally, I signed up as captain on a one-hundred-ton brigantine. Esmerelda was scared and didn't want me to go, but it was the only way I knew to support them. It was ten months before I returned to London, and by then, Esmerelda and Caleb had both succumbed to the plague. I was sickened that I wasn't able to be with them in the end."

Chenoa wiped the tears from Peter's face and sat there looking at this man she had admired for decades. She had no words to soothe his pain.

"Heartbroken by the loss of my wife and young son, and to keep from sinking into another depression, I returned to the sea. The wind in the riggings and the constant slap of the waves on the bow of the ship kept me alert, and fond memories of Esmerelda kept me strong. But she was gone, and I found myself longing for Good Endeavour Farm. It was a touchstone that kept me sane during the years it took before I was ready to retire. Memories of all of you kept me going through squalls and calms, through hot summer doldrums, and hard, cold winters, until finally, I found myself sailing up the bay and into the thriving port of Joppa Towne."

Chenoa took all this in and let it settle in her heart. When he finished, she shared with him the atrocities that her family had faced, the first of which had been at the hands of other Indian nations. That was followed by the era of the spread of European and African diseases that took so many native people's lives. Those events were followed by the terrors of the white colonists' endless invasion of her country. She shared how she stayed in contact with all those she had lost and how she kept them alive in her heart.

In their last years together, Chenoa and Peter agreed to a new alliance, one in which they would focus on each of the moments they had left together and pass on what knowledge they had gained to the younger generations on Good Endeavour Farm. At their age, they knew there was no good worrying about the past or the future. It was time to focus on the present.

When Peter's body finally failed him a few years later, the old sea captain took his last breath with his head on Chenoa's lap, surrounded by their family. It was the end of a generation of immigrant settlers who had escaped poverty, disease, and early death in England and had successfully established a foothold in the New World.

A couple of old shipmates showed up at Peter's memorial service. They lived down in Jonestown, next to Baltimore, and had heard of his death through the informal, old sailor's network. They joined right in with the activities, and after a few mugs of cider, the stories flowed out of these rough and porous men like rum down a dry gullet.

The elder of the two sailors, Jock, who had trouble standing up, raised a mug and said, "Here's to the captain. He lived an extraordinary life and was well known around the Atlantic as an honest man and brilliant captain, in good times and bad."

The younger sailor, Derrik, shouted out to Jock, "Tell them about his record with the pirates."

Jock hesitated and then launched into stories of Peter's encounters on the high seas. "Captain Peter only lost two shiploads of cargo to pirate attacks along the Atlantic Coast and never lost a ship. On most voyages he steered clear of ships flying the Jolly Roger by avoiding their hunting grounds in the Caribbean, the Bahamas, and the Capes of Virginia. By taking the longer routes out in the open ocean, he encountered fewer pirates, and when he did, he could usually outrun or outmaneuver them. His ship, the *Esmerelda*, was one of the fastest ships on the seas, and he never overloaded her with cargo. His reputation attracted the best sailors in the world to join his crew."

Derrik continued the tale. "Sailors respected Captain Peter because you could trust the man. He treated us all fairly. When cornered, he had a miraculous ability to talk with the pirates or the privateers, some of whom might have sailed with him before. He always limited his losses, and his crews all lived to sail another day."

Peter's former shipmates requested that they bury him at sea. Chenoa listened and appreciated their suggestion but said that he had made his choice to return to the land. He had told her he wanted to be buried down near the ledge with his brother. The family remembered him for his accomplishments on the farm, the stories from his shipmates, and the sanitized sea stories he had made up for the grandchildren.

After Peter's death, Chenoa changed. Her thoughts grew inward, and she was often heard mumbling or singing to herself in Algonquin. A short time later, she made a large batch of pemmican, full of dried meats, tallow, and berries. The aroma permeated the log cabin for weeks. With smiles and hugs, she gave her goodbyes to her Good Endeavour family, wishing them well, and walked off into the woods along a path that would be locally known for centuries as Chenoa's Way.

Word came back months later that she had visited her sons' families on the Pennsylvania and Ohio border. She took time to teach those grandchildren about the old traditions before saying goodbye to them as well. Then, following in the path of her father as he sought beaver beyond the frontier, she headed west toward the setting sun.

Chenoa's spirit lived on for centuries in the kitchen of the log cabin, on the land known as Good Endeavour, and in the hearts, the deeds, and the stories of the people she had touched.

PART FOUR

Creating America

Robert and Josie

Chapter 17

IRONSTONE RED

1775

O ver time, an increasing number of colonists, but never a majority, grew tired of King George. They felt that their interests were not well represented in Parliament, and they did not like rising taxes. So an increasing number of people started dreaming of becoming free from the whims, tariffs, and debts of an absentee landlord. Debates raged between loyalists, patriots, and the neutral "fence-sitters" in the towns up and down the Atlantic Seaboard and even with settlers in the backcountry.

On Sunday nights at Good Endeavour Farm, debates raged on and on about which direction would be best for the family. Several members tended to be loyalists—the system was working for them—while others complained about taxes and the tyranny of the Crown. Some claimed that politics had little to do with their lives. But as the possibility of war grew, it became an increasingly important question in everyone's minds. It was a scary and an exciting time to be alive. A time for big decisions, ones that would shape the future of every man, woman, and child throughout the colonies.

Twelve-year-old Robert, a great-grandson of Eli and Chenoa's, was caught up in the excitement of the war and was ready to make a big personal decision too. After years of working for his parents for free, he had decided it was time for him to move on to something new. He wanted a job that would contribute to the war effort and put some money in his pocket. Unlike his gentle and shy great-grandfather Eli, Robert was ambitious, and like Captain Peter, he was impatient to get off the farm and find adventures away from home. Fortunately, he had a few things going for him: he had his great-uncle's love for talking with people, and he did not mind hard work.

To be clear, Robert did not want to cut all the strings to his family. He still wanted to live at Good Endeavour Farm; all his family and friends were there. And of course, he had no plans to give up his mother's cooking or family dinners, either. Those hours were the best times of the day, given all the debate that went on around the table. It was just the work part. He wanted to find work somewhere else, just like his older brother had done when he landed a clerical position in town.

Another motivating force for finding a job was that the farm wasn't doing well under Robert's father's stewardship. His father did not have a knack for farming, and, Robert like his father, had no interest in farming, so he decided he needed to find a different career.

On a warm and hazy sort of day, when everyone was complaining about the humidity, Robert was walking back from an errand in town. He was moseying along, checking to see if anything new was happening. If he could just find the right job, he figured he could talk his way into it. Little did he know that his life was about to change.

Now Robert was of average height and weight for a boy of twelve—he still had some growing to do. A boy his size would have been easy to overlook around Joppa, except for his most distinguishing feature, a mane of red hair, inherited from the O'Malley Scotch-Irish side of the family. This allowed most town folks to pick him out of a crowd and recognize him from a distance. Having bright red hair was sometimes a good thing and sometimes not. He got teased a lot as a young boy but now took pride in standing out and being a little bit different from the other boys.

As he walked along the dirt road back from town, he noticed an older man leading a horse. The horse was pulling a sturdy wagon, which was oddly constructed with oversized wheels and extra-heavy axles. Having a deep love for animals, Robert immediately liked the stocky, roan-colored mare and wanted to pet her. "Afternoon, sir," he said to the stranger. "My name's Robert. You have a handsome horse. Mind if I pet her?"

"Well, good afternoon to you, Master Robert. I'm John Wilkenson. Yes, go ahead, but don't distract her from moving forward. She's got work to do."

Robert slowly moved up along the horse's left flank, speaking softly while stroking her rump, back, and neck. "What's her job?"

"She's got to deliver all this ironstone to the new furnace by dark."

"Mind if I walk along with you until we get to the Philadelphia Road?"

"I don't mind at all. I'd like the company."

"What's her name?"

"I call her Maggie. Look at her ears—she's listening to us."

Mr. Wilkenson wasn't as old as Robert had first thought, but he did have a limp. Apparently, that did not stop him from working. Robert rationalized that if a man with a limp could do this job, then he could probably do it as well. He liked Mr. Wilkenson's friendly manner and decided that this might be just the job he had been hoping to find. "I didn't know there was a furnace going in. Where's it located?"

"It's on the Big Gunpowder, downstream from the grist mill. I supply iron ore to the furnace every day that the weather's good."

"You only have to work on good days? That must be great."

"Well, it's not worth it to be traveling on these roads when they're muddy or when it's too icy. The cart might get stuck."

This line of work sounded better and better to Robert, who

struggled to contain his excitement. His mind was bubbling over with questions, but he tried to act like an adult and not an excited child. He glanced into the wagon and saw a collection of large, flat, dark-red rocks ranging in size from cow pies to sacks of grain. They were different than the black rock they quarried on Good Endeavour Farm. "What do they do with these red rocks?" Robert asked.

"You sure are full of questions for a young shaver, aren't you? You sound like you have a lot of grit. I like that. Where's your homeplace?"

"I live up the Little Gunpowder not far from here."

"You should stop by one day at the furnace. It's an interesting operation. They melt the iron out of these red rocks to make pig iron. Then over at the forge, they beat the pigs into iron bars."

Robert kept petting Maggie, trying to hide his increasing interest. He was intrigued; collecting and delivering the rocks was something he could do. "Do they require you to work long hours?"

"They pay me by the pound, so it's up to me when and how much I work. No one's telling me what to do." As they walked, Mr. Wilkenson told Robert all he knew about iron, where it came from, and why someone needed it. It all sounded like alchemy to Robert. It must take some sort of magic to turn rocks into cannons, he thought.

"If there's going to be a war against Britain, we'll require all the iron we can get for building cannon, ships, and other tools of war," Mr. Wilkenson explained. "If Britain boycotts the colonies, we will also have to start making tools for farming and cooking as well."

Just thinking that he could be collecting the ore for building guns to fight the British got Robert excited. He could play a role, even at his age, in winning the war. He liked everything he heard. He stood up straight as an arrow to appear a little bit older than twelve, and asked, "I'm looking for work, Mr. Wilkenson. Do you have any need for a strong and capable helper?"

The man stopped. Maggie stopped. Then Robert stopped. The man took a closer, more quizzical look at the boy and smiled. "Can you lift these rocks?"

Robert walked over to the wagon, lifted two large slabs, one after the other, put them on the ground, and then reloaded them without too much struggle.

Maggie, who had stopped walking during this test of strength, wasn't paying any attention. She took advantage of the stop and immediately started eating grass along the side of the road. Robert went right up to her, took her halter, and encouraged her to get moving again, a trick not always easy to do with a horse pulling a heavy wagon.

As the entourage moved down the road, Robert said, "No problem, sir. I've done hard work and been around animals all my life. I know many of the farmers in these parts, too. I could start any day you need me."

Mr. Wilkenson smiled at Robert. "I need someone I can trust to take the wagon out on days I can't make it. That person must be reliable. You seem to have the confidence to do the job. If you're interested, let's go talk with your parents."

Robert was ecstatic with this turn of events, so without further thought, he led the way up the lane to the cabin. He became a little nervous as they walked up to the cabin door, not knowing how his parents would react. He should have told them about his plans before bringing a potential boss to their home. But it was too late now, so he opened the door, and called to his parents, "Mother, Father, we have company. I would like you to meet someone."

His parents were quite surprised when they came out and saw the man, his horse, and a wagon half full of rocks right on their doorstep.

Robert introduced Mr. Wilkenson to his parents and made his pitch. Then he just stood back, scratching Maggie behind the ears. He decided to just let the adults talk. The job was a good opportunity, but he needed their approval and knew it was best to let his parents come to their own decisions. Fortunately, his father had sensed that his son was ready to get a job off the farm. He also knew of Mr. Wilkenson and had a favorable opinion of him. His father asked, "How are you finding the red stone?"

"I'm visiting all the local farms to collect their ironstone. Many fields and gardens with sandy soils in the Tidewater have slabs of this dark red rock. Since this rock's tough on plows, farmers have moved many of the rocks out of their fields long ago. But every year they find new ones working their way to the surface. Most farmers are happy to direct me to where they've dumped the rocks, as long as I remove them from their land."

Robert's father asked many more questions and then said, "Yes, we have some red rocks on parts of our farm too. Robert could start here. I like that he'll be meeting with and helping the local farmers." He looked at his wife and said, "I think it's a good job for the boy, one that he could do, and it's local."

Robert knew his mother counted on him for working on the farm, and now he watched her carefully. She must sense that he was itching and ready to try new things. She kept quiet, but Robert noticed that she nodded to his dad.

"It would be fine with us if you were to employ our son," Robert's father said, "Just remember, if you plan to sleep and eat here, you'll still have plenty of chores to do."

Robert responded in his deepest voice, "Yes, sir." He didn't want to sound too excited.

One of the reasons his father was interested in a good-paying job for his son was that Joppa Towne was becoming unviable as a port. This was true in many Tidewater areas, from New Jersey to Georgia. Planters had cut down all the trees and insisted on growing tobacco every year. Without trees and the rotation of crops, the rains washed away the precious topsoil, reducing farm productivity and silting in the ports. The planters' ignorance of what they were doing to their lands killed their golden goose.

The Crown had been forced to move the port and county seat to Baltimore, which had a deeper water port where the Patapsco River, Gwynn Falls, and Jones Falls all came together. Many of Joppa Towne's residents moved away to be closer to better jobs in Baltimore. As a result, land and housing prices, as well as business activities, plummeted in Joppa. The racetrack was doomed as people moved away and even Saint John's Church moved to higher ground several miles west in Kingsville. Fortunately, the families living on Good Endeavour Farm had long been rotating crops to maintain the quality of their soil. They found local markets for their produce, but they had to deliver their grains to grist mills and ports that were farther away. Robert was lucky to have found a job in a growing industry not too far from home. He planned to keep it.

Chapter 18

JOSIE

Robert assisted Mr. Wilkenson for the next three months, and then the older man started to let Robert do more and more of the rock collecting and delivering on his own. Wilkenson's limp was getting worse, and Robert had proven both trustworthy and able to do the job by himself. The man charged Robert a fee for the use of Maggie and the wagon, but it became Robert's job to maintain them both. He and his father built a corral for Maggie at their farm.

Robert loved interacting with the farmers. His outgoing nature proved perfect for his job because most farmers had a lonely existence and were happy to talk with him in order to catch up on the local news. They would direct him to deposits of red rock that they knew about, and of course, they knew about every hard, plow-busting red rock on their property. Many were already in piles, but Robert often had to dig the ironstone out of the soil himself.

Over the next three years, Robert worked hard at the job, and people started to refer to him as Ironhead Red, the boy who collects ironstone. At first, he was embarrassed by the nickname but grew to appreciate it as his reputation as a hard-working young man with integrity spread across the region. By the time he was fifteen, he had also earned the respect of the people at the ironworks furnace where he dropped off his ironstone.

Landing the job when he did proved to be timely. The Chesapeake Bay region was becoming famous for iron, and iron became the second-largest export from Maryland after tobacco. Robert had gotten in at the start of a new industry that would help industrialize the country.

✐

During those three years, Robert grew six inches and put on twenty pounds of muscle. He also became the most reliable source around for local news and was happy to take letters and packages to town for a small fee. He was well-known to everyone in Joppa.

One June day in 1778, during the middle of the war with Britain, fifteen-year-old Robert stopped Maggie under the shade of a large white oak. A girl about his age was also resting there. She had long, wavy, red hair and was exhausted from carrying several sacks of grain.

Robert nodded a greeting "Where're you going with those big bags?"

"I'm heading home, but I bought more than I can carry. My name's Josie."

"Hello, Josie. I'm Robert. I think I've seen you before. Do you live just past Bradshaw Road?"

"Yes, in the brick house. How did you know that?"

Robert replied, "Must be the red hair. When it waves in the wind, it's hard to miss. I pass your place several times a week taking deliveries to the furnace. If you like I can put your bags on the wagon and take you to your house. It's on my way."

"That would be great. Thank you."

"Let me move the rocks a bit and make room." As they walked along next to Maggie, Robert asked, "Is your father the judge?"

"Yes, he is."

"Are you sure he would approve of you walking or riding with a stranger? I don't want to get either of us into trouble."

Josie laughed. "You're no stranger to him. He's talked about the young man helping the war effort."

"We all do what we can. Your father must be on the road a lot now that the county seat moved to Baltimore."

"Yes, but the good thing is that he brings me the latest gazettes and books to read. There are more of those available at the new port."

Robert asked her questions about what she had read and her views on the war. He did not want the trip to end.

When they approached Josie's home, she said, "Thank you. It was nice to meet you and get help with the bags. Be sure to give Maggie an extra helping of oats tonight."

"Why don't we do this again?" Robert suggested. "I'm in town every Wednesday when the weather's good. I could carry your bags on the wagon next week . . . if that would help."

"I'll try to meet you at the white oak tree. If I'm not there by noon, my father probably has me tied up on other errands."

"I'll be there by noon. If you come, could you bring me a gazette?"

"I would be glad to. Until next week then."

Over the summer, Robert and Josie were able to meet up once or twice a month and enjoyed talking about life in the colonies and the progress of the Revolution. Josie seemed well-read and had strong opinions about England. Robert knew a lot about the local farmers, the iron furnace, and the commercial challenges facing Joppa. They got along well.

One day Robert said, "I need to expand my efforts into collecting oyster shells. The furnace uses them to remove impurities from the iron."

"My brother might be able to help," Josie offered. "He's a seafood buyer and knows all the local merchants."

"That would be great."

"I bet they would be happy to have someone come in and take away their empty shells. Let me ask him, and then the two of you could meet."

Josie's brother introduced Robert to people who had plenty of shells piled up on their land and along the harbor, which provided Robert an almost endless source of shells. He also carried charcoal to the furnace. However, since the farmers had stripped much of the local area of trees, he had to go farther away to find charcoal at a reasonable price.

1780

As the war dragged on both Josie and Robert began to wonder whether he should join the Continental Army. It was complicated because the work in the iron industry was critical to the war effort, and the company had been training him to do a variety of important jobs at the furnace. At the same time, he felt the draw of military action, and he wanted to play a more significant role in the campaign for independence. Like many young men, he didn't want to miss out on the chance to prove himself in battle.

The decision was further complicated now that they were both eighteen, had been courting for the past year, and had talked about marriage. Josie patiently listened to him debate the pros and cons of enlisting, but she wondered what role, if any, she played in his decision. She had opened her heart to him and was excited about creating a life together. If he enlisted, they would have to put that all on hold for a year or more. Neither of them wanted to do that. It was proving to be a tough decision for both of them.

He was clearly all tied up emotionally trying to figure out what to do. The week before he was planning to sign up, he took Josie down to the ledge and asked her to go away with him.

Josie was perplexed. "You're crazy. One day you want to enlist, and the next you want to run away with me. Where do you want to go? What's the plan?"

Robert, rarely short on words, said, "I don't know. I just don't want to lose you. If I join up, I might not come back alive . . . or you might give up waiting for me."

They both stared down to the river, watching a kingfisher fly upstream, chattering all the way.

Josie was intrigued with the idea of traveling. It sounded like an adventure. But she wasn't so sure about running away. She liked Joppa and had many good friends and family living there. She did not want to leave them all behind. "If you have to go, of course I will wait for you. We've been through so much together. Just don't get killed."

Chapter 20

THE HOME FRONT

As soon as Josie saw General Rochambeau and General Washington marching their armies down Philadelphia Post Road on their way to Yorktown, she had known Robert would enlist. The generals were larger-than-life figures on their tall steeds and in their colorful uniforms. The columns of troops that followed them kept coming and coming—thousands of them. They looked invincible. The whole town gathered along the main route, wanting to be part of the excitement.

Josie shivered and chills raced down her spine as she found herself watching and cheering the troops. When Robert marched by, stepping smartly in line with the others, she cried. A feeling of jealousy came over her as well. The generals were so stunning dressed up in their fancy blue coats and hats. She would have enlisted on the spot, too, if Washington had asked her to join.

At the end of the parade of soldiers, she met a cadre of women who followed behind the troops and supported them in any way they could. They loved the men who were drilling for battle, nursed them when they were injured, and buried those who died. Even that life was tempting to Josie. It was better than being left behind, away from the excitement, and dealing with all the work and the bad conditions at home.

That night she couldn't sleep, so she got up and wrote to a friend in Baltimore.

Dear Elisabeth,

Many of us have mixed emotions. We are terrified to think our loved ones might get wounded or killed. We are also angry that the war is taking them away and disappointed that we cannot go too. At the same time, we are proud of our country and continue to hope that this 'never-ending war' might finally come to a close. The possibility that we might win the war is exhilarating to some and scary to others.

Now that both my brothers have left for the war, I have to run our family's farm, help with household chores, and help raise my younger siblings. It is difficult, as Mother's health is poor and Father is on the road all the time."

Your friend, Josie.

Josie was right. It was a difficult life on the home front during the Revolution. Money was scarce, and a soldier's pay was not great or reliable. The women were often forced to run the family farms and the households on a subsistence level. The Loyalists, who were widespread throughout the planter and merchant communities, made it difficult for women supporting the Revolution to sell tobacco and buy the goods they needed. The British boycott of American goods made it even harder. Life was a daily battle to keep food on the table and the family solvent.

When Josie drove the carriage to town on an errand, she was constantly pestered by the Loyalist men and women. As an unattached young woman who was known as a supporter of the Patriots, she was often insulted, cheated, and even propositioned when trying to make a case for fair prices. Loyalist merchants, planters, and civil authorities treated her badly, partly because she was a woman doing a man's job.

It got even worse than that. There were at least three times when she was grabbed, pulled into an ally, groped, and kissed. Once, when she screamed, she was pushed to the ground while the scoundrel high-tailed it. The third time she was assaulted, she left a few scratches on one man's face and earned the reputation as a wildcat. That helped for a while. After that, she started carrying a knife with her at all times, and at home she kept the family musket loaded and behind the door. It was clear that she was changing a great deal, and she hoped Robert would still love her when he came home. She also grew anxious that he might be changing as well. She was just glad that Robert had not left her with child. Oh, the grief she would have had to endure from all those men and women if she were unmarried and in the family way.

Early November, 1781

The Americans won the Revolution when the British, under the command of General Cornwallis, surrendered to General Washington at the Battle of Yorktown on October 19, 1781. And when Maryland's Patriot troops returned from their victory at Yorktown, Josie was there, standing in the crowds along Philadelphia Road, trying to spot Robert over the heads of the other returning veterans. Everybody was cheering and waving flags.

She was anxious, not having heard from Robert in weeks. Then someone grabbed her arm from behind and spun her around. She saw an older version of Robert and flew into his arms. He was a bit taller, leaner, and bearded, but he was still the man she had been waiting for over the past year.

He hugged and kissed her and then swung her around to look at her. "Will you marry me now?" he asked.

"I would have married you then. But you wanted to go fight your war."

"I did, and now I'm ready. Let's go get your father to marry us today."

"Robert, you know that's impossible. A public announcement must be published for three Sundays in a row. Besides, Father is away on business. And there is a lot I have to do to get ready for a wedding. Let's pick a date in the middle of December. That will give us time to plan this important event and maybe even get to know each other again."

The young couple spent the next three weeks together visiting with family and friends, letting Robert get caught up on how Good Endeavour Farm was doing, and planning the wedding. One of the cottages on the farm was empty, and they outfitted it with furnishings given to them by both families. During their evenings, they had long talks, sharing many of the things that had happened to them while they had been apart.

One night after dinner at Josie's house, Robert sat at the table with Josie, sipping cider and reflecting on the past. He was proud that he had signed up, fought in several skirmishes, and had helped defeat the British. "I was ready for something new after all those years of collecting ironstone. I wanted adventure, and going off to war was a scary as well as an exciting challenge. I'm glad I went."

Josie nodded. "That may be true, but I remember how you tried several different times before you enlisted to get me to run off with you, to go west, to get away from the war."

Robert smiled. "Yes, that was my first choice, but you kept saying, 'All in good time.' That just drove me crazy. That probably made me want to go prove myself in battle even more, so you would want to be my wife."

"It was a pretty hard existence, keeping everything going here on the home front without you men working the fields and conducting business downtown. Women had to do all that work on top of taking care of their children and doing the household work," Josie said. She went on to share how she had been treated in town and the constant fear that she would be attacked. She didn't offer any names, concerned about how Robert might react. Fortunately, now that the Patriots had won the war and they were getting married, those problems and fears would go away.

Robert just listened and then said, "That explains why you seem different from the woman I left behind. I sense you've gained a lot of confidence in yourself, but I also sense you no longer trust men."

Josie looked directly at Robert. "We both grew up a lot this last year. It doesn't mean I love you any less. I'm just looking forward to getting to know you better."

Robert drummed his fingers on the table, trying to figure out how they each had changed and how they would have to adjust so they could live together as a couple. His life over the past year had been all about established authority, drills, and taking and giving orders. Now that he was back, he was ready to be the head of the family. But he now understood that Josie was fully competent at running everything at her family home and probably could run things at Good Endeavour Farm when they married. They would have to find a way to work together and grow to trust and love each other even more. A year was a long time and people change in many ways in times of war.

"I want your advice on the farm and with the merchants in town," Josie told Robert. "But I don't need you to tell me what to do every day. I envision the ironworks hiring you back and you sinking your energies into your work there, leaving much of the farm life to me. As I recall, neither you nor your father enjoyed running the farm anyhow."

Robert smiled, stood up, and pulled her up to him for a hug. "We'll figure it out—there's always plenty to do. I have a meeting with the people at the ironworks tomorrow. After a year on the road with the army, all I want is to settle down here with you and raise a family."

The ironworks wanted him to help retool their operations, and he rose up to manager within a few years. He enjoyed the work, and he and Josie were able to work well together managing the farm. Josie was right; he had less interest in the farm than she did—and she was good at it.

One of his main challenges at the ironworks was working with a mixture of enslaved and indentured staff. He discussed it at length with Josie and decided he had to change that practice.

It was a tough sell to the owners of the company—all of their competition used enslaved Africans. They were concerned that, if they had to pay their entire work force, they would not be able to compete when margins were so small in the post-war years. His case improved when John Tyson, a Quaker, invested in the company and sided with Robert. None of the other investors thought the furnace could be competitive. And Robert knew that if they lost money by making the transition, the owners would shut down the operations, and they would all be out of a job. It was going to be his responsibility to make sure that whatever changes he made were successful.

Robert used Josie as a sounding board as he tried to figure out how to implement the change.

"I'm proud of you for trying to end slavery at the ironworks," she told him.

"It's tough. I know you want me to push on the morality of the issue, but that's not enough. I have to convince the owners—and the staff—that freed men would care more about the quality of the product and would work harder to increase productivity if they benefitted directly from their efforts."

Robert and Josie moved into the main house on Good Endeavour Farm and over the next several years had three children there: two boys, Charles and Daniel, and their little sister, Sally.

One Saturday, Sam, an African neighbor, was helping to re-shingle Robert's house. After having the noon meal in his cabin, the second one down the lane, Sam came back up the hill to finish the shingling job. The lane was now called Bulls Lane because the farm had been converted from tobacco and grain to pasture and hay for dairy cows and beef cattle.

"Sam, join us for a drink of cider," Josie said.

"I'd be happy to, ma'am."

Josie passed a mug of her fermented cider to Sam and continued. "We've been talking about the past few years. How has your life changed?"

Sam looked over at Josie and smiled. "I don't think backwards too often, Miss Josie. In addition to working at the iron foundry with Mr. Robert, there's always so much to do right here on the farm. Like getting shingles on your home before it rains."

"Robert says you've become the best ironmaster in Maryland. How did you get so good?"

"Well, Mr. Robert is the key man who manages all the ore, charcoal, and lime deliveries, sales, and the finances. I just make good iron. I was lucky my granddaddy made sure I was trained to do a range of skills. Once Mr. Robert set me free and I got my papers, I've worked twice as hard as I ever did before. Freedom's a funny thing. You end up working smarter and harder because it's going to directly benefit your family."

Robert enjoyed hearing Sam's views on things because he always spoke his truth. Sam was younger than Robert, stronger, and had an intensity that Robert admired. Sam had probably hammered in twice the amount of shingles as Robert had that day, and Sam hadn't even worked up a sweat. Sam just got the job done, sharing some tricks of shingling with Robert as he lined up another row of cedar shakes.

"Sam takes pride in making the best pig iron and iron bar in the state," Robert said, joining the conversation. "As a result, we get top price for what we turn out. That success has allowed us to buy Sam's wife and children out of bondage as well. They're all free, thanks to his efforts. His example, more than anything I did, helped convince the investors to shift totally to a hired staff. He's the hero."

"I am fortunate with how things are for me and my family today, but I do fear the future," Sam confessed. "A lot of men have been freed, but Maryland's a border state and they're still at risk here. It's tempting for slaves to think they can escape to the North, which makes the plantation owners mistrust every African they see, free or enslaved. It scares me. The white plantation owners have all the money—and the power—and have taken over the state. They could change the laws at any time to do whatever they want. That's not right."

Robert could see the concern in Sam's eyes and knew there was a long way to go to protect everyone's rights. He could only hope that their choice to free all the enslaved workers at the ironworks would inspire other people to do the same.

Chapter 21

TALK OF ANOTHER WAR

1812

Over dinner, Robert and Josie's daughter, Sally, asked, "Mother, what have you heard from Charles? I miss him."

While serving Robert a second helping of stew, Josie replied, "So do I. It's been two years since he left, and we've received only three letters. I wish he would write more often. It's been twelve months since the last one."

Josie's mind seemed to float away from the dinner table. She stared at the fireplace and thought about her older son. Like many young men, Charles got so excited reading Jefferson's report of the Corps of Discovery that he took off to follow in the footsteps of Lewis and Clark. Unfortunately, few of these would-be adventurers were as prepared or experienced as the members of the Corps, and most lacked the skills they would need to survive in the wilderness and in Indian Country.

"His first letter reflected his excitement in making it to Saint Louis," Josie continued. "But his last two letters talked about how tough it was in the territories. I suspect he's out beyond the reach of the postal service by now. Frankly, I'm amazed any of his letters got to us—this country is so large."

"He told me before he left that most adventurers are gone for long periods and not to worry if we don't hear from him for a year or two," Sally said as she rose to get another glass of milk.

"Charles thought he had enough tracking and foraging experience that he could live anywhere," said Josie.

Robert agreed. "We all know he's a survivor. He knows how to farm, hunt, trap, and even speaks a bit of Algonquin. Just you wait and see, he's going to walk right through that door one day, taller and stronger than ever." As he spoke, Robert glanced at Josie. She was lost in thought again, now staring out the window. He knew she greatly missed her firstborn, and like Josie, a small piece of him could never stop thinking about Charles. There had been a big hole in his heart ever since his son left, leaving a noticeable void in life around the table and the farm.

They all knew that Charles had his challenges. His moods could swing quickly, and he was easily angered when things did not go his way. They understood that one reason he had decided to go on this trip was to fight those demons and get a handle on his emotions; he needed to learn how to be with others without lashing out at them. None of them would ever admit it, but when Charles left, they drew a sigh of relief, being at their wits' end on how to help him. They were hoping that he would learn how to conquer his demons or find a life that suited him better than life on the farm. Nevertheless, they all missed him and hoped to get more mail.

Robert brought the conversation back to a more pressing concern. "We have our own challenges brewing closer to home. Our relations with Britain are getting tense again, and your brother Daniel has picked this time to go off and become a sailor."

Robert was right. Things *were* tense. The Royal Navy had begun to impress American sailors from American merchant ships into their royal fleet. To combat this threat, a number of American captains had equipped their ships with cannon and had been raiding British merchant vessels. Robert thought the privateers' actions were similar to poking a sleeping giant in the eye. Britain would want to poke back, and what better place to do that than the Chesapeake—home to many privateers.

"This may blow up into a full-scale conflict, and Britain may one day sail its formidable fleet right up the bay," Robert warned. "They could attack any of the ports on the bay and even the capital in Washington. We need to think about how it might affect Daniel if he becomes a sailor and how it might impact all of us." He turned to his daughter and asked, "Sally, what do you think of Daniel's plans?"

"I agree that it's a dangerous time for him to go to sea. But he has always dreamed of doing so."

Josie looked at Robert and added, "He will be our second son to take off to who knows where. I fear that you might move away one day, too, Sally. I pray that you will settle down close by so we can see you once in a while and help with your children when you have them."

The following week, Robert saw Daniel heading out for a stroll around the edges of Good Endeavour Farm. Robert knew his son was struggling with his choice to go to sea but didn't really know why. At the same time, Daniel appeared to have no friends and no other plans for the future that would keep him in Joppa. Robert was worried about him.

Robert told Sally to go walk with her brother. "He needs someone to talk with, and he's not sharing much with me. He seems to be closer to you and your mother than the men here on the farm."

Sally nodded at her dad and then ran to catch up with her brother. "Daniel, may I join you?"

"Of course. I was just thinking about you. Do you know how much I'm going to miss our walks? You've always been my closest friend."

"These fields and woods hold a lot of good memories. Tell me about your hopes for going to sea."

"I picture sailing as an escape, a life away from prejudices and the expectations of others. Sailing's a chance for me to explore something different with other young men. Maybe I'll end up on a South Pacific island or in some foreign port, far from the rigidity of these mid-Atlantic tobacco towns."

Sally listened, trying to understand her brother's thoughts. One of his concerns was his father's plans for him. Robert was starting to look at Daniel as the likely inheritor of the farm if Charles did not return. But Daniel did not want to take over the farm, so his father's expectations were weighing heavily on him. The homestead was a gift he would not appreciate and would not accept. He thought Sally should inherit it all if Charles did not return.

Daniel was also trying to figure out who he was and what he wanted to be. He knew he was different from other young men. They were all looking for a wife and starting a family, but he had no interest in either. He also knew he was much different from his father and his brother Charles as well. He didn't fit in around the farm or the rest of Joppa. He was drawn to far-away places or at least moving to a large port city. He needed to discover what he wanted to do and find a place where he did fit in.

"I heard you tell Father you were hoping for a spot on one of those new ships they're building in Baltimore. They say they are the fastest and most beautiful ships ever built."

"I did tell him that. I love the beautiful lines of those new ships, but the thought of sailing hundreds of miles out at sea is daunting. My latest plan is to learn to sail by working the bay's tidal waters on a local merchant or market boat. So what if I end up just taking beans to market? I'll meet lots of people, be able to live on shore some of the time, and start on a new life visiting the ports around the bay. Then if I like sailing, I could always enlist on a clipper."

They were quiet for a few minutes as they walked along the well-worn paths of the backcountry.

"Did I surprise you with my decision?" Daniel asked his sister.

"No, I knew you would end up going to sea like Great-uncle Peter. That chest of his in the attic was so much fun to play with when we were younger—all the masks and the colorful clothes. Didn't you read all those books he collected? You seem to have memorized the stories that we heard over the years about his voyages."

"Yes, but whatever I do, I won't stay away as long as Charles. That's been hard on all of us."

"They say Great-uncle Peter sailed away on a ship and didn't return for thirty years."

"I promise never to do that. But with a war in the Chesapeake pending, I need to test myself to see if I have what it takes to be an able-bodied seaman—or even a captain someday. But I can't swim, and I'm not sure if I'll get my sea legs. I get dizzy on the Joppa Towne ferry.

"You'll do fine," Sally assured him.

"If I can't serve at sea, I'll head down to New Orleans or up to Lake Champlain, wherever I'm needed to fight the British."

Sally's last comments to her brother were, "I think you could do anything. I see you sailing up the Mississippi one day, finding Charles, and bringing him home." With that, she headed back to the kitchen to help her mother with dinner.

Daniel continued on his walk, still in a state of confusion as he wondered what the future would bring to someone like him. He walked down and sat on Eli's Ledge—as the family had come to calling the ledge where Eli and Peter had spent so much time. When dusk fell, he headed back to the house. The next day he was off to learn to sail, or cook, or whatever they might have him do on board a ship.

Two years later, in 1814, the British fleet sailed into the Chesapeake Bay. All of Maryland was on edge. Where and when would the British land? Were any of the Chesapeake Bay ports safe from the hundreds of cannons on ships in the British fleet? The British destination became clear as the fleet sailed up a weakly defended Potomac River toward the nation's newly constructed capital.

By this time Daniel had proven himself at sea and had visited many of the ports that now were at risk. He knew the bay waters well and had visited Rock Hall, Annapolis, Baltimore, Elkridge, Havre de Grace, and St. Michaels, as well as Tilghman, Smith, and Tangier islands. To help defend the nation's capital, he joined Commodore Joshua Barney and his fleet of shallow-draft, fortified barges. He wrote to his parents that Barney's strategy made a lot of sense to him, and he had been assigned as captain of one of the barges due to his experience with shallow-keel ships.

Dear Mother, Father, and Sally,

Don't worry about me. The barges are much better suited for the shallow waters of the Bay compared to the much larger British warships which are confined to the deeper channels. I admire Barney. He fought in the Revolutionary War and later served as a squadron commander in the French Navy. I look forward to engaging with the enemy and will come for a visit once this is all over.

Respectfully, Your son Daniel

Daniel's and Barney's barges, as well as the other barges in the American fleet, engaged in a series of strategic skirmishes with the British fleet. It was like a game of cat and mouse, and it turned out to be a delaying action if nothing else. The Americans quickly came to understand that Barney's mosquito fleet was grossly outgunned and overwhelmed. Barney was forced to direct Daniel and the other barge captains to scuttle their ships to keep their cannons and ammunition out of British hands.

After sinking his ship, Daniel and his shipmates made it to shore by wading and splashing through the thick, sucking mud and dense marshland grasses along the banks of the Patuxent River, dragging their cannons with them. They regrouped under Barney and made their way to Bladensburg to join the local militias in defense of the capital.

With most of the United States military fighting on land and at sea along the Gulf Coast, in New York State, and in Canada, the seasoned soldiers from the British Fleet met little resistance in the Battle at Bladensburg, where local militias had been stationed to defend the capital. The battle became a rout with only Barney's flotilla men standing their ground and repelling British advances until the last minute.

When their ammunition ran out, Barney ordered his troops to fall back. The British marched into Washington and set fire to the President's House—which many were now calling The White House—the Capitol building, and nearly every other public building in the city. It was a devastating blow to the new country. The British re-boarded their ships and headed downriver to the main channel of the Chesapeake Bay, where they then turned north.

After this humbling experience with the British, Daniel and his crewmates walked all the way to Baltimore to help defend that city, the likely next target of the British fleet. They all suspected it would be next since the British thought of Baltimore as a nest of thieves, having lost dozens of merchant ships to Baltimore-based privateers.

Daniel made it to Hampstead Hill—later named Patterson Park—just before the fighting started on September 13, 1814. He and his shipmates helped enhance the defenses that ran from the top of Hamstead Hill all the way to Fells Point. Their charge was to protect the city from the British foot soldiers coming from the east. These were the same skilled soldiers who had routed the American forces at Bladensburg.

Daniel watched as the British sailed their nineteen-ship fleet up the Patapsco River and began a well-planned, dual attack on the city of Baltimore. Their first step was to land 5,000 hardened soldiers at North Point so they could march up the peninsula and attack the city from land. After landing the foot soldiers on North Point, the fleet moved into position to attack Fort McHenry and the city with rockets and bombs. Their goal was to weaken the city's defenses and destroy the defenders' morale with an air attack. The ground and sea attacks were planned to happen simultaneously.

While waiting for the British troops marching toward him on land, Daniel asked around and learned that Baltimore was much better prepared than the defenders of Washington had been. The military and the city had been planning complex defensive maneuvers and had agreements in place for militia from other states to help defend the city.

The American troops had already blocked off the entrance to the Inner Harbor. They used a giant chain that stretched across the Patapsco River, along with log-booms and sunken ships to keep the British bomb ships and rocket ships at bay. Baltimore had also built batteries spread along the shore line, and of course Fort McHenry was well located to defend the city and was manned by experienced staff. They were ready for the British.

On the way up the very flat and farmed North Point peninsula, 1,500 American troops delayed the advance of the British for hours and caused many British casualties. The Americans then pulled back to Hampstead Hill. As the British troops advanced, a boy up in a tree took aim at "the man in fancy clothes riding a horse" and fired, wounding General Ross, the popular leader of the invading British force. The boy escaped. The general did not, perishing from the wound.

Simultaneously with the land advance, the British fleet staged a twenty-five-hour aerial rocket and mortar assault on

Fort McHenry. The Americans returned fire. It was a terrifying display of raw power that sent fear into everyone in the city. The explosions were so loud and continuous that Robert and Josie could hear them at Good Endeavour Farm. They walked back and forth on their front porch, worried sick about the attack on their city and wondering where Daniel was at that moment. All they had heard was that Barney had scuttled his fleet and Bladensburg was a rout. It was one of the worst days of Robert's life. He feared America would be back under a British flag by morning.

But Robert was wrong. When Daniel made it home a few weeks later, he told Sally and his parents, "You wouldn't have believed it. I've never seen anything so amazing as the attack on Fort McHenry. It put the fear of a vengeful God into all of us."

"Were you scared?" Sally asked.

"Yes, I was scared. Thousands of rockets lit up the skies, along with ear-splitting explosions. It was deafening. I was totally intimidated and thought that if the British demolished the fort and the city, our troops would scatter. I also thought the ships might aim their rockets and mortars at us over at Hampstead Hill. I couldn't sleep. Nobody could sleep, although we tried to take naps in the freshly dug earthen trenches. All I could think of was how badly this same British fleet and their ground troops had beaten us on the Patuxent, at Bladensburg, and in our nation's capital. We all knew they were a well-trained and formidable force.

"The next morning, when we saw the American flag still flying over the fort, it re-energized everyone's morale. There was lots of hollering. Fortunately, because of the chain across the river, the British warships had not gotten close enough to Fort McHenry or the city to be effective. As a result, the British rockets and bombs ended up doing little damage. I had hope that the Maryland troops might stand their ground."

When the British troops arrived at the Hamstead Hill fortifi-
cations, they encountered 8,000 men bearing arms and manning
over one hundred cannon. The city defenders had built a mile-
long fortification between the invading forces and Baltimore.
These men, native and immigrant, black, brown, and white and
of all ages, were not going to let the British burn their city down.

As the British infantry approached, the defenders stood
should to shoulder, shouting to inspire one another and to intimidate the British. They were ready to repel whatever the enemy
had in store for them.

The British stopped their advance. This was a more formidable foe than the one they had met in Bladensburg. The failure
of the naval bombardment and the presence of so many defenders gave them pause. Then it started to rain. Simultaneously, the
British on board their ships ended their aerial bombardment,
and the British troops on land made an about-face and withdrew
their infantry from the city. A huge cheer went up as they left,
and many of the city's defenders followed the British troops,
taunting them all the way back to their ships. It was a festive
time for the Maryland defenders. They had stopped the enemy
attack on land as well as at sea. Baltimore had saved the country.

Later, Daniel would claim that standing there with thousands of other men waiting for the British was the most moving
moment of his life.

Chapter 22

Railroads West to Ohio

Robert, Josie, and Sally were delighted when Daniel arrived home safely. They all started cheering and applauding him and the other men from the farm who had joined in the defense of Baltimore. Later that week, Robert sat Daniel down, and asked him about his adventures and his future.

"Father, I had a lot of exploits sailing around the bay. I loved watching ships race one another and seeing tall ships from all points of the Atlantic. But I learned that I'm not cut out for maritime life. My future adventures will be on land."

"Why give up your dream?" Sally asked.

"It no longer *is* my dream. I didn't like being crammed into small spaces on a boat full of unkempt men. There were no swashbuckling sailors on any of the ships where I worked. It's not a very exciting enterprise once you get below deck."

Delighted with his decision, Josie urged him to move back in with them or find something close enough so he could regularly come for dinner. They had missed him and wanted him to be a part of their lives again. He thanked her but said he was staying in Baltimore with a shipmate who had become a close friend.

"Well, bring him out to dinner. We just want to see more of you," Josie told him.

"Your timing for finding a job is good," Robert said. "There are more opportunities now that the war is over. I can introduce you to some of the men who run those businesses. Many of them are my clients."

Robert was right. After putting up with all the disruption of supplies from England during the war, Americans now wanted to grow and manufacture everything here at home. In addition to grist and textile mills, iron furnaces and forges, local businesses began mining local natural resources of granite, chromite, copper, gabbro, flagstone, limestone, sand, and gravel. Daniel found work in the offices of several of these quarries for the next few years, but the long-term prospects were not appealing to him.

One night when Daniel came for dinner at the farm, Robert said, "I want to introduce you to people at the Baltimore and Ohio Company. They're building a railway, first from here to Ellicott Mills and then across the three-thousand-foot-tall Appalachian Mountains to the Ohio River Valley. Can you imagine that? We Marylanders are going to open up the West, and you could be part of it."

Daniel's eyes widened. "That's hard to imagine. How would they get over the mountains? I can't believe they're serious."

Fortunately for Daniel, the investors in the railroads were serious. Baltimore had to find a way to compete with New York's recently begun Erie Canal which, when completed, would connect the Hudson River and New York City with the Great Lakes and the Upper Midwest. If Baltimore could connect with the vast grain-growing regions in the new territories of the Ohio and Mississippi River valleys, they would create another major trade route. The pressure was on. The businessmen knew that if they did not create this connection to the West, the town of Baltimore would become a backwater. Robert knew that plans for the railroad were underway because they had ordered iron rails from him for the first leg of the route.

"I'd like to meet with them," Daniel said. "Can you arrange it?"

Robert nodded. "I can. It's an exciting opportunity."

The one trait Daniel inherited from his father was that he liked to do a wide range of things. The railroad business in Baltimore offered him those opportunities. So he quit his job in the quarry where he was currently employed and joined an advance team with the newly named B&O Railroad, working on planning and purchasing rights-of-way before any track was laid. His various tasks required him to travel along the proposed railroad route but kept him in Maryland most of the time, allowing him, to the delight of his mother, to visit his family often.

One Sunday, Daniel came to the farm for dinner, and his mother met him at the door with a big smile on her face. He had arrived in his business attire and appeared quite confident in his demeanor. He was a big company man now and spoke easily and with a sense of authority. She was excited to see him because she was proud of him. However, she had become increasingly concerned about his social life.

After getting him a cider, she offered him the rocker by the window and pulled up a stool. It was a rare opportunity to get to speak with him alone. She quickly got around to asking about his life in Baltimore. He was approaching middle-age and showed no signs or interest in getting married. Wasn't he lonely? She couldn't visualize how he could be happy with a life without a family.

"I often dine with some of the chaps in the company, but I have trouble socializing with people who think so differently than I do," Daniel told her. "Some of them have traditional views on abolition. I find I can't fully trust people who don't believe in the worth of other men."

"Have you joined a church or found interests outside of work?"

"I have no social life, Ma. I work all the time. I do go for walks on Hampstead Hill and around Federal Hill. And there are a couple of taverns where my roommate and I like to have dinner or a drink that tend to have interesting people. But most nights I'd rather stay home and read a good book."

"Well, let me know when you're ready to settle down. There're several engaging women around here. Sally knows a few herself. But most women your age are already married."

Just then, Robert came in after feeding the livestock and saved Daniel from his mother's interrogation. Robert was delighted to see Daniel, and after a few pleasantries, he sat down at the table and asked his son about the railroad business. Josie got up and went back to cooking while listening to the men talk.

"What do your bosses have you doing these days?" Robert asked.

"I've started securing the rights-of-way for track leading west out of Ellicott Mills. The next section will go over to Harpers Ferry on the Potomac. Now, that's a beautiful setting for a town. It's where the Shenandoah and Potomac rivers merge."

"Where are you finding the labor for laying the track and cutting through the rock cliffs along the Patapsco Gorge?"

"We're hiring Irishmen."

Robert had heard that the Scots-Irish were coming here in droves, escaping bad economic conditions back home and looking to own land and practice their religion. He hadn't been to town recently, but he had heard that Irish immigrants were flowing out of ships like rats and flooding onto the streets of Baltimore. There were whole blocks of Irish living down near Mount Clare Station.

Daniel continued. "I love listening to them talk, and many of these men are skilled and hungry for work. I find them much more reliable and hardworking than many of the local men."

"Maybe I should come over there to hire a few for the ironworks."

"I'm sure you could. But getting back to the railroad business, the most interesting development is how we now plan to pull the freight and passenger rail cars over the mountains?"

"I thought the plan was for horses to pull the cars."

"That was the plan. But when I looked at the details, it turns out it will take too many horses. We've contracted for steam engines which are getting more reliable all the time."

"If they work, you won't have to switch out horses every few miles."

"That's right. We'll just have to load more coal and water to run the engines. It's exciting. There's even talk about having a continuous rail system across the country to the Pacific by the 1860s."

Robert just sat there, listening to Daniel's dreams and trying to grasp the magnitude of the plans. All the way to the Pacific! It was hard to believe. He sat back and relaxed, picturing how the railroads would transform the country. The ability to transport people, products, and news, would accelerate westward expansion. He chuckled, thinking of all changes he had already seen in his life. What more might he live to see?

Chapter 23

ABOLITIONISTS

E ver since they met, Robert had always liked that Josie was well-read, thoughtful, and articulate. With time he had also come to appreciate her self-confidence in running Good Endeavour Farm. She had learned how to work with others, especially neighbors, merchants, and the civil authorities, and as a result she had gained the respect of many of the families in Joppa.

Although their relationship had been difficult when he first returned from Yorktown because of their different experiences, he had learned to treasure a partner who would challenge herself and inspire him to be his best. They had become quite the team. It must be the red hair, he thought, although both of them had turned auburn and gray by middle age.

Josie was certainly as well-known as Robert in the greater Joppa community. She was the daughter of a well-known judge, had raised three children, and had encouraged Sally, her youngest, to follow in her footsteps and get involved in the community. People respected Josie for her willingness to speak up on issues that needed to be changed. She had become a model for a modern woman in the new nation.

One night after dinner, Josie sat down at the large walnut table and told Robert what she was hoping to do with the rest of her life. He was always interested in her thoughts, so he sat down, lit up a pipe, and listened.

"It's time to free all the enslaved men and women in this country," she stated. "I can help locally in ridding our community of slavery, and if I can do that, I think there's hope for others, too. We need strong advocates in every community in the country"

Robert was surprised at first. After all the years of hard work, he thought she might be ready to relax, but he should have known her better than that. Ending slavery was a cause that was very important to her. He looked at her carefully while puffing on his pipe. In addition to the graying and thinning red hair, he saw the wrinkles that now made up part of her smile. He saw the calloused hands and noticed she did not stand up as straight and tall as she once did. But he also saw the determination in her to make things better. She had all the skills she needed to inspire him and others to be their best.

His face brightened and he reached out and took one of her hands, excited by her enthusiasm and energy. They discussed ways for her to be more involved in building a more just union and ways where he might be of value as well.

Josie was driven by her experience with African families like Sam's and other freedmen and enslaved people she knew. She thought there was too much hate and fear in this country, but she also thought the mood was shifting and that she could help it change more quickly. She felt this was the great challenge of her generation and knew it was becoming an increasingly important local, state, and national issue.

Her first goal was to organize and inspire the women at Saint John's Church. She encouraged members of the congregation to read pamphlets about the moral imperative of freeing people from slavery. As a group they encouraged the new pastor to use his pulpit to inspire the parishioners to free their slaves.

Along with Sally, Josie attended community meetings where she advocated to free the dockworkers who worked at the port. These longshoremen were of African descent, and she suggested the port buy them from their owners, free them, and offer them their same jobs with better pay.

Although some of Josie's neighbors appreciated her efforts, she found that she and her beliefs were unwelcome in certain circles of society. The planters started to ignore her and the whole family when passing on the streets or attending church. This reaction was not a surprise. She had already tried to discuss the issue with many of them and had found little hope of changing their minds.

This backlash to her efforts disappointed Josie but did not deter her. It reminded her of the way many of these same people had treated her back during the Revolutionary War when she had to run her family's farm. She and Robert discussed her efforts at length, and he remained steadfastly supportive of her activities.

Then one day Josie received a letter.

> To the Residents of Good Endeavour Farm:
> We have noticed that you are trying to interfere with local commerce. You have no right to do this. If you continue in your attempts to steal our property and take our laborers, we will burn down your house and hang your children from your pecan tree. Keep your nose out of the business world! It's a free country.
> The Residents of Joppa.

When she received this threat, Josie was sickened by the level of hatred and violence it suggested. Her gut tightened and she couldn't breathe. Robert came into the kitchen just then and saw her trembling. He took her arm and helped her sit down on one of the wooden stools by the kitchen table. She took deep breaths until she could remove the fear enough to think about her options.

The death threat was an awful reminder for both Josie and Robert of the schism in the community and the country at large. Was her sin really bad enough to incur a death threat against her family? Did her wish to be faithful to her God, nation, and fellow man make people hate her so much that they wished she were dead? Or were these men scared that she might be right and that the cause of freedom might succeed? That thought gave her hope. Josie pondered the irony of the writer's reference to a free country. What a narrow perspective of freedom, she thought. A free country for whom?

Instead of being intimidated by the letter, Robert noticed that her resolve grew more robust. The cause of freedom was important enough for her to stand up to the threats—if only she could find out who made them.

Robert was enraged. He would storm back and forth in the kitchen, demanding to know who would stoop so low as to threaten the lives of his wife and children. What made it even worse was that it must be someone he knew. He considered their options.

The first thing he did was to clean and ready his guns and keep them loaded by the door while hoping the situation would never come to violence. Next, he sadly trimmed all the low limbs of the pecan tree to prevent someone from using them for a lynching. It made him sick to think about what might happen if things did turn violent. He knew he would kill someone to protect his family. In Yorktown he had shot and killed men, and he made this clear throughout the Joppa community. He also sought help in town by talking to everyone he knew in order to increase the awareness of this ugliness buried in the shadows just beneath the surface of their society.

Robert also reported the threat directly to the sheriff. He showed him the letter and pleaded with him to do something to prevent the vile attacks that had been proposed.

The sheriff just shook his head and replied, "Robert, there's nothing I can do unless you can prove who sent the letter and that it's a real threat."

"Of course it's a real threat!" shouted Robert. "You need to send a clear signal to everyone in the county that there will be consequences for sending death threats and even graver consequences for acting on those threats. As the town sheriff, you need to exercise your authority to remind people that we have a society based on laws and that they will be enforced."

"I'm not going to do that," the sheriff replied flatly. "You want me to lock up a wealthy plantation owner or a merchant for sending your wife a letter?"

"Yes. I do. You've got to take action. Our laws and your ability to enforce them are the only things keeping us from being a lawless frontier. Why else would we need you?"

The sheriff bristled. "Don't tell me how to do my job. Go tell your wife to keep a low profile until this slavery issue goes away. You need to make sure she doesn't blow this all out of proportion and make a real mess of things."

"I'm not going to muzzle my wife, and we will *not* be intimidated. This is a moral and a legal issue. I'm asking you to act now before it's too late. This is an opportunity for you to prevent a crime, not just try to solve it after it's occurred."

"I'll think about how to do that, but I can't be interfering every time someone threatens someone else. That happens every day."

"This is not a Friday night brawl. It is a heinous threat to a middle-aged woman, a mother, and an important member of our community. If you don't act, you're putting us all at risk."

The sheriff shrugged. "I don't think so."

Robert got up angrily, almost knocking over his chair. Totally frustrated with the sheriff, he headed toward the door, then he stopped, turned around, and said as powerfully as he could, "Sheriff, with all due respect, you probably know all the people who might have sent this threat. I believe it's your responsibility to work behind the scenes, meet with the perpetrators, and nip this in the bud before it gets out of control." With that, he slammed the door and headed home to Josie.

Josie chose to continue to speak out, and as a result, another note came the following week. This time both Robert and Josie went to see the sheriff but with no better results. Robert and Josie then took the letters to the minister at Saint John's Church. The minister listened, empathized, and consoled but did not promise to do anything except pray for Josie's safety. Robert and Josie were hoping the minister would use the death threat as an opportunity to preach about "loving thy neighbor" and speak out against slavery—or at least against violent threats. Unfortunately, quite a few planters in the congregation did not want to hear that type of sermon, and the minister did not wish to deliver one.

"I have to minister to all my parishioners," the minister told them. "We would not even have a church if the funds were not donated by the plantation owners."

"With all due respect, pastor, you would not have a church if it wasn't built by the sweat and skills of African craftsmen," replied Josie. "Each of us has the capacity to do good *and* evil. I hope you will speak to these men who are sending us these threats. Advise them to focus on their good sides and to stop spreading evil in our community."

Nothing was done by either the sheriff or the pastor, and fear continued to permeate the house every time a letter arrived with another threat. The more they discussed their predicament with others, the more apparent it became that money, coercion, and intimidation ruled the state. This was not democracy. Josie and Robert would have to stand up for the sake of the community, the state, and the cause of freedom. They did not want to live in a community where the bully wins.

One night, Robert was coming home very late and bumped into a young boy coming around the corner of the cabin with a letter in his hand. Robert grabbed the boy's arm with one hand, took the letter in his other hand, and took him inside, where Josie graciously invited the boy to sit down at the table. She made him a mug of chocolate, and then she and Robert proceeded to ask the boy questions.

Being caught had shaken the boy. He claimed to have no knowledge of what the letters contained. "I get paid for delivering the letters, ma'am, sir," he told them. "I need the money to help feed my family."

Josie showed him each of the letters she had received and made him read them. The boy was shocked at the hate expressed in the letters and was embarrassed and ashamed that he had been delivering death threats to this kind, older woman. He had often heard good things about the people of Good Endeavour Farm.

The boy told them the name of the planter who had hired him and promised never to do it again. He asked them not to inform his parents. Robert agreed and then said if the boy needed a job, he should stop by the ironworks—they always needed part-time help—and then he sent the boy on his way.

The following day, Robert and Josie climbed into their carriage and went to meet with the sheriff again. This time with the perpetrator's name.

"Now that we have proof about who's sending the threats, it's time for you to act," demanded Robert.

"I'll speak with the planter who the boy claims sent the letters. I know both the planter and his wife. Unfortunately for you, this planter is well connected, and I'm sure there's no way to change his mind on this matter. He thinks he's above the law, and he probably is since he's connected to powerful people in England. My advice to you is to stay clear of him."

Robert and Josie shook their heads, got up, and left the sheriff's office, disheartened once again. Lost in thought about what to do next, they walked around town in a daze. Every time they passed a building, they looked to see who might be waiting to accost them. It was as if they had lost their freedom to walk around town or their home without fear of attack. Sadly, they headed home, feeling like outcasts. Josie said, "This must be similar to the way Indians and the Africans must feel walking in this town. It's not right. We have a lot of work to do." They had to find some way to resolve this matter so that everyone could live here without fear.

Robert attempted to arrange a meeting with the plantation owner who was writing the threats, but the man refused to meet with them. Robert was irate, not knowing what else to do.

Josie told him that the best option left was for her to go public in a gambit to protect her family by bringing the debate out of the shadows of the town and into the public square. "If I do nothing, this issue will just fester. If I raise awareness among the citizens, and give all sides the opportunity to have their voices heard, the threats might subside. It may help the community come to grips with the issue and set a tone for how to process differences of opinion in the future without threats."

Josie sent a carefully constructed letter to the local paper, *The Southern Aegis*. Even though the paper typically supported the enslavers' views, they agreed to print her letter because they knew an emotional controversy would help sell more papers. They planned to milk the incident for weeks. They also figured that increasing circulation would give them more opportunities to promote their pro-slavery opinions in the future.

When the next edition of the paper came out, Josie's letter was on the front page:

Dear Neighbors,

Members of our family have been part of this community since 1695. We have sold vegetables and grain to many of you and provided good jobs at the ironworks for your sons. We also go to church with some of you.

As most of you know, I have advocated for abolishing slavery for years, first at my church and, more recently, at civic meetings. My family freed the men and women who once worked our farm. We have seen some of you do the same. Thank you. Over the past month, I have received multiple death threats from Mr. James Smythe in response to my efforts. He has threatened to burn our house and hang my children if I do not cease sharing my heartfelt views on slavery. Do we want to live in a town where we let bullies get away with threatening us and our right to free speech? I thought we had a constitution that guaranteed freedom for all and freedom of speech. Unfortunately, Mr. Smythe must not believe that. He wants to take away my free speech so he can continue to profit from the sin of slavery.

I implore all the members of our community to help protect my family by sending letters asking the sheriff to protect us from these threats. If that does not work, please hold Mr. Smythe responsible for any harm done to us.

I also invite you to join me at Saint John's every Sunday after services to discuss what steps we can take to abolish slavery here in Joppa.

Sincerely,

Mrs. Robert _ _ _ _ _ _ _ _ _ _

It was the most widely circulated, read, and discussed letter to the editor that year. Many people were shocked that an influential planter would stoop so low as to threaten a respectable, middle-aged woman and her children. Some were more jaded, not surprised at all that a wealthy planter would do whatever he wanted to intimidate others, control the politicians, and buy his way to gain and maintain power. Citizens wrote letters to the editor in support of both sides. The back and forth went on for weeks, increasing the paper's circulation both locally and statewide. The editorial board of the paper eventually suggested that Josie should cease her public attacks on a fellow citizen.

The controversy in the paper and the fact that Josie was well known, liked, and respected did make a difference. Here was a woman willing to put her safety and life on the line by speaking out against what she perceived as evil. Her efforts inspired others to think about the horrors of slavery and ways to remove it from society.

Josie's decision to go public proved effective. The death threats ended, and more people came to her weekly meetings after church. The culture was shifting across the county and the country. Over time, even the *Aegis* found increasingly barren grounds for its opinions, and a pro-Union editor bought the newspaper. The country's culture was changing. But as always with complex economic and moral issues, it would take a long time to achieve meaningful change.

Chapter 24

BOUNTY HUNTERS

L ate one night, Robert came home and found Josie at the kitchen table with a number of books and pamphlets spread out across the table. "What're you reading?" he asked.

"The essay I'm reading now is by Ralph Waldo Emerson," Josie replied. She slid the pile over to him and continued reading, deeply engrossed in Emerson's thoughts.

Robert picked up an essay called *Nature* from the stack. After he finished, he spoke up, "He has some good ideas. What do you make of all this?"

"I don't know," Josie responded. "He makes me think differently about a lot of issues. I want to hear more."

"Let's go hear him. I understand Mr. Emerson is speaking at the Lyceum at the Unitarian Church in Baltimore next week."

"I would love to. Let's see if Sally can come with us. I'll walk over to her cabin in the morning and invite her."

The following week the three of them went down to Baltimore to listen to Emerson. The beautiful building was packed, and Emerson, leaning out over the people from the pulpit, projected his deep baritone voice to all corners of the sanctuary, inspiring them to think about their lives and the principles by which they lived. He challenged them to live purposeful lives and to create a better society for all. Josie was so moved by Emerson, that she solemnly but enthusiastically signed up to help. She hoped they could make a difference.

Emerson's words inspired Josie, Sally, and Robert to take on more risks and engage even more in their community. They spoke at length with several abolitionist families, who suggested actions they could take to move the cause along. It was empowering being among other families who cared about the same issues they did.

A few weeks later, Robert came home late and immediately walked over to warm his frigid hands by the woodstove. He glanced at Josie, who was usually happy to see him, but she was silent, tending to a steaming pot on the stove and filling three mugs of stew.

Robert looked over to her and asked, "What's going on?"

Josie looked up with a serious expression on her face and stared at him. He tried to read her mind. He knew it must be important enough for her to not want to speak. Then a child coughed, and the floorboards creaked in the room right above his head as if someone had shifted their weight. Robert's face turned pale; his hands shook. He held his breath as he listened for more sounds. "How many?"

She nodded at the tray in her hands that held the three steaming mugs of hot soup. Carrying the tray, she climbed up the stairs to where their guests were hiding, shivering from the cold and fear.

The next moment he heard the sounds of horses snorting and whinnying. Men were coming up the lane. "Stay put," he called softly up the stairs, "and don't make any noise."

Robert took the lantern off the hook by the door and went back into the bitter-cold night. Three white men were riding toward the cabin, leading two other riderless horses complete with saddles and chains. The chains clanged in the night air.

The men appeared to be strangers to Robert and looked like they had been out in the frigid cold and windy weather all day. Their stiff countenance revealed that this was not a social call. They had business to discuss.

Robert spoke in a polite voice, hiding his nervousness. "Evening. Can I be of assistance to you gentlemen?"

"Looking for three runaways—an older man, a young woman, and a child," one of the riders replied.

"Haven't seen any runaways. I would invite you in to get warm, but the wife has a bad case of cholera. Where are you men from?"

"Down round Charles County way. We've been chasing the runaways for five days. Damn fools should have picked a better time of year to run. They'll never get far in this weather."

"I doubt anyone could survive long outdoors this winter," Robert replied. "Where was the last place you saw them?"

"Some riders spotted 'em last night on a creek down Philadelphia Road aways."

"If we see signs of them, who should we contact?"

"Just let the sheriff know. He knows what to do with 'em. When we come back this way, we'll check in with him if we haven't found them by then. By the way, who lives in these cabins along the road?"

"Family. They all work here. I'll tell them to keep an eye out for your runaways."

"It'll be worth your while. There's a bounty on each of their heads."

The men left, and Robert stood there uneasily, watching them go. He knew that if he hadn't been convincing enough, they would be back or, worse yet, might be spying on the farm for the next few days. If it kept snowing, his guests would have to sit tight; their footsteps would be too easy to track. As he went back into the house, he noticed that the wind had come up and was blowing snow off the roof.

Josie was just coming down the steps. "Did you recognize them?"

"No. The one man claimed they're from Charles County—his accent sure sounded like it. Nevertheless, our guests need to stay put a few days until these bounty hunters move on up the road. I told them that you have cholera—to keep them out of the house—so you stay put, too."

"Well, that gives me a few days to put some meat on their bones. They're starving."

Three days later, the snow had melted, and Robert decided it was time for their guests to move on, to get closer to the Mason Dixon Line. They were so close to freedom. But he was worried about taking them on the well-used Philadelphia Road because of the bounty hunters. He was concerned the bounty hunters might return to the area once they gave up looking farther north.

Josie suggested Robert take them up the river valley on what had become known in the area as Chenoa's Trail. As long as the ground beneath the melting snow stayed frozen, it would be passable for a horse and wagon. Another small farm owned by abolitionists lay about a two-day trip upriver. That would get them closer to Pennsylvania. Robert took them in his wagon, covered up with blankets. Four days later, he returned, his first mission completed. They sent an encrypted note of the mission's progress to their contacts in Baltimore.

They would never hear about their guests again, but they had done their small part and could only hope that the family found their way to freedom.

PART FIVE

Rebuilding America

Nathan and Nellie

Chapter 25

An Un-Civil War

1861

Robert and Josie would not live long enough to see all enslaved people freed in the United States, but they continued to champion freedom until their deaths. No matter how much Josie, Robert, Sally—along with thousands of other women and men—campaigned for the end of slavery, the plantation owners and politicians in the South just dug in their heels.

Robert told Josie how disappointed he had become. "This country's in an ugly stalemate. It's all fueled by populist, hate-mongering politicians, and it seems to become more threatening every day."

She had to agree. "I don't know how we're going to resolve the slavery issue. It appears that dialogue and debate, the critical tools of democracy, are not getting us to where the founders hoped we would be. We have failed to use reason and compromise to overcome emotion, prejudice, and greed. It's a sad time for the battered ideals of America. I wish I had more hope that we could resolve this in a deliberative process."

But they couldn't. It would take a Civil War to force the end of slavery in the United States, and yet "The Lost Cause" continued in the hearts and minds of many Americans.

Caleb's descendants fought on both sides of the war. Two brothers moved south before the war to forge and sell swords to the Confederates in North Carolina. One distant relative carried on the Southern cause during the war and for decades afterwards. An avowed white supremacist, he later led a paramilitary group of Red Shirts during South Carolina's violent

1876 election. He then went on to be a populist politician who served for many years as a US senator, as well as governor, continuing to incite crowds with his aggressive and threatening language and virulent oratory of hate. As a result of the split in the family, the discussions around the dinner table at Good Endeavour Farm were spirited and intense leading up to and during the war.

Nathan, Sally's grandson, was pro-Union and often spoke up about the humanity of those who were enslaved. "How can anyone be for slavery? I've worked beside free and enslaved Africans and respect them. I've also witnessed some of the hardships they face in our society. They live in fear of plantation owners, bounty hunters, sheriffs, and many poor whites who treat them as less than human. I'm puzzled and angry at how many people go to church on Sunday and then turn around and treat their slaves—and even freedmen—poorly."

Toward the end of dinner one night, one of Nathan's cousins said, "The plantation aristocracy started the war to maintain their wealth, their status, their supremacy. But wouldn't anybody? Isn't it natural to protect what you have?"

Nathan pushed back his plate and got up from the crowded table. "Yes, that may be true, but is it fair? Why should so much of the wealth be concentrated in so few hands? We have all been working hard to build this country. We should all benefit."

"Aha," Nathan's great uncle Daniel said, "That is the key question lying at the soul of America. Are we a democracy of the people, of all the people, or just some of the people?"

"Hasn't the country been debating that for years without success?" Nathan asked.

"Yes, Daniel replied. "It's time for all of us to go back and read the founding papers of our nation because, if the secessionists win, it could be the end of our democratic experiment, at least in the South."

"So if we don't want that to happen, my generation will have to fight and kill our brothers in the South in order to keep the states united," Nathan concluded.

"Unfortunately, I think that's true."

Nathan sighed. "What an awful situation we find ourselves in."

Five days after Confederate troops took over Fort Sumter in South Carolina, the first violence of the war erupted in downtown Baltimore. A mob of Confederate sympathizers and street gangs, including one called the Plug-Uglies, attacked the 6th Massachusetts Militia as they marched along Pratt Street between train stations. These were the first Northern troops coming south to support the Union's war effort in Washington, D.C. This walk exposed them to large numbers of citizens, many carrying guns, and many who were Southern sympathizers. Citizens representing both sides started shouting at each other and at the troops. Shooting broke out and four soldiers and twelve citizens were killed in what became known as the Pratt Street Riots.

Following the riot, tension was palpable on the streets, at business establishments, and in homes all around Baltimore. War had begun—again—and the people of Baltimore were choosing sides. All interactions became a question of who you could trust. Were your neighbors, bosses, and sons supportive of the Union or were they secessionists and traitors? The lines of society and business were being redrawn.

Nathan knew men who joined the street gangs and others who joined the Union Army. He tried to follow the issues so he could better understand why people made the decisions they did. Some local militias, such as the Howard County Dragoons, reported to Baltimore to help maintain order but refused to sign their allegiance to the Union. They were dismissed, and they headed south to join the Confederate cause. Not able to rely on local militias to keep Maryland in the Union, Lincoln stationed federal troops and cannon on Federal Hill with guns overlooking the town.

At the start of the war, Nathan worked long hours at the ironworks, where everyone was busy equipping the Union Army. They were a key player, being so close to the nation's capital, and their contract with the Federal government was crystal clear: they were not authorized to sell any supplies to the Confederates. Moreover, the company had to clear their employees to ensure there would be no sabotage by Southern sympathizers within the ranks.

In addition to internal threats from employees, the ironworks' bosses feared attacks on their operations by Confederate sympathizers, of which there were many in Maryland. After the riots in Baltimore, the plant management assumed they would be attacked and required all their employees to bring muzzle-loading muskets or pistols to work for both daytime and nighttime shifts. The staff took turns serving as sentinels and practiced defensive drills every morning. Confederate raiding parties did attack other mills, bridges, and ammunition depots across the state throughout the war, but Nathan's site was spared. However, the fear of an attack made Nathan even more pro-Union than he already was. Based on his friendships with freed and enslaved men and women at Good Endeavour Farm and the ironworks, he had concluded that slavery was a curse on all men.

Good Endeavour and other farms along the Philadelphia Road did well during the war. The local troops bought all excess grain, fruit, vegetables, and livestock from the farmers. But Nathan and his young, male friends did not fare as well. They were the generation destined to fight the bloodiest war in the nation's history. Their lives would be full of drilling, marching, eating rations, and catching malaria, which was rampant throughout the South. And they had to fight and kill each other when the time came.

Near the beginning of the war, Nathan told his uncle Daniel, "I'm resigning my job tomorrow and joining the Union Army."

"Are you sure that's what you want to do? I know they need you at the furnace."

"It's what I think I have to do to help win this war, keep our country intact, and end slavery."

"It's going to be ugly. . . and yet, I wish I was going with you. I have always been glad to have served the country back in 1814." Daniel reached out with both hands and held Nathan's shoulders and, with a tear in one eye, said, "Take care of yourself and write us whenever you can. We will treasure every word you write. I'll save every letter you send and will look forward to hearing more on your return."

Nathan enlisted the next day. He was strong and disciplined from working on the farm and at the ironworks and was an excellent shot. But he loved working with animals, so he signed up to be a veterinarian. During his years on Good Endeavour, he had become the go-to person for taking care of the animals. He had the touch that made him good at it. His grandparents had also shared a little about natural remedies with him. That knowledge came in handy on his way to Yorktown. After setting up camp each day, he would wander through the local woods in search of useful plants for man or beast.

As a veterinarian, Nathan was assigned to take care of the horses, oxen, and mules needed to transport food, supplies, cannon, and injured soldiers. His commanding officer also called on him to take care of sick or injured cows, sheep, chickens, and pigs that were constantly being acquired to feed the troops.

When his regiment encountered its first massive battle, his colonel yelled at him, "Forget the damn animals and fix up my soldiers. I need everyone in this battle right now."

There were never enough surgeons to handle all the wounded men. The injured were often dropped off right in the mud or dust in front of Nathan's tent, which served as both his bunk room and as an operating room.

When Nathan told his colonel that he had no experience with people, the colonel replied, "The only difference between men and animals is that men are better at killing each other and that's the top priority right now."

Fortunately, Nathan worked alongside a freedman with far more medical experience than he, and Nathan picked up many of the steps needed to stabilize a wide array of wounds.

His work evolved to amputating human legs and arms and distributing any available amounts of alcohol or morphine that he might have. His tools included a suitcase of surgical supplies, including sharp knives, saws, an axe, morphine, and bandages—whatever he could get his hands on.

The days and nights during and after a battle became a haze of blood, agony, and death. He rarely had time to change his bloody clothes or remove his mud-caked boots. During large-scale engagements, he had to forget his veterinarian responsibilities completely while he quickly dispatched sick or injured animals directly to the kitchen butcher to use for dinner.

In addition to treating injuries encountered in battle, the troops sought him out to help them deal with widespread illnesses. Between battles, he spent much of his time treating pneumonia, typhoid, dysentery, diarrhea, scurvy, and malaria, in addition to an array of festering wounds and blisters. It seemed to Nathan that a large part of his job involved pleading with the generals to procure drugs for all the casualties of war. There was never enough quinine to reduce the symptoms of malaria, and he administered copious amounts of opium gum, laudanum, and morphine to help soldiers deal with their most severe bouts of pain. As some of the men recovered from their wounds, they found they were addicted and began to beg for and steal drugs. He had to post a sentry on the drug tent.

During multiple-day engagements, his colonel would order him to get the troops back into the fight as soon as possible. These demands, along with long hours, sleepless nights, deaths, and diseases took their toll on his health. The only things keeping him sane between the terrifying nightmares and the horrific reality of war were his dreams of the golden wheat fields of Good Endeavour Farm and his own growing use of morphine.

Nathan had signed up for "90 days of duty," but with so many people dying, he could not leave his brothers-in-arms to suffer. His ninety-day commitment slowly and painfully stretched to four years.

1864

Nathan's great-uncle Daniel had lived a long life, and in retrospect, he figured it may have been too long. Sickened by the horrors of the Civil War, he wished he had passed away years ago so he wouldn't have to read or listen to firsthand accounts of the savagery of the war from wounded soldiers he met.

After his roommate passed away, Daniel was lonely and moved back into the big house at Good Endeavour Farm so the family could take care of him during his waning years. Daniel was not used to so many people around and often would not attend Sunday dinners. He would seclude himself for days, not speaking to anyone in the family. Other times he would take off to Baltimore for a night or a week and never mention what he was up to.

Nathan had always liked the older man, even though he thought Daniel was a bit odd. At times Daniel would be elated upon his return. At other times he would dissolve into sulking, drinking, and yelling at his creator about the loss of so much young life in the war. After reading letters from Nathan about battles where thousands of men were maimed or killed, Daniel would fall into some dark place. All he could think about during those times seemed to be the loss of so many young men he would never have the chance to meet and who would never grow up to live full, if not always normal, lives. Daniel never finished a letter from Nathan without sobbing. This Armageddon had no redeeming value. It was nothing like the glorious war his father, Robert, had returned from in the 1780s or his own war in 1814. The Civil War was a bloodbath going on for far too long.

During these lonely, lost hours of Daniel's last years, he sought solace by drinking and having dinner at one of the taverns along Joppa, Bradshaw, or Philadelphia roads. He often met someone at these establishments to spend the evening with. There were older men like himself to talk with, but Daniel preferred the company and promise of younger men, always asking them about their dreams and desires in life. Most of the men were like Daniel, escaping the loneliness and the horrors of the day. Sometimes, these evenings would end in angry, drunken scenes. At best, Daniel offered his drinking partner some level of solace or even physical comfort.

One night in 1864, he ginned up a conversation about how long the war would endure with a striking, younger man with blue eyes. They both agreed the killing had to end. After discussing the massive bloodshed of the war, the subject came up about what might be the most effective way to bring an army's operations to a halt.

"I don't see why both sides haven't engaged in more strategic attacks," Daniel told the young man. "The railroads deliver most of the troops and supplies to the Union armies. You would think these supply lines would be the prime targets for sabotage by the South."

"Can you give me an example?" asked his drinking companion.

"Just consider the BW&P—the Baltimore, Wilmington, and Philadelphia Railroad. The Magnolia Station is right over here near Joppa Towne. They have hundreds of miles of track exposed and only a few troops defending the bridges. It wouldn't take many raiders to overpower them, destroy the bridge, and disrupt the flow of supplies and reinforcements for weeks, maybe months."

"It couldn't be that easy," argued the young man. "It must be well guarded this close to Washington. I bet there are troops at both ends of the bridge."

"From what I understand, they're mainly on the south end, leaving the northern end vulnerable to attack. I think they're short-handed."

"Well, I guess they can't defend every bridge, and I doubt the Confederates would come this far north." Shortly after that, the younger man stood up, paid his bill, and politely excused himself. "Thanks for the company."

Daniel was sad to see him go and asked, "Can you stay for another drink?" But the younger man shook his head and strode out of the bar.

It was late, so Daniel decided to take a room at the inn. When he went down for a late breakfast the next morning, he noticed quite a buzz among the other diners. "What's all the commotion?"

"Haven't you heard? A branch of the Confederate Cavalry, operating under a local man, a Major Harry Gilmor, hit the railroad bridge near Joppa Towne last night. According to one of the Union soldiers who escaped, they made a real mess. The Confederates tore down the telegraph lines, dumped train cars full of supplies into the Gunpowder River, and damaged the track and the bridge. It'll be months before they can make it safe for train traffic again. What a terrible time for this to happen. It's going to lengthen the war by many months."

"Oh god! Who's this Major Gilmor?"

"Those who have met him say that he's a rather dashing

young man with piercing blue eyes. Some people said there was somebody here last night who looked like him."

"Here at the inn?"

"Yeah. He talked with men at the bar, evidently looking for information about the war. After leaving here, he must have rallied his raiders and headed over to the bridge. After the attack, they disappeared into the night. It was one of the most daring and effective raids of the entire war."

Daniel stood there by the bar, stunned. Thanking the man, he decided to skip breakfast and get away from the inn as fast as possible. All kinds of questions shot through his head as he rode home. Could the man he had drinks with be one of the raiders? Was he the major? Was it possible that Daniel was to blame for the idea, the target, the raid's success? Daniel did not know and would never know but made a pact with himself never to tell another soul about the possibility that his words had aided the South in their cause—a cause he firmly despised.

Daniel kept looking over his shoulder while nervously urging his horse to go faster. He knew that he was exposed out on the open road. If someone remembered him talking to the young man with the blue eyes, he could be thrown in jail or even hung as a conspirator, a Confederate strategist, or even a traitor. A deep sense of guilt permeated his whole body as he accepted that his alcohol-induced chatter and his desire to entertain the dashing young man may have extended the war by months and increased the number of young men who would die.

Daniel's remorse was so great that he swore to himself never to be so glib when talking to others; he did not want to cause any more harm. In fact, after leaving the inn, he went directly back to Good Endeavour and rarely left the house again. The shame of it all hovered over him and overshadowed all the good he had accomplished in his life. He cut off contact with most members of the family and just stayed in his room.

The guilt must have still been with him when he went to his grave less than a year later, because his final act was a sad and unresolved chapter to his lonely and secretive life. He was found one morning on the frozen ground, having fallen to his death from the second-story window of the addition.

He was old and unsteady, and relatively unimportant, so most people accepted the cause of his death as an accident and moved on. They had other things to worry about. But the immediate family was puzzled—things did not quite add up. It had been a cold morning, and the window would not have been open. Several relatives thought he might have taken his own life. Suicide could easily have been a possibility since he had kept to himself and had been depressed for months.

However, upon going through his papers, family members found a couple of unsolved questions that made them stop and wonder about his lonely life. The first was a series of receipts for large donations made to the local veterans' homes and hospitals. They had never heard him talk about these donations and wondered what might have prompted his largess.

Then, upon examining his daily journal, they found that many entries had been ripped out or crossed out, including entries up to the day he died. They found fragments of the journal pages with burnt edges in the fireplace. On the largest piece of charred paper left in the fireplace were the words, "I did it." No one in the family could figure out what might have occurred that was important enough for the old bachelor to write down and then remove. It was a sad and puzzling end to a long and secretive life.

Chapter 26

HEADING WEST

1865

Nathan made it through four horrifying years of war in one piece physically, but emotionally, he emerged as a broken man. He was also struggling to kick an addiction to morphine that he had used to fight the pain, the exhaustion, and the horrors he faced while working around the clock to save men's lives under terrifying and unsanitary conditions. At times during the war, he had tried to take solace in the arms of one of the women following the troops but in his mental condition found it a shallow, meaningless episode.

Even though he had dreamed for the past four years of returning to Good Endeavour Farm, he was in no condition to go home; he was too shattered. There was no pride in his soul, and he could not imagine any family celebration that would open his heart again. He was not ready to face all the family's questions about the war. Death and destruction swirled through the gray matter inside his head. His daytime reality and his nighttime terrors were a mix of skirmishes and major battles punctuated with names that caused fear to rise in his heart: Bull Run . . . Shiloh . . . Antietam . . . Vicksburg . . . Gettysburg.

Nathan needed to discover a way to clear his foggy mind, rebuild his emaciated body, and find a new way to rekindle his spirit as well as fight the convulsions of withdrawal. Once discharged, he sent a brief letter to his parents letting them know he was alive and that it might be a few months before he would return home.

Then, with only a rucksack, a musket, and his discharge pay, Nathan turned west, following the well-worn trail left by so many others needing to escape or seeking their fortune. Along the way, he encountered many white men, black freedmen, Mexicans, Indians, Creoles, Chinamen, Frenchmen, and others speaking in a variety of languages. Some of the men were damaged, missing arms, or limping on injured legs, their haggard looks reminding him of the men he had taken care of during the war. There were men in tattered gray uniforms and others in blue. He didn't stop to talk with any of them. He had nothing to say.

Nathan left the war with a deep distrust of his fellow man and shocked by what ordinarily good people could do to each other in battle. Nightmares of his field hospital overrun by Confederates or accidentally shelled by his own Union artillery haunted him for weeks. His mind and body were constantly on alert, and he often found himself jumping at loud noises and looking back over his shoulder as if someone were tracking him. Like him, many of the men he encountered on the worn trail were heading west to find a reason for living. He understood that most men he met might not be bad people unless they were hungry, scared, or greedy, and then they were a threat. Everyone was hungry.

Other men he encountered were just evil, looking to rob him of anything that might be hidden on his body or in his possessions. In an effort to protect himself, he wore a scowl across his face, sharpened his knife out in public several times a day, and ignored them all while holding his rucksack tightly to his side. To further deter any surprise attacks, he found himself constantly scanning the horizon to see if anyone was lying in wait for him.

Following dirt trails, Nathan walked across Kentucky to the muddy Ohio River and boarded a flatboat that would carry him downstream to the Mississippi. There he caught a rickety, old, steam-powered paddle-wheeler that carried him up the Mississippi River to St. Louis. The cheapest ticket gave him access to the lowest deck, but he avoided going indoors because of the awful stench from the livestock in the ship's hold.

He sneaked upstairs, but it was no more welcoming. Most passengers there were losing their money at gambling tables and to pickpockets. Nathan watched one game of five-card draw erupt in a dispute that ended in a shooting and a man thrown overboard. The massive, churning river swallowed the man whole, along with all evidence of his life's journey—another pruned limb of a family tree leading to nowhere. As much as he wanted to help the accused man, Nathan had to accept that the land where he was heading, like this riverboat, had little room for justice. He would have to learn how to survive out in these lawless territories. It was times like these that he felt a deep sense of loneliness and a long, long way from Good Endeavour Farm, and he wondered what the hell he was doing in this lawless land.

While venturing on these dangerous steamships and in these treacherous waters, Nathan chose to keep his own company. Standing in the bow of the paddle-wheeler where the breeze was freshest, he could keep his eyes on the other passengers. But most of the time, he found himself watching the swirling, brown waters while leaning against one of the weathered, wooden poles that supported the upper deck. The powerful currents, the sheer magnitude of these mighty rivers, and the range of debris floating downstream mesmerized him. The Little Gunpowder Falls was nothing more than a twig on a grand oak compared to the Mississippi, a river so broad that it was hard to discern the exact location of its far shore. He struggled to envision the vastness of a land that yielded this much water and silt to the sea every single day of the year.

Nathan took an older steamship up the much more treacher-ous and log-strewn Missouri River, which carried him westward to Independence, where he disembarked. This town was the last reliable place to stock up on victuals that would carry him across the plains. It felt good to be standing on land again. He had wondered whether he would ever get off the rickety old paddle-wheeler alive. Walking the streets of Independence allowed him to explore the shops as he tried to determine what other essentials he might need for this third leg of his trip. The following morning, he set off, walking west on the Oregon Trail. His goal was to get to the Platte and South Platte rivers and eventually reach the mountains. Once he started walking, he never looked back.

Nathan trudged by—and tripped over—an endless sea of ruts, broken wheels, cracked yokes, and broken-down wagons with a half-century of names, dates, and curses etched into the discarded boards. The rusted iron and wooden remains revealed a weathering record of previous souls who had passed this way. Souls, similar to himself, searching for their futures. The trail was a composite of the empty footprints left by beaver trappers, immigrants on wagon trains, miners, ranchers, and soldiers discarded after years of war.

Everywhere Nathan went he saw roadside residue that looked well picked over by man and beast. These remnants of numerous failed journeys and the resulting graves constantly stared him in the face. He felt they were fellow travelers trying to reach out to him from the past and warn him of the challenges to come. Like soldiers lost in battle, Nathan felt deep sorrow for those who might not have made it, but he was not deterred. He carried on because it was all he knew to do to escape the past. Walking into the uncharted territories with the hope of seeing the mountains gave him a new goal in his life, something different that he hoped would ensure that the past four years would not haunt him forever. Unlike his settler ancestors, who had to pay for passage to the New World, he was already here. All he had to do was walk . . . and survive.

One day, in search of clean water, Nathan left the trail and discovered an abandoned homestead lying in the middle of a slightly northern sloping terrain. The soil was less baked than in other places he had passed, and a few volunteer vegetable plants had self-seeded and were still producing an unseen but meager harvest. These hardy plants offered him the first fresh food he had consumed in weeks, aside from the foraged weeds he had collected along the way. A tiny spring and a creek offered him adequate water, so he took his hat and scooped up the fresh water to ease his parched lips and throat. On one scoop he caught three minnows, which he chewed and swallowed after spitting out the tiny bones. For the first time he sensed that he was over his withdrawal period and felt a deep gratitude for the fresh water and the vegetable volunteers. There was nothing else he craved except what nature was offering him.

While bent over, picking beans and squash, a coarse braying came from a thicket a little way off. As he turned toward the sound, two black vultures took flight from the thicket. Nathan cautiously walked over to see what was producing the loud sounds and found a small, bony donkey stuck in the brambles, his worn leather halter caught on a fallen tree limb. "Hello, little man," he said softly. Look at the mess you got yourself into."

He squatted on the ground for a few moments, soothing the tired and frightened beast. Then he moved slowly into the thicket to unravel the halter from the limb. He succeeded after a short effort, and the skinny animal walked right into the stream and drank his fill. Then the donkey began grazing on the grass along the stream banks, not anxious to go anywhere. Nathan thought he must be parched and ravenous but also decided that the donkey appeared to be sure-footed even though he looked like a bag of bones.

As Nathan relaxed and watched the donkey eat, he was comforted by the calm presence of this other living creature, one that posed no physical threat to him. The donkey was another feral soul like himself, trying to live off the land. After weeks of lonely travel, avoiding others, he felt a deep desire for companionship. He continued talking, putting the donkey at ease, and then went over and found him easy to lead. The name scratched on the leather halter was "Buddy."

They both spent the night by the stream, with Nathan taking the opportunity to wash his clothes and his body. In the morning, he searched the grounds of the homestead, finding a blanket, two cotton sacks, and a rope. He filled the sacks with the vegetables, picked as many apples as he could find in the abandoned orchard, and tied half the weight onto the donkey's back and the other half on his own. Nathan wondered why the settlers had given up the farm, the donkey, and this way of life. Could it have been an Indian attack, disease, or did they just give up one day and head back East?

Man and donkey headed back to the main trail and then west, the warm morning sun on their backs. Nathan led Buddy with the rope and found himself talking with the donkey from time to time. There were many topics Nathan had locked up inside his heart that he now tried to articulate. Just talking released a great deal of buried angst. Even though they moved at a slower pace at first, Nathan was delighted with the company and pleased to be sharing the weight of his load.

After about a week, Nathan noticed that Buddy had put on some weight and was no longer just skin and bones. They were getting along fine, foraging on the run, but things got drier and drier as they went west. Fortunately, Buddy was able to nibble on the grasses they passed, and Nathan shot a few rabbits. Buddy didn't seem interested in the meat.

In Nebraska Territory, Nathan stopped at a saloon, a simple

clapboard affair, burned by the sun and etched by the wind and in need of repair. The saloon was just the first of a dozen buildings along the sides of a dusty, manure-dotted path. Looking around, he didn't see any people out on this hot afternoon. But the shade provided by the saloon was welcoming. He tied Buddy up to a rail at the watering trough on the shaded side of the saloon and cautiously went inside.

The old, weathered proprietor sitting behind the equally weathered bar did not move but eyed Nathan for a moment and then asked, "How can I help you, young feller?"

Nathan's eyes had to adjust to the darkness as he looked over at the barkeep. "What can I do to earn a good meal?"

The man took a look at the longing in Nathan's eyes. "Looks like you were in the war, son. Can you shoe a horse?"

"Sure can. I grew up with horses and served as a veterinarian and a surgeon in the war. I've shod and un-shod many a horse, alive and dead. Just show me the patient."

Once he finished shoeing three horses, Nathan came inside and sat down to his first real meal in weeks. Another older man sitting quietly in the corner got to talking with him. "I hope you don't mind me saying this, but you look a little road weary," the old man said.

Nathan nodded.

"My name's Hans Schmidt. I'm farming just over the ridge from here."

"I'm Nathan. I'm heading west. It's a lot longer trip than I figured."

Hans laughed. "That's why we stopped walking west and put down our roots here in this little valley. Why don't you come out to my place for a few weeks of quiet and recovery? You can't walk to California without a break. And, truth be told, I could use a little help and can give you a bunk and meals. I'm an honest man. The barkeep can vouch for me."

Nathan gave this some thought as he finished his meal. "I think I would like that."

The man smiled. "Let's go then so we can get home before dark."

They went outside to hook up Hans' two horses to his wagon. Buddy was tied to the back of the wagon and, without carrying a load, could keep up with the horses' pace. The wagon creaked, the horses snorted, and a dust cloud, kicked up by the wheels and the animals' hooves, followed them out of town and the whole way home to Hans' farm.

There were few landmarks in this vast grassland, mainly just cottonwood trees growing along the banks of dry arroyos and meandering creeks. The trip took about an hour, during which he learned that the man was of Swedish and German descent and his wife, French and Danish. When they crested the hill overlooking the farm, the man explained how he came by the land and how he and his son-in-law had built two sod homes and a sod storage shed. He lived in one of the homes with his wife, and the second was for his daughter and her husband, who was still away at war. When Nathan asked about the man's son-in-law, all he heard was, "He hasn't returned home yet."

"I suspect my folks are saying the same thing about me," Nathan replied.

Hans' wife, Bertha, and their daughter, Nellie, greeted them as they arrived at the farm. The two women were strikingly different. The plains had sapped much of the life out of Bertha. She was strong-looking but seldom spoke. She knew how to work but rarely shared a smile.

In contrast, Nellie, who looked to be a few years older than Nathan, was warm and quite engaging. She was tall and strong looking like her mother but had that rare gift of being able to listen, empathize, and share her own perspective in a conversation. She had inherited that gift from her father.

Looking around at the sparse buildings and expansive views, Nathan was surprised at how brown everything was compared to the greenery of home. He figured that Hans would have to grow different crops here than at Good Endeavour Farm and then water as much as he could. This farm would require a great deal more human labor than back home, and he noted that all three of his hosts seemed incredibly fit. Their once-pale complexions were tanned and freckled, their hands calloused, and their bodies strong. They owned a single team of horses to help plow the land and carry water. They kept a coop full of chickens out back. Everything else they ate grew from the ground.

Hans' family treated Nathan well, and he grew fond of them. They let him sleep in the storage shed, but he preferred to sleep under the stars on clear nights. The Schmidts were the first people he had spent any time talking with since the war, and he learned about the hardships they had endured to eke out a living from the land on this desolate plain. Homesteading here on the nearly treeless plains was a lot different than the challenges his ancestors had faced clearing the land of thousands of old trees.

Hans kept Nathan busy, and Nathan quickly grew to love the plain's grand views and big skies that were often filled with fast-moving, puffy clouds. But he struggled with the solitude, dryness, howling winds, and the dust storms.

One night, Nathan woke up screaming, looking for a place to hide from the Confederates who had overrun his encampment in his dreams. No one mentioned it the following day, but he told Nellie about his dreams a few days later. "I'm sorry for the night-time screams," he said. "I'm hoping this trip west will help me get past the carnage and fear from the war."

After two weeks with the Schmidts, Nathan told Nellie and her parents, "I want to thank you for your warmth and hospitality, but I have a deep need to keep moving."

"You're welcome back any time, son," Hans told him. "Always things to do where I need another pair of hands."

Nellie smiled at him and gave him a warm hug. "I hope you find what you're searching for. I also hope you'll stop by here on your way back east. Safe travels."

Nathan left the soddies with a renewed sense that there were still many fundamentally good people all around the country. Those two weeks with Hans' family were a solid start to rebuilding his faith in humankind.

After a couple more weeks of walking, with Buddy now carrying most of the load, Nathan woke one morning to a crystal-clear day and a dramatic view of what appeared to be a long, continuous wall of mountains to the west. The mountains were large, but it was hard for him to comprehend how big they were from this distance. Over the next few days, he was transfixed by the snow-covered peaks. Never in his life had he seen anything so spectacular, and he could not take his eyes off their white and green beauty against the dark blue skies.

The mountains grew taller and even more majestic with each day's travel. He'd had no idea about the natural beauty of this country before beginning this journey. The sketches and paintings he had seen in magazines back home did not come close to doing justice to the beauty of the land on the horizon. There was no way to describe the scale and beauty of the West in mere words. You had to experience it with your whole body.

Although he couldn't be sure if they would ever receive it, Nathan posted another letter to his parents in the next town he passed. His heart was opening up, and he wanted to give his parents hope that he was recovering from the war. He also wanted to share his impressions about the vastness of the land that he was experiencing on his journey.

September 15, 1865

Dear Mother and Father,

I am sorry I did not come home right after my release from the Army and that I've been remiss in writing to you. I've had to clear my mind and relearn who I am. I trust that you and the rest of the family are well. I'm doing better. I have just made it to the mountains of Colorado and am overjoyed by their majestic nature. I cannot express myself well in words right now, but there is a stirring in my soul, which has been dead for many months. I make you the promise that I will regain my strength, will keep in touch, and hope to be home by the time the snow flies at Good Endeavour.

Nathan, your loving son.

Nathan left the well-traveled Oregon Trail and followed the South Platte River right up to the base of and then into the mountains. The higher he and Buddy climbed, the more there was to see. The more he saw, the more he wanted to see. That desire kept driving him up into the mountains. The country to the east that he had been traversing for the past month seemed flat, brown, and worn down in comparison to the mountainous terrain. The rocks beneath his feet were rough, loose, and active, as if the mountains were lifting him up, up, up to touch the clouds while shedding the crumbling boulders into the depths of the valleys below. This land would be brutal to farm.

Early the following day, Nathan found a little glen with lots of grass and a gurgling creek and tethered Buddy with a good length of rope to a snag. Storing his rucksack and musket inside a dense grove of trees, he climbed and pulled himself up the sloping rock face until he found a ledge to rest on, thousands of feet above the plains. He drew in the clean, cold, mountain air with each breath and blew out what he imagined to be the stale, malarial air from deep within his lungs. He hoped he would never again have to revisit those malarial swamps throughout the South.

Some of the pain from those four years in the South flowed out of his body as well. Feeling energized, he shouted as loud as he could and listened to the echoes bouncing off the valley walls, repeating and then disappearing into the evergreen-blanketed valley. The shouts carried his damaged self away, far away from his life in the present. He found himself repeating the phrase, "The war is over. The war is over. I survived, but now it's over."

As he stood there listening to the echoes dying away, Nathan noted a silence surrounding him so deep that it reached into his soul. A silence so quiet that all he could hear was his heart beating, pumping blood through the veins in his ears. Yes, he was alive and he was here, now, on top of a mountain, in awe at the magnificence of nature and smiling at the beauty all around him.

Then the silence was cut by the distant cry of a single, solitary, golden eagle as if it were calling to Nathan to come out from his shell and not stay buried in the past. The eagle was offering him a doorway to the present so Nathan could come out and enjoy the moment in this magical place.

It became clear that he had been dwelling in the past and not thinking of the present or the future or all the wonders of the world. It was so simple. He had to start listening to the here and now and start living fully in this moment in time. A broad smile filled his face, a cloak of anxiety washed right off him, and he spun around on the ledge. Laughing for the first time in months, he proceeded to climb up to the mountain's crest.

As he peered over the edge upon reaching the summit, a strong gale buffeted his face. He looked out across the deep, spectacular valley before him and saw a large, boiling bank of dark clouds tumbling down from even taller mountains to the west. They appeared to be racing toward him. The avalanche of menacing clouds was dramatic to behold. He had never seen anything like it. But he quickly understood as the valley filled up with clouds that he had better take cover. Turning around, he started down the leeward side of the ridge, back to where he had come. Within a matter of minutes, the sun disappeared, and the storm buffeted the mountain peak and engulfed him with white-out conditions.

Fortunately, an overhanging outcrop offered him refuge just in time, and he pushed his body way back into the crevice, back deep into the warmer womb of the mountain. The snow came like surf, filling the cave, drowning him with white foam, and insulating him from the colder windchill he would have faced if he had remained out in the open. Wrapping his arms tightly around his chest and pulling his legs up into a tight fetal position, he wondered how many other people had taken refuge from a storm in this crack in the earth.

An hour later, the skies cleared, the temperatures warmed, and his bluish-white blanket of snow brightened to yellowish white from the sun's penetrating rays. Nathan dug his way out of the remaining snow and into a world transformed, changing from browns and yellows to white ridges and green valleys. The lakes were blue again, reflecting the sky, and everything was fresh and bright. Like a world reawakened, the sun warmed his flesh. He stretched his limbs and shouted with joy. In some strange way, he had a sense of being reborn.

Slowly and carefully, Nathan worked his way back down the now-slippery slope, anxious to get back to Buddy before darkness set in. He returned exhausted to the glen, where Buddy was still eating, just as the sun set. There had been no snow at this much lower elevation, so he crawled into the hidden little fortress where he had stored his musket and rucksack. The tree-lined nest was full of dry pine needles, a soft mat that would ease his tired muscles. Burrowing beneath the fragrant needles, he drifted off to a deep and dreamless sleep.

The next morning, Nathan awoke with Buddy lying by his side, keeping them both warm. It was the first time he had slept through the night since the war ended. No nightmares, no screams. He had shed an enormous load and deliberately chose to leave all the bad memories from the war in the mountains. He had awakened full of energy and even more connected than ever to the land and all the world around him.

Buddy and Nathan slowly descended from the mountains and made their way to a small-town Nathan had seen from the ridge. Walking into the town, he learned the residents called it Boulder, Colorado. He stopped at the blacksmith shop and the stables, where he got part-time work and stayed a few weeks until he knew for sure that he had healed something that had been broken in his heart. Nathan enjoyed working with his hands; it was comforting because it helped calm him and allowed him to be useful to someone else. But he wondered if he should stay here in this transient community where he knew no one. Starting over in a new place was not his goal. He had come west wrestling with the past, needing to clear his head of wartime atrocities, and he had done that. Now it was time to head home, back to Maryland, back to Good Endeavour and the future he had dreamed about all his life.

The land that Caleb and his sons had carved out of the wilderness was calling to Nathan. The land that Chenoa and Eli, Robert and Josie, and so many of his other ancestors had cared for was still there, just waiting for him to return and work the land. He had seen only a tiny part of the West and loved it, but now he felt the tug of home and felt well enough to return to family, friends, and the farm. Unlike many of the other people he had met on the trail, he was not a vagabond. He had roots, and those roots were important to him. There were things he wanted to do with his life, and he could only imagine doing them on Good Endeavour Farm.

With a solemn vow to return, and a majestic image of the mountains lodged in his brain, Nathan and Buddy turned their sights around and, early the next day, headed into the morning sun. They went back the way they had come, back along the South Platte to Nebraska, back to the saloon that was still good for a hot meal. But at that point, Nathan hesitated. He felt an inner pull to visit the Schmidts; they had been so good to him. But he decided to keep moving to get home to Maryland before the snows came.

"Please give Hans my best the next time you see him," Nathan told the barkeep.

"I know they'd love to have you stop in. Hans always needs an extra pair of hands."

"I'd love to see them all too. But I've got to get home and would hate to impose on their hospitality again."

"Suit yourself. By the way, did you know that Hans' family has been in mourning since about the time you left? They got word that Nellie's husband died in Texas in one of the last battles of the war."

Nathan felt a pang of sorrow for these good people. He wondered what was to become of Nellie. "What terrible news . . . I guess I should take the time to visit them after all and offer condolences to her and her parents."

Nellie and her folks were delighted to see Nathan walking over the ridge with Buddy. Hans and Nellie walked up the lane to meet him and took him back to their home for a meal. After dinner, they showed him the letter they had received from the US Army. Hans had guessed the truth because he knew his son-in-law would have come home as soon as he could to a wife as special as Nellie.

"Did you get some of the darkness of war cleared out of your head by going west?" Hans asked Nathan.

Nathan smiled. "Starting with my stay here with you, the trip helped turn my focus to the present and the future and what I hold important in my life. I'm looking forward to seeing my family again and seeing how things have changed on the farm."

After dinner, Nathan sat down on an outside bench, pondering his future while looking at the myriad of stars that filled the heavens from horizon to horizon.

After putting away the dishes, Nellie came out and sat down beside him. They were quiet for a while, just enjoying each other's presence. Guests were few and far between on the plains. Then Nellie spoke up. "My husband and I built this house together, and then he went away for over two years. I often wondered what he would be like when he returned from the fighting. I knew he would be a different person, and I was a little fearful that he might have changed a lot. But I never let my mind wander too far about what I would do if he never came back. I miss him and the life we had."

Nathan held her words for a few moments and then responded, "We don't know who we'll become when we're tested by tragedy. All we know is that we will change. Let's hope that we'll all change for the better." He started thinking about the people he missed. "I think it's good to miss someone. It means they touched you deeply. I hope you have fond memories of your husband that will stay with you throughout your life."

"I do relish the good times we had together," Nellie replied.

"I've been gone from our farm for four years—I was just a boy when I signed up. I know that I changed quite a bit during the war. And now in the last two months, I've changed again."

After a few more minutes of silence, Nellie whispered, "Aren't the stars beautiful?"

Nathan nodded. "The nights when I looked at the stars during the war, all I could think about were the things I would do if I survived. So many of the men around me didn't make it.

A lot of them died in my arms, as well as a number of civilians. Oddly, I feel I owe it to them to make the most of my life now."

"I think you will."

That night Nathan slept out under the stars, trying to make sense of his future, thinking of his family, and thinking of Nellie. The following day, Hans said he had a few projects that needed two men. Nathan was happy to help. The list grew each day.

After the first week, Nathan told Nellie, "You're the first woman I've been able to talk with about the important things in life. You helped me deal with my nightmares when I first came through here. I don't have them much anymore. I want to thank you for that."

Nellie smiled. "Our talks have helped me a lot this week too. I think I'm seeing things a little more clearly each day. There's a lot more living ahead for both of us."

"It helps to share transitions with someone you can trust. This has been the first time I've been able to talk about the war without being overwhelmed with negative thoughts. I'm sorry I went off and told you all about my childhood home too. That had to be boring for you."

Laughing, Nellie said, "I like listening to you reminisce about the past and hearing about your dreams for the future. To hear about how much Good Endeavour means to you tells me a great deal about you and your family. The stories help me understand your decision to go back East."

At the end of the second week, Nellie asked Nathan to help her bring several buckets of water up from the creek. On the bank Nathan stopped and took in the full range of the subtle colors of the land. It was not the mountains or even Good Endeavour Farm, but it had an aura all its own, especially at sunset. Looking at Nellie under the fading pink skies, he saw a beauty similar to the landscape—she looked like a princess of the plains. His heart stirring in his chest moved him to action.

Walking over to her, he took her hands in his. After listening to the meadowland birds for a few moments, he looked down into her eyes and said, "I'm ready to head home. It's time for me to get on with my life."

"I'll miss you," she said, looking up at him.

Searching for the right words, Nathan said, "Nellie, I know it's a lot to ask, but will you come with me? I have this feeling that we could build a good life together."

She smiled and squeezed his hands.

"Will you marry me and come live with me in Maryland?"

Nellie waited a minute, looking first down at the insects fluttering around the ripples in the creek. She turned over his calloused hands and then gazed directly at his sunburned face and wide-open eyes. "You are a good man, Nathan. I feel like I can trust you. I also think we would be good together." After a pause, she continued. "I have two concerns that I want to share with you before answering."

"Yes?"

"I haven't lived in an area with lots of people before. I've grown up enjoying the solitude of Nebraska, and I don't know how I will react to the East. It's a little scary, but I think I'll adjust. I also want you to know that although we tried, my husband and I didn't have any children. I don't know if that will be any different with you . . . I hope it is. I would love to have a large family one day."

Nathan lifted her hands and kissed them a bit awkwardly and then replied, "My mother likes her solitude too. She often retreats into the farm to be alone and watch the timberdoodles at dusk. We have a hundred acres and a river, so it's a great place to enjoy the quiet. I also hope that we'll have a family. But if that should not happen, there are always children around that we can help raise."

She looked at him and said very calmly, "Then, yes, I accept your offer."

Nathan pulled Nellie into his arms, looked into her eyes, and gently kissed her. Then they held each other as if they had found something that had been missing in their lives for far too long. They were a little hesitant holding one another, a bit self-conscious and new to each other's smells, tastes, and contours. But it felt so good to hold and be held by someone they thought they could laugh with, work next to, and, hopefully, raise a family with. It wasn't long before their bodies relaxed into each other's embrace, the warmth flooding their bodies, erasing some of the pain of the past few years. A real sense of hope, excitement, and the future started to percolate in their hearts.

Nathan smiled and, with a twinkle in his eyes, asked, "Do you think we can get married in the next two weeks? I'd like to head east before the snows come."

She laughed. "We're pretty informal out here. There's a community event this weekend in town. We can arrange for the preacher to marry us then. It might cost us a chicken or two."

Nathan beamed and then his face morphed into a more serious expression of concern. "How disappointed will your parents be if you move away?"

"I'm sure they'll miss me terribly. I bring a lot of joy to their lives. But Dad liked you the first time he met you, so that's good news. I'm sure that's why he brought you home. Mom will be happy for me too. She always says that all women need a man. Of course, they would love to have you stay here. But I understand. You have a lot more to return to back East."

Long after dark they finally headed back to the sod houses, with Nellie holding Nathan's hand and leading the way.

When Nathan asked Hans for Nellie's hand in marriage, the older man was so happy for his daughter that he cried. It was a bittersweet moment, for he was sorely disappointed that they would be heading off to Maryland. Nellie's mother was more stoic. She had been expecting that Nellie, now that she was widowed, would leave soon to find a new life someplace out West. They were happy they had gotten to know Nathan and they liked him. Nellie's mother embraced her daughter, wished her the best, and promised to write every month.

Their last week on the plains of Nebraska Territory went by in a dust-storm blur. Neighbors stopped by to wish Nellie the best, the traveling minister married them on the weekend in return for a hot dinner, and then it was time for Nathan to take his new bride home to Good Endeavour. He got caught up in the excitement of it all and in his growing love and appreciation for this woman he had married. But he also had a growing curiosity about how things had changed back home and how he and Nellie would fit into life on the farm in this new post-war world.

Chapter 27

CREATING A HOME

Nellie and Nathan left Buddy with the Schmidts and took a stagecoach east. The last leg to Baltimore was by train, passing through Harpers Ferry and Ellicott Mills along the B&O route laid out by Nathan's great-uncle Daniel. Having telegraphed ahead, they were greeted by Nathan's parents upon arrival at the Baltimore station.

His parents looked old; after all, it had been four stressful years since he had seen them. They had worried about him constantly during the war and then even more so when he didn't return right away, and they were greatly relieved that he had finally come home. So many sons and daughters had moved away or gone to war and never returned. They were reunited with a flush of tears—it was so good to see their son once again.

They welcomed Nellie warmly and then drove them home in the family's carriage. The long ride gave Nathan's mother plenty of time to ask Nellie all about her family and life on the plains. It gave Nathan a chance to catch up on how the family was doing on Good Endeavour. It felt so good to be sitting with his folks once again.

The first thing Nathan did when he got to the farm was to fall to his knees in the garden and grab large handfuls of topsoil. He closed his eyes and brought the soil close to his face so he could absorb the familiar smell, feel the moisture, and remember the fertility of the land. Letting the friable, organic-rich soil sift through his fingers and fall back to the ground, he knew that he was truly home. He had returned to the land where he had grown up, and he was reconnecting to the plants, trees, water, land, and the air on Good Endeavour.

Standing up, he brushed the soil off his hands and trousers and took in all the views as he walked over to the house. All through the war, he had known he would return, known that he would spend his life on Good Endeavour. What he hadn't known was that he would come back with a healthy, wholesome, and loving wife to start a new life together.

The entire family was excited, and all of them came up to the big house to welcome him, celebrate his return, and welcome Nellie into the family. One of the small cabins was available, so the newlyweds moved right in. Family members would stop by throughout that first week and drop off home furnishings.

Nellie was thrilled to have so much support, and she dedicated much of her time to meeting the family and fixing up the cabin, which wasn't much larger than her sod home on the plains. She listened, watched, and learned a great deal about the farm, the family, and the patterns of life on Good Endeavour. Living here was distinctly different than her life in the Nebraska Territory—more people, more water, and more trees. But after a few weeks, Nellie told Nathan that she felt loved and supported by his family. She was enjoying all the activities, and to her surprise she even liked the chaos of Sunday gatherings.

In addition to falling in love with Nathan and his family, Nellie told Nathan that she was falling in love with the tall trees, rich soils, and the frequent rains; the lushness was so different from the drylands where she had been raised. She would stand in the woods or down by the stream, letting her body absorb the moisture drop by drop. It would dampen her pores and fill her lungs with the refreshing cool air. The humidity was like a salve, a soothing ointment that softened her body and nourished her soul.

One evening when they were getting ready for bed, she told Nathan, "I feel the dust of the plains flushing out of me the longer I live here in the East . . . I love the moisture on my skin."

She quickly adapted to the wetter climate, and on hot days in the summer, she walked with Nathan down to the river, where they took off their clothes and floated with the current around the boulders. After a refreshing swim they often took a walk up the stream valley and through the woods. She relished these times when it was just the two of them, and she could show her affection to this man who was now her partner sharing a whole new life. Nellie had liked Nathan from their first meeting and had helped him through the bad times, and now she was starting to appreciate him for all his gifts. She especially loved the way he was learning to care for her. She liked that he always took time to listen and show his appreciation of who she was and who she was becoming.

Nathan's sisters embraced Nellie as one of the family, which put her occasional bouts of homesickness in perspective. This was the most family she'd ever had, the most people she'd ever known. But at times it was too much, and she had to get away from the activity in and around the main house. It was at those busy times that she would seek out her mother-in-law to go for a walk where she would either just enjoy the solitude of the farm or ask for advice.

Nellie did miss her parents and wrote every month to share the news from Good Endeavour. She never missed a month understanding that she might never see them again.

Dear Mother and Father,

How are you? I miss you both very much and wish we could be together again. It was a good decision to marry Nathan and move here. Nathan is a good man, and his family has welcomed me warmly. I am intrigued with the country here in the East. It is so green and moist. Nathan's sisters have helped me learn to tend the land, raise food in the garden, and identify the plants and animals in the forest—all so different than

*those found in Nebraska Territory. This family has taken excel-
lent care of the land for generations.*

*We live in one of four log cabins, each about the size of your
sod home. There is a bigger home here where Nathan's
parents live. Every Sunday, the family gets together to eat,
socialize, and plan out the work for the following week. They
work well together and have plenty of family stories to share.*

*The only challenge I've faced was a rough bout of malaria,
but I recovered and am pleased that I moved East with
Nathan. His sisters are taking good care of me.*

*Please write. I want to hear from you, and I will try to send
updates when I can find the time to write. I want you to know
that no matter what I say about my new home, I promise that
I will never forget the two of you and our home on the plains.*

Love, Nellie

Nathan's first priority upon returning home was to get a full-time, well-paying job off the farm. He had known too many farmers who had lost their land after a couple of bad harvests and did not want to rely solely on the farm's success for his and Nellie's livelihood.

His father agreed, especially since the extended family had been running the farm just fine. He offered suggestions to help Nathan find a new career. "Nathan, why don't you set up a veterinary shop? There's a need for a good vet around these parts."

Nathan said he wanted nothing to do with operating on man or beast—he had seen enough blood for a lifetime. His first thought was to apply at the ironworks; it was the only business he remembered close to the farm. But then one of his cousins piped up and asked if he had heard about the new cannery that had been constructed just down the road.

Nathan raised an eyebrow and looked at his cousin, wondering if he was serious. He had eaten canned beans in the army but had little knowledge of the process. All he knew was that it was convenient to open the tin-plated, wrought iron cans, and that canned food seemed to last forever.

Nathan was intrigued and asked his cousin many questions. Then, early the next day, he saddled up his father's horse and went over to look at the new canning operation. He met the man in charge, told him something of his background, and asked questions about the future of canning. The possibilities seemed limitless. Over the past couple of years, local farmers had converted their operations to raising acres and acres of tomatoes, beans, and fruit to be sold directly to the cannery.

The man in charge was impressed that Nathan had run a field hospital for four years, and he offered Nathan an assistant manager's job, which Nathan gladly took.

As it would turn out, Nathan was smart to accept the job at the cannery. Canning food became a big business in the late nineteenth century all around Baltimore and Maryland's Eastern Shore. It was an excellent opportunity for Nathan to be there at the beginning of a new industry. He settled down to a relatively stable life centered around his new job, the farm, and the family—just what he had dreamed about during the awful war years and on his trip west.

Life on the farm quickly absorbed Nathan and Nellie. Of course, Nathan had a full-time job, so his primary role was helping his father on the weekends to plan and market their products. Drawing on his wartime experience, he also provided limited medical care for the family and the animals. Nellie was much more involved in the day-to-day gardening and farming operations and Sunday cooking duties.

Just as it appeared that everyone's roles and responsibilities were getting squared away, tragedy struck. Nathan's parents insisted on going to an important town meeting on a snowy day. The horse and the horse-drawn sleigh slid on an icy bridge. The sleigh flipped over into the stream and his parents were swept downriver. A neighbor who had seen what happened came running up the lane shouting, "Nathan, there's been an accident. Your parents are washing down the river."

Nathan, along with several other men, ran down the lane with a rope. They found his parents hung up in an ice floe and log jam and pulled them to shore. They had stopped breathing. Their bodies were ice cold. No matter what he tried, it was too late. Both his parents were dead. Nathan went into shock lying there, holding them both and trying his best to warm them up. His brother-in-law brought a carriage to carry them to the family plot down by the river, where they were buried.

Even though everybody had experienced tragedies before, they were shocked and horrified that the two people who had been at the heart of Good Endeavour for decades were instantly lost at a relatively young age and to an accident that, sadly, could have been avoided.

Nathan took the loss especially hard, having missed out on being with his parents for the past four years because of the war. There were so many questions he wished he had asked them. He also knew that Nellie was desolated, having come to think of them as her substitute mother and father. It was a sad time for the family, and it took several months for the farm to adjust to their loss, new leadership, and to run smoothly again.

This was also the time when Nathan introduced Nellie to the ledge overlooking the Little Gunpowder Falls. She immediately understood its value to him and others who found it a place of contemplation and decision making. It was much like the spring back in Nebraska where Nathan had proposed to her.

Now that the big house was empty, everyone agreed that Nathan should move in there with Nellie. The two newlyweds were hesitant at first, but after several months of mourning, they moved their things to the big house, and Nathan took over the role of farm manager with help from his uncles. By default, Nellie took over hosting Sunday dinners, and Nathan ran the after-dinner meetings where farm and family decisions were made. The cooperative farming system first set up by Chenoa and Eli had kept the farm an effective operation even through bad times, and Nathan was determined to continue their policies.

The most significant impact of these changes fell on Nellie. Fortunately, she had been helping her mother-in-law in the log-cabin kitchen since she had arrived at the farm, so with the help of her sisters-in-law, she was able to make things work. With time, she eased into the role of hostess of Good Endeavour.

It wasn't long before she pulled Nathan aside and told him, "Nathan, now that I'm in charge of the kitchen, I sense a growing kinship with the women who have toiled here before me."

"You mean my mother?"

"Not just your mother. I find myself smiling whenever people talk of Molly, Chenoa, Josie, or other keepers of the kitchen. It's like we all become one. Every time I wipe down the counters, restock the cabinets, or polish the old walnut table, I start thinking of them. I'm also thinking more broadly about the range of important issues discussed around the table. Maybe I'm just growing up, but I think those women of the past are helping me, speaking to me, all the time."

Nathan just smiled. He was delighted that she had settled into life at Good Endeavour.

❧

Nellie and Nathan were no sooner lodged in the big house

than the family had another death. Nathan's cousin, Ruth, whose husband had died in the war, took sick and succumbed to smallpox. Their two children were left as orphans. Nathan's sisters had been passing the children back and forth while Ruth was sick but didn't have room for them on a permanent basis. It was a sad time.

Nellie had been thinking about the children as she had watched Ruth slowly slipping away. She went out to meet Nathan as soon as he got home on the day of Ruth's passing. She took his arm and walked him down to the ledge so they could be alone. He looked at her, intuitively knowing what Ruth's fate had been that day. Nellie nodded, her face reflecting a deep loss that conveyed the tragedy of it all. "Nathan, sit with me a moment. There's a lot to take in." She leaned against his shoulder, trying to give him a few moments to relax from work and absorb this new loss. "I know you're still mourning the death of your parents. I am too. I also know that Ruth was like a little sister to you. I am sorry for your losses — we'll continue to mourn their passing as long as you want."

She paused for a few moments before continuing. "But right now, I think we need to talk about the children. I'm concerned about them being in limbo for too long."

"I agree we need to address that question. What're you thinking?"

She looked at him, knowing he was as deeply concerned about the children as she was. She knew he felt it was his responsibility to come up with a solution and suggest it to the family. After all, he was now the manager of the farm and had always been close to Ruth and her husband. It made sense for him to step in and find the best resolution for them all.

Nellie waited for him to think about the options and then moved ahead with what she had been thinking. "I would like to take both of the children under our wing. We could adopt them.

It might be the only way for us to have a family, and I think it would be the least disruption of the children's lives. They have already come to know us. What do you think?"

Nathan had been thinking the same thing all week. He had a decent job and had always wanted children, but he was just getting used to being married. Learning to live with and loving Nellie was one thing. Having a wife and two children would be even more challenging. He hadn't thought the responsibilities of fatherhood would happen this soon. But he wanted to step up and do this for the children and especially for the children's now-deceased parents. Ruth and her husband had been his childhood friends, and they would love to know that Nathan and Nellie had taken their orphaned children into their home.

He thought about his childhood and all the children who had grown up on Good Endeavour. It was a great place to raise children, and right now, the big house was largely empty. "Nellie, I'm most concerned about you. Are you ready for this? It will take a lot of your time and attention. It's not as if you signed on to help out with the whole family."

"I know. But after wondering since I was first married if I would ever have children, yes, I'm ready. I've carried the sorrow of being childless for years now. This will be a good way to put that ache aside once and for all and become a mother."

He saw in her eyes the same desire, common sense, and resolve that her eyes had conveyed when he proposed to her. He knew then that she was committed to making their marriage work, and he knew she would make this instant family work as well. Sensing that she wanted to do this as much as he did, he stood up and said, "Well, it makes sense on so many levels. We've both had smallpox, we have room in the big house, and we have plenty of support from other family members." He reached down and took her hand with a big smile. "Let's go pick them up from my sister's house and take 'em to their new home with us."

They each carried a child up the hill, and by that evening, they were putting two scared little children to bed and trying to figure out how to become a family overnight. They stood side by side, arms around one another, and watched the children fall asleep. They had the family they had dreamed about and knew that aside from these few precious minutes at night, their quiet times together as a couple had come to an end.

Nellie took to caring for the children easily, and her love and attention must have filled some of the emptiness the children had from losing their parents, because they were lively and joyful children. Nellie was now anchored even more solidly in the community. She was fortunate that there was always some other experienced mother in one of the cabins to answer her questions, support her instincts, and confirm that everything the children did was indeed normal.

Over the next few years, Nathan and Nellie conceived three children of their own: twin girls and a boy. The two boys shared a room, as did the twin girls. The oldest slept in with Grandmother Sally.

The twins were the most significant challenge, with Nathan and Nellie taking turns at night pacing the hall with babes in their arms. The whole family learned to sleep while listening to creaking, pine floorboards, and crying, colicky babies. But the house was full of life and laughter, reminding Nathan of his own childhood days.

Nathan's solution to every problem with the children was to take them outside, day or night, summer or winter. They would quickly calm down as soon as they sensed the outdoor air. He knew he was not the first man in his family to quiet a child by taking a walk in the woods. Like his father before him, he would take them on walks around the farm, telling them everything he knew about the world around them. Later in their lives, he would take them on adventures to explore every corner of the farm and for long hikes up the river. He loved teaching them the songs and sounds of the owls, kingfishers, foxes, and deer. It was as if he were channeling the knowledge and stories passed down from Chenoa.

Now that every bedroom in the big house was full, Nellie immersed herself in raising her five children. Watching them grow up together was total chaos at times, often noisy, and equal parts exasperation and joy. Fortunately, the children were never at a loss for playmates. They could always find one in the main house or in the cabins down the lane. On rainy days the children roamed the bedrooms, attics, great rooms, kitchen, and cellar of the big house. They all had their favorite hiding places. In addition to each other, they often found bats hanging in the attics, black rat snakes in the cellar, and flying squirrels in the eaves.

Unless the weather was horrible, the children spent all their days doing chores or exploring the great outdoors. Until they turned six, each child was expected to be within sight of at least one of the houses. From age six to nine, they had the run of the farm, from the orchard to the cliffs and down to the river's edge. The older children were responsible for the younger ones, and of course, each adult on the farm kept an eye on them all. Any infractions or disagreements could be brought up in front of the whole family at Sunday-night councils. The fear of that made it easier to resolve issues among the children in a timelier fashion.

One year when Nellie's birthday was coming up, Nathan struggled to find something special to show her how much he appreciated all the things she did. After thinking long and hard about what to do, he decided to buy her a decorated ceramic chamber pot set in a polished oak stand. This would save her from going out to *Eli's Privy* in the middle of a cold night. He had seen one advertised in a woman's magazine she had bought and was sure she would like it.

When he gave it to her, she laughed. "You must have confused me for one of those fancy ladies from the city, not a dusty old lady from the plains." She took a good look at it and added, "I'm sure this will come in handy on cold and rainy nights."

Nellie's next challenge was to create a plan for educating their five children. One idea she particularly liked was to teach her children through acting out historical or literary plays. Along with parlor games and reading, performing plays for each other and for guests had become a popular way people entertained themselves during the end of the nineteenth and start of the twentieth centuries.

The best actors joined professional acting troupes and provided a range of performances at town halls across the country, including ones that produced rowdy vaudeville and burlesque shows. Nellie loved the more gentile melodramas put on by dramatic touring companies. She was inspired by the plays she had seen as a young girl and credited them as the reason she had developed a deep love of reading and learning. She was determined to pass her love of learning on to her children.

After the children were in their bedrooms one night, she sat Nathan down by the fire to discuss her ideas. "I've been thinking quite a bit about the best way to educate our children, something in addition to their chores or reading the Bible. Most of them know the basics of reading and writing, but they need to be inspired to learn a wider array of things. They will need as much education as they can get to meet the changes they'll face in the future."

Nathan agreed. "They also need more structure in their lives," he added.

"I want to inspire them to love learning by having them read, memorize, and perform plays—right here in our living room. Just think of the skills and discipline they would develop."

Nathan got up and started to stroll around, picturing the children putting on plays. "I could see it being a good way to teach them how to work together, take turns, and speak with confidence. They would learn about the importance of practice and discipline. I like the idea. But they need to learn arithmetic and science, too. They need to be prepared to take over the farm one day."

"I don't know how to incorporate those subjects yet, but I agree with you. Just living on a farm should offer plenty of opportunities to discuss and test scientific principles, and maybe you can share with them how we keep our books and manage the land. I think we can do this."

Nellie ordered copies of plays and invited the other children on the lane to join her classes. Nathan directed the students on how to design and build a stage at one end of one of the largest rooms in the addition. At first Nellie directed the children to memorize amusing poems, songs, and monologues and then to act out simple, one-act plays with one another. Acting came easy to some of them, while others struggled. They all learned by watching one another perform. Once the older ones got proficient and excited, the rest quickly followed suit.

Before long, Nellie was holding after-dinner events on the first Saturday of each month, and as the children improved, she opened the performances to family and neighbors and moved to weekly shows. She told attendees that the "cost of admission" was the donation or loan of books for the children to read, help with the wardrobes and sets, or offering to teach a subject or craft they knew well. The library started to grow, and most every child read the books and magazines that were collected.

The children also had to create and color broadside playbills and post them at the store on Philadelphia Road to alert the neighbors to the next event. One neighbor gave Nellie an old upright piano, which she and Nathan repaired. Nellie learned how to play and now accompanied each performer. The quality of the performances improved dramatically with a well-tuned piano to keep the tune moving along.

Nathan watched with pride and amazement at how quickly Nellie's stage-direction talents developed and was intrigued by how she kept the children engaged in all aspects of putting on a performance. She taught the children their numbers and geography by challenging them to figure out the costs of keeping a traveling troupe funded for a year.

As a sign of appreciation, and to provide her with more inspiration for her work, Nathan would take Nellie to town-hall performances when well-known, dramatic companies came through nearby towns.

"Nellie, guess who's performing at the Havre de Grace Opera House next week!"

"Is it somebody I should know?"

"Yes. Uncle Milton! I saw broadsides posted all around today. We've got to go."

"Let's take the two older children. They would get a lot out of it, even if he is a bit overdramatic."

"What? My uncle—overdramatic?"

Nellie laughed. "I wish he'd stop by and meet all the children. It would mean so much to them."

"I'll ask him."

The Nobles Dramatic Company came to the opera house and performed for six nights. Uncle Milton and his wife, Dolly, had quite the flair for acting and inspired the two older children by belting out the lines and the lyrics to the songs so everyone in the town hall could hear them. The supporting cast was not nearly as good, missing a few lines and mixing up the sets for one show. But, all in all, it made for a fun evening.

The following week, the two older children who had attended the show ran around the house and the yard, re-enacting the plays they had seen. All the children amazed Nellie at how quickly they memorized their lines that week, making her wonder if one day they might be seduced by the acting bug and run away to join a touring group of actors themselves.

Uncle Milton accepted Nathan's invitation to stop by Good Endeavour on the following Sunday, when no public per-formances were allowed by the local churches. He made his appearance at the farm dressed in stage attire, evidently to main-tain his theatrical presence. He insisted on listening to each child as they took to the temporary stage in the living room. Proud parents and their nervous, budding actors lined the walls, and at the end of the performances, he praised the performers and claimed, "We are all actors in search of a stage."

When it was time for Milton to leave, he turned to Nellie and said, "Keep encouraging the children, my dear. They'll remem-ber these plays forever. No matter where they end up in life, they'll use the skills they're developing here." He presented Nellie with copies of the dozen plays he had written and then left with a flourish as everyone came outside to wave goodbye as the carriage left. The children were in awe. Nathan understood. It was the closest that many of them would ever get to royalty.

As the children grew older, Nathan sensed there was a need for greater exposure to more subjects, especially the sciences and current events. He subscribed to *The National Geographic Magazine*, which all the children and most of the parents eagerly devoured. It contained a wide array of pictures and arti-cles about animals and people from all around the world and dramatically expanded the children's knowledge and sense of wonder.

Nellie agreed with the need to stay current. Like many women of that era, she had a growing interest in politics and social movements and wanted to pass that interest on to her children as well. To further immerse herself and her family in the culture and the issues of the times, she subscribed to *Harper's Bazar (later changed to Bazar)*, one of the first weekly magazines in America. It was a good choice, for this magazine was one of the first national magazines to present a range of ideas to its readers. Aside from fashion, it covered topics such as the Conservation movement, widespread political corruption, and the concentration of power and wealth during the Gilded Age. The magazine was just what Nellie had hoped for, both for herself and the children.

For the rest of her life, Nellie devoured every issue of *Harper's*, from the fancy front cover designs to the ads on the back cover. The magazine fed her mind with a great deal of fodder for discussion, debate, and enlightenment. The children engaged in debates on many of the topics, and Nellie was always tearing out stimulating articles to educate and inspire them, her husband, and her community as needed. Nellie became well known at home and in the community for saying, "Let's see what *Harper's* has to say about that."

It was an exciting time for Nellie and her friends because their lives coincided with the Progressive Era of ideas from 1896 through 1916. This social action movement, led by middle-class women like Nellie and her daughters, focused on cleaning up corrupt government, modernization, family, education, and women's suffrage. Nellie told Nathan that she might be able to contribute to these causes by writing letters to the editors of local and national papers. She began a campaign, writing in favor of women's suffrage, an effort she continued supporting over the next several decades.

Chapter 28

IMMIGRANT NATION

1900

N athan, now fifty-eight, was always looking to hire more good men and women to work at the cannery. Fortunately for him, a flood of immigrants from Europe descended on Baltimore around the turn of the century. In fact, the city had become the second-largest hub, after New York, for immigrants coming into the United States, with a million men, women, and children coming through the immigration center at Locust Point. But hiring good men was tricky. They often did not speak English, and many of them had deep-seated, centuries-old hatreds for immigrants from other European countries.

Many of these men and women had started their journey in Eastern Europe and then made their way to the port at Bremen, Germany, before sailing to the United States. Baltimore received an influx of Poles, Lithuanians, Bohemians, Ukrainians, Hungarians, and Russian Jews. Italian, Irish, and Greek immigrants arrived at Baltimore from different points of departure. Most of these often-penniless immigrants were competing with each other and with earlier European and Africans immigrants for jobs at the city's canneries, garment factories, steel mills, and shipyards. This mix of cultures created enormous challenges to the residents, businesses, and city governance. Nathan, like most other people, developed his own biases against immigrants from certain countries and religions based on his experiences with men from similar backgrounds. He had come to believe that immigrants from some countries were more hot-headed than others and could not be trusted.

On one hot Sunday, the usual mix of family members came to Good Endeavour for the noontime meal. Everyone had brought something to share. One man of German descent brought beer he had made to share with the others. German beer had replaced cider in many homes by this time.

Sundays were always a great chance to catch up with one another and get to know new family members, some of whom were first-generation immigrants. Nathan tried not to let his biases show and welcomed all guests of his children and their children.

After the meal, Suzie, Nathan and Nellie's granddaughter, said, "I'm hesitant to bring this up, but I don't know what to do. I would love to hear everyone's thoughts on the hatred I see displayed every day at the garment factory and what I can do about it."

"Go ahead, Suzie," Nellie told her. "Tell us what you're feeling."

Everyone stopped talking and listened to Suzie's attempt to describe her fears. "People I trust and admire are mistreated and are not allowed to advance just because they're Greek, Polish, Irish, or Jewish. There's a constant flow of snide comments and even physical abuse. I saw one woman sabotage another woman's work—a dress that was beautiful and painstakingly made and with perfect stitches."

"If you spoke up and defended your friend, are you worried you might get hurt or lose your job?" Nellie asked.

"Yes, or worse. I'm tense all the time, and it's not just about me. It's impacting the quality of everybody's work."

Several young men and women nodded in agreement and some described similar experiences.

Nellie spoke up after listening to everyone. "I'm glad you told us. I think it's awful."

"If it's affecting safety, production, and quality, you have to find a way to tell the managers," Nathan added. "If I were your boss, I would want to know so I could fix the problem. Hate can poison a workplace. I try to understand what drives my employees, and before I put a new man into a well-functioning team, I test him out to make sure it will work. I find it's often about personality and background."

"I agree," said Nellie. "It's hard to change someone's prejudices and fears, but each of us needs to be aware about what we say, how we treat others, and even what we laugh at— especially when the joke is at someone else's expense. We should never lose sight of someone's humanity."

"Some people try to succeed by climbing on the backs of others," Nathan said. "They don't understand the importance of collaboration. Our success at the plant comes from teamwork, not just competition. But hate is often inbred in people . . . it's hard to heal."

"Does anybody hate us?" asked Suzie.

"I've received hate mail due to some of the letters I've written," Nellie admitted. "Some people don't like my opinions and try to scare me into silence."

"Are you scared?"

"I was once. The first hateful letter was intimidating. But that was their goal—to shut me up. I decided I was not going to let them win by bullying me. I try to be more understanding in what I say, and ironically, that has made me more effective. People have come to know and appreciate that I try to understand the key points on both sides of an issue."

"When one of your ancestors, Eli, married Chenoa, a Native American, it caused quite a stir in Joppa Towne," Nathan said. "Just the idea of an Indian living nearby created fear and distrust."

"I've heard stories about her. I've always been proud that she was a member of the family," said Suzie. "How could anyone have hated her?"

Nathan sighed. "They never took the time to get to know her as a person. It's often hard to accept other people's perspectives and actions without knowing their backgrounds—we all grow up under different situations."

"Some of you descended from Chenoa and, as a result, have Indian blood," Nellie told everyone. "How does that make you feel?"

There were murmurs all around the room. A number of the people seemed surprised at this part of the family history. One of Nathan's nephews said, "I don't think that's something we should tell people. It's not that I don't like Indians, I just don't want anyone to know I have Indian blood—they might hold it against me."

"You can choose how you handle that knowledge," Nathan said. "As for me, I'm like Suzie. I take pride in it, and I think it makes me more sensitive to the struggle that all types of people face. I think that knowledge makes me a better manager."

There was an instant hush around the table when Nellie announced, "When I was in Nebraska, I shot an Indian. He was breaking into my sod storehouse, and I feared for my life. It turned out that his family was starving. I didn't know that. Fortunately, he lived. We learned that our government had forced his people off their land, and they could no longer feed their families. Now I have a greater respect for Indians, and yes, I'm proud to be part of this family with Indian blood."

Nathan redirected the conversation. "Getting back to Suzie's predicament, let's make an agreement that we will help new immigrants get adjusted here quickly so they can become hard-working citizens and good neighbors."

"But it's so hard, Grandpa," protested Suzie.

"Not as hard as being an immigrant parent, struggling to feed your family, learn English, blend into our culture, and learn the ropes of a new job. Now *that's* hard."

Like many managers, Nathan faced these issues every day. He struggled to understand the personalities, fears, and prejudices of the men and women he employed and tried to treat them fairly. However, it was nearly impossible to treat everyone equally because it was their different personalities and diverse talents that made them so valuable on a team.

A few weeks after the discussion with Suzie, there was a commotion on the cannery floor. Nathan jumped out of his chair and ran down the open stairs from his office, which overlooked the vegetable processing operations, to see what was happening. All he could see was chaos. Two men were fighting and everyone else was gathering around and watching while trying to stay out of the fray.

"What the hell's going on here?" he bellowed as he tried to assess who was in the fight and how to stop it.

Two men were at the core of the chaos. They were circling each other like two hissing, crouching bobcats and paid no attention when Nathan ordered them to stop. One was a huge man waving a two-foot steel crowbar in his right hand, while the other was a small, wiry man wielding a bloody butcher knife. They were spitting a cascade of venomous ethnic slurs at each another. The man with the crowbar was bleeding from a nasty cut on his left shoulder, but he never took his eyes off his enemy. Like a trained gladiator, he was waiting for a false move by his nemesis so he could attack.

"Back off, back off, let's cool down a minute," Nathan shouted in his deepest authoritative voice, his face and ears turning bright red. Even though he was in charge in theory, the two combatants didn't care. In fact, they didn't seem to notice him at all. Their eyes were locked on each other, looking for that advantage to rush in and kill the other man, intent on killing or being killed. Was the fight the result of something serious or was it only based on a minor infraction of some unwritten code?

At that moment the knife-wielding man charged, but this time the bleeding man was ready for him and cracked him on the side of his head with the iron bar. The petite man staggered for a moment, trying to maintain his balance, and then fell backward into the crowd of onlookers. They cradled him and then pushed him back up on his feet. He wobbled and then stumbled toward his opponent.

Nathan waved his arms, trying to keep them separated from one another. "Stop it. Do you both want to get killed?" When the combatants continued to ignore him, he shouted to the other men standing around watching the melee, "Help me. We've got to stop them."

The bigger man with the bar swung again and knocked the knife out of the stunned man's hand. That's when Nathan moved in. "Grab 'em!" he ordered.

Nathan and a man in a white apron charged in and wrestled the big man to the floor. They wrenched the bar from his hand while pinning both of his muscled arms to the slippery, blood-covered concrete floor. Two other men grabbed the man who had wielded the knife. He was wobbly from being hit in the head and now was cradling a broken hand. A small and agile young woman grabbed the bloody knife that had slid under the tomato-prepping table and took the crowbar from Nathan.

"What should we do with them, boss? It's going to take a while till they cool off," the white-aproned man asked.

"Lock 'em up in empty storage bins . . . just keep them far apart from each other. Someone needs to stay with each of them till they calm down. Where's Jane? Get her in here with her medical supplies and see what she can do. I want to see how bad the cut is." He then turned to his secretary and said, "Contact the sheriff to come pick up both of these men."

Nathan turned his culprit over to younger and stronger staff members, straightened his tie, and tried to mop up his white shirt, which was covered in a mix of blood and tomato stains.

"Now, who saw what happened?" he asked. "How did this escalate to a near-tragic level so quickly?"

The majority of the employees he interviewed suggested both men were at fault. Nathan knew they were two of the more aggressive employees in the firm, but he had tried to work with them because they were both quite skilled and hard working— just what he needed. It appeared that no one thing had started the fight; it had been brewing for days. Nathan fired them both but said they could come back when they had a year with another firm without any violence reports.

The sheriff and a deputy arrived and took charge of the two, telling Nathan they would be locked up for a week. After they had calmed down, he would release them back to their families where they would disappear into the morass of immigrants on the streets looking for work.

That night, when Nathan came home carrying his stained clothing, Nellie looked up from setting the dinner table where she had just set out a mug of hard cider and a steaming pot pie. "Oh god, Nathan, what happened?"

"We had a fight on the floor of the production facility today. Two hotheads. One got cut up pretty badly, and the other took a blow to the head with a crowbar."

"Was anyone else hurt? Were you in danger?"

"No, but we all were scared. The fighters were dangerously mad and exploding with hate. You should have seen the fire in their eyes. My hands are still shaking just thinking about what they might have done to each other."

"I'm surprised that the threat of losing their jobs—and maybe even their lives—didn't keep them in check," Nellie said. "Don't they have families to feed?"

"Yes, they do. That's the sad part. I'll send the families a case or two of canned food, but that won't last them long. But I can't worry about them anymore. I have to dedicate all my time to rebuilding the team. They were key workers and our production dropped badly today. We had to throw out bushels of tomatoes that didn't get canned, all because of them. We can't let production drop any further or we'll all be out of a job."

Chapter 29

Saving America

Nathan spent time walking in the fields at the end of each day. It proved to be a good way for him to relax and ponder the best solutions to challenges at work and on the farm. During this part of the day, he weeded, attended to blights, and constantly tried to predict the weather. Timing was everything on a farm, so the family always debated the optimal time to plant, harvest, and sell their crops.

Nathan encouraged the family to follow the best scientific methods for restoring the quality of the soil and selecting what to plant. He became an advocate of the work of George Washington Carver at Tuskegee University in Alabama, the most prominent black scientist of the time. Nathan enthusiastically read and diligently followed Carver's teachings about the importance of crop rotation. He shared these practices with his children and their classmates, figuring that everyone should know how to farm. He was often heard saying, "According to Carver," or asking himself, "What would Carver do?"

In addition to keeping an eye on Good Endeavour, Nathan watched with increasing concern how rapid population and industrial growth around Baltimore was eating up the valuable agricultural lands and hardwood forests.

Discouraged by the destruction he witnessed, he sat at the kitchen table and wrote a series of letters, lobbying the governor to preserve what remained of Maryland's forests. He was delighted when the governor finally hired the first state forester to acquire land for future state forests and parks along the

Gunpowder, Patapsco, Pocomoke, Savage, and other rivers, as well as the Appalachian Mountains in Western Maryland.

The country was beginning to respond to a new breed of conservationist—like Nathan—who saw the need to preserve forests, wetlands, meadows, rivers, and the Chesapeake Bay for food, animal habitats, and the health and enjoyment of future generations. The governor understood that these common resources were valuable and, therefore, set up a process to manage them for the benefit of all the people of the state.

But it wasn't just the loss of the forests that kept Nathan up at night. The Industrial Age had arrived. Along with all the benefits it provided consumers, it had a deleterious impact on the land, the streams, and the air that nobody was talking about. Even his cannery produced waste and used a lot of energy to sterilize its food, so consumers did not get sick. Contaminating the river was not as big a problem when he was the only local business on the river. But now dozens of businesses dumped their liquid and solid wastes into the streams, exhausted smoke and gases into the air, and buried trash in ever-larger trenches on the land.

"All the local streams like the Little Gunpowder Falls are getting clogged with waste," Nathan told his wife.

"I remember the last time we went for a swim," she replied. "The river stank. I decided I didn't want to go there to swim again. It's a real shame."

"That's because we now have slaughterhouses, tanning operations, mills, furnaces, power plants, canneries, and other manufacturing businesses dumping their wastes in it. And that's in addition to all the runoff from new homes, businesses, and barnyards."

Nathan knew these practices were an affront to nature and a clear health threat to people downstream and downwind. He lobbied the governor and business owners, urging them to set up agreements against dumping wastes in streams. But his efforts had little effect. He hoped he was at least raising consciousness and planting the seeds for future action. Behavior change often takes a long time to implement.

Nathan also became concerned about the loss of birds and animals in Joppa and across the state. Wolves, elk, mountain lions, bison, passenger pigeons, herons, and Carolina parakeets were overhunted for their meat, skins, and feathers and were now rare if not extinct in Maryland. He had a growing desire to fight for the preservation of their habitats as well as his own. He could often be heard saying, "We need to find a way to work with nature, not just destroy it."

Nathan told Nellie, "I need to find a way to save Maryland and the country from the gross excesses of humankind."

Nathan's love for America and his desire to protect it had grown ever since his trip west. The perspective he gained by riding on America's mighty rivers, walking under the expansive skies of the plains, and climbing to the top of the world in the Rockies had stayed with him ever since he had come home. He chose that rejuvenating trip, not the trauma of war, as the defining point of his life. It helped him define who he was and what issues were important to him. His family, his community, and living in balance with the land were his guideposts, and he tried to intertwine all those values into everything he did.

With time he grew even more concerned about how the West was being over-exploited. The battle for water, land, timber, food, and mineral resources became the most debated, contentious, and deadly civic battles of his era.

The destruction of the West had started with the desire for land by the growing number of people living in the East, a desire fueled by the continuous flood of European immigrants from that overcrowded continent. This resulted in a genocidal war against the native people who occupied those lands. Nathan read in horror and with a growing sense of doom as the government systematically contained and eradicated the Indians in order to steal their lands for farming and development of the mineral resources beneath them. The killings made him angry, as did the way people either ignored or justified and supported the government's actions. He often paced back and forth in the hallway or on the porch, mumbling to himself, wishing there was something he could do.

More and more often, his face would turn red with frustration, and he would grumble to himself. He finally went to Nellie, needing to talk through his anger. Nellie was eager to listen because she had become concerned about Nathan's sanity; she had never seen him so upset. She assumed he was struggling with the Civil War demons of his past and thought she might be losing him to some mental state beyond her control.

Sitting at the kitchen table, Nathan stared at the well-polished grain in the black walnut surface and asked Nellie, "Are we Americans so scared, so insecure, and so greedy that we can't find a way to share this vast country with the people who have lived here for thousands of years?"

Nellie, busy at the old stove, did not turn around but replied, "People have different experiences and perspectives. I remember growing up in Nebraska Territory with a great fear of Indians. It was dangerous for us on the frontier. We were always under the threat of attack."

"Perhaps because I have Chenoa's Indian blood in me, I'm more sensitive to this outrage than others," Nathan said. "But I'm angry that we're all complicit in these horrendous actions by not speaking out against our government's policies."

"You need to turn your anger into some sort of positive action, Nathan. Go take a walk down to the ledge and think about what you can do."

Nathan sighed and after a few moments got up, put his coffee mug on the counter, and headed down toward the Falls. He found his favorite rock, the highest one, sat down, and closed his eyes. Visiting the ledge was comforting. Sitting there looking down the steep slope to the Little Gunpowder reminded him of the time when he had been struggling about going to war on that very same spot. He always felt surrounded and supported by his ancestors whenever he came here to think through a decision.

Nathan sat there as if he were in a trance, watching the sun set, wondering what the future would be like if the United States didn't monitor and curtail the exploitation of the fragile lands all across the country. It would be a dismal future with no birds, no animals, and no trees. There were plenty of examples in the *National Geographic Magazine* of thriving cities of the past that had been destroyed by man and now lay buried just beneath the sands of time. There was no time to waste if he was going to save the West—*This day had to be another turning point in his life.*

He went to find Nellie. "Just like Josie's campaign for emancipation, and your campaign for women's rights, I'm going to start a campaign to inspire men and women to speak out on what we're doing to our lands."

"That's a tall order and a worthy goal. Let me know what I can do to help."

Nathan knew it was a tall order, but as he saw a path opening for him, his attitude began to improve. His cheeks lost their bright redness, and he even stopped pacing. He looked at Nellie's bent back as she methodically washed the dinner plates. She was a model of someone who could work hard all day long and still find time and energy at night to take action on a scale much larger than the farm.

"I can do this, Nellie. I will compile a few words, share a few ideas, and help expand people's views on living in balance with nature.

"It could take years of effort," Nellie warned him.

"I know. But if not me, then who will do this? Will there ever be a better opportunity to save America? Adding my voice will probably be the most valuable thing I can do with the rest of my life."

Shortly thereafter, Nathan retired from the cannery. He was no longer a young man, and he wanted to focus on the farm, the family, and his writing campaigns. He read widely, and whenever he was inspired, he would slip away up the narrow wooden staircase to the quiet spot in the attic of the cabin where Nellie wrote her letters. With no windows in the old attic, he would light his way with a candle and often spend hours composing letters to others.

Nathan sent letters to John Wesley Powell, Gifford Pinchot, and editors of key newspapers. "Saving America" became his rallying cry. He was supportive of programs to restore the West and the preservation of lands as parks. When his articles started appearing in *The Century Illustrated Monthly Magazine*, where John Muir published his seminal land advocacy work, he knew he might finally be making a difference.

Nathan was delighted when the government began hiring several hundred Buffalo Soldiers from the Civil War during the end of the nineteenth century to serve as park rangers at Yosemite, Sequoia, and General Grant National parks in California. It was a big step and a clear message about treating black men and women fairly. The Buffalo Soldiers' jobs were the same as white rangers, which included evicting timber thieves, putting out forest fires, and building roads and trails. He wrote a number of articles about them and the work they did.

Nathan was ecstatic when Teddy Roosevelt, an outdoors man

and conservationist, ran for President. Nathan tried to engage more people to support Teddy and to encourage better conservation across the country.

Once elected, Teddy Roosevelt began to preserve national lands, finally setting aside hundreds of millions of acres of land, expanding the role of the federal government to include owning and managing lands for use by everyone. Every time Roosevelt announced another step toward conservation, Nathan would call out, "Nellie, he's done it again. He's listening."

The creation of the national parks stopped the big syndicates from over-timbering and overgrazing the land, but Nathan was saddened to learn a few years later that it also displaced some of the homesteaders and Indians who had lived in those areas. The Buffalo Soldiers were ordered to fight Indians who did not want to leave their ancestral homes and hunting grounds. Nathan struggled with this outcome. He was happy the lands were saved but sickened that his action may have contributed to the removal and killing of more Indians.

Nathan was learning how difficult it was to create and enforce legislation that was fair and effective for all. He was also learning how morally complicated most decisions in life can be.

Chapter 30

The End of One Era
and Start of Another

D isaster struck Baltimore when a fire, started by a discarded
cigarette, destroyed much of the downtown in 1904. It was
the most significant fire in America since the Great Chicago Fire
of 1871.

Although fires were common in cities built with wood, Nellie
and Nathan were shocked at the extent of the devastation. *The
Baltimore Sun* said that 1,500 buildings had burned and another
1,000 had been damaged. Nathan and Nellie could see the
flames and smoke from the porch at Good Endeavour, and once
the smoke stopped, they ventured down to the city, wondering
what they could do to help. All sorts of charred debris filled the
streets and sidewalks. They started coughing and had to cover
their faces with handkerchiefs.

Upon seeing ash-covered men, women, and children rooting
through the smoky remnants of their homes, Nellie turned to
Nathan. "Our children have moved out and are raising their
own families. Let's open our home to those families who have
lost everything—we have the room."

Nathan nodded. "I'll go down to the relief station and offer
them three spare bedrooms."

Like Nathan and Nellie, the whole community came together
to help and to rebuild the city. People of all races and ethnicities worked shoulder to shoulder with one another. The mayor
announced that any healthy man could get a job cleaning up the
city. The goal was to push all the debris into the Inner Harbor

to clear the streets and lots so everyone could get to rebuilding as soon as possible. This decision to fill along the sides of the harbor created more land for building the new downtown.

Nathan and Nellie were amazed at how quickly the city grew out of the smoldering rubble. Over the next two years, the city came back stronger than ever and with many more modern conveniences and amenities than before.

Coincident with the rebuilding of Baltimore was the consolidation of many different energy utilities into The Consolidated Gas, Light, and Electric Power Company, which became the major power utility in Central Maryland. Their ability to generate and distribute cheap electricity, steam, and natural gas had a dramatic effect on residential, farm, and industrial life in Maryland in the early decades of the twentieth century. It changed everything. Easy access to cheap power resulted in much greater efficiency, many new inventions and appliances, lower labor costs, around-the-clock production, and more free time especially for women working in the home and on the farm.

The energy utility company hired Nellie and Nathan's grandson, Thomas, an electrical engineer, to head up their new business development department. It was a big challenge and a great opportunity for Thomas, and he couldn't wait to talk with his grandfather Nathan about the job.

The following Sunday, the always properly dressed and unflappable Thomas showed up in the latest Jos. A. Banks suit—quite a dapper sight for his Good Endeavour cousins who worked the land with their hands. They kidded him about his stylishness but were all good-natured about it. They were proud that he was on the management team of one of Baltimore's biggest companies, and as such, he was rarely seen without a tie, suit, and hat. He even went bass and trout fishing, quail hunting, and helped harvest raspberries and vegetables from the garden while wearing a suit. Years later, when they became fashionable, he would wear a seersucker suit, bow tie, and a straw hat in warm weather.

The family still set up the picnic tables under the shade of the spreading pecan tree. Upon his arrival, Thomas hugged his grandmother warmly, shook his grandfather's hand, and greeted all the rest of the family with a smile and a wave. Nathan then cornered him and asked all about the new job. "Sounds like you are off to a good start."

"Yes, the electrification of a major city is going to be a real challenge. But we have a great team."

"What will they have you doing?"

"We plan to connect every business and home in and around the city to our electrical grid, including, one day, both the cannery and Good Endeavour Farm. Just image the impact that will have. And not just on the wealthy. Everyone will have access to inexpensive power with a flick of a switch. All homes and businesses will have clean and safe lighting, heating, refrigeration, and a whole host of time-saving appliances. It will be a big boost for everyone. Cheap electricity will transform our civilization."

Nathan was excited for his grandson. This opportunity was similar to his own entry into the cannery business in the late 1860s and his great-grandfather Robert's entry into the iron ore business in the 1780s. "Keep us posted. Your grandmother and I have ridden every electric trolley in the city, and once you get electricity out here in the country, we want to try every new electrical appliance they make. We can't wait to get one of those newfangled ice machines. Could you imagine having an iced coffee, an iced tea, or a mint julep on a hot summer afternoon like today? Now that would be paradise."

_ᘒᘧ_

Thomas did not make it to the farm for too many Sunday dinners, but he kept in touch, and he did help build the utility company into a major corporation. He enlarged his staff and then decided he needed someone to run the public relations for the entire firm. Nathan advised Thomas to contact an old family friend, Ira, who had just retired after helping consolidate 400 smaller utilities into Public Service Electric and Gas in New Jersey.

"Ira, I need your help. I would like to hire the best public relations man you know."

Ira just laughed and said, "The best PR person I know is a woman."

"What? You know a woman running all the public relations for a major company?"

"Miss Nelson is the most talented and effective person I've seen in the business. If you're serious about bringing in the best, you need to talk with her."

This was a surprise for Thomas. Very few women had managerial level professional careers outside the home. Thomas, however, took Ira's advice and invited Miss Emma Nelson down on the train from New York to meet with him and see the company.

On the morning of the interview, Thomas was sitting behind his large cherry desk, wondering how awkward it might be to have a woman—no matter how professional—manage such an important department. How would his clients and his colleagues accept her presence in such a position?

He didn't have long to contemplate that question, as Miss Nelson flowed into the room, precisely on time, in a very professional but stylish floor-length dress and broad-brimmed hat. Thomas, being quite stylish himself, recognized New York City fashion when he saw it.

The receptionist had not known what to make of her, so Emma had simply greeted her warmly and then glided by her with a royal smile as if she owned the place. She had an air of relaxed self-confidence and warmth. Thomas smiled despite himself and stood up graciously, offering her a comfortable arm-chair. He had never seen anyone like her before. "Miss Nelson, good morning. How was your train ride down from New York?"

Emma took her hat off and set it down on a side table, revealing tightly curled blonde hair. She sat down on the chair, exhibiting excellent posture as if she were sitting for a photograph. Thomas noticed that she was quite buxom, and that without the hat, she was shorter than he had first thought.

Emma perused the room, noticing that everything was quite orderly. She noted Thomas was impeccably dressed in a dark, three-piece tailored suit. She also noticed he had a gold pocket watch and matching cuff links. She smiled at his shaved head that hid his red hair, but his rust-colored eyebrows gave him away.

Returning her attention to Thomas, she answered his question about her trip. "The engines get louder, the seats get softer, but the food never seems to change."

Thomas smiled and relaxed a bit more, appreciating that Emma had a sense of humor. She had succeeded in putting him at ease with her smile and her quip about trains. "I'll treat you to some proper cuisine at lunch. After all, we are on the shores of the Chesapeake Bay. We can dine on oysters, crabs, fish, or terrapin."

She nodded but did not reply.

"Now, tell me how you got into public relations? Ira speaks highly of you."

"I was raised by my aunts who ran the Andrews Dramatic Company in Toledo, Ohio. I spent ten years on the road performing with them, writing scripts, and helping the advance man advertise our shows. It was all about public relations, and Uncle Clarence was one of the best."

Thomas was quite intrigued with this part of her resume, knowing that he also had a connection in the acting arena. "Goodness, your troupe must have been quite good to have had a ten-year run."

"My aunts were good, and each of us worked hard. Every week a different town and, often, a new play."

"So you will probably be quite comfortable speaking with our potential clients . . . most of whom will be men."

"Why, yes. In fact, one of my aunts and I later became co-editors of the country's first woman-owned newspaper. That job was all about interviewing, writing, and marketing our paper to the public, local businesses, and to ad agency representatives—most of whom were men."

Thomas smiled at the response. "Tell me, Miss Nelson, do you still like to write?"

"I'll always be a writer. I think it is just something that's in my bones. I've had articles printed in newspapers, magazines, and in *The Smart Set*, H. L. Mencken's literary magazine. You might know of him since he wrote for *The Baltimore Sun*."

"Yes, I know Mencken," Thomas replied. "He's a very opinionated man and a very sharp editor. You've done well to get his approval."

Emma deftly changed directions back to the job interview. "Tell me about the goals you have for this department, the budget, and the challenges you currently face."

Thomas got up from his chair, walked around his desk, and invited Emma to join him by the large window overlooking the harbor. He pointed out the Patapsco River, the bay, and landmarks around the harbor such as Fort McHenry, Federal Hill, Little Italy, and Sparrows Point. He then identified, with noticeable pride, the locations of current clients and the firms that had not yet signed up for their service. "Our goal is to be the supplier of gas and electricity to them all."

Emma turned to him and said, "Sounds like a challenge worthy of my efforts. I look forward to learning more and meeting other members of the staff."

Emma impressed Thomas in more ways than one. It was pretty clear to him that she understood business, the need to work with the public, and the need to be profitable. She exuded a particular maturity and professionalism that put others at ease, and she could quickly boil down a subject to the key questions.

He also admired her as a woman. He understood Emma was one of those community-minded modern women who cared about social issues, much like his grandmother Nellie. Emma and Nellie would certainly get along well. By the end of the day, he decided that Emma would be just the right person to challenge him and the company to be their best. She joined the company a few months later.

The 1920s

Nathan died in 1920. Since his travails during the Civil War, he had accomplished a great deal, and when asked about his life, he never spoke of the war. He only talked about his successes on the farm, at the cannery, and in the conservation movement, crediting his accomplishments to his trip west and marrying Nellie.

Seeing his body and mind both failing, Nellie stoically accepted that it was time for him to go. She would miss him, but she could see his touch everywhere she looked around Good Endeavour Farm. They had done a lot together, not the least of which was to raise five children and help raise twenty grandchildren. When he passed, Nellie was there holding his hand and remembering what she had said all those years ago when he proposed. "You are a good man, Nathan, and yes, we were good together."

Nellie received letters from the White House, the governor, and conservationists around the country when they learned of Nathan's failing health. It was heartwarming to hear how they credited him with helping gain bipartisan support on bills that preserved rivers, lakes, seashores, and mountains for future generations. Shortly before his death, Nathan was lobbying for the Olmsted Plan to connect Druid Hill, Clifton, Wyman, and Patterson parks with Jones Falls, Herring Run, and Gwynn Falls in a continuous greenway around Baltimore. He hoped that this series of parks would be accessible by trolley so that all families could use them to escape the heat, smells, and diseases so common in the city in summertime.

"Many years ago," Nellie began as she looked around at the people attending his memorial service, "out on the windswept plains of the Nebraska Territory, where I met Nathan, he was a broken man. The Civil War had damaged him, and he was looking for a way back to health, a way back to everyday living. Visiting the West helped him regain purpose in his life. He dreamed of a country where we took care of each other and took care of the land—a place where we all had access to the beauty of nature and job opportunities. I loved Nathan for his passions.

"In addition to preserving and restoring the land, Nathan helped many Americans achieve their dreams. He took numerous steps to treat people fairly and give them a chance, both in his business and in our community. This is now our challenge. I hope each of you will remember the work Nathan did for conservation and equality and will carry on these campaigns in his memory."

A few years after Nathan died, Nellie set her pen aside because her eyesight was failing. She asked a grandson living on the farm to help her seal off the attic above the log cabin. That was a space that had been special—even sacred—to Nathan and Nellie for years. It was their place, an area that allowed them to express their views freely and to make a difference in the larger world. It was also where they kept copies of all their private letters and papers related to many causes and the family's history.

Nellie had grown more fearful during the Great War, and now she saw even more hate permeating political discourse, both domestically and abroad. A wave of intolerance, fascism, and greed was flowing over the country, and she had been receiving an increasing amount of hate mail attacking her mix of progressive and moderate views. She didn't know how far this wave of ugliness would go, so she closed off the room so that no one would find and use the letters against her family. She hoped that a family member would find them one day in the future and appreciate their value as part of the long struggle to preserve the country's natural resources and gain equality for all.

1925

When Nellie died, the service held at St. John's Church was packed. The stone walls, stained glass windows, wooden beams, and wood ceiling echoed the crowd's murmuring and the louder voices of the speakers. People came from all around Baltimore to pay their respects. She had empowered many men and women to educate themselves and speak out on social and economic issues.

Suzie, Nellie's oldest granddaughter, got up to speak first. "I've learned so much from my grandmother's example that I don't know where to begin. Above all else, she had a rich generosity of spirit that impacted all who knew her. She helped me understand that even though there are many sources of hatred in the world, there are things I can do to help reduce hate whenever I encounter it. She also taught me to take the time to understand and acknowledge other people's views. Thank you, Grandmother, for setting such a great example."

An older woman stood up next. "Nellie was an influential voice in the Suffragist Movement, a woman who did not march or speak at rallies in her later years but was one of our strongest voices in the press. Susan B. Anthony once said in a letter to Nellie that her words touched our lives deeply. I am so happy Nellie lived long enough to see the Nineteenth Amendment pass and that she got the chance to vote."

Chapter 31

THOMAS AND EMMA

E mma was so dynamic and comfortable to work with that Thomas spent more and more time with her and they often went out to lunch. One weekend, he suggested they take a day trip on the electric trolley system as an important way for Emma to get to know the city. She concurred, but it quickly became apparent to both of them that they enjoyed each other's company and a sense of adventure in addition to work.

Emma was fascinated by the trolleys and how they connected everything together. Several trolley lines took passengers right into the country where they could hunt and to resorts at Bay Shore, Gwynn Oak Park, and Electric Park. Thomas and Emma made sure they rode all the lines, and they often spent the afternoons and evenings swimming, fishing, dining, and dancing.

Emma learned that Thomas was an accomplished fly fisherman, and he learned that she was an elegant dancer. They also paddled canoes up the estuarine rivers of the Chesapeake and shot clay pigeons at trap and skeet ranges. In the evenings they dined in Greektown, Little Italy, South Baltimore's German district, and the Irish sector and shopped at Cross-Street and Lexington markets. Thomas dressed in a suit and tie for all of these outings, and Emma wore dresses, even when eating oysters or paddling a canoe.

One night, according to her diary, they were out for the evening and found themselves sitting on a rock ledge overlooking Ellicott City. This was a quaint and whimsical historic town on the western terminus of the Baltimore electric trolley system. As the sun set, a diamond ring magically appeared in Thomas's hand as he offered Emma his hand in marriage.

As a writer, Emma had been keeping a diary where she had diligently recorded their courtship to that point. The last entry in her diary that night was crossed out, leaving anyone reading it to question what she might have said in response to Thomas' proposal or what else might have occurred that she chose not to share.

They were married in New York, where she had family and friends. Emma stepped down from her job, and in short order they started a family. Thomas continued working for the power company for the next forty years.

After Nellie passed, Thomas and Emma and their four sons moved into the main house at Good Endeavour. It felt to everyone like a changing of the guard from one generation to another, from one century to another. After all, Nellie had lived there for fifty-nine years, from 1866 to Nellie's death in 1925.

Thomas updated the entire house to twentieth-century standards, installing indoor plumbing and the latest electrical appliances, including a walk-in freezer. Emma turned the living room into a salon for hosting Thomas's business associates, as well as writers, musicians, actors, and other celebrities. She acquired a gramophone and, over the years, purchased a collection of shellac and vinyl albums. Good Endeavour hosted live performances by students and faculty from the Peabody Institute and Johns Hopkins University, held seances, and Emma directed plays for many years for the Ladies Guild.

When the stock market crashed in 1929, it was a challenging time in America. Fortunately, Thomas' job kept them solvent, and they continued to live at Good Endeavour. The Great Depression was hard on many family members who lost their jobs and their homes. Relatives needing a place to stay sought refuge on the farm. Thomas and Emma welcomed anyone who asked to come stay in the house, in the cabins, or to pitch tents in the woods. Owning the farm helped them ensure that none of their family members went hungry. It was a viable farm, and with more hands to help, more food could be planted and harvested. Thomas expanded Molly's vegetable garden and converted more fields to raising livestock.

Fortunately, the fruit orchards, nut-bearing trees, and hedgerows full of berries, planted many years before by Captain Peter and William, had been well taken care of by successive generations. The produce grown on the farm helped feed the families living there during this time. Family members pumped groundwater from *Phillip's Well,* which helped improve productivity. During these challenging years, the family constructed hutches and raised thousands of chickens, rabbits, ducks, and turkeys to eat, barter, and sell.

Facing Dust Bowl and other disastrous agricultural conditions, President Franklin Delano Roosevelt directed General Douglas MacArthur to create a tree army to plant three billion trees on lands denuded by overgrazing, over-farming, and clearcut lumbering. Even though Thomas may not have liked the idea of big government, he was very supportive of these reforestation efforts, offering support and land from the power company whenever needed. Two of his unemployed nephews who lived in the cabins on the farm and who were close to Thomas and Emma's sons joined the Civilian Conservation Corps. One was assigned to the Patapsco State Park straddling Baltimore and Howard counties, and he shared his experience in a rare letter home to his parents. Thomas's brother showed him the letter.

April 1933

Dear Mother and Father,

I'm doing fine. There are 200 of us here at the Avalon camp near Lost Lake – just up the Patapsco River from Elkridge, Maryland, and downriver from Ellicott City. We have been building trails, planting trees, and constructing pavilions in two sections of the park called Orange Grove and Glen Artney. We're using rocks that we're quarrying from the hillsides that remind me of the black rock cliffs overlooking the Little Gunpowder. These buildings are solid and should last forever.

It's been hot, and the work is hard. We toil all day long and have to follow strict regulations just as if we were in the Army, but at least no one's shooting at us. Most of the fellas are honest and hardworking – I've found it fascinating to work alongside men from different backgrounds. I didn't know that I had biases about people from the city and other countries. I am ashamed about that. I've learned a great deal after working and living with these men. I've grown to respect most of them even when they don't agree with all my views.

I hope our work is making a meaningful impact and helping to revitalize the country. I also hear rumors that Germany is gearing up for another war. If they do, most of us here are ready to follow General MacArthur – to Europe if needed.

Let me know if you're not getting the $25 checks each month that Uncle Sam is supposed to be sending you. I hope it helps. The $5 I get to keep doesn't last long, but then again, there isn't much to spend it on here at camp.

Respectfully,
Your son, Amos

The 1940s

Thomas and Emma listened in horror to their large Majestic radio every night after dinner as the Second World War broke out in Europe. At first, Emma was dead set against sending troops to the war, but by the time Pearl Harbor happened, she and basically everyone she knew understood that troops in Europe, Africa, and the Pacific would be necessary to stop fascism from taking over the world. She was scared for the people already fighting abroad and for her family and wondered how they might end up supporting the war effort. Rumors were rampant about German U-boats off the coasts of America. No one was taking that lightly.

America responded to the fascist threat by starting the biggest manufacturing push that had ever taken place in order to arm its allies. All sorts of businesses geared up in Maryland and across the country. In addition to his work at the utility, Thomas had become the president of the National Electric Light Association and was deeply engaged in helping to standardize, update, and coordinate electric supply and delivery across the country to meet all the demands of the booming manufacturing sector. To help achieve the country's goals, he worked long hours and was proud to be part of a national effort with such global consequences. The National War Board also recruited him to help manage projects in Pittsburgh and Baltimore in support of the war. The danger was clear: everyone would have to sacrifice and work together to help defeat the Axis nations.

Men of most races in Baltimore were engaged in the war effort, as were many women who had never worked outside the home or off the farm. These men and women built hundreds of Victory ships, tanks, planes, jeeps, and weapons to support the Allies. By the time the Japanese attacked Pearl Harbor, America was already heavily invested in the war effort.

The land on many small farms, including Good Endeavour, lay largely fallow during the war. Thomas, of course, had no time to work the land, and many of the men and women who had farmed his land during the Depression had gone overseas to fight or had landed jobs in wartime manufacturing. In addition to the loss of farm labor during the war, less farm equipment was being built, and fewer replacement parts were available to keep older equipment working. The country was focused on supporting the war and had converted the tractor and farm-machinery plants to war-production plants.

Because of all the competing needs for manpower, it was a tough call whether to enlist in the armed services or not. Every time Thomas's four sons, their wives, and children came to share a meal, the war came up for discussion. The families would pool their ration card stamps and coins to get enough food for all of them for these dinners. Thomas would give the blessing for the food, family, America, the Allies, and the men who had already been deployed. Once everyone had been served, Emma would start the meal with a question about the war. She wanted to know what her sons were thinking about their roles in the conflict.

At different times each of her sons had discussed enlisting, but she thought they were all too old by the time the United States entered the fight. She did not believe that men in their thirties with wives and children at home should be sent off to the war, especially if they had war-critical jobs right here at home.

At one of the Sunday dinners, Thomas started the conversation. "We've made a tremendous contribution building the equipment our allies need to fight the fascists. I don't know if they'll need all our men as well."

Andrew, the third son, spoke up. "Father, they'll need everyone they can get on all fronts. It's not just about building more planes. Who's going to fly them?"

Thomas got up from the table, walked over to the fireplace, and emptied the ashes from the bowl of his briar-wood pipe by tapping it against the brass andirons. "It's more productive if you focus your engineering knowledge on delivering the best planes in the world rather than cracking up a single plane over Germany or Japan."

"Don't worry about me," Andrew replied. "I tried to sign up to be a flyboy, but they rejected me. They didn't want people with glasses to fly fighters, gliders, or even the Flying Fortresses."

Andrew was a good example of a man struggling with his patriotic duty. As a boy, he had been inspired to fly by the aviation career of Howard Hughes. When he grew up, he bought a Piper Club with a group of friends. As talk of war increased, he joined the Maryland Civil Air Patrol and practiced drills with them on weekends, thinking he would end up training others to fly or get to fly himself. The government did contact him to buy his plane for training purposes but did not want him as a pilot because of his poor eyesight. He was gravely disappointed; it had been a lifelong wish to participate in dogfights and become a flying ace.

Andrew also had an essential manufacturing job in Baltimore. He had started his career in 1936 as a chemical engineer for American Smelting and Refining Company's local copper smelter and refinery. ASARCO refined copper, an essential metal for generators, motors, and radio circuitry, as well as brass to reduce corrosion on jeeps, tanks, and planes. Andrew would end up spending the entire war trying to boost copper production, which had to increase fivefold to meet wartime needs. The Baltimore facility became the biggest copper plant in the country, and Andrew worked his way from chemist in the laboratory to being in charge of the smelting and refining operations.

When the war was over, many returning veterans found jobs as part of the post-war boom. They did not return to the small family farms where they grew up because they no longer needed a farm to achieve the American Dream. They bought homes in the suburbs, which meant they needed to buy cars, and they started raising families.

It was an exciting time. The country had proved that it could accomplish great things if everyone worked together. Immigrants from many nations and people of various colors had all fought in the war, and many had come to respect one another. It had taken the country almost a hundred years and two world wars to heal many of its differences and to recover from the devastation of the Civil War. America was now at the peak of its power and prestige, and the world was watching to see what it would do next.

PART SIX

Adjusting to Change

Andrew and Kate

Chapter 32

A MID-TWENTIETH-CENTURY FARM

1952

Once Thomas and Emma passed away, Good Endeavour Farm became available for sale. All four of their sons had moved away and three of them did not want to move back. But Andrew was different. He felt boxed in living in his suburban cottage and was looking forward to a new challenge. It was an exciting opportunity to him that he might be able to raise his family on the farm where he had grown up. His dreams were full of plans for Good Endeavor.

Although Andrew's hairline was rapidly receding, his body and mind were both in good shape. He was of medium build, and at thirty-seven, he was strong and quite energetic. Most of his free time was spent outdoors, especially hunting and fishing. The farm would be a great place to pursue his dreams of being outside and raising his two children in nature.

The engineering side of his mind made him scrutinize the numbers before he decided to move. He quickly understood it would be a challenge to turn a profit on such a small farm in the mid-twentieth century. Like many of his predecessors, he would have to keep his off-farm career at the copper works and hope to break even or make a small profit on the land.

Andrew imagined all sorts of grand plans for the land, plans he told himself he could implement in the evenings, on weekends, and during vacations. He also knew that his plans could only succeed with the full support of his wife, Kate. So Andrew set out to convince her that this was a fabulous opportunity for her and the children. It might not be easy to convince her, he knew; she might not see it the way he did. After all, she had grown up in a small town, liked their current suburban neighborhood, and loved having lots of friends nearby. Convincing Kate to move into a 16 room house on a hundred acres could be a formidable challenge.

Kate, an athletic brunette with shoulder-length, wavy hair, generally supported Andrew's dreams but was a bit more cautious. It had taken her a while to adjust to his last dream—marrying him and moving all the way from Western Massachusetts to central Maryland. She was still trying to get used to the humidity and heat that descends on Maryland in the summertime. Nobody had prepared her for July in Baltimore.

Over the past ten years, however, she had grown to love living in their bungalow just off York Road in Towson. Yes, it would be nice to have another room or two, but a whole farm was not on her radar. But time was short. They had to decide.

One evening a few days later, after their two kids were in bed, Kate joined Andrew in their modest living room to discuss the move. She brought in a plate of freshly baked hermit bars to share, the strong, gingery aroma quickly filling up every corner of the room. They were one of her New England specialties. They both smiled as they took their first bites.

Andrew was on his second cup of after-dinner coffee and started sharing his excitement with Kate. Normally, he was a man of few words except when he was excited about something. That's how Kate knew how important the farm was to him—he was never too tired to talk about it. And now the time had come. They needed to make the big decision about moving there or not.

"Andrew, that all sounds great, but I like it here. I like the community we've built. We'll have to drop out of the bridge clubs and the dance parties. With two little kids in tow, this would be an even bigger challenge than when I agreed to marry you."

"I hope you think *that* decision worked out well," Andrew said while reaching over to take a second hermit.

"Of course. I just don't want us to bite off more work and risk than you or I can handle."

Andrew had always placed Kate on a pedestal ever since he had met her at a Johns Hopkins spring dance. She meant a lot to him, so he always took the time to listen to what she had to say and what she wanted to do. But that did not mean they had an equal relationship. He made most of the big decisions because he was the breadwinner, and buying the farm would be a big decision. But he wanted and needed her full support.

He looked at her and said, "I know this is a big step for you. It's a big commitment. It's also a wonderful opportunity. Just picture the children growing up with nature all around. They'll have their own horses and can join a 4-H club. We'll all go down to the Little Gunpowder to fish and swim on hot days. We'll have dogs, cats, and pet lambs. We can't do any of that here in town."

"I love that image of the kids playing outside," Kate admitted, "but right now they're too small to enjoy it or even be safe. Edward's only two and Betsy just turned four. They won't be much help to you on the farm for quite a few more years. I'm worried about the trouble they could get into with all the large animals, buildings, and equipment. Can't we wait until they're older?"

Andrew drummed his fingers on the end table. He knew what he was getting into—he had grown up on Good Endeavour and knew it well. Kate, on the other hand, had never lived on a farm before. She would be taking a big gamble on this new way of life, and he needed to assuage her fears.

"You're right, they are young, but my brothers and I all thrived on the farm. You can see how excited our children are whenever we visit there. They love the animals, the barns, and the wide-open spaces. They'll learn what they can do and can't do pretty quickly. And we won't have to worry about them wandering out on York Road like we do here."

"I'm also concerned about how much of your time it will take. You'll be working two jobs—we'll never see you."

Andrew didn't want to say it, but he knew that working outside on the farm would not be work to him. It would help clear his head of all the challenges he faced at the plant. It would clear his lungs from the pollution he was exposed to in the bowels of the copper smelter. And of course, he secretly hoped to make the farm profitable one day so he could achieve his dream and become a full-time farmer.

Kate continued. "We also don't know anyone in Joppa. There's no walkable neighborhood—we'll have to drive everywhere. When I discuss this with our friends, they think we're vanishing back into the wilderness."

Andrew listened to her fears and acknowledged her concerns; they were real. At the same time he thought she was partly intrigued by the idea and was just making sure he had considered all the angles and the challenges. In the end he figured she would trust him on this decision.

"We'll also be safer if there's another war or pandemic," Andrew pointed out. "They won't bomb us out there in Joppa. We can grow our own food, drink our own spring water, and heat the house from our own woodlot.

"I'll make you this promise. First, we'll continue to come into the city to see our friends. Second, we'll build a bigger local community. We'll make Good Endeavour a vibrant place where friends and neighbors will want to come see us, enjoy the country, and to see the animals. They'll fall in love with the farm just like our children have. And there's plenty of room for your parents and the rest of your family to visit us. If we look at the big picture, you have to agree it's a wonderful opportunity. It's all manageable, and this may be our only chance to move there. Let's do it."

Kate did not answer. She held her tongue with only a slight grimace that revealed her concerns. She had done her best and now was out of ammunition, so she decided she would have to make this work for their family. "I just hope you know what you're getting us into," she said as she stood up. "I'm heading to bed."

Kate went to sleep that night full of fear and the excitement associated with setting off on a new adventure. She called her parents the next day. They thought Andrew must be crazy — people were *leaving* farms not moving *to* them.

Andrew stayed up for several more hours that night, sipping and finishing his third cup of coffee, eating the last hermit, and looking at the details on the plat of the farm. There was a great place that he circled on the plat where he would build a fishing pond.

When he finally went to bed and fell asleep, all his dreams for the farm kept swirling through his head. It also seemed to him that the farm had been calling for him to return ever since he had left it to study chemistry and engineering at John Hopkins University. Now that he was finally coming home, he thought he heard a voice, the same voice he had heard before, beckoning him to return. A big smile stretched across his face. He was on his way home.

One of the things Andrew loved about Kate was that once she had committed, she was fully on board. So on moving day she was ready. In fact, she was the first one to climb into their wood-paneled Willys station wagon. On their way, all the familiar street names called out to him, names not just reflecting his past but also the history of Joppa and the Maryland colony.

They headed east on Joppa Road and turned north onto Route 1 up to Saint John's Church in Kingsville, where he took a right onto Bradshaw Road and left onto Old Philadelphia Road. Andrew could almost imagine watching General Washington, wearing a blue uniform, a black tricorn hat, and riding a white horse, leading thousands of men south on their march to Yorktown.

The family crossed the Little Gunpowder Falls and took a left onto Bulls Lane. Andrew drove the car slowly along the yellow sand and gravel road. The kids climbed up front to sit on their parents' laps. They crossed Piney Run and waved to the Sargables working in their vegetable garden. Theirs was the closest house to Good Endeavour. These were the neighbors who had been feeding the animals for Thomas during his last years. The Willys station wagon continued up the lane to the main house looming large at the top of the hill. It was a festive time for them all.

Hoppy, the farm's resident black cocker spaniel, greeted the family with a wagging tail and a growl as they walked up to the front porch. It was his porch and his home that he was defending. He knew Andrew's family but was confused with the loss of his owners and all the moving of boxes and furniture. Andrew noticed that his son, Edward, got the message and gave Hoppy a wide berth. Hoppy would rule the back porch even after Andrew started breeding English Setters for hunting quail and grouse.

Andrew couldn't contain his excitement and swung Kate around as if they were dancing. She had to smile in spite of herself, glad that he was so thrilled about his decision.

They unloaded the Willys, adding the boxes to the ones already stacked in the kitchen by the moving company. Andrew then walked around the inside and outside of the house, making a list of work that needed doing. The kitchen required modern appliances again. Equipment that had been state of the art when first installed by Thomas in the thirties was now out of style and out of date. The house, fences, and barns all needed coats of paint, and the mile-long lane leading from the main road needed grading. He wondered if Kate would learn to drive the tractor and help maintain the lane. He thought maybe she would enjoy that and could fit it in between the children's naps. Then he thought better of that idea, or at least he needed to test the water and see if she had any interest in outside chores.

That was as far as he got with his list because, as he approached the barnyard, it came alive as the animals began mooing, bleating, and whinnying. The one-hundred-acre farm had come fully stocked with animals, so there was plenty to be done from the get-go. The livestock sounded hungry, so he headed over to feed them. It was time for him to re-immerse himself into life on the farm. He was now responsible for feeding all the animals twice a day, 365 days each year. The animals were not going to be shy in letting him know when they were hungry. Andrew smiled and got to work. It was good to be back.

Kate had her own epiphany as she watched Andrew disappear into the barn. She later told her closest friends that she felt a pang of jealousy in her heart at that moment, wondering how a farm could stir a sense of competition for time and the attentions of the man she loved.

A shriek of delight mixed with fear brought her attention back to the children. They had corralled a six-foot black rat snake in the front yard. She distracted the children from the snake and ushered them inside the house. The snake disappeared into the hollow trunk of the ancient Royal Paulownia tree that stood prominently off to one side of the house. For just a moment Kate wondered how many snakes lived in the hollow tree, in the basement, and throughout the house.

After Kate focused the children's attention on opening boxes in their rooms, she took a moment to look around the inside of the house. The eighteenth-century addition felt cavernous with its nine-foot ceilings. She walked around, getting a renewed sense for its two staircases, two hallways, six porches, library, and large, wavy-glass windows. The white plaster walls and wooden-framed windows were bare except for picture hangers and empty curtain rods. Everything needed painting.

She was drawn back into the kitchen and sat down at the old walnut table, remembering family stories. For centuries this one room and table had been the hub for the house, the family, and the farm. She was comforted sitting there and picturing her mother-in-law in command of the stove. Connecting with all the family stories made her feel like this was where she now belonged.

Kate quickly snapped out of that trance and looked around. Mountains of cardboard boxes, sitting on the well-worn, pine-plank floors, surrounded her like a fort and waited for her attention. It was time for her to start opening and sorting their possessions. This was her job: creating a home, organizing a kitchen, and building a foundation where her children could thrive. Even on that very first day, it was quite clear that the inside of the house was to be her domain, and the outside would be Andrew's. It just made sense. There was plenty of work that needed their attention in both arenas.

On that first morning, Kate's attention focused on finding the boxes with food supplies to make lunch, Lincoln Logs, toy horses, and toy trucks to entertain the kids and, before bedtime, finding the boxes that contained the sheets and towels. She mixed herself a cold-coffee milk, her favorite drink, to whet her whistle and to help her feel more at home here at Good Endeavour. Then she got busy.

Over the next few months and years, Andrew spent all his free time caring for the farm. He knew the land was tired; it was considered to be a spent-dirt farm, full of clay subsoils and weedy flora. This was no surprise. He knew the land had been plowed and disked for 250 years. By now most of the rich topsoil had been washed down Piney Run and into the Little Gunpowder. Like many mid-twentieth-century farms, it was more a window into the agricultural past than a productive, profitable business.

But Andrew had plans to change all that. Like his ancestor Nathan, he wanted to become a good steward of the farm, rebuild the topsoil, and make the farm a local source of food. At some point he planned to make it a place for the community to visit as well. He wanted to make it productive once again and defend it from the negative impacts of growth that he could see happening all around him.

To rebuild the farm's productivity, he needed a plan, so he committed with the county Extension Agent to following FDR's Soil Conservation Service advice every step of the way. Each year, he religiously rotated crops, spread nutrients, and created rain-infiltration berms on steep slopes. He even planted millet and buckwheat around the edges of the fields to encourage quail to return. As a dedicated steward of the land, he would give it his best shot.

Within a matter of weeks after moving onto the farm, Andrew and Kate faced their first big farming decision: what to do with 1,000 turkeys? Andrew remembered feeding the birds as a child but did not remember how they were processed and marketed. All he knew was that whenever he or one of his hunting dogs came close to the pens, the large white birds erupted in a wave of garbled gobbling with their high-pitched voices.

"It sounds like a thousand-member community choir warming up—with no one directing and no one on key," commented Kate.

The birds that came with the farm were now almost fully grown and slated for market in four weeks. They lived in the same raised turkey pens that had been built during the Depression to keep the extended family fed. Now they had become the farm's main cash crop. But how does anyone butcher, dress, pluck, and deliver a thousand freshly slaughtered birds just in time for Thanksgiving and Christmas dinner tables? Andrew had to decide whether to sell live birds wholesale— which was easy but barely covered their expenses—or skip the middleman and kill and dress all the birds themselves and then sell them directly to their friends and neighbors.

That evening after they put the children to bed and were sitting down around the kitchen table, Andrew told Kate his plan of selling the dressed birds directly. She raised an eyebrow and looked at him. It sounded like an impossible task to this young mother from the quaint little town of East Longmeadow, Massachusetts.

"Andrew, we have a thousand birds. Who's going to clean them all? It will take weeks. Who's going to buy them? We don't have that many friends. I can't even envision the effort it will take to butcher, sell, and deliver all those birds."

"I'll talk with the neighbors, see what they've done in the past," Andrew assured her.

Kate clammed up, got up from the table, and went to wash the dishes. All she could think of was wrestling a single turkey into the oven on Thanksgiving Day—it never fit. With no previous experience with dressing turkeys, she had no way to comprehend the challenge. It all sounded crazy to her. She had envisioned getting to know the neighbors by attending teas and playing bridge, not standing around in the shed butchering turkeys.

To learn about processing the turkeys, Andrew walked down the lane to talk to Margaret and Vernon the following morning. The Sargables lived in the first cabin out the lane, were the oldest residents on the farm, and were experts on processing all kinds of domestic and wild game . . . and roadkill. He remembered Margaret and Vernon to be a little gruff and getting on in years, but they had always been trustworthy neighbors.

He found the old couple harvesting squash in their extensive garden. Margaret did the talking for both of them. "We'll bring a team up there starting the Friday before Thanksgiving and then again five days before Christmas. We'll clean and dress your birds for you at a flat rate per bird, paid daily in cash."

"Will you help sell and distribute the birds as well?"

"Nope, that's your job."

The color must have gone out of his face because Margaret quickly added, "You should put an ad in the *Aegis* and *Jeffersonian* newspapers a week or two ahead of time. That's how they've done it in the past—it seems to work out okay. People know about our turkeys."

This discussion gave Andrew the confidence he needed. This had been an ongoing business for the past two decades. It couldn't be that hard.

Kate was still nervous about the whole thing. "Who's going to deliver these birds? You work all day."

"People living close by will pick them up. I bet I can get a bunch of orders from the Engineering Club down in Mount Vernon, so I'll deliver the birds there. We'll also hire a teenager to help deliver them to our friends in Towson. If this works, it will pay our mortgage for the year. That would be nice."

After more discussions around the table, Kate finally agreed to sell retail this year and then re-evaluate whether they would continue after that. Kate was a worrier, but she was also a doer like Andrew. She jumped right into action, placing the ads, sending printed postcards to all their friends, and putting the word out to their old church in Baltimore and their new church in Kingsville. What better way to let their friends know where they were living now and let the Joppa neighborhood know that she and Thomas were the new farmers at Good Endeavour.

Kate was right to be wary—much of the work fell to her. Even before the Sargables had cleaned the first bird, she was on their party-line phone, answering questions and taking orders while trying to keep the files organized and an eye on the kids.

On the Friday before Thanksgiving, the chaos began. Margaret and Vernon and six other neighbors showed up at 8:00 a.m. in ragged, blood-stained aprons and with a collection of sharp knives. They went right to work boiling water on a coal-fired stove in the barn and organizing an assembly line. It was a continuous process from dawn to dusk with a million downy pinfeathers floating like mist through the air. Hot, wet feathers accumulated like strata on the ground. Andrew, who had taken the day off from work, helped catch the live birds and orchestrated the delivery of fully dressed birds to families in town. Kate sold birds to the long line of purchasers coming up the driveway, handing the dressed and bagged birds through front-seat windows so no one needed to get out of their cars.

The crew walked down the lane that night, exhausted and covered with feathers and blood, but they were all there early the next morning, stoking the fire and sharpening their knives. The team met their goals for Thanksgiving and came back for Christmas as promised. They were glad to have the work and extra cash for the holidays. Andrew and Kate got to know these neighbors well and gave them each a turkey. They also met a blur of new neighbors who came to the farm to buy turkeys from 9 a.m. to 9 p.m. It was a busy week of twelve-hour workdays.

Each of the neighbors had something to say when they came to buy their birds.

"Andrew, you're all grown up. I've been buying turkeys from Good Endeavour for years and remember you when you were just a little sprout."

"My grandfather loved your birds. Kept the family alive during the Depression."

"Can I order my Christmas turkey now?"

"Hope you will keep up the tradition." In just six weeks, Andrew and Kate became the new faces of the farm. They had jumped into a farming life that had been there for decades, centuries even, and they were now a part of a much bigger community. But after all the focus on turkeys, Kate decided that no matter how good a turkey might taste, she was going to bake a ham for Christmas dinner.

As Andrew and Kate's son, Edward, grew up during the 1950s, he considered the large, two-story grain shed, the hay and livestock barn, and every other building on the farm to be his domain, especially after he and his mother came to a truce about his freedom. Now, at seven, he could go anywhere around the buildings as long as he always responded to the bell, when she rang it. The agreement also stipulated that he would get "all his chores done every day and would show up for meals on time." That part was easy, he never missed a meal.

The large, faded-green barns and smaller sheds on the farm served as the stage for the imaginary stories he acted out after school and on weekends. Many of these were based on characters from the comics and television such as Tarzan, Zorro, Spiderman, Popeye, and Westerns. He also added pirates, when he started hearing stories about them from his mother.

But these buildings were also central to operations on the farm. Each fall after the family held its annual corn-picking/ pig-roasting event, they would shovel the corn into one of the large, wire-mesh, mice-proof grain cribs. Then when the oats and barley were ripe the following spring, a neighboring farmer with a giant combine harvester came to harvest and bag the grains. It was an exciting day as Edward helped mix the grains with molasses, minerals, and last fall's corn to produce a nutritious feed for the animals.

Mixing the grains was a noisy and dusty production that yielded dozens of fifty-pound burlap feedbags full of a richly aromatic grain mixture. He and his father would then tie the bags tightly with baling twine and drag them back into the other mouse-proof grain crib. Edward thought the feed smelled almost good enough to eat. As he got older, he developed a sweet spot for molasses-flavored, homemade oat and pecan granola, which looked, smelled, and tasted much like what he had fed the animals over the years.

The second floor of the grain shed looked like a museum of antique farm equipment. It was a great place for Edward and his friends and cousins to explore. It was filled with retired, dust-covered farm equipment once needed to run the farm with horsepower. Brown and black leather saddles, reins, harnesses, single- and double-tree yokes, and bridles hung from the beams and the walls.

Edward and his sister, Betsy, made good use of the horse-drawn sled for two and the black leather doctor's carriage that sported canvas sides and roof. Betsy harnessed the steadiest ponies and trained them to pull wagons, carriages, and floats for special events like Fourth of July parades in Kingsville and in the Joppa-Magnolia community.

The large hay and livestock barn lay just west of the grain and equipment shed. It had a walk-out basement at the south end and pens and stalls for sheep, cows, pigs, and horses. When Betsy and Edward were old enough, they took over the chores and diligently fed the animals—rain, snow, or shine—before and after school.

The ground at the north end of the livestock barn had been built up to create a "banked barn" where horse-drawn wagons and, later, flatbed trucks could drive up and into the loft to unload bales of hay. The floor of this cavernous hayloft measured fifty feet by fifty feet. It was thirty feet high and was outfitted with thick, woven ropes, a pulley system, and rusty iron claws for grabbing and moving hay bales. The system could swing bales of hay to all corners of the barn using a rusty metal track mounted just below the roof. When not being used for hauling hay, Edward and his friends would swing from the rafters while shouting Tarzan-like calls.

Each summer, Edward watched as this monstrous cave above the livestock barn was slowly and laboriously filled by the family with 2,000 bales of cured hay from three cuttings from the fields. Then he and his sister would empty the loft, bale by bale, morning and evening, over the winter as they fed their hungry animal friends a sweet, musty memory of summer.

One weekday evening in June, with the skies dripping with humidity, Edward heard his father speeding up the gravel lane in his '57 blue and white Chevy sedan. Thinking there must be some emergency, he headed over to meet his dad. The dogs came too, running in circles and excited by the commotion. The car door creaked open, his father jumped out and slammed the door shut, and shouted to Kate, "Rain's coming. Hold off on dinner. We'll need you driving the flatbed."

Andrew hurried into the house to change out of his suit. Kate turned off the stove and the timer and changed clothes as well. They all had serious looks on their faces, knowing they needed to get the hay into the barn before the rains came or they would lose part of the spring crop and have to buy hay from others the following winter. If the bales got drenched in the fields, they would mildew. If they put them away too damp, they could smolder and might burn down the barn. This wasn't the first barn built on this spot. Farming was tricky.

Edward pulled on a long-sleeve shirt, tough dungarees, and canvas gloves so he wouldn't get scratched from the brambles in the hay. He looked around for his sister. "Where's Betsy?" he called to his mother.

"Ring the bell. She's probably off riding, but she'll hear the bell." The old cast iron bell sat on a twelve-foot repurposed telephone pole. The bell often hosted hornets, which streamed out after Edward whenever he pulled on the rope. He rang it five times: their *all-hands-on-deck* alarm. Then he dropped the rope and sprinted away to avoid getting stung.

Andrew yanked open the rusty front door of the seldom-used '37 Chevy flatbed truck and chased away a bright orange corn snake and several large spiders and wasps who were living there. Not even attempting to hand-crank the old engine, Andrew released the handbrake, put it in neutral, and then started to push the truck, one hand on the steering wheel and both feet on the ground. Edward ran over to help. They pushed as hard as they could, rocking the tires back and forth in their dried clay ruts in an attempt to get the ancient vehicle moving down the lane.

Finally, the bald tires jumped out of their ruts, and the whole antique truck began to creak and lazily roll down the gravel lane as if it were an old bull just waking up from a long nap. Andrew jumped up on the running board, sat down on the cracked leather seat, shifted the truck into gear, and popped the clutch. The truck lurched but the engine did not catch. He tried again. The rusty old engine fired and came alive on his third try at jump-starting it. Smoke billowed from the rusted exhaust pipe. Andrew revved the engine several times and then braked to a stop. Every time Edward witnessed this reawakening of the old truck, he thought it looked like a celebration or an ancient rite of passage. One day he would get the chance to start it.

Backing up the hill, Andrew stopped, and Edward filled the truck's gas tank from the pump by the barn. Kate slid in next to Andrew, and when Edward had finished filling the tank, he jumped on back while glancing to the west where the skies had turned dark purple and green. Thunder boomed in the distance. None of them doubted they were going to get soaked—it was just a question of how much hay could they save.

As they approached the newly mowed field, Edward noticed how the rolling hills were dotted with yellowish-tan, rectangular hay bales. Edward hoped the hay was well cured, dry enough not to weigh too much—more like forty pounds each rather than sixty. It looked a little too green to him. Andrew opened the truck's squeaky door with a firm shove of his left shoulder and slid out. Kate shimmied over into the driver's seat and drove slowly, in first or second gear, between the rows of bales. Edward and his dad walked along on either side of the truck, picking up and stacking bales onto the flatbed without the truck stopping.

After three layers of hay bales had been stacked, Betsy showed up in her yellow jodhpurs and black riding boots and climbed up over the hood to her position on top of the bales. She helped pull up and stack the bales tightly so they wouldn't fall off.

Once they stacked the hay five bales high, they headed back to the barn. Betsy and Edward rode on top to hold the bales firmly in place and to cool off with the breeze in their hair and on their sweaty faces. Edward felt like he was on top of the world as he surveyed the fields. Everything he could see was part of Good Endeavour.

They were almost knocked from their perches when the truck drove under the broken branches hanging from the large mulberry tree. The family's black-and-white English setters escorted the truck back and forth from the field to the barn, doing their part helping to harvest the hay.

After the family completed multiple trips to the hayfield and stacked over 300 bales of hay, they were finished and ready for a drink. Andrew parked the truck back in its resting spot next to the barn and walked toward the house. Edward noticed the sweat dripping from his father's sizeable angular nose and the hayseed looking like freckles on his bald head and the back of his sweat-soaked shirt. All Edward could think about was a nice refreshing swim in the Little Gunpowder. He was dreaming of submerging, as long as he could hold his breath, and let the river water wash all the hay dust and seed out of his hair, ears, eyes, and nose. But it had gotten dark, and the river was just too far to go.

It was time for a cold drink and dinner. They were all famished. Kate went in to turn the stove back on and to bring out pitchers of their home-pressed apple cider and grape juice. Edward felt a great sense of accomplishment and camaraderie with his family; they were a team. Life was good. He smiled as the first drops of rain splattered on his face, and then he cheered. They had done it—and it had taken the whole family working together to get the hay in before the rain. He stood there smiling in the rain, shirt off, letting the rain wash him clean.

Chapter 33

IMPACTS FROM THE OUTSIDE WORLD

The Late 1950s

One Saturday afternoon in the middle of a picnic lunch, a thunderous sound came rolling up from the Little Gunpower River. Andrew jumped up, glanced at Kate, and said, "Here they come again. I hope I'm not too late." And with that, he climbed the fence, hustled across the pasture on foot, and headed down to the cliff overlooking the river. He was armed with nothing but a staple gun in his pocket that he had been using for a morning roofing project.

"Be careful, Andrew," Kate called after him.

Edward ran after his father. "What's up, Dad?" he asked when he caught up with him. "What's all that noise?"

Andrew had begun to pant, so he spoke haltingly to Edward. "Every fall . . . a group of men . . . ride their motorcycles along the river. Last year . . . they trespassed on our land, cut our fence, and our sheep got out . . . we lost a few of our best ewes."

"I remember that. Are they bad guys?"

Andrew paused long enough to catch his breath and reply, "I don't know if they even thought about what they were doing or not. It appeared they just didn't think about their impact on us. Just out on a joyride in the woods."

"What are you going to do?"

"I want to talk with them . . . before they do any damage again."

"Aren't you a little scared confronting a whole motorcycle gang out here in the woods? There's just two of us, and it sounds like a lot of them."

"Well, yes, but what else can I do? This is our home—and we depend on the sheep for food and income."

"Call the police."

"I tried that last year. The guys were gone by the time the police arrived. I hope this time we can resolve it by talking with them. I have to believe they are basically good people."

Edward wasn't too sure about his father's strategy. He hadn't heard too many favorable things about motorcycle gangs.

By the time Andrew and Edward got down to the fence, there must have been twenty men on motorcycles, many of which were very loud Harleys. The men were revving their engines, anxious for the leader to cut a way through the understory and the fencing. They had stopped when they saw Andrew coming toward them with a half-grown boy in tow. They stood flat-footed, waiting to see what the farmer had to say. The big man in the lead carried a set of wire cutters in his right hand and had a canvas case with a machete handle sticking out strapped to his back. Several of the other riders carried similar cases.

Edward was sure that his father had seen the wire cutters. Edward's legs were shaking in his shoes. He had no idea what to say or what his father might do to discourage the men from proceeding on their weekend adventure.

Andrew came right up to the big man in front and stopped. "Can I help you?" His voice was polite but firm.

The big man in front, who happened to be covered with tattoos, responded, "Yeah, we're trying to find a trail up the river."

Edward thought for just a moment that the men looked like pirates, with their tattoos, beards, machetes, and bare chests. He wondered if the motorcycle gang might have a similar honor code to the pirates he had been reading about who once terrorized the Chesapeake. He figured they could easily be direct descendants of those pirates.

"Well, there's no trail on this side of the river, as you can see," Andrew replied. "It's too steep here by the cliffs."

"Yeah, those rocks drop off right into the river. It's forced us to come up here to the top of the hill where it's flat just to get around the ledge."

"I understand, but this is my property, and I'm trying to make a living farming it."

The big man took a long look at Andrew and then saw the sheep huddling in the far corner of the field away from the noise. They had stopped grazing; they were petrified.

Another man standing behind the leader said, "For Chrissake, this is all supposed to be public land."

Andrew, as usual, took a moment to choose the right words. "The steep stretch lower down by the river is owned by the state. You should check with the park service down in Annapolis. I think you'll find there's a public trail on the flood plain on the other side, it's much flatter than this side."

"We've come through on this side before. It's more challenging and fun."

"Yes, I know. Last year someone cut this fence with wire cutters, and all my sheep got out. I lost several good ewes. My neighbor had a steer get out the year before, and the steer broke its leg. It's hard enough trying to make a living on a farm these days without losing your livestock."

The big man turned around and spoke to the others. There seemed to be some disagreement. Edward heard a lot of grumbling and cursing. He heard one of them growl, "It's a free country. I should be able to go wherever I want to."

Another one said, "We're not bothering nothing. Let's just keep going."

But the big man, obviously the leader, got back on his Harley and turned it around. "Sorry about your fence. We're just a bunch of guys trying to have a little fun on a Saturday afternoon." He gunned his cycle down the hill and back through the understory.

All the bikers followed, going back the way they'd come, filling the natural, canopy-covered corridor along the river with rolling thunder and exhaust fumes. Edward wondered if that would be the end of the problem or if there would be a different and maybe less reasonable leader next time. Andrew bent over and picked up the NO TRESPASSING sign the bikers had just ripped down. He stapled-gunned it back up on the post.

"You made that look pretty easy, Dad. I bet it could have ended differently if either of you had started yelling."

"You're right. It took me a long time to learn that. Some people think you get ahead by yelling, but I find that doesn't work so well. It's important to treat people respectfully. You rarely know all the facts."

"At first I was scared," Edward admitted. "It looked like the man was ready to stand his ground and defend his actions. Then when you treated him like a neighbor, he calmed down. I think he got it."

Andrew sighed. "I hope so. Let's get back to lunch."

One of Kate's biggest fears as a mom was that her children might contract polio, which had been widespread in the forties and fifties. A vaccine had been created and mass vaccinations began in 1954. The number of cases dropped dramatically over the next few years, thanks to the advances of science and the development of vaccinations and public health programs around the world,

During those years, Betsy did contract rheumatic fever, and the doctor quarantined her in her room. Edward saw his mother pacing back and forth in the hallway, day and night, and watched as she went in regularly to apply cold compresses to her daughter's forehead. The family doctor, who lived in Bel Air, made regular house calls to Good Endeavour to monitor the girl's progress.

Like his mother and father, Edward was scared. Betsy was his only sibling. All he could see from the door to her room was his sister lying motionless during the day, and he could hear her moaning and her restlessness at night. It was a frightening time. All the family knew to do was to wait it out. Betsy recovered, but with a weakened heart.

The following year, Edward was quarantined in his bedroom during the Asian Influenza Pandemic of 1957-1958. He felt like a pariah; he couldn't go to school, and his friends were not allowed to come over to play. All he could do was read. Even his family ignored him. They kept him in his room, put meals on a tray outside his door, and only spoke to him through the keyhole.

One morning, a deep rumbling vibration bounced Edward right out of bed. The whole bed and the walls of his bedroom were shaking. He jumped up and peered through the old, wavy-glass windows and stared wide eyed at the woods behind the house. Without glasses, all he could see were giant yellow and pistachio-green mammoth-like creatures busting their way through the woods, shoving aside both short and tall trees in their path. He blinked twice to clear his vision and grabbed his horn-rimmed glasses before they vibrated off the bedside table.

The wild beasts morphed into yellow and green metal earth-movers and bulldozers that pushed over anything and everything in their way. They churned their way through the trees, into the field, and into *his* backyard, dramatically and permanently destroying the fields and woods along the north-western half of their tract. The machines were invading the farm. Andrew, Kate, and Betsy had all rolled out of bed at the rumbling and watched in silent disbelief as the dissection of Good Endeavour Farm began.

"Stop them, Dad. Get your gun. Don't let them do this," Edward pleaded.

Andrew just looked at him and sighed. "There's nothing else we can do. I've tried."

Edward was angry, so he pulled on his pants and T-shirt, and ran out to watch the big machines transform the mature woods and the lush green fields into two, flat, ribbon-like deserts of sand and clay . . . which would eventually be paved over with asphalt. Men and machines were building a highway, and a big one at that. At that moment, Edward didn't care where the road came from or where it was going. He was just angry that it was chewing up and destroying his farm, his home, his life. All he wanted to do was stop it.

Edward had naively thought that Good Endeavour Farm was safe from the impacts of rapid growth, but as his father explained, few places were. In the case of the highway, the government had come through and claimed—by right of *eminent domain*—forty acres of the farm to build a very small section of Interstate 95.

Andrew explained how it was part of President Eisenhower's ambitious plan to improve commerce and the movement of troops in time of war. That vision had major impacts—both positive and negative—across the entire country. When the interstate project was completed, the country would end up in a vast network of roads that would allow people to travel farther and faster. Unfortunately, the program would also result in the dismemberment of tens of thousands of farms, towns, communities, watersheds, and ecosystems along the way. But after seeing how bad a world war could be, President Eisenhower wanted America to be prepared.

The loss of forty acres felt like a near-fatal wound to a traditional small farm. This new highway was the first significant incursion to the Good Endeavour deed since the original 1695 patent was issued. Edward knew his father was devastated. Andrew had been investing his heart and resources for ten years to restore the farm and its soils, and now his efforts were being trashed. Andrew explained to Edward how he had tried to stand up to this insult to the sanctity of the farm. He had fought the highway's location in court but to no avail. Edward remembered watching his father when he was talking to his lawyers on the phone. It was unnerving for him to see his father's normally pale complexion turn so red and his voice get so loud while seeking some avenue for stopping the disruption of his farm.

Each member of the family had their opinion of what to do. Kate had suggested that it was time to move now that the bucolic rural setting they loved would be destroyed. Betsy's reaction was to spend more time riding, fearing they would move and leave the horses behind. Edward took it all in quietly but made a pact to fight back. He would prowl around the highway construction site after school every day and on weekends when nobody was there, trying to decide what he could do to slow or stop the highway's progress. He figured if all the kids along the route took some action, it would make a difference. He even wrote a letter to *The Aegis* to get more people engaged. It was his first attempt to influence others by writing a letter.

Edward started his terrorist campaign with minor tactics, just enough to let the construction teams know they were not welcome. His first act was to relieve himself on the gigantic tires on the large earthmovers. This was a mark telling everyone that this was his land. On another day, the local police caught him on his bike, knocking orange and white barrels down hillsides. They cornered him while he was trying to make a run for it with his bike. He could have escaped on foot, but he was loyal to his bike and refused to forfeit it.

The policeman got out of his cruiser and confronted Edward. "What the heck are you doing?" he demanded. "This is government property. You can't be out here damaging it."

"It was my family's property, and they stole it from us. I want to stop it."

"You can't do that. It's all approved, and it's way too big a project to stop now. Give me your name and address."

Edward pointed to the barns and the house. "I live right there."

"Go tell your dad and mom that you now have a record for vandalism. If I catch you here again, I'll take your bike away and talk with your parents. There will be serious consequences if you cause any more damage. Do you hear me?"

"Yes, sir. But I'm not a vandal. I'm trying to send a message."

"Message received. Now get out of here. I don't want to see you on this site again. I'll be watching."

Edward lay low for a week, planning his next step and building up courage. He now knew having an escape route was critical. He didn't want to lose his bike, so he left it home. When he returned to the site, he climbed up on a large Euclid earthmover. Six of these forty- to fifty-foot-long machines had been parked overnight, nose to toes, in a line. Somehow, he found the key on the one he climbed up on and figured out how to start the engine. When it rumbled alive, he almost bounced out of the heavily cushioned driver's seat. He covered his ears with his hands—boy, it was loud. It sounded and vibrated like a gigantic cicada. Edward could not imagine spending the whole day in the cockpit. It must mix up your innards, he thought.

These machines possessed a tremendous amount of destructive potential.

Edward tested the control levers. One engaged with a lot of effort, and his steed rammed into the vehicle in front of him. It didn't move, but Edward's earthmover's wheels started spinning. A little more tinkering and he forced the gears into reverse, which resulted in him smashing into the vehicle behind him. Next, he wondered if he could aim the earthmovers toward the cliffs overhanging the valley and then jump off at the last moment. Fortunately, he could not turn the beast enough to break out of the column. Realizing he was making too much noise, he killed the engine and got the heck out of there, concerned that the cop might catch him again and lock him up this time.

On the next day of his rampage, Edward broke into a large supply of dynamite. He quickly understood that his campaign could easily get dangerously out of control, so he went home to think about it.

That night after his mother had gone to bed, Edward sat down at the walnut table and told his father about his attacks on the highway construction site. He thought his father might appreciate his efforts to save the farm. Andrew did not. "Edward, you're better than this." He proceeded to tell Edward what could happen if he continued espousing violence. "There are several things worse than losing part of the farm. One would be to lose you to an accident. The second would be you losing your freedom and living in jail."

Andrew also talked about how to get things done in a democracy without taking the law into your own hands. "You don't always win, but you can make a difference. Once you turn to violence, however, it weakens your cause, the rule of law, and our democracy."

Edward slowly began to appreciate there were multiple ways to make a difference in this country. His father was clear that resorting to violence or intimidation were not tools he should consider. Those actions just make you a terrorist.

Edward worried that his father might forsake his dreams and move off the farm. But Andrew wasn't going anywhere. He looked at his son and said, "Your grandfather often told me to work hard for what you think is right and adjust your course as needed if things change. I'm not giving up the farm. This has been our family's land for a long time, and I refuse to roll over and become roadkill on this highway to the future. I hope we will never have to sell this farm."

Andrew met with the county extension agent in Bel Air and with the state forester in Annapolis and then created a plan to respond to this four-lane scar across the land. He decided to plant evergreen trees, thousands of them, in a sixty-foot-wide swath between the farm and the highway. Andrew's goal was to create a natural buffer on the farm to block the view, the noise, and the exhaust from the highway. Some people laughed. It would take years to plant all the trees and even more years for them to grow into an effective barrier. But Edward understood that his father's decision was a way to turn his anger into action. Action that would, with time, result in long-term benefits to his descendants, the ecosystem, and his neighbors.

Andrew drafted his immediate family to plant trees each spring break during the sixties, seventies, and eighties to meet this lofty goal. They started each day with a hearty breakfast and then marched out to the barren highway right-of-way with Andrew giving directions to his fledgling tree army. "Okay, let's go. Edward, you and Betsy complete the grid we laid out yesterday. Your mother and I will lay out the grid for the rest of the week."

When Edward arrived at the grid, he pulled up a stalk of orchard grass to chew on and scanned the fields. There was a large area to plant, but he was game. The project gave them all a goal and a vision to think about. It made him proud that they were accomplishing something of lasting value. They were building *a forest*, much like what his uncles had done when they joined the CCC during the Depression.

One day, Andrew took Edward to the Avalon part of the Patapsco State Park and showed him the thousands of acres of forests that members of the CCC tree army had planted back in the thirties. "Your generation is the beneficiary of their efforts so long ago. Like them, we might not see the fruits of our labor, but someone will one day, and they will smile and wonder who planted the trees."

In five short years the first seedlings his family had planted to block the sights and sounds of I-95 were taller than Edward. They had grown so well that they were crowding one another and needed thinning. Andrew decided to sell about 300 trees per year as Christmas trees to his friends and neighbors. The family had suspended the raising of turkeys by then due to the tighter health regulations on meat processing, so Andrew figured they would have plenty of time around the holidays to sell trees. Kate agreed with a great deal of relief. She figured that selling 300 trees would be far less stressful than processing, selling, and delivering 1,000 fresh turkeys. Besides she had experience now about farming and was more comfortable in taking on new ideas.

So, once again, the family got busy getting the word out.

"I'll run the ads in *The Aegis, The Jeffersonian,* and *The Sun,* and I'll send postcards out to our turkey-buying, corn-picking, and church friends' networks," Kate offered.

Andrew smiled at her and then turned to Edward and Betsy and said, "Edward, go build and paint a *Cut-Your-Own-Tree* sign and install it along Philadelphia Road at the end of the lane. Betsy, go buy a dozen handsaws over at Anderson's Hardware and Farm Supply and make sure we have plenty of baling twine handy for tying trees onto cars. Then we'll have to wait and see who wants a fresh, local tree as opposed to those shipped in from North Carolina or Western Maryland."

To Edward it was exciting to launch a new business; it was an adventure. It was also the right thing to do, maybe even the best use of the land. But they had to wait to see if the neighbors would be interested. There were no other Christmas tree farms in the area. Would there be interest? Would they even break even, given all the effort they had already invested?

At eight on the Saturday morning following Thanksgiving, the dogs started barking. Edward ran outside and saw that several carloads of people had already arrived to see them, explore the farm, and get a tree.

Edward locked up the dogs for the day and went to see the early arrivals. "Happy Holidays. Great to see you. Here's a map to where you can find different tree types. We have fir, spruce and pine."

The visitors essentially had all the same questions:

"What kinds of trees do you have?"

"How do we do this?"

"Do I have to cut the tree myself?"

"Didn't this used to be a turkey farm?"

Edward tried to answer everyone's questions and wanted to stay and chat with the people, but several more cars were coming down the lane. It was like that all morning. By noon the farm bustled with families—many coming out from Towson and some from Joppatowne—the new, 1960s, suburban community built right over the top of where Old Joppa Towne had once prospered.

The number of tree customers kept growing over the next two weekends as word of mouth spread the news of a local place to buy fresh trees. Parents would bundle up their children even on cold days to bring them out to the farm. The children ran around, squealing upon seeing the animals, and then the whole family would stroll or run through the fields to find the *perfect tree*. The entire month was a festive time on the farm, especially when it snowed.

For the next thirty years, Decembers at Good Endeavour were abuzz with excitement. Dressed in their long johns and over-alls, Andrew and Kate welcomed customers and offered coffee, cookies, and hot chocolate. Edward and Betsy—and, years later, spouses and grandchildren—participated in this family tradition of helping customers cut, drag, and tie trees onto cars.

A tree farm might have demanded a lot of time and hard work throughout the year— mowing, trimming, and spraying—but in December it provided a great deal of fun and camaraderie. Edward loved it because it was another project that engaged the whole family, like bringing in the hay.

Once again, the Good Endeavour family had adjusted to the times. Andrew took a bad situation and turned it into a new business and neighborhood event. Cut-Your-Own Christmas trees became the farm's new cash crop and provided the family with a viable business that they could manage on their own. Andrew concluded that since tree farming helped restore the land, employ the family, and serve the neighbors, his ancestors would be proud.

One chilly evening in October, right at the beginning of dinner, Betsy asked, "Do you know what they have us doing at school?"

"Are they running you through safety drills?" Andrew asked as he reached for the meatloaf.

"Yes. When we hear a specific alarm go off, we're told to crawl under our desks and not look out the windows. It's all about the Russians attacking us with missiles. It's terrifying."

Andrew, as usual, took several moments to respond. "We're trying to get the Soviets to remove nuclear warheads they have in Cuba. There's a standoff at present."

Edward piped in. "Should we be worried? Some of the kids at school act as if it's a big hoax."

Andrew finished his last swig of beer and looked right at Edward. "It's no hoax, but it's unlikely they'll attack us. Take the drills seriously—it's always best to be prepared and know what to do."

Edward squirmed in his seat. Betsy said, "But the news is all about how scared folks are. Thousands of Americans are building fallout shelters. Are we going to build one?"

"We're not building one at this point. We're hoping diplomacy will work," Andrew told her.

"But if we wait it may be too late! I think it's all pretty scary."

Andrew tried to explain about how doomsday scenarios are always scary. He claimed that one reason they had moved to the farm was to be self-reliant if need be. But he made it clear that he didn't think it would come to that. "The Russians have nothing to gain by attacking us," Andrew said. "Our ancestors used to be scared of Indians, pirates, and vigilantes. Now it's warheads in Cuba, bioterrorism, and at some point, lasers in space."

"I feel like we're growing up in a dangerous time," Betsy told him. "I think the older generation is letting us down, passing on all these bad problems with horrific scenarios."

Her statement took all the air out of the room. Edward understood that his sister was challenging their parents.

Andrew took quite a while to formulate his answer to her

challenge. He explained that was often the perspective of younger generations as they struggled to understand a complex world. "My generation had to face the impacts of two world wars, the stock market crash, the Great Depression, the rise of fascism, nuclear weapon proliferation, bigotry, and the domestic nightmare of the McCarthy-era witch hunts and blacklists. There are always external and internal threats to democracy and security. We have to take them all seriously."

"What can we do?" Betsy asked.

"Keep up with the news. A lot is going on in the world," Kate said.

"Change is inevitable and continuous," Andrew told his daughter. "You need to study hard so your generation can deal with the changes of the future."

Despite hearing about all the bad news in the world, Betsy and Edward still had a busy and pretty good life on the farm. Each of them had a list of chores each week, and they took over all the feeding and care of the animals.

As she got older, Betsy started to take longer and longer rides with her horse on the trails along the Little Gunpowder. One day she came back and talked about two boys she had met on one of the trails. She spoke about new paths they had introduced her to and how much fun they had together.

"Who are these boys?" Kate asked. "Where do they live?"

"Don't worry, Mom. I think you might know their parents. They live over on old Joppa Road and keep their horses at Mrs. Roger's farm. Anyway, they've invited me to go on the next trail ride with the pony club. You can check it out if you want, but I'd like to join."

"Well, you can go if it's an organized club, but take your brother with you. He might enjoy it as well."

Betsy rolled her eyes. Edward sensed that he was being sent along as a chaperone to protect his big sister. But he did enjoy trail riding, it was much more fun than riding around a ring. It involved climbing ridges and crossing streams. The most fun was when riders turned their steeds around and headed for home at the end of a trail ride. This was a signal to the horses that food was waiting for them back in their stalls. They shivered in anticipation and then would explode, galloping full blast through the woods with their riders hugging their steeds' necks and tucking their heads in as close as they could to the manes. That adrenaline-charged feat was exhilarating, dangerous, and scary. The goal for the rider was to avoid being jabbed or knocked off their mounts by tree branches. The riders had to trust that their horse would not get too close to a branch. Betsy and Edward had a pact that they would never tell their mother about these hazardous flights through dense woods.

After Betsy and Edward joined the pony club, Andrew offered to build a ring in the front field for the club to practice in. Kate agreed, thinking it would be safer for Betsy to spend time in their front pasture with other kids rather than out all alone on the trails.

The ring was used as a practice area for training ponies, learning to ride, jumping, and dressage. The front field also proved to be the perfect size for hosting events, so everyone agreed that Good Endeavour would host the first Joppa-Magnolia Horse and Pony Show the following spring.

Edward was up early on show day as the first horse trailer came rumbling in Bulls Lane to the farm. He welcomed the riders who were members of the club, chatted for a few minutes, and then directed them to the parking area. When he looked back down the lane, he saw a variety of vans and trucks driving up the hill. The traffic increased, sending up a continuous cloud of dust. The family was floored at the turnout. No one had planned for so many horses, people, and dogs running around the farm. The riders came from all over Harford and Baltimore counties and even Pennsylvania. Edward was excited that their show had drawn so many riders. Andrew and Kate looked at each other and commented on how fortunate it was that they had enough room for everyone and that it had not rained.

Betsy sat at a makeshift table built out of an old wooden door balanced on two sawhorses. She registered riders and horses for specific events as they arrived. There were a lot of classes; it was going to be a busy day.

Kids from seven to seventeen unloaded their mounts and began to prepare them with currycombs and brushes. There was a lot to do to make each animal look its best. Some contestants even took the time to braid and put bows in the manes of their mounts. The grooming routine was an effective way to calm both rider and horse.

The show judge, Doc Leffler, and the local veterinarian, Doc Burley, arrived, as did the Joppa-Magnolia Fire Department ambulance in case someone needed them. Riders would sometimes fall off their mounts, especially while jumping, so it was good to have medical personnel handy at a show.

Kate's and Andrew's job was to greet people with a smile, answer questions, and fix problems as they arose. As the numbers increased, Kate grew nervous, trying to second guess what might go wrong. "Andrew, we don't have room for all these people. We'll run out of food, ribbons, and places to put them all." She was also concerned that some people had brought dogs that might scare the horses.

"I think we're in good shape," responded Andrew. "It's a nice group of people and everyone seems responsible and willing to help out. But now I better get down to the ring and welcome folks on the loudspeaker."

"I'll enlist several younger children to hand out ribbons," said Kate.

When Edward finished directing traffic, he opened the concession stand. The pony club sold coffee, donuts, and sodas for five cents, hot dogs for ten cents, and hamburgers for twenty-five cents. Of course, they didn't have enough for such a big crowd, but the food lasted through lunch. Edward was starving already, so he devoured two jelly donuts covered with confectioner's sugar and immediately got the powdered sugar all over his shirt.

It was not long before he noticed a buzz of nervousness mixed with seriousness permeating the riders, their parents, and the horses as the crowd assembled. A practice ring had been roped off where the riders warmed up their mounts and practiced their *voice, rein,* and *leg signals* to their mounts.

Everything seemed well organized. Andrew had locked up his English Setters so they would not excite the horses, and, fortunately, the people who brought dogs with them kept them on leashes. There were only a few instances where horses tried to bite or kick one another.

Then the hour for the show to begin arrived, and the loudspeaker came alive with an ear-piercing screech. Several horses shied, a bit skittish of the crackle of the speakers, but their riders quickly calmed them down.

Andrew's voice carried across the field. "Welcome, everyone, to Good Endeavour Farm. I hope you have a great time here today. Please see me if you have any questions. I will now turn the microphone over to today's judge. We're happy to have Doctor Leffler from the University of Maryland Extension Service."

Dr. Leffler took the microphone and described the plan for the day. He then welcomed entrants for the first event to enter the ring one at a time, proceed at a walk in a clockwise manner around the inside of the ring, then stop and hold their mount. Dr. Leffler then entered the ring, took careful notes on what he saw, and then instructed the rider to trot and then to canter. Jumping classes would follow.

Betsy waited for her turn and then entered the ring. She always entered sitting tall in the saddle and dressed in her yellow jodhpurs, white blouse, and black riding hat and crop.

Edward heard her talking to Bunny, her youngest and greenest pony. "Let's go. Easy, girl. That's it. Don't worry about the other ponies. This is our ring. Just a nice gentle walk to get comfortable."

Dr. Leffler called out in his deep baritone, "Trot."

Betsy gathered her reins, leaned forward, squeezed her thighs against the saddle, and started to post in tandem with Bunny, who was always happy to oblige her rider by shifting her tempo up a notch. Several times, Betsy had to rein Bunny in. The mare was full of oats and always ready to go into a canter, her next gear. She pranced a bit, but Betsy pulled on the reins and Bunny dropped back to a trot fairly quickly. Dr. Leffler, who never smiled, glanced up at Betsy, pleased that she was able to control her excitable steed. He had been at a cross-country race the month before where Betsy, riding Bunny, had won the Hunt Club Cup. He knew she was fast.

Betsy had spent many afternoons working her ponies in the ring, which paid off. She won several ribbons in different events throughout the day. Edward was proud of her.

The last event of the day was the cart-driving competition. Betsy had been looking forward to entering this event. It would be her first experience showing Bunny pulling a cart. She had been working with Bunny, walking behind her with long reins and cart-pulling tackle and teaching her voice commands. She had also used the same gear with Bunny to pull in Christmas trees from the back fields. But Betsy had never actually hooked Bunny up to a cart with wheels. She thought for some reason that this might be a good time to try.

Betsy connected Bunny to the old sulky and lead her across the grass to the gravel lane. Bunny was okay, her ears perkily looking ahead, listening to all the people and watching other horses and ponies. As soon as she pulled the sulky onto the gravel, however, the wood and metal wheels started to make a racket on the loose stones, and she spooked. Her ears went straight back, and she launched herself at a full gallop, ripping the driving reins out from Betsy's hands and pulling the bouncing sulky behind her.

Edward froze with his jaw hanging open, wondering how this could be happening. He knew Bunny was fast—he had ridden her—but he was now mesmerized at how quickly she flew around the field, pulling a rapidly dismembering cart behind her. He understood immediately how dangerous the situation was with so many people running around trying to get out of her way. How could he stop her? Where might he corner her and calm the runaway pony? Maybe he could corral her in the ring. No, she was too fast for any human intercept. There was no outfoxing or stopping this beautiful but terrified bay mare.

People and horses scattered in all directions, many seeking shelter inside the ring as Bunny flew around the *outside* of the ring. She headed back toward the barn where she disappeared. Along the way an unsaddled horse joined her in the race. Edward sprinted toward the barn. Betsy joined him in the search, and they finally found Bunny gasping for air, wedged back in a high corner of the dark hayloft.

After helping unhook what remained of the sulky from the scared pony, Edward took the halter of the horse beside her and led her back to her owner. Betsy spoke gently to Bunny to calm her down and then removed all the rest of the broken tackle. She led Bunny to her stall in the barn, where Doc Burley checked her out. She was fine except for scratches, but the cart was wrecked. Edward returned to the ring area where everyone was catching their breath. The show was officially over, and the riders began to reload their ponies and horses into their vans.

Edward knew better than to voice it, but he thought it had been an exciting way to bring the first horse and pony show at Good Endeavour Farm to a close. He was tired and hoped to sleep well that night. But no such luck; his subconscious kept rehashing the sulky race in his dreams.

Chapter 34

Social Reckoning

The 1960s

The sixties was a time of significant steps forward on human rights, including greater integration in schools, colleges, and some workplaces, residential settings, and religious institutions. Chenoa, Josie, and Nellie would have been especially pleased by the reckoning. After all, they had helped sow the seeds long before. But they would have been disheartened that these next steps had taken so long and were still so challenging to implement.

Watching the debates on television made Edward wonder what role Good Endeavour and his ancestors might have played over the years in the current racial makeup of the Joppa community. Mandeville was an enclave of black and mixed-race families living adjacent to and just to the east of his family farm. Some of the neighbors living there may have descended from men and women who had worked on Good Endeavor, either as slaves or freedmen. Some of them may be relatives—he just didn't know.

When Edward was growing up, the Mandeville residents lived a largely separate and unequal life compared to white families in adjacent neighborhoods. The children of the Mandeville neighborhood were bused twenty miles to a colored consolidated school in Hickory, near Bel Air. That school had far fewer resources allotted to it than the white public schools such as Old Post Road Elementary or Edgewood High School that Betsy and Edward attended. Not going to the same schools resulted in little interaction between the adjacent neighborhoods. Edward had not even met any of the kids in Mandeville, although he had met several of their parents when they stopped by to talk with his father about hunting on Good Endeavour or helping out on the farm.

But now, in 1964, all public schools were mandated by law to integrate so all children would have equal educational opportunities. He was puzzled that it had taken 200 years for colored people to get the vote, and it had been another hundred years to get these children included by law in the mainstream public school system. It then took ten more years from the landmark 1954 Supreme Court decision to finally integrate schools in Harford County. Edward couldn't understand it. It felt like a travesty of justice in a democracy built on the ideals of equality. How could the country be so slow in providing equal education for all its people?

But it was not just the school systems that were segregated; so were many aspects of Edward's life. No colored people attended St John's Episcopal Church. There were none in any of the pony clubs or pony shows he attended or the Boy Scout troops. He also could not remember ever seeing black families coming to buy turkeys or trees, even though they had helped prune the trees in the summer and butcher the turkeys in the fall. He also could not recall a person of color in his house except his father's business associates from other countries and women hired as babysitters or to help his mother with ironing and laundry. There was still segregation throughout society. Maybe school integration could start the change that was needed.

While watching TV the night before the county-implemented integration at Edgewood High School, Edward, who was now fourteen, was agitated about the hatred present in the country. "Why are people so scared about integrating our schools?"

Andrew took a moment to get a cup of coffee and formulate an answer. "As a boy growing up, we rarely ever talked about race. It seemed to be the nature of things to accept the way things were. It was a class society and most people knew where they fit in. I don't think we had any appreciation for how much people in power stacked the deck so they would stay on top. That certainly applied to colored people, but also Jews, Italians, Irish, Polish, Chinese, and women. I think that's all changing now, and I think that will be good for everyone.

"I'm guessing that some white men and women are concerned they might lose out if things change. Therefore, they keep fighting change by dragging their feet or rigging the system and the elections to benefit themselves."

"I've heard people argue that there's a finite amount of wealth, and if you have more people at the table, your slice of the pie will be smaller," Betsy said.

"Is that true?" Edward asked.

"No, I don't believe that," Andrew told them. "From what I've seen, we all do better if everyone has the opportunity to do their best and succeed. And if that happens, the pie will be bigger."

"I'm so glad we're discussing this topic," said Betsy. "Everyone seems to be scared to talk about it because there are so many opinions and so much prejudice. There are also a good number of oppressed people who don't want to talk about the past. I can't blame them."

"Do you think there will be problems tomorrow when the school buses pick up all the colored kids in Mandeville and other areas?" Edward asked his father.

"I hope not," replied Andrew. "Both white and colored people are concerned about that. Hopefully, this step of integrating the schools will help everyone get to know and respect one another."

"I have to admit I'm a little nervous about tomorrow," said Edward. "It's the first day of the school year—for both white and black students. What should I do, Dad?"

"Your job is to treat everyone fairly. I trust you will welcome the new kids when they show up."

"But be careful. You never know how anyone will react," Kate added. "If you like, I'm sure that Betsy's friend who's picking her up tomorrow morning would be happy to drive you to school, too, at least on the first day."

Andrew glanced at Kate and then turned to Edward. "I think you both need to ride the bus. It should be just a day like any other."

Edward tapped his fingers on the top of the table. He tried to understand what his father was telling him. Yes, it was a historic day, but more than that, he sensed his father thought that some of the kids on the bus might need his perspective to calm other kids down. But how could he do that?

Edward was keenly aware that some of the kids at school were quite prejudiced. He had heard ugly statements from a couple of them on his school bus. Their hateful talk and bragging scared him much more than anything he had heard from people of color.

It was also fairly common to see people displaying their Confederate flags as if they were still fighting the Civil War a hundred years later. He had heard grownups talking about how some of this anger had bubbled up recently at the local school board meetings. He knew it was an awful remnant of the past that might seep to the surface at any moment. After all, Confederate sympathizers like John Wilkes Booth and even some of Baltimore's Plug-uglies had lived not too far away from Good Endeavour. But now the law of the land mandated that the schools integrate, so he hoped the years of debate were over.

ᴈ৳ৎ

The next morning, Edward walked hesitantly out Bulls Lane to catch the bus on Old Philadelphia Road as usual. The birds still sang and the scent of fall was in the air, but nature was not distracting him from his thoughts that beautiful, sunny morning. He knew that today might turn out to be anything but routine, and he had started his walk early to make sure he was at the bus stop on time. He felt as if he had a date with destiny and planned to welcome the new kids as they boarded the bus.

On the way Edward stopped in front of his gregarious neighbor's home. Morris, a light-skinned black man, lived in the third house out the lane with his wife, Lillian. They had a garden behind the house and a natural spring behind that where they got their water.

Seeing Edward, Morris walked down the hill from his porch. "You be careful today, you hear. Be nice to those new kids riding your bus. I know some of them, they're good people—from good parents. They're more scared about getting on that bus today than you are."

Edward nodded and assured Morris that he would welcome the new kids. He hadn't even thought about how the new kids would be reacting. Of course, Morris was right—he often was. Edward thought about this for a few moments and then waved goodbye and walked on down the dirt lane. As he walked, he kept going over in his mind what he thought might happen and what he would do if it did. He hoped that some of the other kids might listen to him.

He also thought about the different types of people he had encountered at school in the past. Edgewood High School served Edgewood Arsenal, the local military base, so there was already a range of ethnicities and students with different skin colors in his school. They all seemed to fit in fine. Among the spectrum of classmates he knew, some were friendly . . . and some were not.

Some were bullies and some were shy. Some were bookish, some were jocks. It didn't seem to have anything to do with skin color or nationality.

Oliver, one of the neighborhood's white kids who lived in a rundown house, joined him on the way to the bus stop. Edward's whole body tensed because Oliver was just as likely to meet you with a hard punch to your bicep as he was to say hello. Most kids thought he was a bit crazy and a bully. But Edward had discovered a good side to him as well—they both liked exploring the woods after school. Edward also knew Oliver lived with his parents and a bunch of younger siblings in a two-story house that was in great need of repair. His father often did not have a job and drank too much. Oliver had a tough life being the oldest, and he rarely had money for lunch.

Edward held his breath, waiting for the punch, and then relaxed. Oliver was in one of his quieter moods, probably contemplating a problem at home that took up all his attention.

As they came up to the bus stop, about six kids were there already, all from the new homes that had been built along Bulls Lane. One of the bigger kids was going on and on about how bad integration would be. No one said anything, they just stared off into space. Edward finally had enough of the boy's remarks. "Stop it," he said. "We should welcome these kids to our school. They're our neighbors."

A silence descended on the group of kids as they looked down the road, hoping the bus would arrive. The big kid who had been complaining came over and stood inches away from Edward's face, close enough that Edward could see the blonde stubble on the kid's sunken chin and the meanness in his eyes. The kid clenched his hand into a fist and shouted at Edward, "Who says?"

Edward's whole body froze, and he tried to remember what his dad would do in a case like this, what could he say to calm everyone down. He didn't know. Maybe it was too late.

Before Edward could say anything, Oliver came over to stand next to him. "You heard him. It ain't right to curse them. They're all just kids like us. Give 'em a chance."

Oliver's support of Edward's comment was helpful. It was obvious he was scared at what Oliver might do. Oliver's evil, reckless reputation preceded him, so the boy just grunted and walked over and pushed to the front of the line, mumbling a couple of slurs under his breath. He wasn't about to mess with Oliver.

"Thanks. I think he was about to deck me," Edward said under his breath.

"I think you had guts to say something. I hope he'll think twice before doing anything stupid on the bus."

"But how about the others?"

"After your performance, I bet no one else from this bus stop will say anything either. They might even be thinking about what we said."

Fortunately, the bus arrived a little early. When the kids boarded, Edward chose to sit halfway back to see how things would unfold. The bus driver, who happened to be colored, was all smiles. She lived in Mandeville and was picking up her son and taking him to the "good" school for the first time. Edward held his breath when they stopped at the colored neighborhood just up from Bulls Lane. They had never stopped there before. He had never driven or walked back this lane.

The white kids were quiet and nervous as the new kids boarded. When one girl asked if this bus was going to Edgewood High School, the driver nodded with a smile. The new kids boarded slowly and sat in the back. As they passed his seat, Edward noted they came in all shapes and sizes, just like the white kids. He waved his hand in a subtle greeting and tried to catch their eyes, hoping to offer them a simple welcome as they passed by. A few of them made eye contact but nothing more. One tall, skinny girl about his age caught his gaze and held it for a moment. He smiled, hoping he had lessened her fear a bit.

After a few tense minutes of riding the bus together, Edward noticed what he took as a collective sigh of relief. They were all just kids on their way to school. Some didn't want to be there, but most were excited about the first day of school. Most of the kids just looked out the windows.

Later that day, he heard that there had been no violence and no intimidation reported on any of the buses going to Edgewood High School. The school and the community had taken another step toward the greatly delayed but largely peaceful integration of American public schools. Of course, there were examples of verbal protests at other schools that showed up on the *Evening News* that night. But not in Joppa.

Within a few weeks, the new students were acting like the other kids—talking, changing seats, chewing gum, and poking fun at each other. By the end of the year, they were part of school life. However, the colored kids and the white kids tended to congregate in different parts of the cafeteria at lunch and different parts of the gym for evening events like school dances.

But in school Edward noticed white and black students starting to speak to and getting to know one another, and at school events, everyone cheered for whoever made the baskets or performed the solos. After years of not being treated equally by the dominant white culture, this was one more step toward racial acceptance and inclusion. But there was still a long way to go.

ASARCO on Strike! When one of the bigger employers in Baltimore went on strike, it made headlines. Edward sat at the kitchen table, nervously reading the articles in *The Baltimore Sun* and watching the news on TV. This was his father's copper plant in the news, and he was concerned for his father's safety and was impatiently waiting to talk to him that night. Edward had missed him the previous night when his father had come home late and again this morning because he had left before the sun was up. But tonight, he would catch him even if he had to stay up past midnight.

Edward knew that things at work had been tense for his father, but he had not appreciated that the whole plant would shut down. It was getting serious. Over the last two days, hundreds of employees had either stayed home or joined the picket line, threatening not to return until they got a better deal. The strikers were painting management as the *bad guys*. This upset Edward and the family. His dad was clearly management, and Edward had difficulty thinking of his dad as a *bad guy*. He wanted to know more.

Edward watched as Andrew drove in the lane and walked up to the house, clearly exhausted after a twelve-hour shift at the plant, his third one in as many days. "Dad, what's going on at work? I want to hear all about the strike."

"Let's get some dinner into us, and I'll tell you what I know. But then I'm going to bed. I'm tuckered out."

Kate told Andrew he should take advantage of the strike and take a few days off to rest up, but Andrew explained there was no way he could do that. He was part of the skeleton crew left at the plant, all of them non-union employees. It was up to them to manage the slowdown and cessation of all production. That meant shutting down the furnaces and all of the refining processes. It was a big deal to stop all operations and their intricate supply chains designed to produce high-grade copper 24/7. They could not afford to shut down for long with huge cargo ships backing up in the harbor full of copper ore from around the world.

Andrew hated strikes—they were so wasteful and dangerous—but he understood their value in some circumstances. He just wished everyone could sit down and work out what needed to be accomplished.

Edward was full of questions about the issues, opinions, and threats he had read about in the papers and was fascinated with it all. At the same time, he was quite concerned with the increasing number of threats leveled at the managers. He wanted to know why this was happening and if his father would be safe crossing the picket line.

The family sat down to eat, and Kate served up a pot roast, baked potatoes, and tomato aspic. Her face was grim, her hands were fidgeting, and anytime his parents were standing close together, she hugged Andrew tightly as if she didn't want to let him go. She was worried about what was happening and wanted to hear when it might be over. But nobody had an answer to that. The potential for violence scared her, as did the uncertainty of whether the negotiators could resolve it at all. What would they do if the plant shut down and Andrew lost his job?

After dinner Andrew got a beer and tried to relax. "I went in early today to avoid the strikers, the crowds, and the news media. But they were there, too, waiting for us, like an ambush, and it was tricky getting through the gate. The last thing I want to do is call in the police or the National Guard, but we may need to. The crowds are growing and getting rowdier."

"The paper said there were hundreds of people at the gates," Edward told his dad.

"We estimated at least three to four hundred people at around ten a.m. Some of the strikers I recognized, but many of the people I've never seen before. They were all carrying signs and chanting. Labor supporters from other unions and other plants all around the city are showing up. Those are the strikers who might resort to violence. I don't think our people would hurt us."

After a short lull in the conversation, Kate said, "I got several calls today about the strike. Two were from local TV stations, and two were ugly threats."

Andrew looked at her, quite alarmed. "That's a mess. I sure don't want you dragged into this cesspool. Who would do that? Don't answer next time it rings."

"I only pick up to see if it's you calling or maybe a call from the school about the kids."

"If it's a threat, just hang up on them as soon as you can."

Kate just stared ahead.

"The papers say that whatever the outcome of these negotiations, it will set the standard for manufacturing across the city," said Edward. "They said that's why your workers are getting support from all over."

"A lot is riding on the decisions we're making."

"Were you at risk of getting attacked or beat up at any point in the day?" asked Kate.

"It was intimidating to see the anger and the size of the crowds when we went in today, but no, I never thought I was in physical danger. But a few dozen hourly employees who weren't union members crossed the picket line, claiming they needed to work to feed their families. Two of them got roughed up before we could get them through the gate. Not a very pretty picture."

Kate's face was tight with concern. She kept busy serving, eating, clearing the table, and cleaning up the dishes. After dinner she went to sit in the wicker rocker by the window, apparently wanting to be close to Andrew but probably not knowing what to say.

Edward guessed his father wasn't telling them everything, seeing how scared his mother was. "There was good coverage of that fight on national TV," he told his father. "Some people in the crowd were calling them scabs."

"WBAL reporters were pushing us hard as we tried to enter the plant, trying to get us to comment on the progress of the discussions," Andrew replied. "We couldn't tell them much since the negotiations are directed by the company lawyers in New York and the union bosses and their lawyers from Washington, D.C. I spent my day creating a list of recommendations for the ASARCO lawyers to use to address issues that I thought had real substance and value to both the employees and the company."

"Like what?"

"Well, the plant is getting old and needs updating if they are keeping it operational. We all know that. There are health, safety and pollution issues that also need addressing, and that could be done at the same time."

"Why not just fix them and save the headaches and the risks of a strike?" asked Edward.

"Because it's costly. It's all about balancing the cost of upgrades, market projections, and short- and long-term profitability. We have to make a profit, or headquarters in New York will shut us down. As you know, it's not just the copper industry. Most businesses are facing increasing competition from foreign manufacturers with modern plants. America is at risk of losing its industrial base. It's a tough call for all the old plants we have in this country."

"The mayor seems to be quite involved. Whose side is he on?"

"The mayor says he wants better conditions and better pay for the residents of the city. But he knows very well that it would be devastating to the city if all the big manufacturing plants shut down. Big plants like Bethlehem Steel, ASARCO, Allied Chemical, Kennecott, and Alcoa have been the backbone to Baltimore's growth for more than a century."

"What's going to happen?"

"In past strikes, discussions have gone on for weeks and sometimes months. Then the lawyers end up agreeing to a compromise that we'll have to implement. It's complex and often doesn't achieve what was intended or needed by either side."

Andrew was right; it was a complicated business. Copper ore arrived by ship into Baltimore from all around the world, mainly from Peru, Mexico, and the Southwestern United States. The ore then has to be crushed, melted, and refined and then sold to a vast array of markets.

Andrew explained to Edward that many of the jobs were dangerous—and not just around the acid baths and the molten-metal casting. Asbestos was widespread at the facility, and everyone knew it was dangerous. The men who performed the more dangerous duties were paid more relative to other workers because they had to be more skilled, very careful, and reliable. Safety was a key issue and became even more so when one of Andrew's key men fell into a hot acid bath.

It was a business that also generated large volumes of chemical wastes that were affecting the health of the employees and the residents across the city, as well as the quality of the bay. Even Andrew had high levels of chemicals in his blood. All of these concerns needed to be dealt with by the negotiators, so it was a real balancing act. To put it in perspective, health and environmental issues were not high on the list of important tasks back when the plant had to grow so quickly at the start of the war. But now things were different, and the government was passing regulations to get large manufacturing companies all across the country to upgrade and clean up their operations.

Management and the labor union negotiators struggled over the optimum ways to balance pay increases with the costs of health and safety, environmental, and productivity issues. Both sides knew that ASARCO couldn't afford it all, it was just too expensive. They had to compromise somewhere.

"What about the workers? What do they want aside from increased wages?" Edward asked.

"They're just like everyone else. They want to be treated fairly and have opportunities for advancement, irrespective of race or ethnicity. That's been difficult at times, but we've made some progress on merit pay and upward mobility over the last decade."

Andrew was right. Ten years prior to this strike, all the management positions and the supervisor/foreman jobs at ASARCO were held by white men. Over the past decade, the company had moved the best people into those jobs, regardless of skin color.

"Now, our foremen are all colored, reflecting the workforce, and as a result, operations are running more smoothly than ever," Andrew said. "We're trying to open up opportunities in upper management as well, and we're seeing more applicants of color for lab and engineering positions. I take it as part of my job now to make sure we hire and train African Americans for management positions."

The strike at ASARCO dragged on, resulting in a great deal of lost revenue for the company and the employees. The crowds on the picket lines grew in number and the strikers became more desperate with time. One morning, as Andrew tried to walk into the plant, a man grabbed him by his suit jacket lapels and pulled him into a face-to-face standoff.

Andrew took a deep breath, and once he had collected his wits, asked, "How can I help you?"

"Agree to our terms," the man growled.

Andrew didn't know what to do but had been trained not to push back with force. He noticed the media moving in, hoping to catch an even more serious altercation. Before Andrew could say anything, one of the local union leaders, a man named Bill, came over and pulled the angry man off him. Bill turned to Andrew and their eyes locked on each other as they silently acknowledged that tensions were peaking and close to getting out of hand. Andrew straightened out his jacket, nodded to Bill, and entered the gate.

One of the news cameras had caught the incident and the clip showed up that night, both on local and national TV.

When Andrew returned to the parking lot at the end of the day, he walked to his car, the last one in the lot. He stopped with a sense of shock and disappointment, and his body shook. Someone had thrown a brick through his windshield. Not a good wrap-up for a difficult day. He took a deep breath and then cleared out the glass from the front seat. He got in and drove his sedan—with no windshield—all the way to the Chevrolet dealership in Kingsville.

Once he got there, he called Kate. She arrived fifteen minutes later to pick him up and take him home. She was petrified; she had seen the TV clip of the assault and now there was this violent vandalism. The violence shook her up and made her think it was time for Andrew to become a full-time farmer. She did not want him to go back in to work the next day and mentioned this as they drove home and then again after dinner. When Andrew said he did not want to talk about it anymore, she shut down emotionally, went to their bedroom, and refused to speak with anyone.

Andrew dreamed about being a full-time farmer too, but he did not mention that to Kate or anyone else. His primary focus at this point had to be on ending the strike and then restarting the whole smelter and refining operation—no mean feat. But when he tried to relax, his thoughts went right to the farm. He had unfulfilled plans for Good Endeavour, and just thinking about having time to pursue them was good for his mental health during this desperate time at work.

The strike was finally resolved after six long weeks, with both sides claiming victory. "We'll see how this all turns out down the road a few years," Andrew told Kate. "There are still large issues that need to be resolved, issues that were avoided by both sides in the settlement."

Although Edward had been concerned for his father's safety, he found the details of the strike to be a real education about business and about working with others. He learned that reality was always more complicated than it appeared on the surface, and this made him want to learn as much as he could about what made people tick.

Even months after the strike, Edward continued to ask questions, trying to absorb how his father's business world worked. He was so curious that his dad invited him to visit the plant for a day and walk through the buildings once things were back to normal. Andrew wanted Edward to see each of the major processes and meet the men who ran the operations. He also wanted Edward to have a real hands-on experience in a manufacturing plant that would bring geometry, chemistry, business, and psychology popping off the page and into real life. Edward was excited about skipping a day from school and getting to see the plant firsthand.

"Here, put these on," Andrew said as he passed Edward a pair of plastic safety goggles, a white hard hat, and ear protection—similar gear to what he and his dad had begun to wear while cutting trees on the farm. "The required use of this health and safety equipment was just one of the outcomes of the strike."

They left the offices of the management team, walked through the clean chemical lab where Andrew had begun his career, crossed the moonscape-like industrial yard, and entered into a series of big but run-down buildings. On the tour, Edward was amazed at the vast scale of the operations. As he followed his dad, he felt like he was crawling through the bowels of the earth, watching the different metals flow like lava and glow like the sun. The rooms looked like poorly lit subterranean caverns large enough to house the largest Mesozoic dinosaurs. These sheet-metal caves were filled with fire, smoke, and dust that filtered the sun's rays from the windows in the roof arching high overhead. Edward felt like he had been exiled to Dante's inferno.

At one point, Andrew waved to a man to join them. "Bill, I'd like you to meet my son, Edward. Would you mind telling him what you do here as the foreman of this operation?"

"Glad to. Nice to meet you, Edward. Your dad and I go way back. We've seen a lot."

Andrew stood back a few feet, letting Bill and Edward talk.

"I tell the men what to do and make sure they have what they need to get it done," Bill began.

"What part of the operation are you responsible for?"

"We purify the copper. Once the metals are melted out of the ore, it's poured into molds, cooled, and sent to us."

"How hot do you heat the ore to get it to melt?"

"We use natural gas furnaces that reach twenty-three hundred- and fifty-degrees Fahrenheit."

Edward couldn't really comprehend that temperature.

"Then we use electrolysis to remove gold, silver, platinum, tin, and other metals to get the copper pure enough for most uses."

"What? You produce gold? Dad, you never told me that. What do you do with it?"

Bill laughed. "We sell a lot of gold to the dental industry. Of course, I pocket some of it to buy my next haircut." Bill's eyes twinkled as he smiled at Edward and then winked at Andrew.

At the end of the tour, Bill said, "You should come work with us this summer. We always need hard workers around here. My son's coming in while he's off from school. But I bet your old man has you working on the farm."

"He sure does. He always has a long list of chores for me to do."

"Ha, he's famous for his lists around here, too."

Edward thanked Bill for showing him around and shook hands with him warmly. He noticed that Bill had large calloused hands; he guessed they were from years of working in hot and rough conditions. On the way home, Edward said, "Everyone seems to work well together. I didn't notice any left-over animosity from the strike. Did you have to fire anyone?"

"Not this time, but a few men moved on to other positions. Most of the men were glad to get back to their jobs. Bill, for example, is a strong union man, and he's also very professional. He's a leader. I don't think either of us holds a grudge about the strike, although we didn't always like the tactics on either side."

"He looks familiar. Was he on TV during the strike?"

"Yes, he pulled that angry man off me."

As one of the strike organizers, Bill had been trying to keep order and keep people safe at all times. Andrew respected him a great deal because Bill cared about the quality of his work and the people who worked for him. For his part, Bill fully appreciated that they were all in it together. He knew the company was trying to balance multiple needs, and every week, he brainstormed with Andrew on how to make things better. They were trying their best to keep the plant running in the face of increasing competition. Neither of them had any idea how long they were going to be able to keep the plant going.

PART SEVEN

End of an Era

Edward and Jessica

Chapter 35

CONFRONTATIONS

The kitchen had remained a constant, central to life on Good Endeavour Farm for centuries. But America was changing dramatically just as Edward was coming of age. The most significant changes in kitchens all across the world were the installation of telephones and television sets.

The TV created the bigger disruption in the family's lives because they all watched it together, right before, during, or right after dinner. At Good Endeavour, instead of quiet dinners where Edward and Betsy dodged questions about their days at school, the family sat there night after night, riveted by images of extreme and often horrifying events happening around the world. The *Evening News* brought all types of challenging stories right into the kitchen, the soul of most family's homes.

Edward learned a great deal from watching the news and listening to Walter Cronkite deliver the stories without a great deal of partisan bias. Watching the pictures and hearing different perspectives about the world helped his studies at school come alive.

So there they sat, night after night, mesmerized by the flickering images on the screen. The pictures got more upsetting when they replaced the black-and-white TV with a full-color model with a larger screen. It was shocking to be sitting in their peaceful home watching body bags from Vietnam, petroleum spills on California and Gulf Coast beaches, and fires lit by social rage burning in the inner cities all across America. Edward found the images upsetting and wondered what sort of world he was growing up in. Combining that imagery of horrors around the world with leaks proving that the government had been lying to the American people, and proof that some politicians were using dirty tricks to win elections, it was no surprise that Americans' confidence in their government dropped precipitously during the sixties.

These events clearly eroded Edward's confidence in all branches of government, along with unregulated capitalism and even his fellow man. He came to appreciate that American democracy was a fragile concept that needed support at all times. But what could one person do about it? That was the big question bouncing around in his head.

One night in late summer, when the myriad of issues bubbling in the American cauldron got Edward down, he shouted at his dad, "How can you watch this and not be enraged? Why aren't we doing something about it?"

When his father did not quickly respond, Edward stormed out of the kitchen, slammed the door, and followed the well-worn trail down to the ledge overlooking the Little Gunpowder. Seeking the solace and serenity that he often found in nature, he closed his eyes and listened to the crickets clicking in the woods. Hearing whispers of night floating up from the river helped to clear his mind, and his heart rate began to settle.

What must have been a half-hour later, his father found him sitting on the ledge and sat down beside him. Neither of them spoke a word for what seemed an eternity.

Eventually, Edward said, "Sorry, Dad."

After a few more minutes, his father replied, "I am too." He paused then said, "You ask good questions, many with no easy answers. But you must keep asking them until you find a way to contribute to a better and safer society. When you go off to college, there will be many options for you to pursue. Pick one or two and sink your teeth into them. You'll develop skills you will then be able to use to make the world a better place."

"It's so perplexing to think about the complexity of each of these issues. I have no idea at this point what I might end up doing," admitted Edward.

"My father often told me that in addition to taking care of our family and community, there are two other guiding principles in life. First, you should do your best to value and treat all men and women equally, and secondly, you must take care of the land because everything depends on the land. It's not easy, but if you can find a career that will help achieve those goals, you will make a contribution to the stability of our society. We can't solve everything, but we can certainly find opportunities where we can contribute to the greater good."

After another twenty minutes, Andrew stood up. "Sitting here on these rocks has given our family good advice, but they aren't getting any softer. I'll see you back at the house."

Edward sat there for another hour, and as he sat, his vision of the future became clearer. He agreed with his father. He wanted to find something constructive to do with his life. It was a tragic time, but it was also a time when many people were stepping up and speaking out. It was a time of reawakening for America. People wanted to know the truth. They wanted to get involved. Edward wanted to be a part of that change. He was ready to leave the farm and develop the skills he would need to meet those goals. He stood up and stretched, took one last look at what he could see of the valley in the dark, and started up the trail, back to the farmhouse and his family and forward to an unknowable future.

1967

At seventeen, Edward left his old life behind and took off to attend Franklin and Marshall College in Lancaster, Pennsylvania. It was an exciting time to be on his own and have the opportunity to face critical issues on a vibrant campus. Many of the students he hit it off with were asking tough questions and looking for answers too. With all the provocative ideas floating around during classes and in late-night discussions, Edward started to understand how democracy could work. Its success depended on a serious search for truth and the testing of different ideas.

The years he was away at college proved to be a challenging time for America and for democracy. He watched as violence dominated the news coverage. First there were the shocking assassinations of Bobby Kennedy and Martin Luther King. It was difficult for Edward to make sense out of these heinous acts. It seemed to be a backlash to the progress made on civil rights earlier in the sixties.

Then there were the police riots at the Chicago Democratic Convention, the ongoing war in Vietnam, the election of Nixon, the Watergate scandal, and the proliferation of thousands of nuclear warheads.

Fortunately, there were high points, too, such as the landing of a man on the moon, Woodstock, the first Earth Day, and the bipartisan passage of badly needed environmental laws. But the lies, prejudice, and greed of the people in charge began to rip apart the social fabric of America, leaving the country's *contract with the people* raw and exposed. Fortunately, Edward did learn during these times that there were many amazing things humans could accomplish if mankind could just find ways to work together.

Edward's knowledge of the world grew dramatically as he engaged in a variety of courses and attended lectures by visiting scholars. He also learned more about people, human nature, and current issues by participating in demonstrations, teach-ins, and rallies. Many of these were focused on human rights, threats to our environment, and the Vietnam War. These issues were important to him, and he listened as people expressed a range of perspectives, raised questions, and shared their concerns and their dreams about the future.

Not surprisingly, Edward was most drawn to issues and courses centered around being a better steward of the planet. Taking care of the land was in his blood, and environmental destruction threatened all forms of life on the planet.

Because Edward's father was a good steward of the land, Edward had not fully understood how badly humans were abusing the land, the air, and the water all around the world. He learned how common waste-disposal practices were damaging not only people's lungs and blood chemistries but also the ocean's acidity, the atmosphere's temperature, and the planet's biodiversity—all of which were critical to people's health.

Edward became particularly concerned about how the Earth was losing its Goldilocks climate that had made the land and humans so productive for thousands of years. This shook him to his core. The historical data and trends were clear. But what could he do about it? He did not want to fall into the plight of people who were so overwhelmed by the data that apathy set in. He decided that one thing he could do was to help people, governments, and organizations manage our resources and disposal practices better in order to reduce the damage to the land and our climate. This goal was far bigger than just Good Endeavour, but it would help small farms and people everywhere.

1970

Edward pursued a range of classes to help him better understand what was happening to the Earth and was diligently working towards a career he thought would be meaningful. Then in the spring of his junior year, news leaked out that Nixon was secretly and illegally bombing Cambodia and Laos, which represented a dramatic expansion of the Vietnam War. A war the president had promised to end. Once again, the president had lied to the American People.

On hearing the news from a roommate, Edward grew angry and felt constrained in his tiny dormitory room. Needing to get out into the open air, he went outside, thinking he would either walk on the Quad or in the woods around the west end of town.

But instead of the peace and quiet he had sought; he found the Quad abuzz. It was quickly filling up with dozens of confused and angry students flowing out of the dorms and shouting against all the lies. Someone ran an extension cord out of a dorm window and hooked up a microphone and amplifier to it. Students got in a line to speak.

Edward listened as fellow students discussed what they had heard and what options were available to protest this escalation of the war. Many felt betrayed and thought America had already lost too much treasure—in lives extinguished and resources wasted—for this seemingly never-ending war.

The crowd grew to hundreds of students, all gathering to listen to the latest news as it came across the Associated Press wires and to hear perspectives about abuses of power, threats to democracy, and pleas to "bring the boys home."

One speaker Edward knew from one of his classes suggested that the participants turn their anger into educational efforts with people in Lancaster, as well as their families and hometowns. Speakers encouraged the students to get involved in community-organizing efforts to help boost voter turnout and to lobby politicians. Another student shared her knowledge of non-violent protests and civil disobedience theories based on King, Gandhi, and Thoreau.

By noon the crowd had grown to around 600 people, and the local news outlets were now reporting that people from all over the city were rallying downtown. Reuters News reported that students at other schools, church congregations, and various civic groups all across the country were also pouring out onto the streets. Edward heard shouts all around him of, "Let's go! Let's go! Let's go!"

Finally, Edward thought, someone calling for action, a concrete destination—a march to Penn Square in the city center. Maybe the politicians would listen if enough people came together. According to the news, this was now part of something much greater than a few angry students. There was a global response to the government's illegal actions, and maybe, just maybe, it could make a difference if he joined in as well.

The campus newspaper editor had a handheld, battery-operated microphone and shouted, "Follow me." Edward heard people cheering and could sense the excitement of an emotionally charged crowd as it moved slowly forward, amoeba-like, toward the center of the old town. His adrenaline surged. He was still angry but was also excited that so many people cared and were trying to find a way to learn more and express their concerns. He shouted and waved to students he knew, encouraging them to join the march.

The attendees of the morning's speeches flowed out of the Quad and into a two-to-three-person-wide column, chanting, "End the War," and "Bring them home," as they marched across campus. Edward met up with a friend from one of his classes. Jessica was a tall, strawberry-blonde freshman who was well spoken and cared about many of the same things Edward thought were important. They had only hung out a few times, but he was intrigued by her passion about life, and they had hit it off immediately. But today, she was angry—almost to the brink of tears—about what government leaders were doing and lying about in the name of the American people. He gave her a hug of support and said, "Let's join the march. Maybe we'll find ways to take action and stop the war."

"Okay. But let's stick together. Who knows what might

happen downtown. I've never been in the midst of so many riled-up people before."

As the line of protesters snaked across the length of the old 1787 campus, hundreds of other students and faculty members joined the march. As angry as people were about the expansion of the death and destruction in Southeast Asia, there was a real sense of camaraderie among the marchers. They held out hope that they might be able to change the direction of the country.

The positive energy on campus was dampened a bit as Edward and Jessica, along with other students, left the ivy-draped, old brick buildings and started down James Street. This was a residential street with mature trees and lined with old brick rowhouses with white marble steps and dark slate roofs. It was like he and Jessica were going back in time as they marched down the tree-lined streets of this pre-Revolutionary War town. He wondered if there had been previous demonstrations here by the Abolitionist or Suffragette movements back in the nineteenth and early twentieth centuries.

Edward watched as older residents came out of their row-homes to see what the ruckus was all about. They stood on their front porches, overlooking, and in some cases only inches away from, the sidewalk. Many of these older residents had scowls on their faces. It was apparent to the conservative townspeople that these teenage marchers, clad in baggy blue jeans, with their scruffy, unkempt hair and handmade anti-war posters, were from the college campus. It became apparent to Edward that many of these people did not share his anger with the president and were, in fact, not happy that the students were demonstrating against the war and invading their usually quiet street.

But the students were not alone. They were being joined, and the march was being bolstered, by other city residents. Well-dressed families with preschool children and even older retirees had joined the march because they also believed the war must end.

As Edward and Jessica walked and chanted, they encouraged all the bystanders they passed to join the march. A few people waved and smiled at the procession and a few joined. Then several middle-aged men cursed them, which disappointed Edward. One older man with greased-back white hair, standing on his elevated porch in his threadbare T-shirt, didn't respond to Edward's invitation to join the march. But he did take the time to spit on him. Edward stopped walking, stood his ground, and shook with anger, disgusted that he now had this man's saliva on his face and hands. "Why the hell did you do that?" Edward shouted.

The man spoke gruffly, yelled, "Keep moving," and then ignored him.

Jessica pulled at Edward's arm to keep him focused on moving downtown. "You can't let one old man stop you or distract you from our goal. We want to be reaching out to people who might listen, who might not yet know what's happening."

"He spit on me. Did you see the hateful look plastered across his face? And he doesn't even know me."

"He knows you're attacking his president, and he's probably scared of all these people in the streets. You're disturbing his neighborhood, and he's not happy."

"All I want to do is talk with him."

"I doubt he'd listen, and this is probably not a good time—both of you are angry."

Edward didn't have the time to respond, as his attention was distracted by a group of young men intentionally walking against the flow of the march, shoving Edward and others out of their way as they passed, and shouting, "Get off our sidewalk, freaks."

Edward's face turned red. His primal instinct was to push back. Fortunately, the training he had received earlier in the day about non-violence, and Jessica's firm grip on his arm, kept him in check. Then one teenager, sitting on a porch with his mother, hit him with a half-full can of beer. Edward threw it back, but other marchers told him to settle down before he escalated the situation. Nobody wanted this demonstration to backfire.

"Don't let them get under your skin," Jessica pleaded. "Hold strong to the non-violence pledge you took this morning, or everything might get out of hand. We're concerned citizens, not rioters. Don't give the government any excuse to shut us down."

Edward took a few deep breaths. "That's harder than I thought it would be. But I do remember seeing my father during a strike, and he had somehow kept control of his emotions. He told me once to always treat a potential adversary with empathy and respect, especially if you don't know their whole story." Edward sighed. "I have a lot to learn."

Their spirits and their comfort levels rose as they entered the town square, which was already clogged with other citizens protesting the war. The square was packed like a full house at a rock concert. Smaller groups were working their way down the side streets to join the main branch of marchers. The masses feeding down the side streets looked like dendritic streams coalescing together as they approached the sea.

Edward's face was radiant, his body tingling with adrenaline. Scanning the crowd, he guessed that thousands of people from all parts of the city had already come to the rally. This spontaneous, anti-war march was more widely supported than by just a few hippie students. People of many backgrounds had come out on the streets that day, and it turned out to be a turning point. A growing segment of the public were sick of the lies and sick of the war.

Edward saw numerous church delegations with banners and a large group, some in uniform and some not, with American flags. They proudly carried a sign saying *Veterans Against the War*. Another group had a black *Prisoners of War/Missing in Action* flag. A small girl carried a sign saying *Bring My Daddy Home*.

Speeches in progress were amplified by a powerful sound system mounted in the back of a pickup truck. The square was packed. Edward worked his way closer to the front but then turned around to see if Jessica was behind him. And just like that, she was gone. She was nowhere in sight, apparently separated from him by the swirling crowd of bodies.

Calling her name drew no response; it was just too noisy to be heard and too crowded to be seen. That worried him. They had agreed to stick together, but now she was gone and he wasn't sure what else to do to find her. They would surely find each other when the crowd dissipated, but she hadn't wanted to be separated. Hopefully, there wouldn't be any violence.

The speakers shared new information about the war and offered ideas that Edward thought were well-developed moral and political arguments for taking action. They were hoping that a flood of letters and phone calls to each member of Congress might help bring the war to an end and bring the country back to its senses.

Edward listened to the talks and signed several petitions to his congressional representatives for about an hour. Everything was calm and orderly. Then, all of a sudden, the rally was interrupted by a group of over a hundred counter-protestors. They charged in and tried to drown out the speakers with their chants of "Commie go home" and "America—love it or leave it." They waved both American and Confederate flags.

Aside from the few altercations on the way downtown, it had been a peaceful and inspiring rally in Penn Square. Now everyone who had gathered was being threatened. Chills went up Edward's spine. This new group was following a different playbook than the non-violence strategy being encouraged by members of the initial crowd. The newcomers acted as if intimidation and coercion were preferable to the democratic process of public protest and debate. They had discarded the concept of the rule of law that was at the heart of American democracy.

The vigilantes swelled forward into the crowd of peaceful demonstrators, squeezing them even tighter than before. A scary and claustrophobic sensation overwhelmed Edward, and his whole body crouched down a few inches, preparing for a fight-or-flight reaction. A strong urge in his gut was encouraging him to get the hell out of what might turn into an ugly scene. But the crowd that had engulfed him moved forward like a large, crashing wave, carrying him with it, pushing back on the counter-protestors as a natural response to being squeezed. It was impossible to move against the turbulent flow.

Moments later, Edward found himself face to face with the devil incarnate. The young man was about his age, with short blond hair and dressed in camouflage. His face had turned bright red with yelling and shoving, and he had a dazed glint in his eyes. His muscular arms were swinging, apparently trying to hit everyone in his way.

As one of his fists glanced off Edward's cheek, Edward grabbed and immobilized that arm, bringing their faces to within inches of each other's growling mouths. Gasping for air, Edward could smell the man's sweat, hear him grunt, but had no idea what to do next. He was shocked at how quickly he had turned to using force to combat force and how the afternoon had escalated from an informative, non-violent protest to this melee. Who were these guys?

Watching this violent element take over the crowd, the mayor got up on the back of the truck holding the speakers and told everyone to leave. "You've made your point. We'll pass the message on to your elected officials. But it's time to go home before there is any more violence. In a gathering this large, we cannot protect you. Let's continue this debate in the halls of Congress."

Just at that moment, police officers grabbed Edward and the counter-protestor and pulled them apart. Uniformed reinforcements had arrived from the suburbs and dragged people from both sides away from the contact zone. Edward paused to catch his breath and then slipped away and disappeared into the crowd, leaving it up to the police to deal with the devil.

It was time to find Jessica and head back to campus. He was saddened to think that he had lost her. She must have dissolved into the retreating crowd flowing out of the square and back to their homes.

Then there she was, standing off to one side of the square on a limestone bench, calling to him. He waved and inched over to her. She was smiling, obviously happy to see him. They both had stories to tell about what had happened to them after they had become separated in the crowd. As it turned out, she had rescued a crying toddler and found his panicking parents. They had each gained a clear appreciation for what could go wrong in a mob.

As they turned to head back to campus, Edward noticed the police now had sharpshooters on the rooftops and were using walkie-talkies to coordinate and direct their efforts. Personnel carriers entered the square; the police were clearly planning on making arrests. It was time to go, and the crowd dispersed.

Edward was shaken by the physical encounter but also energized by the turnout. Jessica thought that, considering the number of people who had shown up to protest, they had made their point. Both felt a sense of accomplishment. They had been part of a thoughtful protest that, for the most part, had been successful and orderly. The community had come out and had sent a clear message to the president and to Congress. The challenge now would be to keep this anti-war alliance together and growing. There wasn't anything more they could do that day, but Edward decided to use this newfound energy for writing letters and motivating others.

Over the next few days, Edward and Jessica met numerous times to share what they had experienced in the march, pleased to have someone who had been there and who would listen to them and help process their emotions. They also followed the news of the anti-war movement across the country, trying to figure out what they could do next to end the war.

One of the most tragic events that happened that year on the home front occurred a few days later at Kent State University in northeast Ohio, where a dilapidated wooden ROTC building was set on fire during a protest. The National Guard was called in, and they used tear gas to push students back toward their residences. Members of the Guard fired thirty-six shots into the crowd of seventeen- to twenty-one-year-old students. Tragically, four students were killed and nine others were wounded.

The nation exploded upon the news that the National Guard had attacked and killed unarmed students. Edward and Jessica could not believe it.

"It could have been us!" exclaimed Jessica.

"The students were villainized by the authorities and randomly shot by some members of the Guard," Edward said. "It's an awful example of the misuse and abuse of power."

As a result of what happened at Kent State, the students at Edward's campus once again gathered on the Quad and decided to repeat their march to the city center to protest that misuse of power. Fortunately, this second march was scheduled as a night-time candlelight vigil in memory of the deceased and injured in Southeast Asia and at Kent State. As a result, this second march included a wider range of people from across the political spectrum.

"Edward, we need to go back downtown to honor the dead and injured and see if we can get everyone to agree on ending the war," Jessica urged.

"You're right," Edward agreed. "Things have got to change in this country."

Once they got in line and started marching, they were amazed at the number of people who had shown up. It was a much bigger turnout than before. Church groups were handing out candles, hundreds of them.

"Jess, take a look back at campus and then down James Street. There's a line of lights stretching all the way from campus to Penn Square."

"There are also lines of people coming from all corners of the city," Jessica replied. "There must be twice as many people this time."

This somber march seemed to help knit the divided communities together. There was no violence or anger on the way downtown, and speakers tried to unite rather than divide the participants.

It pulled Edward and Jessica together as well. At the start of the march, she held on to his arm in order not to be separated. It was also a time to think about the people who had died or were injured on both fronts of the cultural war.

As they entered the square, Edward reached out and took her hand and held it tightly. When she looked at him and smiled, he laughed. "I don't want to take the risk of losing you again."

They continued to hold hands during the rally and then walked hand in hand in silence all the way back to campus. This quiet and emotional evening was responsible for bringing them closer together, and it made them value their lives even more than they had before. They were also grateful and encouraged that so many people seemed to agree that something had to be done.

In response to the widespread demonstrations and the political backlash across the country condemning the government's actions, hundreds of colleges, including theirs, decided to shut down for the rest of the semester. The schools wanted to create space and time for greater discussions on what could be done to repair the social fabric of America.

Jessica and Edward spent the next week together wrapping up the semester and spending all their time talking about the war, the marches, their letter-writing campaigns and their plans for the summer and beyond. They felt fortunate to have found each other to care for and to listen to, someone they were beginning to trust with their deepest feelings.

One thing they discussed was whether they could both stay in Lancaster together that summer. Unfortunately, jobs were hard to come by during the recession and they both had committed to jobs back in their home towns. Edward was frustrated and angry that they had to part ways for the summer. They had begun to grow close, and it seemed like a long time to be apart. They agreed to write to each other and made plans to be together in the fall. On the final day in Lancaster, they got up, had a quick bite, and then Edward took Jessica to the train station. They didn't talk; they didn't know what to say. Both felt they wanted to be together but neither knew how to convey it or make it happen.

After a long hug, Edward stood on the platform, waving, as Jessica's train pulled out of the station. He wished that he was going with her. His whole body trembled, then he bolted, his legs flying as he ran along beside her window for the whole length of the platform. Jessica was crying tears of joy and longing. He stood at the end of the platform, waving, and once the train was out of sight, he turned and headed for home.

When he got back to Good Endeavour, Edward continued to follow the news, study the issues, and reflect on his actions. In addition to having discussions with family and friends, he contacted his representatives and wrote letters to *The Aegis* and *The Baltimore Sun*.

His job with a local construction firm allowed him to engage with his fellow laborers, who held a mix of opinions often quite different than his. These discussions helped him learn how a person can disagree with another on a variety of issues and still respect and enjoy each other. It proved to be an excellent opportunity to listen and gain an appreciation for the complexity of most issues.

The day after he came home, Edward sat down at the walnut table in his usual place closest to the fireplace. His parents took their seats at the ends of the table. Where does one start, he wondered. How does a kid home from college encourage his parents' involvement in changing people's minds about the war?

"What do you think about Nixon's expansion of the war?" he asked.

"I'm more concerned about your involvement in these marches and your safety," Kate told him. "There must be a real danger living on campus. Why else would they close your school?"

"Don't worry about me. What I want to know is, what are you doing about this illegal war and the thousands of people dying in Southeast Asia? It needs to stop."

"The war is a huge problem," Andrew agreed. "And you can certainly voice your concerns. But if you chose to join demonstrations, you need to be careful. Any large gathering can turn violent. It only takes one zealot to burn down a ROTC building, and then as we saw all hell can break loose."

"I understand how they can get out of control, and I appreciate it must be scary for you. I'll be careful. But what else can we do to change the president's mind."

Andrew sighed. "Don't get me wrong, protest and debate are part of being a democracy. It reminds me of your grandmother Emma and other ancestors who took to the streets in support of abolition, woman's suffrage, and honest government. But when a group uses violence to get their way, they've crossed the line. They become terrorists and their actions often produce a back-lash that makes progress harder."

"Well, I'm planning to write letters all summer, and I hope you will too. We need you and your generation speaking up on these issues as well. You carry far more weight than I do. There are lots of people who know you." Edward didn't know how much headway he had made with them, but when the discussion petered out, he headed down toward the Little Gunpowder. He needed time alone.

Sitting on the ledge overlooking the river valley, he tried to put the vision of his future back together again. He wanted to stay involved in these national and even global issues—everyone's voice was essential to keep democracy alive. But he did not want to make politics his career. He was focusing his academic studies on how to fix the serious environmental issues the country faced. A healthy environment and a livable climate seemed so fundamental to everything else.

While working that summer, Edward constantly thought about Jessica. He missed her smile, her touch, her enthusiasm, her thoughtfulness, and their discussions. Did she have anybody to talk with about the turmoil in the country?

Phone calls were out of the question because of the cost of interstate calls and the lack of privacy on a single, centrally-located, household landline. Writing was his only real option for sharing his thoughts with Jess, so he got out a pen and paper. The words just flowed from all the emotion pent up in his body onto whatever stationary his parents happened to have. The words, sentences, and paragraphs he wrote were his efforts at sharing all his thoughts with her and his dreams for the future.

About a week later, he received a long letter in the mail from her in which she shared some of her dreams as well. This letter made him miss her even more, so after checking with his parents, he wrote her another letter, inviting her to visit Good Endeavour.

1971

The following winter when Edward came home for January Break, his parents were glad to see him. He had spent the Christmas holidays with Jess and her parents and now had only one semester remaining before graduation.

Andrew laughed at how long his son's hair and beard had grown. "You must have been studying too hard to find time for a haircut and a shave."

Edward smiled. "I have no line item in my budget for barbers, in fact, I have no budget. But you're a good one to talk. Look at those sideburns. You'd fit in easily on campus."

Kate shushed them both. "I'm offering free haircuts after lunch. You both need them. My specialty is a crewcut, of course."

Father and son glanced at each other in alarm. Edward rolled his eyes. Andrew figured they both could slip out after lunch and pay Ray a buck each for his services at the local barber shop.

After eating, the family lingered around the kitchen table, talking about the farm, and then the discussion drifted to Edward's future. "There's a scientific revolution going on in our understanding of the Earth and man's impact on it," Edward told them. "I find it fascinating to be part of it all. My professors are encouraging me to continue my studies in graduate school. They believe that protecting the environment and preserving our climate are the most important issues facing humankind."

"Maybe you could do a thesis on the health of the soils here on Good Endeavour," Andrew said.

Edward laughed. "I'm happy to offer some ideas, but my work will be dealing with environmental issues on a regional and even a global scale. I've been studying these fascinating new NASA satellite images of the planet. We've never had this ability to look at the entire Earth from space before. The extent of the damage we've done to this planet is jarring. Almost everywhere you look, man has destroyed past civilizations and damaged important ecosystems."

"Your ancestors would be proud of you," replied Andrew. "They too were concerned about the land, and one of your great-uncles, a man named Nathan, lobbied to preserve and restore land all across the country."

"I hope I can carry on the campaign, reduce the impact of our actions, and restore what we've damaged. There's a great deal more to do."

Kate had been listening quietly to her son's dreams. When there was a pause, she said, "But what if you get drafted? You lose your deferment once you finish your senior year. You may have to delay your plans to go to graduate school? She was concerned and was right to be.

Edward had been discussing his options and his duty in long talks with Jess, since they were both hoping on a future together. There were multiple options; he knew he could enlist before graduation and be committed for three years, or he could pursue his graduate degree and wait to see if his lottery number came up in the draft.

Edward thought back to that tense night the previous year when all the students had gathered around the only TV set available in the dorm. The room had been full of smoke and crammed with young men sitting on the floor, on couches, or standing shoulder to shoulder up against the walls. It was a somber group that watched their destinies unfold on the flickering screen. As each birthdate was announced, you could hear the groans, curses, and screams around the room. The students themselves were safe so long as they remained in school, but each man in the room had brothers or close friends whose lives had just been drastically altered by the luck of the draw. Several claimed they would leave school to enlist in the navy or coast guard, but many swore they would refuse to serve and would leave the country.

Halfway through the evening, Edward had started to relax as the lottery dragged on. Then his birthdate was called. It was #183 out of 365 possible dates. Not too good, but nobody knew what the manpower demand would be when he graduated and became eligible to go fight a war on the other side of the planet. It was sobering.

Edward pulled his attention back to the present. "You're right, Mom, but I've decided to go on to graduate school after I get my undergraduate degree this summer. In the meantime, I'm getting on with my life." We'll just have to wait and see what happens with the war.

"If you do go into the military, where do you think you'd like to serve?" Kate asked.

"I don't know. It's hard to know what's right. I've looked into the Army Corps of Engineers. I have skills that would be useful there."

"Like your experience on earthmovers when they built Interstate Ninety-five?" asked Andrew.

"Very funny, Dad. If they find out about that, they may throw me in the stockade."

"But the war *is* ending," Kate said. "Nixon says he has a secret plan for getting us out of Vietnam honorably. It may all be over by the time you lose your student deferment."

Andrew snorted. "I'll believe that when I see it." He clearly had less faith in what the president said than Kate did.

Edward's last semester at college passed slowly. He was on edge a good bit of the time but buried himself in his courses. He and Jess grew closer and continued to lobby to end the war.

Edward graduated from college, worked all summer, and then entered grad school at Syracuse University in the fall. It was a rigorous program but he made it through the first semester. It was exciting. As the end of the year came, they celebrated. His number had not been called. Edward remained eligible to be called up but fortunately, the mood in the country was shifting away from an army of conscripts toward a professional army.

Jess transferred schools to be with Edward, and he buckled down in pursuit of his graduate degree. Two years later, on the same day that he successfully defended his graduate thesis, he was hired by an environmental consulting firm, and most important of all, he proposed to Jess.

1974

The environmental laws passed by the US Congress became the tools Edward and his peers used to assess and clean up tens of thousands of contaminated properties all around the country. They also helped change standard business practices to reduce waste and its impacts to the air, the land, and the water. It was a time of significant transformation as the country moved from a culture of exploitation of land and our other natural resources at any cost to their restoration and reuse. This change resulted in considerable benefits to human health and to the American economy over the next several decades.

One Sunday after dinner at Good Endeavour, Andrew turned to Edward and said, "You must be excited to be part of the revitalization of America. All my career, the short-term bottom line was paramount. We obviously didn't want to pollute anything but always assumed that our wastes would just be diluted in the air and water. After all, the Earth's a big place. But we were wrong. There are so many of us now, our practices have to change."

"Managing our resources better is a huge challenge," Edward replied. "I'm glad to be part of it."

Kate looked at her son and smiled. "Now that you're getting married and have a good job, are you planning to stay here with us?"

"No, I need to be closer to the office. Jess and I have fallen in love with a small farm on the edge of the new planned city of Columbia, Maryland. It's about an hour away. We're intrigued by James Rouse's vision for this new town."

Rouse, indeed, was trying to make money by creating a self-sustaining city designed to respect the land. Another of his goals was to create an environment for the growth of people from all walks of life. These visions rang true with Edward, who had grown up with the same ideals of protecting the land, building clean communities, and treating everyone equally. Edward was delighted to discover that the two most successful aspects of the town were the amount of open space that had been protected and the broad diversity of people who chose to make Columbia their home.

In addition to raising their two daughters, Jess had the privilege of teaching English as a Second Language to young people who had emigrated to the United States. She became a surrogate mother to many of them, teaching not just the language but also helping them learn the culture and traditions of America. Jess was passionate about helping immigrants meld into life in America and become productive citizens, hopefully with less rancor than in previous eras.

ঔ৮

One Sunday evening when Jess and Edward came to Good Endeavor for dinner, Andrew asked Edward, who was finishing a piece of sour cream apple pie, "Did I tell you that the copper works is shutting down?"

Edward was taken aback. The plant was one of those places that had always been there in his mind and in family discussions. It had been operating for over 150 years, and he assumed it would always be there. But it should not have been a surprise when he remembered how polluted it was. "Oh my, Dad. How will this affect you?"

"They've offered me a job in Texas or at one of their new overseas operations. But we're not moving. I've chosen to retire and dedicate all my time to farming."

Edward was having a hard time adjusting to this news. He sat up straight in his chair and looked right at his dad's face to see how he was taking the news. Andrew's face was relaxed. In fact, he looked relieved. "You've always wanted to do that. Are you going to be able to keep the farm going without the income from your job?"

"As long as we can grow and raise most of our food and sell trees, we'll be fine."

"You've lived frugally most of your life, and I've always respected that. What will you miss most about the copper plant?"

"I'll miss the people—we have a great team. But I won't miss the smoke, the labor/management disputes, and the red-hot acid-bath fumes. Every time I smell sulfur, I think of the friend I lost in the acid bath. It was a dangerous place to work, and I'm sure my body is full of tellurium, sulfur, zinc, and the other chemicals we used at the plant.

"Thinking back to the war years, it was a scary time. I have a lot of pride for what we accomplished, meeting the wartime needs for copper and brass."

"How did the strike settlement a few years back play into this decision to shut down the plant?"

"That's a good question. To end the strike, the company agreed to fund more safety projects, improve the health care package, and pay higher wages. That was good for all the employees in the short run."

"How about funds for cleaning up the site?"

"No funds were left to clean up the site or reduce the pollution going into the air and the harbor. Both sides went for immediate pay raises versus longer-term security."

Jess had been listening intently. "So what happened?"

Andrew explained that when the Environmental Protection Agency and the state told them they had to comply with the new environmental laws, the company management in New York decided to shutter the plant in Baltimore. They moved their operations to other sites that had fewer people living downwind, weaker rules, lower pay rates, and no union.

"Unfortunately," Andrew explained, "as we predicted, the other manufacturing firms here in Baltimore followed our lead. The city lost a large part of its industrial tax base. The settlement should have left funds for cleanup, but nobody at the time knew if the new environmental laws would have any teeth. It turned out they did."

"What's going to happen to Bill?" asked Edward.

"The mayor's hoping that people like Bill will be able to move over to the hospitality business as the Inner Harbor becomes a tourist destination. Bill tells me that he will probably work in a cleaner environment but for lower pay. I'll miss him." Andrew stood up to stretch. "I predict that many manufacturing plants all across the country will be moving overseas to countries where there are fewer environmental laws, less enforcement, and lower labor rates. It scares me, but those talking heads on TV claim globalization will be good for us. I don't know about that."

"That sounds like a terrible outcome," Jess said. "What can we do to prevent that from happening?"

Andrew turned to face Jess and Edward; his expression serious. "Your generation's challenge is to convince people, governments, and businesses around the world to work together. It's going to take all of us to reduce our negative impacts on the planet and our climate. That's going to be a tough job that has to be done sooner rather than later. We can't wait decades before we act."

Edward and Jess just sat there, trying to take it all in.

Chapter 36

LAST DAYS ON THE FARM

2000

Over the waning years of the twentieth century, Edward watched as both his parents and the family homestead deteriorated. The smaller, post-I-95 version of Good Endeavour became less productive and less integral to the family's fortunes. When the post-war generation across the country grew up, they moved away from the family farm for college, marriage, and job opportunities. Agrobusinesses and large corporate farms were now meeting most of the needs of the exploding population. As a result, fewer people were reliant on the small farms that had proved so critical to the settlement, growth, and the social and economic fabric of the country since the first colonists settled on America's shores.

There were so few farms left in Joppa that feed and agricultural-supply stores closed up and moved away. Others had transformed into nurseries and landscaping-supply companies to serve the needs of suburbia. What was left of Joppa was slated for high-density residential development. The rapid post-war suburbanization of America was gobbling up the land and sweeping away forests, historical landmarks, and small farms—like Good Endeavour—that had stood for centuries.

Edward spoke to his parents about hiring help to run the farm or moving them to a retirement home. Andrew and Kate, however, were not going anywhere, choosing instead to "age in place" and let the land go fallow and revert back to meadowlands—a rapidly disappearing habitat.

As he aged, Andrew slowly cut back on farm activities that

he could no longer perform safely by himself. When it got to be too much, he sold off the animals, leaving only a handful of his hunting dogs for company. After breakfast, he would often feed the dogs and then spend the morning in the woodworking shop in the back of the equipment shed, making tables, knife holders, cutting boards, or bread boxes to give to friends or family members.

Over time, Andrew grew shorter, more bent over, and walked more slowly. He told Edward that there were times during the day when he thought he heard a cow moo or a horse whinny. At those times he would stop what he was doing, turn around, and wonder if he had accidentally left a gate open or the water running.

During his afternoon naps, he often pictured his children, or their children, climbing in the hayloft or galloping a pony up the lane. When reflecting on these moments, it would come back to him that there was no hay in the barn, and the water to the barnyard and sheds had been disconnected for years. But his fifty years of memories on Good Endeavour kept him engaged to the end of his days.

Edward and Jess watched as dementia set in. They were increasingly concerned about Edward's parents living all by themselves or even driving. What if something happened? One day, it did.

Andrew didn't come in for lunch, so Kate rang the bell. After a few minutes, she started to worry and then turned down the burner on which the soup was simmering and went to look for him. Once outside, she heard the fifty-year-old John Deere tractor running in the collapsing tractor shed, so she made a beeline toward the sound. Of course, Andrew couldn't hear the bell if the tractor was running, so she took a deep breath and calmed down.

As Kate approached the shed, however, she noted that several of their setters were clustered attentively around the tractor, and they barked when she arrived. She found Andrew trapped underneath the spinning left-rear tire. The thick tread had dug into the soil and the axle was now hung up on the ground. Kate didn't scream or panic but got right to work turning off the engine and trying to pull Andrew out. He was alert but could not move his leg, so she hustled back to the house to call an ambulance.

In a matter of minutes, the EMTs arrived in their shiny red-and-white ambulance with yellow and red lights flashing. They had come from their post at the local Joppa-Magnolia Volunteer Fire Station and both knew Andrew and Kate.

The team leader came up and asked, "Andrew, how did you get under there?"

They quickly extracted Andrew from beneath the tractor, put him on a gurney, loaded him into the ambulance, and took him to the emergency room at Franklin Square Hospital, where the doctors stabilized him over the next week. Then they sent him to a rehab facility. With time, he recovered the use of his damaged leg but was never quite as spry again. This incident shook up Kate, who thought it was time to move, but Andrew did not see any reason to leave the farm.

About a year later, Andrew and an older friend were out one weekend, taking turns cutting down a tree with a chain saw. The blade got hung up as the tree rotated and tilted in the wrong direction. Perplexed about what to do next, they headed in for lunch. As they hobbled away, talking about difficult trees they had felled in the past, the tree spun around and fell on them both, breaking several vertebrae in Andrew's friend's neck. Andrew escaped with only bruises and cuts where he was hit by the branches that pushed him to the ground.

It was the final straw for Jessica and Edward. It was clear to them that his parents needed to find younger help on the farm if they were going to stay. Andrew agreed to hire help if he needed it but still refused to leave Good Endeavor.

While Andrew worked in the shop, there were many days Kate sat in her wicker rocker, knitting or playing a hand of solitaire. Occasionally, she would glance down the lane to see if anyone might be coming for a visit. She would linger in the memories of times past when hundreds of people had come for turkeys, horse shows, and Christmas trees. She had lived a different life than the one she had expected, but then most people do. When asked by Jess, Kate said she would have to agree that it had all turned out pretty well.

Andrew continued to get around and sold cut-your-own trees up to his last days on the farm, but it was no longer the big community event it had been in the past. Friends and neighbors would still stop by now and again, not just to buy trees and dogs but to talk about the old days on the farm.

"I remember the farm during the Depression. Your family raised some fine turkeys."

"Whatever happened to Bunny? She was the fastest pony in the county."

"Any hunting dogs for sale? Your setters could hold a point for minutes on end."

One Saturday morning, Jess and Edward came to Good Endeavour for breakfast and were sitting around the old walnut table with mugs of fresh-pressed sweet cider—not the hard cider their ancestors drank. Edward pointed out some of the marks he had made on the polished kitchen table as a kid. They all laughed at the stories of divots and burn marks they recognized.

"It's important to know that we all leave our marks wherever we go," Andrew told them.

Edward looked at him and smiled. "That's so true, Dad. In fact, I was wondering if after breakfast you could show Jess a few of the 'marks' you've left here during your tenure at Good Endeavour."

Andrew agreed, so after finishing their drinks, they all went for a walk through the back fields, accompanied by an armada of dogs.

Andrew spoke as if reliving his years on the farm. They walked along the sinuous, 1,000-foot water-retention berm he had built with his tractor and plow back in the fifties. It helped to slow the flow of water and topsoil across his fields. When they got to the last field, he pointed out his extensive reforestation efforts, the natural, multiflora hedgerows, and described the manure he spread and the cover crops he planted to enrich and hold the soils. It was clear that he had done much to improve the land, the habitat, and the quality of water flowing into the Little Gunpowder Falls and the bay. Almost to prove his point, Andrew whistled the increasingly rare, 'Bob! Bob-white!' call and within moments a quail returned the call from a not-to-distant hedgerow.

Edward's fondest memory of his parents on the farm were from that day walking home from the back fields. Andrew and Kate were ahead of him and surrounded by their English Setters. Edward was happy just watching them from a distance. He stopped and smiled as his parents strolled, hand-in-hand, across the land that had been their "good endeavour."

Kate succumbed to stomach problems that winter, and Andrew experienced a series of mini-strokes and died of old age soon after. The farm—their farm for fifty years—was ready for new inhabitants. Unfortunately, once Andrew and Kate passed on, no one in the family was in a situation where they could take over the property. They were deeply involved with their careers and communities elsewhere. So now, God forbid, the land was up for sale to buyers not related to the family for the first time since the family had acquired it in 1695.

In fact, no one stepped forward to buy and farm the land. Agriculture was no longer the highest use of small family farms around burgeoning cities. Like many other areas, the rapid population growth around Baltimore had turned the once rural community of Joppa into a sea of homes. Many of the new residents spent much of their leisure time inside their homes, playing digital games, and developing online communities. Instead of working on a farm or foraging in the woods, the youth of the twenty-first century stalked the digital universe.

There was also no interest in saving and rebuilding the farmhouse, which was slowly collapsing, or the small cabins along the road which the state had recently condemned. The trees—last business on the farm—were now up to fifty feet tall and no longer income generating. Edward had to smile as he noted that the 30,000 trees they had planted were serving as an effective sound and visual barrier between the highway and the farm. The forest they had built was a fitting tribute to his father's vision and efforts.

As his father would have liked, Edward tried to entice the Maryland State Park system to acquire and preserve all or part of the land to add to Gunpowder State Park. The ledge still had a beautiful view of the valley and the falls. But even though the state was interested, the farm was not high on their priority list. The only taker was a local developer who had already acquired the two empty farms adjacent to Good Endeavor.

Edward fully appreciated that the loss of the land to suburbia marked the end of the farming era of the family farm. It was the end of living off the land for many families all across the country as their farms were swallowed up by the growing population.

The era that had begun in the late seventeenth century when Caleb and Molly's family carved the farm out of the wilderness had come to a close.

Before selling the farm, Edward removed those furnishings and mementos, collected down through the centuries, that he thought the family might want to keep. He loaded them in his van, took them home, and stored them all in his basement or attic. He saved the books from his parents' library and kept the old walnut table to use in his home office.

In his last review of items, Edward discovered dozens of one-act plays and monologs that his grandmother Emma used to entertain guests back before radio and television. Not all that long ago, he thought. He discovered monologs written in a heavy Irish brogue and others in Italian slang. He recognized them because his father had often recited them to him in a theatrical voice, having memorized them as a child eighty years before.

Along with these treasures, Edward kept all the old letters and family records that he had never taken the time to review. There must be something of interest in the boxes that had been saved down through the generations. Someday, he might have time to read them all.

Edward retained a local auctioneer to sell the rest of the items, but being curious, he decided to be present throughout the estate sale to see who was buying his memories—and hoping the buyers might have their own stories to share about Good Endeavour.

The sale occurred on a chilly, late fall day. The grass was quickly trampled by the auctioneer's team bringing a constant flow of furniture and equipment out of each of the buildings. The treasure-seeking buyers hustled about in their attempt to see and assess the value of everything they liked before the bidding began. Edward stood anxiously on the sidelines, his hands clutched behind him, as he watched hundreds of pieces of his life sold off to strangers following the rhythmic cadence of the auctioneer's enticing chant.

The horse-drawn sleigh, the covered doctor's carriage, tractors, paintings, trucks and antique furniture from past generations brought good prices. Other items, such as the porcelain fermentation vats and canning jars, did not. It was sad not to know the stories that went along with each of the items. He wished the antiques had eyes and mouths that had recorded the events of the past, so they could share their stories with him.

As hard as it was for him to watch items disappear into cars, trucks, and vans, it eased his sense of loss to watch the buyers' enthusiasm as they bid for items he no longer wanted. He hoped they would cherish their purchases; they were clearly rejoicing over their newly purchased booty.

Invisible to most people in attendance, Edward mingled with the crowd, listening as they shared why they had bid on an item, what it might be worth, and what they planned to do with it. It reminded him of how excited his mother, Kate, had gotten at auctions and flea markets as she nervously bid on items over the years.

As Edward watched the array of artifacts disperse into new homes and lives, he decided that he had to know more about his ancestors. If anyone was ever going to tell the stories of the past, it would have to be him. And yet, there was so much he didn't know. How was he going to put a coherent story of the past together without more detail and research? It would be a gargantuan task.

Glancing around the farm, he wondered if there was more to find on the homestead before they demolished it. Maybe behind the walls and beneath the floorboards. Where would someone have buried a time capsule, if there ever was one? Where would a sea captain have buried his treasure? He didn't know, but he wanted to find out. He set that thought aside. It was something to think about after all this chaos of the estate sale was over. The house wasn't going anywhere, at least not anytime soon.

At the end of the twelve-hour ordeal, after the last car had disappeared down the driveway, Edward gave a sigh of relief and took a good look around the empty farm. It looked so different without its livestock, equipment, furnishings, and its people. Even the dogs had gone to new owners. The farm was naked, stripped down to its bones, and it looked its age.

As he walked around, he could hear voices of the past, murmurs from his ancestors. He felt a great loss—something that would be hard to convey to others. It would take time, but maybe he would write the family saga. It might be the best way to honor the past, get on with his own life, and pass the family stories on to future generations. That just might be the best way to keep the family's roots alive.

He turned toward his van and headed home.

Epilogue

The 2020s

E dward drummed his fingers on the black walnut table. It was a habit he had picked up years ago, possibly from his father . . . or maybe his grandfather. It had always been a quick way to clear his mind.

Tonight, he found himself reflecting back some twenty years to when Good Endeavour had been demolished. The discoveries of the time capsule, the chests, and the other attic gave him a trove of treasures that he added to the artifacts and stories his family had saved. It was quite an extensive collection and gave him enough of the bones of the family's history for him to write the book he'd been planning for years. His goal was to capture the essence of the Great American Experience on a small farm in Maryland and to understand some of the difficult choices that our ancestors made.

He was assisted in writing the book by the presence of the black walnut table that had become his partner and his muse. The table had been in the kitchen of the log cabin throughout all the historical events at Good Endeavour and, therefore, he had this gut feeling that it was helping him write about the people who had gathered around it in the past. It had become his inspiration and his sounding board. The table had become his writing companion.

Edward eyed the laptop on the table, which was still open with his final manuscript just waiting for him to press SEND. Yes, the book was complete and ready to go to the publisher. But now he just wanted to reflect one last time on what he had learned from his research and what he had accomplished with the book.

He stood up and went to sit in his mother's wicker rocker by the window. He glanced at a couple of colorful masks hanging on the walls—gifts from Captain Peter. He smiled at the framed and mounted family tree that Eli had drawn. He then switched off the overhead light in his study, sat down, and closed his eyes. The house was quiet, the windows were open, and he listened as the calls of a flock of Canada geese pierced the cool night air.

Writing the book had helped him develop a clearer picture of who he was and why he was so passionate about taking care of the earth and seeking justice for all. His research revealed that these issues were not new and required constant vigilance. His generation had made strides on both fronts, but there was so much more that needed to be done.

One way he had learned about the past was by taking lifeless names off a weathered family tree and breathing life into them. He accomplished this by projecting the family's set of traits, behaviors, and personalities back in time. This allowed him to re-energize his ancestor's names into active characters who laughed, cried, argued, fought, and loved within the context of both the family stories and the nation's history. He then let the characters speak for themselves as they came alive on the page.

His goal was to understand the decisions they made, not to judge them. The resulting stories captured what life could have been like during challenging times in America's history. He hoped their choices would help him deal with the moral dilemmas that the country still faces.

After an hour spent dozing off and on in the rocker, Edward opened his eyes and pulled out Captain Peter's gold pocket watch to check the time. It was late. As he passed the seventeenth-century walnut table, he leaned over the twenty-first-century laptop and pressed the SEND button. He closed the lid, switched off the light, and headed to bed.

Author's Notes

I wanted to honor our collective ancestors who participated and who continue to participate in the Great American Experiment. To do that, I have woven in elements of the lives of people from different ethnicities and races to illustrate how important they were in building the country, but I do not pretend to do their stories justice. My goal was to humanize our collective ancestors and to bring life to the stories of the past.

I have tried to use appropriate names for characters that reflect the range of perspectives and usage throughout history. This was a challenge. I hope it will have the desired impact on the reader that our ancestors often thought, behaved, and spoke differently throughout history, as we continue to do today.

This book of stories is further limited in that it only follows one branch of one family tree. Many other branches of the same family did not prosper, and often, their historical records disappeared. I also appreciate that the relative "successes" of the family central to this book were due in part to a society that favored white colonists and, later, white Americans, over all others. This novel could therefore be seen by some as a case study in white male privilege in America. That may be true. Many others were not treated as well.

These stories offer the reader a historical insight into the critical issues of our time. They reveal how hard it has always been to make and maintain progress in a politically, socially, economically, and morally diverse society. I hope these historical examples help each of us find our better selves in living out our lives in the twenty-first century.

The Bones of the Book

These stories of the people and the events in this book were woven from a variety of sources. They include many of my own family's genealogical records, diaries, family Bibles, correspondence, artifacts, and maybe most importantly stories. The book benefited from a variety of published works including *Spes Alit Agricolam,* by S. F. Tillman, a book on family genealogy from 1225–1938, *Sunrise/Sunset, a True Tale,* by H. R. Parker, Derby and Miller, 1854, *Town Hall Tonight,* by H. R. Hoyt, 1955, and *A Little Girl Goes Barnstorming,* by F. N. Tillman, 1939. Many diverse sources and tangible items helped the author ground the fictional stories in facts and give them life. The author encourages everyone to engage in a similar project and then use the past to better understand the present and the future.

Note from Author

If you enjoyed this book, would you please consider helping spread the word by:

1. mentioning it to others
2. leaving a review or rating on Amazon or Goodreads
3. inviting me to do an interview, blog, zoom, or to present a talk in person

You may email the author at: **ned@sustainable.us**.
Thank you.

Printed in the USA
CPSIA information can be obtained
at www.ICGtesting.com
LVHW061343130823
755091LV00001B/47